URSULA MOLLER'S LIST OF REGRETS

HAZEL WARD

Hope St Press

www.hazelwardauthor.com

1

IT WAS COMING

There was a slight cooling in the air. Ursula stopped what she was doing and looked across the allotments. Yes, definitely a touch cooler. Most people wouldn't have noticed but when you spend all your time outdoors, you become attuned to the changes. No matter how small, the variations in light, temperature, and atmosphere are noted and acted upon. Sometimes, before you even realise you're doing it. Because you and Nature have become inseparable. You are a cog in its wheel and in return, Nature gives you this instinct. This protection. Samuel's words, not hers. Although she was para-phrasing. If he were here now, he'd be teasing her for making it sound fancy, and then he'd look up at the sun slipping below the skyline and tell her this was his favourite part of the day. It used to be Ursula's too, but lately it just brought out the melancholy in her.

She snipped off a handful of ripe strawberries. They'd make a nice treat for when she got back from watching the sun go down over on Samuel's old allotment. It was an evening ritual that she'd been following too long to stop, even though it added to the melancholy.

She heard her phone's muffled ringtone and abandoned the strawberries to search for it inside the shed. It had stopped ringing by the time she found it hidden in with the packets of seeds she'd made up for next year, but the caller ID was still on the screen. Andi. How long had it been since they'd last spoken? Six months? More like eight. Ursula was about to call her back when the phone rang again. This time, she answered it straight away. 'Sorry I missed you, I couldn't get there quick enough.'

'It's Pablo. He's gone. Left me.' Andi must have included that last bit to make it clear that gone didn't mean dead. It was always best to clarify. Especially with Pablo.

'Are you sure?' Ursula stopped herself from saying, this time. Are you sure this time?

'It's not like before. We didn't have a fight.'

'Okay. Is there anything I can do?'

Silence, finally interrupted by a sigh. 'You haven't seen him then?'

'Me? Why would I see him? Did he say he was coming to Birmingham?'

'No. I guess I'm clutching at straws. You'll let me know if he turns up though, won't you?'

'Absolutely. Have you spoken to the kids?'

'They haven't heard from him. He's not in his usual haunts either. Sorry, Urs. I just had to check.'

'If you need me…' Ursula left the sentence hanging, not ready to say what she would do if Andi did actually need her.

'I've got to go. I'll call later. Or tomorrow.'

'Anytime. You know that. Anytime.'

'Yeah. Sorry, I'm not myself right now. Bye, Urs.'

Ursula still had the phone to her ear even though Andi had cut the call. She was looking out of the window at the sky. She'd missed the sunset but that wasn't what was troubling her. It was the air. It had changed again. She went outside to get closer to it. The rain was coming, that was all it was. A storm maybe. She should go home before it started, but she knew she wouldn't.

The rain was still falling when she pulled into her driveway. She got out of the car and her eyes were immediately drawn upwards to Anton's office window and the shadowy figure that dominated it. It was too dark to see his expression but she knew it would be disapproving at best. A rustling in the hedge behind made her jump. It was just a neighbour walking the dog, but she still shot inside and locked the door. Ursula wasn't usually like this. The call had set her on edge. She was worried about Andi but, of course, it was more than that.

She went straight upstairs to get ready for bed and stopped at Anton's office, its door closed as usual. Her fingers brushed the handle but she didn't open it. 'Pablo's left Andi again.' Nothing. He never replied, never made a sound, but she knew he'd be watching her from the window in the morning when she left the house.

The night was spent battling against her racing thoughts. It was hard enough to sleep in this house at the best of times and Ursula was no good without proper rest. Daylight came as a welcome relief. It was all the excuse she needed to get up and go to the allotment.

On the way out, she grabbed a sleeping bag. She kept a camp bed stowed in the allotment shed. It came in handy when Anton got too much. Sleeping over wasn't allowed but seeing as she was always there before and after anyone else, no one noticed.

As soon as she arrived, she drew the curtain across the shed window, laid out the camp bed and snuggled into the sleeping bag.

The morning was nearly gone by the time she woke up. She made a cup of tea on the camping stove and took it outside to the bench in the middle of her plot. Now that she'd slept, Ursula felt better. Stronger. Ready to face the worries that had been piling up since yesterday. If it really was over between Andi and Pablo, she'd have to go to her. It was the right thing to do, but it would mean she'd have to leave the allotment which didn't bear thinking about. She packed that thought away. There were more pressing things on her mind at the moment. Because if Pablo had gone, where exactly had he gone to, and why did Andi assume he'd come to her?

Pangs of hunger gnawing at her stomach finally made her leave the bench in search of something substantial to eat and she set off for the nearest café. It was Saturday, the allotments were busy which meant lots of chats as she followed the path to the front gate. It took twice as long to get there, but she didn't mind. It wasn't as if she had anywhere else to be.

The café was full of young people. Students probably; it was close to the university. The guy behind the counter nodded at her as she walked in. 'Garden breakfast and a black coffee?' He'd been working here for about three months, long enough to remember her order which was as regular and unchanging as she was.

'Yes please.' Ursula didn't know his name. To her, he was just the young guy with the beanie. To him, she was probably the woman who always ordered garden breakfast and a black coffee. Or possibly the woman who always came in on Tuesdays, Thursdays, and Saturdays. Or even a combination of the two.

She squeezed onto one of those long communal tables, beside a group of young girls who were taking up more space than they needed. They were planning their night out. It took her way back to when she and Andi were that age, the careful planning that went with their nights out. Particularly when it came to the clothes they were going to wear. Ursula had been expecting to hear from Andi again last night but there'd been nothing. She dropped her a quick message to ask how she was and if she'd heard anything. There was no reply by the time her food came, or when she left, the girls still talking about the amazing time they were going to have tonight. Or after she'd popped into the supermarket to buy some bits for later.

Ursula walked back along the street, past the café, the nail bar, and the vape shop. Something made her stop at the estate agents. Something often made her stop at this particular estate agents. They were always posting leaflets through the door telling her people were queueing up to buy the house. It was a tantalising notion but appealing as it was, she knew it was impossible. Anton would never allow it.

Following an afternoon of doing very little, Ursula went home. Normally, she stayed at the allotment as late as possible, but today wasn't a normal day. Her routine had been broken and she was feeling jittery enough to leave while it was still light. As expected, Anton's expression was one of disapproval. You'd have thought he'd be pleased to see her home early, but when could she ever please him? She ignored his displeasure and tried Andi's number. The call went to voicemail, leaving her to speculate on why she wasn't picking up and whether it had anything to do with Andi's need to check if Pablo was with her. More than likely, it was because he'd come back, all smiles and sorries. Yes, that would be it. Andi would have welcomed him home with open arms and Ursula wouldn't be needed after all. She was okay to carry on doing what she always did. Except that didn't feel right anymore. There was a change in the air. She could feel it as easily as she could feel the variations in light, temperature, and atmosphere. Something had shifted but she couldn't put her finger on what it was. She just knew it was coming, and she wasn't going to like it.

The phone started to ring. Andi, at last. 'Sorry I didn't get back to you, Urs. We've had a minor crisis here. Someone not behaving nicely.'

'Pablo?'

'No. I have spoken to him though. He's definitely not coming back. There's another woman.'

'Oh, Andi. I'm so sorry.'

'Yeah, well at least I know where I stand now.' She was trying to make a joke of it, the way she always did when she'd been hurt.

'I'll come.' Ursula bit her lip. How could she have said that so easily with so much at stake?

'Would you? I could really do with an old friend right now.' Andi's voice was faltering and wobbly. Ursula had no choice then, whatever it took she would have to go.

'I'll come on Tuesday,' she said, before she could stop herself.

Andi had said goodbye ten minutes ago, but Ursula's mind was still whirring. There wasn't one day in the last six years that she hadn't been to the allotment. Not one day. And now she was going away, leaving it and the house behind for God knows how long. And of course she was leaving Anton too. How was he going to take that?

'I'm going to Bala,' she called out, her voice pinging around the empty house. 'I said I'm going to Wales.' She listened out for the sound of crashing upstairs or even the roof falling in, but it was the same as ever. Dull silence. Anton was a very unresponsive ghost. In fact, he was the same in death as he was in life. Boring.

She sat hunched up on the couch. Tuesday. She'd promised Tuesday. What had possessed her? But she already knew the answer. Andi had possessed her. Wasn't that always the way? Andi had always had this uncanny way of making Ursula say the most surprising things, whether she'd wanted to or not. Right from the very beginning.

2

THE DAY WAS HERS – 1978

Maybe it was the way the light slipped in through the in-between bits of the curtains and tickled her eyes open. Maybe it was because she turned over and switched the radio on and 'Supernature', the song she couldn't stop dancing to, happened to be playing. Or maybe it was because she was about to start her first job. It could have been any or all of these things but from the moment she woke up, Ursula had this feeling the day was going to be special and straight away, she was out of bed and on her feet knowing that everything she did in the next twenty-four hours was going to be monumental. Because some days you just know, don't you? Some days you can be absolutely sure that nothing whatsoever is going to go wrong. That is, until your mum opens the door with a foul look on her face, and then the perfect bubble is well and truly burst.

'Ursula, we do not all want to hear that bloody song every minute of the day.' She meant herself really, since they were the only two people who lived in the flat, and Ursula most certainly did want to hear it every minute of the day.

'It's not my fault it's on the radio.' She held up her hands, her feet and hips still moving but her mum's fingers were already on the dial, turning it down to a low hum.

'Hurry up. You don't want to be late on your first day. We can travel in together.'

Ursula was about to say no we can't, thank you very much, but then she remembered the sacrifice that had been made to get her this three-month trial and realised how important it was to her mum that she didn't mess it up. A lot more important than it was to Ursula. Not that she wasn't grateful; she really wanted to work in fashion. It's just that she'd seen herself in a big fashion house in London, not in a crappy little shop, on a crappy little street in Birmingham. Even the name, Ethel Street, sounded like somewhere her nan would go to buy a new girdle. But none of that mattered now because she was still feeling like fantastic things were waiting to happen, so she wasn't in the mood for hanging around. Even if it meant travelling into town with her mum. Anyway, the shop might not actually be that crap, if the name was anything to go by. Talulah.

The thing about Talulah that had swung it for Ursula was that they didn't just sell brought-in fashion. They made their own designs on the top floor of the shop. According to her mum anyway. Ursula hadn't been inside yet. But this was why she'd spent ages deciding what she was going to wear today. A pair of skin-tight trousers, a blouse with an oversized collar and a waistcoat, all of which she'd made herself. They'd been picked to show off her sewing skills. She desperately wanted to work on that top floor.

To her surprise, her mum didn't offer an opinion on her outfit. Ursula wasn't sure whether this was good or bad. But as she zipped up her knee-high boots, the opinion came: 'Are you sure those boots are wise? You might be on your feet all day and it's not actually cold.'

Ursula shrugged, trying not to look too pleased that the criticism had validated her choice. Her mum actually had great taste in clothes but no self-respecting nineteen-year-old wanted full-on approval from a parent. 'It'll be fine.'

'Please yourself. Come on. We should be able to make the eight o'clock if we get a move on.'

As they stepped off the train at Moor Street, the rush of people heading in to work pulled them towards the station's exit. After a lifetime at school and one miserable year at college, this was all new to Ursula and it was a bit of a thrill. Also, 'Supernature' was still running in her head and she had to try really hard not to dance all the way along the platform.

Her mum walked with her along New Street, talking non-stop about the need to make a good impression. At last, she turned off at Bennetts Hill, leaving Ursula alone to deal with the butterflies dive bombing her stomach. It gave her the chance to stop and check herself in a shop window. Annoyingly, her left boot was bunching at the ankle. She pulled it up, smoothed down her waistcoat and trousers, and told herself these were the clothes that would get her noticed. 'Today will be a day I'll remember for the rest of my life.' She breathed in, closed her eyes and started counting. If she could get to fifty without breathing out, it would be a sign that everything was going to be perfect. The madness in her stomach was easing off but she gave herself a bonus ten for double insurance.

At sixty, she let her breath out and opened her eyes. The first thing she saw was a man staring at her from a few doors away. He was wearing a dark grey suit, a shirt with pale blue stripes and a blue-grey tie. His shoes were so polished, the sunlight was practically bouncing off them. Ursula noticed all of these things because her dad had been dressed almost exactly the same the last time she saw him. This man had short dark hair, also like her dad, but he was younger than her dad. And good looking. Still too old to be staring at her though. Thirty maybe? It was hard to tell because he looked so serious.

She was used to men looking at her. It was being tall. It made her stand out. Also, she'd been told she was pretty. She didn't know about that, but she did get her fair share of men and boys staring, whistling, or shouting things after her. Usually, she ignored them but today, because of that feeling that had been with her since she'd woken up and because her mind was still on a 'Supernature' setting, she crossed her arms and raised her eyebrows. Instead of turning away in embarrassment, the man smiled and all of a sudden, he didn't look like her dad anymore. All of a sudden, she was the one that was embarrassed. Ursula swung around and even though she was walking in the wrong direction, she headed back up New Street to go the long way round to the place of her new employment. For the next three months at least. Providing she didn't screw things up.

The butterflies were back by the time she walked into the shop. It didn't help that she nearly fell over her new boss, Cassandra Fry, who was kneeling by the door rubbing at something on the carpet. Cassandra jumped to her feet and, in the space of a few seconds, looked Ursula over, paying special attention to her face. Probably trying to work out which of her parents she looked like these days. Ursula could have told her both, she had her mum's colouring and her dad's features. But that would have made things awkward and things were already awkward enough.

'Ursula! How long has it been?'

'Ten years, I think.'

'Ten years? No wonder you look so grown up.' Cassandra fixed a smile on her face, the kind that looked like it really didn't want to be there. There was every chance she'd forgotten Ursula was coming. Unless she'd changed her mind about giving her a job. There was definitely a chance of that.

'Mum said she spoke to you about me working here.'

'Yes. Yes she did. Sorry. It's just that you look so...' So much like him. Ursula silently filled in the gaps of what Cassandra was trying not to say. 'Anyway, welcome. Gill did explain it's a trial period, yes?'

'Yes. Three months.'

'Exactly. Look, I have an important client due anytime now so Andi's going to show you around. Go through to the back and you'll find her upstairs. Where did you get your outfit from?'

'I made it myself. Except for the boots, obviously. Is it okay?'

She walked around her, scrutinising every stitch. 'Not bad. Gill said you were good.'

Ursula nodded, all the time thinking about how much it must have taken for her mum to come in here and ask for this woman's help. 'What should I call you, by the way?'

'Hmm?' She fiddled with the buttonholes on the waistcoat. 'Oh, Cass or Cassie. Never Cassandra.' She pulled a silly face and Ursula remembered how Cass used to make her laugh with those faces when she was little, before things went wrong. Before Cass chose a side.

The important client arrived and Cass's attention was

drawn away. Ursula found the stairs and went up to the next floor. The first door she opened revealed a kitchen. Next to it was a small room with two green-velvet armchairs and a curtained-off area. She'd passed the changing room downstairs, so she guessed it was a fitting room for clients like the one Cass was talking to now. On the other side of the landing was a toilet, and another room filled with racks of clothes. That left only one at the end, making it at the front of the building. The door was slightly ajar. Ursula pushed it fully open and walked into a big light-filled room. In the centre was a long, high table. Laid out on it were pieces of material cut into shapes. Workbenches with sewing machines faced the two side walls. Above them were shelves, some stacked high with rolls of material and others with labelled boxes. One of those boxes had been left open on the table. Inside it were rows of cotton reels in different shades of green. Dotted around the room were four dressmaker's mannequins with pieces of unfinished clothing fastened onto them. Ursula's eyes were on stalks. This was no crappy little shop. This was heaven.

Sitting at one of the workbenches was a girl with black spiky hair, red tartan bondage trousers and a T-shirt with the sleeves cut off. She was hunched over a piece of forest green velvet, hand stitching it. Ursula wasn't sure if the girl had seen her so she took a couple of steps closer and when that didn't get her noticed, she coughed.

'Yeah?' said the girl, without looking up.

'Are you Andi? Cassie said you'd show me around.'

'Just a sec.' She carried on stitching for a few minutes then laid the material down on the workbench. 'Come on then. What's your name again?'

'Ursula Fry.'

Andi frowned and straight away, Ursula was worried she'd sounded too stiff and full of herself. She'd been here less than half an hour and she'd already made her first mistake.

'Fry? Same as Cass. You related or something?'

Oh, so the frown had been for a different reason. Or possibly two reasons. 'Kind of I suppose. She's my aunt, my dad's sister, but we haven't really spoken since my dad walked out on us.' Ursula had no idea how that had spilled out of her so fast. She usually kept it to herself. Mistake number two. Bum. Cass obviously hadn't told anyone in the shop. She'd be furious when she found out, and all that grovelling, all that pride swallowing her mum had to endure to get her here would be wasted, because there was no way she was going to last the three months now. She wanted the ground to open up and swallow her whole. Preferably while 'Supernature' was playing so that she could at least die dancing.

'He walked out on you? What a horrible thing to do.'

Ursula stopped thinking about what Cass was going to say and thought about what this girl had just said. No one had ever put it that way before. Mostly, they didn't talk about it at all. Mostly, she didn't think about it, other than it being a statement of fact. Ten years ago, her dad had cut them out of his life completely. Fact. But actually, Andi was right. It was a horrible thing to do.

'What's your favourite song this week?' said Andi, as if she hadn't just slung the most profound insight at Ursula's feet.

'Oh, 'Supernature'. I can't stop dancing to it.'

'Yeah, that's a good one.' She began to sing the chorus and the next minute they were both dancing. And suddenly, Ursula had that feeling again. The one that told her this day was hers and she was going to remember it forever.

3
———

GHOSTS AND HABITS

There were days when Ursula wondered whether, if she could she live her life over again, she would never have worked at Talulah. Today was one of those days and, like every other time when this regret plagued her, she came to the conclusion that no matter how many times she went back, she would always choose Talulah. Because without it she would never have met Andi and, in spite of everything, life without Andi was just unthinkable. But of one thing she was certain. If she had the chance to go back to that first day, she would make sure that this time, she'd say goodbye to her mum at Bennetts Hill and just keep on walking. No stopping to check her reflection in a window, or to make a deal with herself about perfection. Just keep going until she reached the shop. That much she was clear on.

Why she was having one of her regretful days today was no great mystery. It was the feeling that had settled in her gut from the moment Andi told her about Pablo. But what had started off as mild disquiet had ramped up to full-blown panic immediately after Ursula had offered to go to Wales.

That was three days ago. After endless conversations with herself about the need to break out of her routines, the panic had settled back down, but the sense of foreboding was still there, and it wasn't going anywhere. It was only her determination to save Andi that was keeping her from backing out. Although quite what she was saving Andi from wasn't clear. Was it from despair or from Pablo? Now that Ursula thought about it, they were one and the same thing.

She cut into a piece of cheddar, the sound of the knife echoing through the empty air as it escaped the cheese and smacked against the plate. It made her teeth grate. Empty echoes always made her teeth grate. She topped the cheese with a slice of apple and bit into it. Habit made her chew soundlessly and, not for the first time, Ursula reminded herself it was a habit that needed to be broken. She picked up a stray cheese crumb from the table and dropped it onto the plate. Another habit. There were so many of them. Perhaps she should write a list of the things that needed to be broken. Or fixed. She'd begin one as soon as she was settled in Wales. Anton would approve. He'd always been a big fan of lists. At that thought, a devilish tut came out of her mouth and made her flick the cheese crumb off the plate, sending it skidding across the table. He definitely wouldn't approve of that.

The last nub of cheddar, the remainder of the apple, and the dregs of a pot of Greek yoghurt finished off her meal. It wasn't what she normally had for breakfast but she was using things up since she didn't know how long she'd be away.

The chair scraped on the floor as she stood up and Ursula knew that it didn't matter which room you were in, you would have heard it. Triple glazing kept the outside sounds outside and the house was supposed to be noise free. It had been designed for silence, but there was one design flaw that was obvious to Ursula, with her non-architectural brain. Downstairs was completely open; there were no dividing walls between the functional areas. The upper floor had individual rooms but they didn't stretch as far as the dining area which was two storeys high. So sounds carried and noises broke through, like small acts of defiance. The idea of it conjured up old memories that made her smile and just because she could, she grabbed the back of the chair and dragged it up and down until even she found it too much.

She put the chair back in its place and looked up to the very top of the house. 'Quiet enough for you?' she shouted, so loud it bounced off the roof's interior and boomeranged back to her. Her gaze followed the two-storey wall of glass all the way down from the ceiling to the ground floor. On the other side was the garden, immaculate as ever. She paid someone to keep it that way. It was how Anton liked it.

She washed and dried the breakfast things, put them away and threw the last bits of rubbish in the dustbin. There was almost nothing left to suggest she'd ever been here, except the imprint of her shape on one side of the leather couch. Although you'd have to look really closely to see it, even after years of occupation. And the cheese crumb, of course, still sitting mutinously on the table, willing her to break the habit of an almost lifetime.

A blackbird's song greeted her as she opened the front door. One step across the threshold and she'd be in a different world. And yet... Ursula sighed, strode back to the table and picked up the cheese crumb. Bloody habits.

She locked the door, tossed the cheese in the blackbird's direction, and walked to the car, determined not to look back. She almost made it too. But as ever, her resolve wasn't strong enough. Her gaze sought out the same window that always drew her attention whenever she came and went. Anton was there, of course he was, his eyes boring into her. Ghosts and habits. She'd been ruled by them for so long that she couldn't imagine life without them.

It was still early when she reached the allotments and, as always, there was no one else there. Ursula loved the busy parts of the day here most of all. Those were the times when there was always someone to stop and chat to, and a quick chat was all it took to make you feel a bit less alone. But these quiet times had their benefits too. There was a comfort in the peaceful solitude that came with the beginning and end of the day. Samuel had told her that once. He'd been a great lover of solitude. Even so, he'd often allowed her to share his.

She followed the path to her plot, abundant with vegetables waiting to be picked. New potatoes, leeks, parsnips, and purple sprouting broccoli went into a box, along with three cauliflowers, two spring cabbages, and some garlic. The box was full but there was plenty left on the plot. Her friend Clyde would make sure the ripe produce didn't go to waste. He was taking care of everything while she was away. He'd be here in half an hour, so there was still time for a little solitude. Ursula stepped back onto the path and squeezed through a narrow gap in a nearby hedge. The gap had been wider once and the hedge tidier. Behind it were four more allotments, although it was hard to distinguish one from the other these days. They'd been left to run wild after Samuel died because the council couldn't make up their minds whether to rent them out or tarmac over them to extend the car park for the leisure centre next door. It was a dreadful waste, and yet Ursula was secretly pleased. It might look a mess but at least no one else had stamped their mark on it and erased Samuel.

She sat down in the garden chair that was a permanent fixture outside Samuel's shed. This was the place where she held her evening sunset vigils and even when there was no sun, she still came. Ursula closed her eyes and imagined Samuel was with her, two old friends enjoying a quiet moment together. If she concentrated really hard, she could feel him next to her, smell the earthy scent of him after a day's work on the soil. At least she liked to pretend she could because the one ghost she would have given anything to see, eluded her. Samuel was gone, and all she had left of him was this straggly patch of weeds and her memories. 'I wish you'd taken me with you,' she whispered and, from somewhere deep within her heart, he replied: *'So do I, Ursula.'*

Something wet touched her hand and made her open her eyes. It was Colonel, Clyde's dog. His big, damp nose knocked against her bare skin. He was hoping for biscuits. Colonel was always hoping for biscuits. She ran a hand over his long black coat, just as Clyde appeared from the gap in the hedge. 'I thought you'd be here. You want me to go away?'

'No, your timing's perfect.' Ursula looped her arm in his. 'Let's find a biscuit for Colonel.'

Clyde shook his head. 'That dog's gonna lose so much weight while you're away.'

Colonel was at her heels looking very sorry for himself. She gave him another pat. 'Poor boy. In that case, I'd better give him two.'

With the biscuits dispensed there was little else to do and Ursula had no more excuses to linger. Clyde carried the box of vegetables to her car and put them in the boot. He pushed his straw trilby back on his head a little and looked her squarely in the eye. 'You gonna be okay, Ursula?'

'Yes, it's not that far.'

'You'll let me know when you've arrived safely?'

'I'll message you as soon as I get there.'

'Call me anytime.' His face settled into that grave, protective expression that had somehow become his normal countenance since Samuel's death. With her anyway. It wasn't his natural look and she missed it. He'd been the dry, straight man who was never far away from a tell-tale giggle, the Ernie to Samuel's Eric.

She pecked him on the cheek. 'I'm just going for a short break to help an old friend.' Clyde didn't look convinced. She couldn't blame him; she was having a hard time trying to convince herself. 'But yes, I'll call you. If only to see how Colonel's getting on with his biscuit-free starvation diet.'

She waited until Clyde was almost at his allotment before taking one last look around. Some might think this place was just plots of land for people to grow flowers and food, but they'd be wrong. It was a community, a way of life, a haven, and she was already feeling the wrench of leaving it. Sadness was creeping over her. The melancholy was back again. But her best friend needed her and that topped everything. Even if it meant walking away from the place that had been her sanctuary for so long. Even if the thought of that made her want to scream in terror.

4

A WRENCH AND A REUNION

The scenery after Birmingham was in a gradual wind down. The motorway slid into the A road without any great fanfare and at first, it was difficult to see any discernible difference. It was almost by stealth that the evidence of big city living slipped away. Every now and then, Ursula thought she'd left it behind but a drive past a retail park in Shrewsbury, or smoke billowing from the factories of Wrexham made her question that. It wasn't until she reached a village called Froncysyllte that it began to feel truly different. From then on, her surroundings became more enclosed by hedgerows, alive with small birds, and trees that reached out to each other across the narrow road. Hills and valleys fanned out before her, spring flowers on their last legs mingling with the lush early summer greens, and their only interruption was the occasional pretty town or village. They made handsome travelling companions and despite the huge effort it had taken to leave home, she was enjoying the drive.

She'd been so lost in the journey itself that she was almost surprised to find she'd reached Bala in a little over two hours. It didn't seem long enough to get to somewhere that was so different to the place she'd left. And yet here she was. In fact, she'd gone too far. Her instructions had been to turn off and take the lake road, but she was already in the centre of the small town. As she had time in hand, she decided she might as well stop and take a look around. Besides, it was just after eleven-fifteen. She normally had a morning break around this time. Coffee, a biscuit, and a chat with whoever was passing her plot.

Bala's high street was a mix of grey stone and painted buildings. Cottages sat alongside shops, pubs, hotels and chapels, many of them dating back to the Victorian era at the very least. Possibly longer. Ursula was shamefully ignorant on historic architecture. Not that it mattered. No one was going to test her on it, and all she really needed to know about this place was that it had the air of a town that was well-loved by those who called it home.

She carried on past several cafés that even in early June were quite full, and found one that looked empty. A push of the door explained why. It was closed. She went to try her luck further along, but before she'd taken more than a few strides, the door was flung open by a woman with the same kind of full-figured, voluptuous body Andi had been blessed with in her prime. 'Sorry, love. We're a bit late opening this morning. We're having a problem with the hob. I'm very limited as a result, but I can do you the best coffee and scone in town.' She was middle-aged but when she smiled, the dimples in her cheeks made her younger.

'Coffee and scone is perfect.' She took a table by the window and watched the faintly blue sky turn to overcast within minutes. Then, with hardly any notice at all, spots of rain were marking the glass.

'It's just a shower. Be over before you know it.' The woman was coming towards her with the coffee and scone. 'Here for a holiday, are you?'

Ursula pulled her attention away from the weather. 'Yes, you could say that.'

'Staying long?'

'Maybe. I'm not sure.'

The woman nodded and remained fixed in the same spot. Perhaps she was waiting for more information. Ursula didn't volunteer any but gave her a placid yet blank smile. Anton used to call it her veil, which was clever of him to notice, since she used it to hide behind.

The café door opened and brought with it a gust of wind and a tallish, broadish shape hidden in a hooded waterproof coat. The woman shot off after her new customer, leaving Ursula's scant information to remain a mystery. 'It is you under there then, Howard. I can't do your usual, my love. The hob's broken. Gareth's looking at it now. I can do you a scone or a sandwich. As long as it's cheese or ham.'

'I'll take a ham sandwich and a coffee. Thank you, Megan.' The deep, baritone richness of the man's voice sounded too much for the little teashop. Like it was out of place. Which, of course, it was. The man was American. As far as Ursula could tell anyway. He had, after all, only spoken a handful of words before taking a seat on the periphery of her vision, so that she was aware of his presence but would have needed to turn to actually see him. She chose not to turn and concentrated on cutting the scone in half and buttering it.

A further enquiry from Megan on the man's morning walk delivered a reply that confirmed he was almost definitely American, even though he seemed to be a local.

'I was just saying to that lady over there, it'll be over before you know it. She's here for a holiday. Doesn't know how long, mind.'

'I guess those are the best holidays.' He sounded as though the words held no great interest for him, as though he were just going through the motions of conversation in order not to appear rude. Ursula couldn't help herself then, she had to turn her head. But Megan was already on her way back to the kitchen and the man was reading something on his phone.

He was older than she'd thought, with a greying hairline that framed his face and lost itself in a shock of grey-black African hair that was longer than a crop but too short to be classified as properly long. He bent his head a little closer to the phone and his heavy-framed glasses slipped down to the very edge of his nose. He took them off and, as if suddenly aware he was being watched, looked straight up at her. It was too quick for Ursula to do anything other than smile that placid, veil smile that Anton hated so much. The man's mouth twitched. His head gave a nod, so subtle she almost didn't see it. Perhaps that was because she was thinking how tired he looked. Or perhaps it was because she was thinking of someone else.

'One Americano and one ham sandwich. Rain's stopping now. I said it would, didn't I?' Megan breezed in and sliced through the impasse.

Ursula cut the scone into quarters, put one in her mouth, and was already chewing soundlessly before she realised it.

Megan had been right, the rain had gone as quickly as it came, although the moody sky was refusing to budge. Ursula had driven back to the turning she'd missed on the way into Bala and followed the road that ran along one side of the lake, past the clutch of cottages she was looking for. The satnav was slow in finding her position so it was more by luck than anything that she came across the faded sign for Amnawr at the foot of a single track road.

The grey, stone house was much bigger than she'd expected and should have been imposing, but the surrounding hills and trees made it seem less so. Ursula pulled up between an old van and a much newer SUV and got out to get a proper look at it. It had been in ruins when Andi and Pablo bought it. As soon as they'd got it into a liveable state they took in paying guests, some of them permanent. Pablo liked to joke it was a commune. That was Pablo for you.

Ursula retrieved the box of vegetables from the boot and headed for a wide stone step that led to an oversized front door. Andi opened it before she got there. Her silver hair was pinned into a messy bun and she was wearing one of those big fisherman's jumpers over her jeans. It made her look rounder than she probably was. As it had been six years since they'd actually seen each other, Ursula couldn't be sure. She put the box down on the step. 'I'm here.'

Andi took Ursula's hands in hers. 'So you are. Hello, mate.'

5

WELCOME TO AM-NAWR

They stood on the step for a while taking each other in. It had been too long since they'd been this close physically and they'd both changed enough for it to be noticeable. Age did that to you. Life did it too. Eventually, Andi let her hands drop. 'It's good to see you. Come in and let me show you around.'

Ursula picked up the box of vegetables. 'I brought these from the allotment. I thought you might find a use for them.'

'Wonderful. We grow veg here but not too successfully. Not lately anyway. Maybe you can give us some tips? Let's start with the kitchen. We can drop these off in there.' She set off across a wood-panelled hall that was as big as a room. Ursula trailed after her, looking this way and that, noting the cobwebs dangling from the ceiling and corners. Anton would have hated them. Actually, he'd have hated everything about this house.

'Watch the cats,' said Andi, just as two small creatures skittered across Ursula's feet.

'You have cats?'

'Not just cats. Here we are.' Andi took the box of vegetables and put them down on a long table in the middle of the room. It immediately made Ursula think of the sewing room at Talulah. It was probably that table and the worktops and shelves around its outer edges. Talulah's room didn't have a Belfast sink, an Aga, or a Welsh dresser but in a funny way, it felt very much like that first day. Except she and Andi were young then, their lives unmapped and unspoilt.

'What's your favourite song this week?' said Andi, her face as straight as the first time she'd asked her. She must have realised what Ursula was thinking.

'Oh, 'Supernature'. I can't stop dancing to it.'

They caught each other's eye and, for a moment, all the sorrow, all the grief and heartache they were both caught up in melted away. They opened their mouths to sing the chorus, but then they could already hear it. Just not in the way they remembered. Suddenly, a man's head appeared from behind a door, round and bald with chubby, red cheeks. Seconds later, he was sashaying across the floor, singing. It was absurdly high-pitched and off-key, and it was hilarious. Their laughter seemed to be all the encouragement he needed to keep going and it wasn't until he nearly tripped over a fleeing cat that he stopped and grabbed his side. 'Bloody hell, I've got a stitch now. Sorry ladies, I couldn't resist it.'

'You're forgiven. Ursula, this is Don, our resident comedian. He's doing the cooking today,' said Andi.

His head jerked back with a look of outrage. 'Today? I think you'll find I do the cooking every day. Which is why I was skulking in the pantry when you came in. Welcome to Am-nawr, Ursula.'

Andi pointed to the box of vegetables. 'Look what Ursula's brought. They're from her allotment.'

'Excellent. Now kindly sod off and let me get on with my creations. Lunch will be served at one, as usual.'

'He's very funny,' said Ursula when they were back in the hall.

'Yes, he is. He's one of the good guys.'

'Are there bad guys here then?'

'Define bad.' Andi stared at a spider weaving a cobweb in between the banister posts. 'I suppose Esme can be a bit edgy but she's like that with most people, so don't take it personally. You're all right though, aren't you, Urs? You're not letting things get you down?'

'Never mind me, what about you?'

She looked up and sighed. 'Let's just say I'm glad you're here.'

The downstairs rooms were open to everyone. Aside from the kitchen, there was a lounge, a quiet room that doubled as a library, and a small TV room. Upstairs, the four permanent residents had their own private rooms, leaving two guest rooms, and two bathrooms. Andi showed Ursula the one that had been allocated to her. 'It overlooks the vegetable garden. I thought you'd like that.'

Stepping in from the dark landing was like leaving a tunnel on a sunny day. It wasn't so much that the sun had finally come back and filled the room, it was just that the room itself was like a summer's day at its best. The walls were of the palest yellow hue that reminded Ursula of the light at the beginning of the day, before the sun got to full strength. If the colour itself wasn't enough to lift your spirits then the hundreds of hand-painted wild meadow flowers that covered them surely were.

'The previous occupant was an artist who was recovering from some mental health problems. She said this was her therapy,' said Andi.

'It's extraordinary.'

'It's one of the prettiest rooms in the house. Esme's been after it, but we decided to keep it for guests. Shall I leave you to unpack? Lunch is in the kitchen. It's always at one but Don will sound the gong. It's his little ritual.'

'You get on well with him?'

'I suppose so. He's been great since Pablo left.'

'Has Pablo been in touch since you spoke to him the other day?'

'One or two messages. No explanations. I hate myself for saying this, but I miss him.'

'I know.'

'Do you miss Anton?'

'I often think of him.' How could she miss someone who'd never really left? Andi didn't know that though. No one did. Ursula kept his hauntings to herself.

'That wasn't the question. Sorry, I shouldn't have asked. It's not as though it's the same thing. Anton didn't leave you.' Andi squeezed her arm. 'I'll see you downstairs.'

Ursula waited for the door to close before giving the room the once over. A double bed with a small table either side, one wardrobe, one chest of drawers and a washbasin. All a little ancient but perfectly functional. She went over to the window. Someone was working in the garden below. A woman. Esme, perhaps. Esme who was edgy around most people, and an artist recovering from mental health problems. Andi had a knack of attracting people with issues.

She looked further out, beyond the garden to a hill that dwarfed everything else around it. Sheep, white woollen puffs occasionally flashing a glimpse of black leg, moved easily along its slope. There was nothing else, just green pasture, darker green trees and the sheep. Apart from ... was that a figure standing there? Yes, she thought it was. Her mind raced back to home, to the window of Anton's office and she wondered if he was still there, expecting her to come home tonight. Then, once again, she recalled that morning in 1978, nineteen years old and on the cusp of life. And she wondered how that life might have turned out if only she hadn't stopped to breathe.

6

HIS OTHER FAMILY – 1978

Ursula was working in the shop again, tidying up the rails. She was halfway into her trial period but Cass still only let her loose in the sewing room a couple of days a week. And even then, she was only given the most basic tasks under Wanda's supervision. As often as she could, she wore clothes she'd made herself to show that she really did know how to sew, but it made no difference. It was so frustrating.

When she first came to work at Talulah, Ursula assumed Cass was the dressmaker, but she'd been wrong. Cass designed the clothes and Wanda made them. Wanda knew everything about sewing, but she was quite old. Fifty-six. That was why Cass had brought Andi in, so that Wanda could teach her everything she knew before she retired. Andi was twenty, a year older than Ursula. She'd been here nearly two years and apparently she was still learning. Ursula wished she'd been here two years. She wished she hadn't wasted a year at college learning to be a secretary when all she wanted to do was sew. But her mum had insisted she had something to fall back on. In the end they'd reached an agreement that if Ursula did a year of college and still wanted to sew, her mum would speak to Cassandra about giving her a job. So Ursula knuckled down and learned shorthand and typing. But even before the year had been over, she was nagging her mum to go and see Cassandra.

Last week, she'd tried to get her to speak to Cass again about letting her spend more time with Wanda, but her mum had refused. As far as she was concerned, she'd got Ursula in and it was up her to prove herself now. Of course, it wasn't the real reason she refused to speak to Cass again. The real reason was because of the things that happened when Ursula's dad walked out. He didn't just leave them, he cut them off, and so did his family. Including Cass, who'd been her mum's best friend as well as her sister-in-law. They'd lived in a big house in Four Oaks that they couldn't afford anymore and not one of the Frys lifted a finger to help. So they had to move in with Nanny Graham. Ursula had slept in the room her mum had slept in as a kid, until her mum got a job and they were able to get their own flat.

So yeah, her mum was bitter, and Ursula supposed she was too. Especially since she'd started talking to Andi about it and had realised it wasn't normal for that to happen. But not so bitter that she wouldn't jump at the chance to properly work here. Because in spite of everything, she'd come to love working at Talulah, and she'd come to love working with Andi and Wanda. And Cass wasn't too bad either, if you didn't listen too hard to that nagging grudge.

Andi came downstairs and nudged up to her. 'Can't have lunch with you. Cass wants me to cover.'

Ursula swore under her breath. Cass could easily have managed on her own. It wasn't like they were ever rushed off their feet. Talulah was too expensive for that.

Cass was serving someone at the till. She walked the client out and then made a beeline for them. Straight away, Ursula was worried that she'd heard her and was about to sack her on the spot. Andi was always telling her not to be so sensitive but it was all right for her. She wasn't on a trial and she hadn't spent the last ten years of her life wondering what she'd done to make the Frys hate her so much.

'Ursula, could you do me a favour when you go out? Could you pop into Boots and pick up some photos for me?'

'Yes, absolutely.' She sounded ridiculously over-enthusiastic, but she couldn't help it. It was the relief making her act like a complete brown-nose.

'She'll need an extra quarter of an hour for that,' said Andi.

'What? Oh yes, obviously. Take an extra fifteen minutes,' said Cass before waltzing off into the back.

'That was too easy. Should have asked for half an hour. She's desperate to get those photos back,' whispered Andi.

'Not desperate enough to get them herself though,' Ursula whispered back.

'Oh no, far too beneath Madam Cassandra.'

'What's the rush anyway?'

'She's been hanging around Barbarella's and the Rum Runner taking photos of that new look. They're going to be the inspiration for her next collection.'

Ursula screwed up her face. She didn't know which new look that was.

Andi tutted. 'You've got no idea what I'm going on about, have you? Right, we're going to the Rum Runner on Saturday. You need educating.'

.   .   .

It was a good job she had an extra fifteen minutes because the queue in Boots was ridiculous. You'd have thought everyone would have had their holiday films developed by now but not so. It took ages to get Cass's photos, leaving Ursula just enough time to rush back to the shop before her break was over. But not before sneaking a crafty peek at this new look she was clueless about. Because, when it came to fashion, Ursula was endlessly curious. Besides, if they were going to the Rum Runner on Saturday, she'd only got a few days to find something that wouldn't make her stand out in the wrong way.

She took the photos out of the packet. Carefully holding the edges so there were no smudges, she sifted through pictures of girls and boys dressed like something from another time. There were pirates, highwaymen, Pierrots, bodice-wearing Marie Antoinettes, and so many more. She could have been looking at a fancy dress party, except that wasn't what they were about. They were so strange and fantastic that she nearly screamed with excitement. Only a few left. She couldn't wait to see what was in them. She picked up the top photo and put it at the back, her eyes greedily searching the next one. But this wasn't a nightclub photo, it was in someone's house. Cass must have taken it to use up the film roll. A man, a woman and two girls. A family photo then. Only the thing was, the man was her dad. A bit older than Ursula remembered him but definitely him. Which must mean her dad was also their dad. Which also meant these girls were her half-sisters. They looked too much like her not to be. And then it occurred to her that they were only a few years younger than her. So that could only mean he already had another family when he walked out on them. Ursula went cold, then hot and clammy. The photos slipped from her fingers. She watched them falling but there was nothing she could do to stop them. It was like everything was slowing down and the floor was getting closer. But then someone caught her arm and she was back in real time again.

'Are you all right?' The voice was calm and strong. For a moment, she thought it was her dad. But then she remembered where she'd seen that face before. Her first day. The man by Bennetts Hill.

'Yes, thank you.' She pulled her arm away and reached for the photos scattered about the floor. To her horror, some of them had footprints stamped across them. She snatched them up as fast as she could, panicky tears running down her cheeks.

'Let me,' said the man. He took them from her and wiped each one with a handkerchief before returning them to the packet. Then he shook the handkerchief and held it out for her. 'I am afraid it is quite dusty, but I have only one.'

'They're my boss's. She'll go mad.'

He smiled, like he felt really sorry for her. 'Come. I'll explain.'

Without saying another word, she let him take her out of the store.

'Where do you work?' His accent was different. Sort of English but not really English.

'Ethel Street. Talulah.'

'Ah. That explains it.' He didn't say, but she knew he was talking about that first time they'd seen each other.

When they reached the shop, he held the door open for her. Ursula skulked in, a grovelling, snivelling mess. She couldn't look at Cass who rushed over to her. 'Ursula, what's happened?'

'I'm afraid it is all my fault,' said the man. 'I was rushing and knocked the photos out of her hand. Of course, I will pay to have them redeveloped.'

Cass flashed him an angry glare. 'That won't be necessary, thank you.'

He nodded and thrust a small card into her hand. 'In case you change your mind. Goodbye, Ursula.'

'Bye...' Ursula trailed off, fully aware that she sounded pathetic but she was thinking about the look Cass had given the man. If she did that with a total stranger, what the hell was in store for her when he left.

'Anton. My name is Anton Moller.'

Before he was even out the door, Cass pulled Ursula away and bundled her upstairs to the kitchen to be left with Wanda who insisted a cup of hot sweet tea was needed. Everyone was fussing over her as if she'd had a fall. Ursula drank the tea and made herself go back downstairs to face the music. Might as well get it over with.

Cass was on her own in the shop. 'Are you okay now?'

'Yes. I'm really sorry about the photos.'

'No. I'm sorry.' Cass didn't say what exactly she was sorry for but she obviously didn't believe the photos just happened to fall out of the packet when that man bumped into her. She knew Ursula had been looking at them and had seen the one of her father and his other family.

Before either of them could say any more, the shop door opened. It was a client, come for a fitting. 'I never agreed with it. I want you to know that,' said Cass. Then she turned to the client and greeted her with a smile that was big and broad, and completely fake.

7

PLUNDERING THE DISASTER FUND – 1978

The rest of the day was spent trying not to think about that photo. It helped that Cass sent Ursula up to the sewing room for the afternoon. Guilty conscience probably. But that meant Andi was needed in the shop, so there was no one to confide in. Although in truth, Ursula didn't know if she was ready to tell anyone yet. But when they finished for the day, the first thing Andi wanted to know was what had really happened.

Just hearing the question was enough to make her feel sick. 'I don't want to talk about it.'

Andi shrugged. 'Okay.'

'I looked at Cass's photos.' Oh right, so her mouth wanted to talk about it even if her heart didn't.

'Is that all?'

'There was one of my dad in there.'

'You're kidding? Then why would Cass ask you pick them up?'

'I don't know. Maybe she forgot it was there. Or maybe she didn't expect me to look at them.'

'Well it was a crappy thing to do. She must have known there was a chance you'd look.'

'He has another family. Not just that, they must have been born before he left us.'

'No! But that's … I mean, shit. That's awful. That's really, really awful for you.'

Ursula's eyes began to sting and then before she had a chance to stop herself, she was crying.

Andi put her arm around her. 'Sorry, mate. I didn't mean to upset you.'

'You didn't. It's him. How could he do that to us?'

'I don't know him, but my guess is it's because he's a selfish bastard. Do you think your mum knows?'

'Not sure.' It was another thing Ursula had been trying not to think about.

'Are you going to ask her?'

'I dunno. What if she doesn't?'

'If you were her, would you want to know?'

Ursula didn't have time to answer because the station was just ahead and her mum was waiting outside. 'Do I look like I've been crying?'

'Your eyes are a bit red, but I think you'll get away with it. I'll see you tomorrow.'

They split up, Andi heading for her bus and Ursula getting ever closer to the station. In her first week at Talulah, her mum had waited for her every day but since then, they only shared the journey home if her mum had been delayed at work. It was too much of a coincidence to imagine that was why she was here today. The look on her face when she spotted Ursula backed up that theory. She was smiling, but it wasn't her natural smile. And her eyes. Yes, her eyes most of all gave her away, the tension in them, the searching look that lasted too long.

If Ursula needed any further proof, the train journey provided it. They hardly spoke. And when they did, it was about the weather or how full the carriage was. Not the kind of things they normally talked about.

As soon as they were home, her mum put the kettle on. This much at least was normal. A soothing cup of tea before starting the dinner. That was her routine. When she was still at school, Ursula used to look forward to this time, her mum coming back from work and relaxing with a cuppa while telling her funny stories from the office. But there were no funny stories today. 'Cassandra called me at work. She told me what happened.' It was always Cassandra these days. Before everything changed, her mum only ever called her Cass or Cassie.

'I didn't know she had your number.'

'She has it for emergencies. She thought this was an emergency.' Her mum pulled two chairs out from the kitchen table and pointed to one of them.

Ursula poured the tea, put it on the table, and sat down. 'Did you know about his other daughters?'

'Yes.'

'Before he left us?'

'A few days before.'

'How?'

'It doesn't matter.'

'It matters to me.'

Her mum touched the bridge of her nose and closed her eyes. 'Their mother told me. His other woman, I mean. She came to the house. Took great pleasure in it too. Even showed me photographs.'

Ursula sniffed away the tears that were threatening to burst through. 'Why didn't you tell me?'

'I hoped we'd come to a civilised arrangement eventually and then we could explain you had sisters. By the time I realised that wasn't going to happen, you'd already lost so much, I just couldn't do it. I always meant to tell you when you were older. I didn't expect it to come out this way. Bloody Cassandra. Stupid, selfish and thoughtless as ever.'

'Cass said something to me after. She said she never agreed with it. She was talking about his other family, wasn't she?'

Her mum snorted. 'She might not have agreed with it, but she kept it to herself. She knew he had two lives long before I found out and she said nothing. We were best friends, first and foremost. At least we were supposed to be. I held her hand through heartbreak after heartbreak, but it meant nothing. When it came to the crunch, she chose his secret over our friendship.'

Ursula didn't want to cry anymore but she really wanted to scream. 'I hate him, and I hate Cass. I never want to go back there again.'

'Sleep on it, my love. I know how much you like it there. And you've got this new friend, Andi. You get on well with her, don't you? Tell you what. Let's not cook tonight. Let's go to the Grecian. We can pretend we're on holiday and we're all glammed up after a day on the beach.'

Ursula could just about remember holidays like that. Long golden beaches and warm turquoise seas. 'Can we afford it?'

'We'll take it out of the disaster fund. I think it qualifies, don't you?'

.   .   .

Ursula was woken by the alarm. She switched it off and lay still, listening to the sound of her mum moving around the flat. Except for when she was out with Andi, last night had been one of the best times she'd ever had. Perhaps it was because her mum had treated her as an adult, rather than her little girl. They'd even shared a bottle of wine. After a couple of glasses, her mum had told her so many funny stories, just like she used to back when Ursula was a schoolgirl waiting to hear the next instalment of office gossip. And then out of nowhere, her mum spoke about her first job, working for the Frys and how she and Cass became friends. She even mentioned the first time she saw Ursula's dad, Bernard Fry, and how she couldn't believe her luck when he asked her out. Typical of her. She couldn't see what was obvious to everyone else. Bernard Fry had been the lucky one. Right up until he threw it all away.

Yesterday had been momentous. Not only because she'd had a great night out with her mum, but also because she'd found out two secrets that explained a lot. The first had been that other family. The second had been the true extent of the rift between her mum and Cass. And if she'd ever imagined there might be a time when they'd be reconciled, she understood now that it was unlikely. She'd given up believing her dad would come back just after her thirteenth birthday. There were only so many times you could hang around the letterbox hoping for that one card that granted you forgiveness for whatever it was you'd done wrong. But she supposed she hadn't given up hope that one day he'd turn up out of the blue and tell her he was sorry for all the years, all the birthdays he'd missed. She'd been stupid and childish, she could see that now. He was never coming back. He was never going to apologise, or tell her he loved her. He had all the love he wanted from his other daughters. And even if he did, she knew she'd tell him to fuck right off.

Her mum knocked the door. 'Are you up?'

'Yeah. Be out in a bit.' Last night they'd talked about Talulah and how much Ursula had been enjoying working there, until yesterday. Her mum had said to think long and hard before throwing it in just because of what happened.

Ursula's finger hovered over the radio while she made a deal with herself. If 'Supernature' was on, she definitely wouldn't tell Cass to stick her job. She pressed the button. It was 'British Hustle.' Hmm. She went to the bathroom, then joined her mum in the kitchen, still trying to make up her mind.

'Just in time. Isn't this your song?' Her mum turned the radio up. It was 'Supernature'. A sign. It had to be.

'I thought you didn't like it?'

'It's growing on me. Are you going in to work?'

'Yeah. I've decided I'm going to carry on. Unless Cass gets rid of me when my three months is up.'

Her mum smiled. 'She won't do that.'

As usual, they travelled into town together and parted ways at Bennetts Hill. Ursula had nearly reached Ethel Street when she heard her name being called. It was the man, Anton. He was on the steps of the building she'd seen him by on that first day. She waited for him to catch up with her. He was about the same height as her so when they stood face to face, it made it easy to see what an unusual blue his eyes were, like the turquoise seas of those holidays she could just about remember. Maybe it was his golden tan that made them stand out so much. Whatever it was, she couldn't look away from them.

'Ursula. Hey. I just wanted to ask how you were.'

'I'm fine. All mended. Thank you for looking after me though, and for lying to my boss.'

'I was just there. You needed help. Anyone would have done it.'

'I don't think so. Some miserable sods just left their footprints and walked on.'

He smiled, as if he was trying hard not no. 'They came off with a little rub.'

She nodded, remembering his handkerchief. Who the hell uses handkerchiefs these days? 'Yes they did. Well, thank you again. I'd better go or I'll be late.'

'Of course. Would you ... would you like to go for a drink? After work, perhaps?'

'Oh. Yes, all right.'

'Tomorrow? I can meet you here when you finish.'

'Okay, Anton.'

'You remembered my name.'

'I did.'

His face broke into the sweetest, shyest grin. It took Ursula back to that first morning when she'd thought he looked like her dad. How could she have been so ridiculous?

8

ESME SETS HER STALL OUT

Oh that smile of Anton's in those early days. So shy and unsure. So heartbreaking. Funny to think that he'd rescued her with those photos. In those first few months, it often felt like she was rescuing him. Although she couldn't have said what from.

Ursula thought she could hear a baby crying close by. Andi hadn't mentioned there were children here. She packed the past away in the dark corners of her mind and pulled herself back into the present. The figure was still up on the hill but the woman in the garden was gone. Another of those cries was interrupted by the sound of a gong coming from downstairs. Lunch must be ready.

Something brushed past Ursula's legs as she opened the door to go down. A third cry announced that whatever it was, it was in the room. She followed the sound to her bed. A black cat, long, sleek and skinny, was perched on top of it. 'Well, hello to you,' she said, but the cat had already curled up into a ball and closed its eyes. She left the door ajar so that it could get out and went downstairs.

There were four people in the kitchen. A young man was scrubbing his hands at the sink and a young woman, the same one from the garden, was standing by the table watching Andi and Don set out the plates.

Don pulled out a chair for Ursula. 'Come and eat. It's just a simple leftover collation. Nothing too elaborate.'

The young man dried his hands and gave Ursula a friendly nod. 'Hi, I'm Brett.'

'And this is Esme,' said Andi.

Esme took a seat next to Andi and said nothing. Don and Brett sat down too but there were still empty places at the table. One of them would have been Pablo's, of course. Ursula noticed everyone except Esme was looking at her. They were probably expecting her to say something. She ignored her inner nervousness and put on her veil smile. 'Hello everyone. I'm very pleased to meet you. Thank you so much for welcoming me into your home.'

'You're in my room,' said Esme, without looking up.

Andi leaned closer to Esme. 'Esme, you know that's not true.'

'I wanted it.'

'Tough. We took a vote and you were outnumbered. That's how democracy works,' said Don.

'I don't mind moving.' Under the table, Ursula stroked her left wrist with her right thumb. Her pulse was racing and she was trying to calm it down without drawing attention to herself.

Andi held up her hand. 'That won't be necessary. We decided as a group that we wanted to save it for guests. Didn't we, Esme?'

'Yes. I was just saying, that's all.' Esme sent a scowl Ursula's way and Ursula was reminded of something Andi had said in one of their calls about someone not behaving nicely. It didn't take a genius to guess who that someone was.

'So, the bad news on the bothy is it's worse than I thought. The good news is I can make it good but it's gonna to take me a while,' said Brett, ignoring Esme's outburst. Unlike Don, he was English, from the London area probably. Esme too. Ursula wondered if they were together. They'd be an odd couple if they were.

'Brett's trying to repair a bothy that's been falling down for ages.' Andi directed the explanation at Ursula.

'I've got a few hours spare if you need some help,' said Don.

'Cheers. Howard said he'd give me a hand as well,' said Brett.

Howard. Wasn't that the name of the man in the café?

Andi piled some salad onto her plate. 'Howard's one of our other guests. He visits every year. He doesn't always come back for lunch.'

'I think I saw him up on the hill earlier,' said Brett.

Andi nodded. 'Yes, that would make sense.'

If Esme's rudeness over lunch was anything to go by, then Andi had been playing down her apparent edginess. In the space of an hour, Ursula had been on the receiving end of at least five separate dirty looks. But years of practice had made her an expert at ignoring dirty looks. It was the sudden verbal attack that had shocked her and made her wish for the safe haven of her little allotment. It was just after two-thirty. If she was back there now, she'd be making a coffee to sit outside if the weather was dry, inside the shed if it wasn't. Her afternoon routine, coffee at two-thirty with another biscuit and her thoughts. But she wasn't there, she was here with Andi and these strangers and, thankfully, lunch was over. Esme had stomped off somewhere, presumably to have a big sulk. The men had gone to the bothy and Andi was promising a tour of the grounds. Ursula went back up to her room to fetch her boots and coat. Her return roused the sleeping cat. It jumped down and rubbed against her legs, pushing its head into her hand as she stroked its glossy fur. She had to watch her step as it followed her downstairs, winding around her legs and nearly tripping her up.

Andi was waiting in the hall. 'Ah, Charlie's made himself known to you, I see.'

'He's been sleeping on my bed. His name's Charlie?'

'Charlie Big Potatoes, actually. Don named him.'

'Is that because he thinks he can do whatever he likes?'

'Not exactly, but that's not a bad description of him. He belongs to someone else. We're not sure who, but he likes to pop in and eat us out of house and home. No, the reason Don called him that is because he hasn't lost his manhood yet. He's still very much a Charlie Big Potatoes.'

Charlie Big Potatoes followed them out of the house and found a bench to sit on by the vegetable garden. In actual fact, calling it a garden was overselling it. It was more of a sorry-looking patch with very few edible vegetables. Andi noticed her looking it over. 'It was better when Pab was managing it. Esme looks after it now. When she's had time to get used to you, perhaps you can give her some advice. I think she could do with some. Maybe tactfully.'

'Understood. How long do you think it will be before she gets used to me?'

'Hard to say. You can never tell with Esme.'

Andi took her around the rest of the garden, pointing out

the chicken run and a small field with a few goats. Once they were out of the garden, they were in a meadow walking towards the hill that Ursula had seen from the bedroom window. She looked up at the spot where the figure had been standing earlier, the figure she now knew was the mysterious Howard. That was a relief. For a while she'd thought Anton might have followed her here. It sounded ridiculous but she knew better than to underestimate Anton.

A trek along a beaten path took them a little further up the hill to a small tumbledown building. What was left of it was made from grey boulder-like stone. Brett and Don were busy taking apart the remainder of the back wall. Their progress was being monitored by a sheepdog, its white coat splattered with black, grey and bluish patches. On seeing Andi and Ursula, it ran over to them, its tail wagging excitedly.

Andi patted the dog's back. 'This is Esteban. No sign of Howard yet?'

Brett shook his head. 'I think he's still up there. I guess he'll come down when he's ready.'

Andi gazed upwards. 'Well, I hope he doesn't leave it too long. There's another wave of rain coming in and this one's going to last all night.'

The rain had already begun by the time an electric-blue Corsa joined the other cars on the drive. Ursula was on her own in the lounge, sending her promised message to Clyde. A fire had been lit and the smell of burning coal filled the room, making her think for the first time in years of the house in Four Oaks. They'd had a big fire in the lounge, or the sitting room, as her father had called it. He'd been very keen on calling things by their proper name. Yes, he'd been a man who liked things done properly. Unless it came to himself. He was very much above his own laws in that regard.

She heard the front door opening and two accents. One, the dulcet, lyrical sound of a Welsh woman. The other, a man's, deeper, American. The lounge door opened. Megan from the café bustled in, followed by Andi and Don. 'Nearly ran over him on the road, I did. Daft sod. I told him this morning, don't be out late, there's a storm coming. Didn't I tell you, Howard?'

The American walked in, his face and hair wet. 'You did, Megan, you did. I guess I just got carried away.' He saw Ursula and gave her another of those barely perceptible nods.

'It's a good job I was on my way home, otherwise you'd have been soaked to death by the time you reached here. Anyway, I can't stop. Gareth's doing a paella tonight. I told him, it's hardly Mediterranean weather, but you know what he's like when he gets an idea in his head.' Megan took a breath and spotted Ursula at the same time. 'Oh, it's you. I did wonder in the café this morning, didn't I, Howard? I said, I wonder if that's your new guest.'

'And you were right. You must be Ursula. I'm Howard.' He shook Ursula's hand. She watched his fingers closing around her palm, his knuckles bulging and looking like they might burst out of his skin. They made her think of her old friend Samuel and the way he would pluck a delicate seedling between his long, thick fingers and replant it as though it were the most fragile of treasures. Which of course it was, as far as Samuel was concerned.

. . .

Dinner was a strain. Esme was intent on making Ursula feel unwelcome and no one seemed to notice except Don who was clearly irritated on her behalf. Howard said very little and was constantly checking his phone. Brett was out, and Andi's head was obviously somewhere else. All the way here, Ursula had imagined a big reunion with Andi. She'd expected tears and a long heartfelt talk, and perhaps that was what Andi had planned for this evening but Ursula didn't have it in her to wait around for it. Esme's behaviour was beginning to get to her. She wasn't equipped to deal with such animosity. Neither was she equipped for so many new encounters. She'd known there were other people living in the house but she hadn't imagined they would be quite so present. They were like a family, and a very fractious one at that. It was all a bit too much. When the meal was finally over, she made excuses about being tired after her long drive and went to bed.

9

DEFYING THE ODDS

Ursula was woken by an alarm call that could only be Charlie Big Potatoes. His plaintive miaow was coming from some-where very close but, this time, it wasn't from the other side of the bedroom door. Nor was it from the wardrobe or from under the bed. There was only one other place he could be. She drew the curtains back and, sure enough, there he was perched on the sill. He glared at her with such comical outrage that she just had to open the window for him. 'Do come in, Mr Big Potatoes.'

The cat stepped in, leaving a trail of paw prints behind him. She wiped it away with a tissue and tried to dry his paws before he made any further mess. It earned her a bite that pierced her skin but it soon stopped bleeding when she ran it under the cold tap. Charlie stuck his head in the running water and began lapping it up. Ursula turned the flow down to a trickle and went back to the window. The rain had been almost non-stop throughout the night. It had left a heavy mist on top of the hill, but it looked like it might be clearing up. At dinner last night, Don had said it was a tradition for all newcomers to take their first trip up that hill alone. That was before the atmosphere had gone so far downhill that no amount of polite chit-chat could rescue it, and before she took fright and fled to her room. Ursula was cross with herself for doing that, but not entirely surprised.

Having finished his drink, Charlie Big Potatoes jumped onto the ledge and pushed his wet head against her, his purr almost as loud as his cry. She rubbed the back of it, making him push even harder. Ursula smiled. 'I'm going to make a deal with you, Charlie. If the sun comes out by the time I'm washed and dressed. I'm going to climb that hill.'

The sun had come out when she and Charlie got down to the kitchen. The two cats that she'd nearly fallen over on the first day were tucking into their breakfasts. Charlie nudged the smallest one out of the way and stuck his head in the bowl. Without a word, Don put down another bowl for the little thing and it carried on eating.

To her surprise, Megan came in through the back door with a basket of eggs. 'Not too many today, Don. The rain must have upset them. Morning, Ursula. Got any plans for today?'

'I thought I'd climb that hill behind the house.'

'Really? Well good luck to you. I hope you've got a warm coat. It can get cold up there.'

'Do you climb it then, Megan?' said Don.

'Not since they forced me to at school, Don. I won't be going up again, thank you very much. Gareth likes a walk up there, mind. He's my son, Ursula. You got any kids, have you?'

'No.'

'No? Well they can be a blessing and a curse. I'm not always sure which. I'm off to work.'

'Don't believe a word of it. She dotes on that young man,' said Don, after she'd gone. 'I'll make you some sandwiches and coffee to take. You never know how long you're going to be when you're up there. It draws you in.'

She found Andi in the library room hunched over a computer. 'Just doing the monthly accounts. Dull but necessary.'

Ursula flashed the backpack Don had given to her. 'I'm venturing up the hill. Keeping the tradition going.'

'You don't have to you know.'

'I think I'd like to do though. It's my small act of defiance.'

Andi took off her reading glasses and rubbed her eyes. 'I haven't heard that for a few years.'

Neither had she until it popped up in her head yesterday morning. How strange that it was making a reappearance when all she wanted to do these days was run away from anything the least bit challenging.

Andi broke her train of thought: 'Who or what are you defying?'

'Not sure. The odds probably.'

'Well I suppose that's a start. It's not that hard really if you take the path by the bothy. Just a steady incline. Brett's working on it this morning. He'll point the way out for you.'

'Okay, see you later.' Ursula slipped on her waterproof and threw the backpack over her shoulder.

'Maybe I should try some small acts of defiance as well.'

She was on her way out the door when Andi said it and she had to turn back round. 'And who or what would you be defying?'

Andi gave her an impish grin. 'The odds. Definitely the odds.'

Ursula smiled and tried not to think about how guilty she was feeling for shooting off on her first proper day here. She was feeling bad about last night too. She should have stuck around and waited for the opportunity for that talk but as well as being spooked, she'd been a bit annoyed with Andi over Esme's rudeness. 'We'll talk later, yeah?'

'Yeah.' Andi slipped her reading glasses back on and resumed her work on the computer. Ursula left her and headed for the bothy.

Brett was working alone but he had Esteban for company. He showed Ursula the best track to take and she set off with the dog on her heels. She turned back to Brett. 'He thinks he's coming with me.'

'No worries. He knows the area better than any of us. He'll come back down when he's had enough.'

Ursula set back off, already worried that she now had the responsibility of making sure the dog returned safely. Esteban bounded ahead, pausing to wait for her at different stages of the climb. Climb was probably something of an overstatement. It was more of a long and winding upward slant that made her only slightly breathless. She picked up her pace on the narrowing track until Esteban steered her away from a squelchy bog. She saw then that she'd veered off onto a separate spur that was taking her nowhere and had to retrace her steps back to the path that went around a side of the hill that wasn't visible from her bedroom window. Here, she saw swathes of old and new bracken that cut through clumps of wispy yellow grass. In the distance was a small building. She headed for it, only realising when she got closer that it was an upended tree. The size and shape of its densely compacted roots had tricked her into thinking it was another bothy. Pity. She could have done with a shelter now that the sun had gone and the clouds had descended. She was wearing her warmest coat but it wasn't enough to keep the cold out.

Esteban was waiting for her by a grove of tall firs at the top of the hill. Ursula caught up with him and saw that he was standing by a construction made of branches stacked together like a small tepee. She crawled inside and pulled him in with her. To think she'd been worried about taking responsibility for him when it was he who was making sure she got back in one piece.

Feeling hungry, she took out the sandwiches Don had made for her. Esteban's ears pricked up as she opened them. She broke off a corner for him. 'Thank you for keeping me safe.' He swallowed it in one gulp. She gave him another and that was gone as quickly as the first. His head bobbed as if asking for the next one. It made her laugh. She hadn't expected to make new friends here, especially the four-legged kind. Not that the other occupants of the house were friends yet. She wasn't even sure they liked her. Although Don seemed kind, as well as funny, and Brett was very pleas-ant. Esme was trickier to define. Howard was the trickiest of all. Over dinner last night, he'd hardly said a word. You wouldn't have known he was there if it wasn't for the fact that he was the sort of man you noticed anyway. But that was just the exterior of him. Inside, he seemed to be shutting down. Ursula knew all about shutting down; she'd been doing it for most of her life. But there had been a time when the opposite was true. There'd been a time when she'd thought she was going to conquer the world. And it had all started with Cass's photos. Discovering that her father had another family should have been the worst thing that could have happened to her. Even worse than him leaving. But as it turned out, it was the best thing. Who was it that said out of adversity comes opportunity? She didn't know, but whoever it was, they were right.

10

GOING PLACES – 1978

Ursula was in the kitchen making the drinks for the morning break when Andi came in and closed the door behind her. 'Is your mum's name Gillian?'

'Yeah. Why?'

'She's on the phone to Cass.'

'Do you know what they're talking about?'

Andi shook her head. 'Maybe it's about the photos, because it sounds like your mum's having a proper go at her. I just took the post in and heard Cass say your mum's name, but after that she couldn't get a word in. Quick, take her coffee down. See if you can catch any of it. I'll do the others.'

Ursula grabbed the mug and shot downstairs to the back room that Cass used as an office. Cass was at her desk facing the room's only window which looked onto the wall of the building behind. That was probably the reason she didn't notice Ursula had come in. That, and the fact that she was trying very hard to interrupt the person on the other end of the line: 'Yes but... I know... But... Would you just let me... Yes, of course, but...'

Ursula stood in the middle of the room, not sure what to do next. She'd got so caught up in the excitement that she'd forgotten she wasn't Andi. Andi would have stayed here, eavesdropping until the call ended, or until she was noticed, whichever came first, and then she would have reported everything back. Ursula wasn't gutsy or cheeky in that way. She was too scared of pissing people off. She coughed like a genteel old lady, polite and hardly noticeable. It went unheard. The next one was a great hacking thing that sounded like she'd been smoking fifty a day for years. Cass nearly jumped out of her skin. She swivelled her chair round and met Ursula's hesitant gaze with red eyes that pierced her non-existent confidence and made her blurt out: 'I brought your coffee.'

Cass signalled to the desk and put her hand over the receiver. 'Go and mind the shop. And close the door behind you.'

It was another twenty minutes before the office door opened. Cass took the stairs so fast that it made the only two customers look up. It must have spooked them because they left straight away, leaving Ursula alone in the shop, trying to work out what her mum had said to make Cass's eyes so red. Andi had to be right. It could only be about what happened yesterday. Because as she'd already worked out, it definitely wasn't to bury the hatchet. Unless it was in Cass's head.

The morning had been dead. There'd been a couple of sales. One client had come in for a fitting, another for an alteration and that was it. Aside from sticking her head out of the office door every now and then, Cass had pretty much left Ursula to look after the shop on her own. When she came out to cover at lunchtime, she looked more like her usual self, but that was because she'd redone her make-up. 'You and Andi can go together as it's quiet. Before you go, could you ask Wanda to come down when she's got a minute?'

The second they were out of the shop, Andi started on the questions. 'So did you catch what they were saying?'

'Not really but whatever it was, Cass was upset. Anyway, there's something else I need to tell you. I'm going for a drink after work tomorrow with the man who helped me when I dropped the photos.'

'I thought you said he was old.'

'Not old exactly. Older. Only one drink though. It's not like I fancy him or anything. I thought I should say yes, as he got me out of trouble.'

'So long as he knows that's the only reason, because he probably fancies the hell out of you.'

'As if.' Ursula laughed but she had a feeling Andi might be right again.

Fifteen minutes before their usual closing time, Cass locked the door and called a meeting in the sewing room. Ursula went upstairs and joined Andi and Wanda who were sitting at the table. She caught Andi's eye and raised her eyebrows. Andi replied with a shrug.

Cass came in with those photos. Straight away, Ursula's cheeks began to burn. Within seconds, her face was so red you could have stopped traffic with it. She couldn't understand why the others hadn't noticed. But they were too absorbed in the photos that Cass was spreading out on the table. All except the one of Ursula's dad and his family. God knows what she'd done with that but it wasn't in the packet anymore. Cass put the last photo down. 'Take a good look at them, ladies. This is the next big thing.'

Wanda picked up a couple. 'Nothing hard there. How long before you have the designs ready?'

'Two weeks, then it'll be flat out after that. I've been thinking for a while the shop needs a new direction. Now we have it. We'll stay open while I finish off the new designs. During that time, we need to move all of our existing orders off the books. Then the shop will close for a revamp while we get the new collection ready.'

'That sounds like a lot of work,' said Andi.

'Yes, but you'll have help. Ursula will be working up here from now on. I've arranged for someone to cover the busy times in the shop. I take it that's okay with you, Ursula?'

'Yes. I mean, absolutely,' said Ursula, her face finally calming down.

'You must follow Wanda's directions to the letter, though. There's no room for error.'

Ursula nodded. She was too stunned to do or say anything else. She stayed that way until they left the shop and Andi brought her back to earth with a loud whoop that turned the heads of people rushing to get home. 'About time. Your mum must have really laid into her.'

Her mum was waiting at the station again. Ursula threw her arms around her, making her laugh. 'It's been a while since you've done that.'

She gave her mum a big sloppy kiss. 'Thank you. I don't know what you said to Cass but from now on I'm working upstairs.'

'I just reminded her of her responsibilities as an aunt and a godmother.'

'Oh I'd forgotten she was my godmother as well as my aunt.'

'Hardly surprising. She's not exactly covered herself in glory in either department.'

The morning alarm came on as usual but Ursula was already up and dressed, she was that excited. She even beat her mum into the kitchen which had to be a first. Her mum took the tea she'd made for her. 'Somebody's keen.'

'That, Mother, is the understatement of the year.'

'Yes well I know you're in a rush to get started, but throwing your cereal down your front won't get you there any faster.'

'What? Oh damn.' She wiped the milk and stray corn-flakes off her poshest top. Now she was going to have to wear her second poshest top. She wouldn't normally have worn either for work but she was going for that drink, and she'd assumed women who went for drinks with men in suits wore that kind of thing. 'Oh, by the way, I'm going out after work so I won't be coming straight home.'

'With Andi?'

'No, Anton.'

Her mum raised her eyebrows. 'Anton?'

'Yeah. It was him that got me back to the shop after I saw the photos. It's nothing. Just a quick drink. I'll be home by eight at the latest.'

Ursula had had the best day so far during her short time at Talulah. She'd spent the morning cutting out and tacking together a trouser suit under Wanda's watchful eye and in the afternoon, she'd assisted with a client's fitting. Even though she'd only held pins and chalk, it was a thrill. And then Wanda had stood back to check her changes and asked Ursula what she thought. It was a small thing but it meant everything.

She stayed behind after closing to put on some fresh make-up and assure herself that her second poshest top looked fine. It didn't actually matter what she was wearing because she was absolutely buzzing and when you're in that state of mind, nothing can go wrong. Things were going her way at last. Who cared if her father was a nasty, cheating bastard? Not her. Because he was nothing to her now and she wasn't going to let him drag her down. She was going places and nothing and nobody was going to stop her.

Anton was waiting for her on the corner of Ethel Street and New Street. His face lit up when he saw her. 'You came. I was getting worried.'

'Sorry. We were late finishing.'

He nodded. 'Is there anywhere in particular you'd like to go?'

She looked at him in his well-cut suit and considered the pubs she and Andi usually went to. She couldn't imagine him in any of them. 'No. You choose. I'm easy.'

'I sometimes go to the Albany Hotel with my colleagues.'

'Okay, let's go there.' She imagined how it would go down if she told Andi and Wanda they were her colleagues. He did have an odd way of talking.

The bar in the Albany Hotel wasn't quite so quiet that you could hear a pin drop, but not far off. There were some people in there, most of them dressed like Anton, but it was as if they were deliberately keeping their voices low in case the bar staff overheard them. Anton steered her to a table that was furthest away from the bar, so maybe he didn't want to be overheard either. Her usual choice of drink was Bacardi and Coke or lager but she was afraid they'd make her look vulgar, so she chose white wine, remembering that had tasted nice when she'd had it with her mum at the Grecian.

Anton took the seat opposite her. She was glad that he hadn't embarrassed her by sitting next to her or trying to hold her hand. 'Tell me about yourself, Ursula.'

'Not much to tell. I'm nineteen. I live with my mum. You know where I work.'

'Talulah. Do you like it there?'

'I like it more now that I've started making the clothes instead of selling them. I want to be a great dressmaker one day.'

'Then we have something in common. I make things too. I'm an architect. I make buildings.'

'I thought architects designed buildings. Isn't it builders that make them?'

He smiled. 'I think you are quite the pedant.'

'Can I ask where you're from?'

Anton took a sip of his drink. She hadn't asked what it was but she thought it was whisky. 'I'm from London.'

'You don't sound like a cockney.'

'I'm not. I was born in London but I've spent most of my life in Sweden. My father is Swedish. I returned to London five years ago. I have lived in Birmingham for three years now.'

'So how old are you?'

'I'm twenty-eight.'

Yes, he was too old for her. Not just in years but all the other things that mattered. He was probably married too. He wasn't wearing a ring but that didn't mean anything. Her dad never wore a ring and look how slippery he was. Besides, if she was going to achieve her dreams, she didn't need a man getting in the way. Especially one as sad and lost as Anton. Because it was obvious that's what he was.

He frowned. 'That is a very interesting smile you have. It's like a veil. I can't begin to guess what's behind it.'

'Oh nothing really. I can only stay for one drink. My mum's expecting me home by eight.'

11

NEW TALULAH, OLD PROBLEM – 1978

Anton was waiting on the corner for her. It was something he'd been doing most mornings for some time now. Since that night they went for a drink, actually. Too often for it to be a coincidence, although at first, he'd tried to make it look as though he just happened to be there. But he'd stopped that pretence weeks ago. Ursula didn't mind really. In fact, if he wasn't there, she missed him. It wasn't like they said a lot, but it was nice to know he cared enough to wait for her. Especially today because it was freezing.

'Good morning, Ursula.'

'Good morning, Anton.'

'You have a new coat.'

'It's an early Christmas present from my mum.'

'I see. I wonder, are you free at lunchtime? I have to buy a gift for someone and I would appreciate some help.'

'I could be I suppose.' She'd refused his other offers for more drinks but this wouldn't do any harm, would it? Anyway, she was curious to see who he was buying for.

His smile was so grateful she wanted to give him a big hug and tell him everything was going to be all right. 'Shall we meet here at twelve-thirty?' He even knew the time of her lunch hour.

'We shall.' She was teasing him with his funny old-fashioned way of speaking, but he didn't seem to mind.

Just before she went inside the shop, she looked back. He was still there, watching her. She waved. He smiled that same grateful smile again. Maybe one of these days she'd ask him why he was so sad. She turned to see Cass watching from the window. Everybody was watching her today. Maybe it was the new coat.

The shop was empty now. The walls had just been painted red, quite a change from the previous pastel colours. 'What do you think?' said Cass.

Ursula stood next to her. 'I like it.'

'It's not too oppressive?'

'I don't think so. You could put something on the walls if you're worried. Some big black and white photos would break it up.'

Cass turned and looked at her, as if she were really, really looking at her. 'That's a great idea. By the way, I've been meaning to say. It's three months today since you started with us. Did you know?'

'Yes.' Obviously she did. She'd been waiting for Cass to mention it.

'So, what do you want to do?'

Ursula asked herself what Andi would say, although there was no need because she already knew what Andi would say. 'I'd like to stay if I can.'

'Good. That's settled it then.'

.   .   .

The first thing Ursula did when she got up to the sewing room was tell Andi and Wanda the news. Andi was over the moon. 'That's just brilliant. Did you ask for a pay rise as well?'

'No. I was just so surprised, I couldn't think about anything else.'

'I would have. She's paying you a pittance.'

Wanda looked up from her sewing. 'We can't all be as brazen as you, Andi. Just be glad she's been given a job. Go and put the kettle on. And don't forget to make one for Cassie. And be nice to her. Less of that scowling. She's got a lot on her plate at the moment.'

Andi put on a scowl and laughed. Wanda shook her head. 'She only gets away with it because she's so good. Anyone else would have been out on their ear ages ago.' She picked up a piece that Ursula had been working on yesterday. 'You've ruched this really well. Who taught you to be so neat?'

'My mum. We've been sewing together since I was little.'

'I thought I recognised the style.'

'You knew my mum?'

Wanda smiled. 'I worked for the Frys before I came here. I remember Gillian on her first day. She was already better than most of the other girls and she was only fifteen.'

'She works in an office now. She still sews though. She made me this coat for Christmas.'

Wanda looked it over, examining the coat as only another dressmaker would. 'Beautiful. It's beautiful. Did she design it herself?'

'Yeah. She's really good at it. I want to be as good as her one day.'

Wanda patted her hand. 'She was always the talented one. Imagine what this place would have been like if Bernard hadn't messed everything up.'

'I don't understand.' said Ursula.

'Talulah was Gillian's idea. Her dream. This business was supposed to be for her and Cass. Cassie was never meant to do it on her own.'

'Tea's up. And I even managed to give Cass hers without mentioning pay rises.' Andi breezed through the door with a tray of drinks and stopped dead. 'Did I miss something?'

'Nothing at all,' said Wanda. 'Now then, Ursula, do you know what a princess seam is?'

All morning Ursula had been careful not to show it, but this new revelation of Wanda's had upset her. She knew the Frys had owned a string of bespoke dressmakers and tailors' shops across the Midlands before opening up a clothing factory. And it was no great surprise that her mum had been one of their star dressmakers. But it was news to Ursula that her mum had been robbed of her dream. Lately, hardly a week went by when she didn't find out some new wrong that had been dealt to her mother by her father and his family, and each new outrage made her hate them all the more. The only problem was, Cass was part of that family. How could she work for her now? Ursula really wanted to talk to Andi about it but as she'd agreed to meet Anton, it would have to wait.

He was in his usual place on the corner. 'Twelve-thirty-five. You're almost punctual.' His smile was enough to break her heart and brighten her mood all at the same time. How was that possible?

'I suppose you've been here since twenty past,' she joked.

'Yes.' He probably wasn't joking. 'I thought Rackham's

would be a good place to start. I believe the lady in question shops there.'

'And how old is this lady, roughly?'

'A little older than me.' Aha, so he did have someone then.

'Is she your wife or girlfriend?'

'My secretary.' His smile dropped. 'Do you think I have a wife?'

'Or girlfriend. You must have someone.'

'Why?'

'Because you're twenty-eight, and a catch.' A catch? She'd turned into her nan. It must be Anton with his old ways.

'I am pleased that you think I'm a catch, Ursula, but disappointed that you also think I'm the kind of man who would flirt with a woman if he was already involved with someone.'

'You've been flirting with me? I didn't realise.'

'Now you're teasing me. Unless, Ursula, you are flirting with me?'

She slapped his arm. 'I am not flirting with you.'

'Pity.'

Her mouth opened wide and she let out a little squeal. 'Anton, you naughty man.'

'I would like to be,' he said, quietly and without looking at her.

They'd reached Rackham's already. He held the door open for her. 'I thought perhaps a scarf. She often wears a scarf instead of a necklace.'

'A nice silk one then. Does she like colourful things?'

'Yes, quite colourful.'

She picked one out with a bright green and navy abstract

design that she knew her mum would like. 'What about this? Would your secretary like it?'

He frowned so much she thought he was going to put it back. But then he said: 'I think it will suit her very well.'

'You know, a colourful scarf would suit you too. How about a nice red one?'

He screwed up his nose. 'Red is such a loud colour.'

'Be adventurous, Anton. You might like it.'

He winced. 'I will try to be. But only because you've asked me to.'

She laughed. Enough thinking about family betrayals. Perhaps this strange man with his funny little ways was exactly what she needed today. 'We're having a re-opening event at the shop next week. Do you want to come?'

'Perhaps. I will think about it.'

After long talks with Andi and her mum, Ursula had decided not to leave Talulah. As her mum had said, she may as well get her training from Wanda, who was one of the best in the business, then she could move on somewhere else. She could even work in London if she wanted. Andi had said: 'Why shouldn't you screw the Frys as much as they screwed you?' They'd said it differently, but they both meant the same thing.

It was as well she'd stayed because they were working really hard to be ready for the grand re-opening. There was the new collection to finish and rails to fill with other outfits that had been brought in. There were last-minute decorations to complete and preparations for the re-opening event. Ursula and Andi had been put in charge of the music, and they'd spent most of their free time making tapes to play on a cassette recorder Cass had bought specially.

Now that the big night was here, Ursula and Andi were in the office. They each had five outfits from the new collection that they were going to model. Wanda was helping them get dressed in double quick time. Cass was in the shop doing her best to persuade the guests to leave them enough room for a walkway, while managing the cassette player.

Ursula stuck her head through the curtain that had been put up to separate the front of the shop from the back. There were too many people in there to see if Anton had come. She hadn't seen him since she'd invited him because she'd been arriving early, skipping lunch, and leaving late, so she still didn't know if he was going to be here. She gave Cass a thumbs up to let her know they were ready. Cass changed the tape and as the sound of 'Supernature' blasted out, Ursula took a deep breath, imagined she was a top model and half-walked, half-danced into the shop to cries of 'Ooh' and 'Gorgeous.' She turned in a circle and saw Anton in the far corner, at the very front of the shop. He was wearing his suit; he must have come straight from work. She held her arms out to show the full effect of her top's billowing sleeves and did another twirl before returning to the back of the shop as Andi came through the curtain.

Ursula strode back out in a silver space-age satin jump-suit with a wide belt as 'The Model' was playing. Anton was still in the corner. She made him smile with a cheeky wink this time. Andi laughed as they passed each other. They were both having a ball. Next, Ursula wore a gaucho outfit, then an Arabian style one, and finally a black lace puffball dress with long black gloves and a bolero jacket in silk that received the biggest applause.

Cass left the music playing and breezed into the office with a tray of drinks as they were getting changed into their own clothes. 'Girls, you were marvellous. Weren't they marvellous, Wanda? Let's have a drink to the new Talulah.'

As soon as their glasses clinked, she went back into the shop to mingle. Andi knocked her drink back. 'I'm going to find some more. You two coming?'

'You girls go,' said Wanda. 'All I want to do is get home and put my feet up.'

They poked their heads through the curtain. The shop was full of expensive looking women in great clothes. 'This is fantastic, isn't it?' said Andi. 'Urs, let's do this when we're older. Let's open our own place like your mum and Cass were going to.'

Ursula laughed, but then she saw that Andi was serious. 'Do you really think we could?'

'Yeah, I do. We wouldn't let anything come between us like your mum and Cass did and, let's face it, we're bloody brilliant.'

'We are, aren't we? We could go to London.'

'Yeah. We could do anything we want. Let's get drunk to celebrate.'

'In a bit. I'd better just say hello to Anton.'

They went through the curtain, Andi to look for more booze and Ursula to find Anton. Before she could go any further, Andi grabbed her arm. 'We should make it a promise.'

'Which bit, opening up our own business or letting nothing come between us?'

'Both of course. And that should be nothing and no one.'

'Okay. It's a promise. Save me a drink, I won't be long.'

Anton was nowhere to be seen in the shop so Ursula went outside where a crowd had spilled onto the street, but it was mostly women who'd had too much to drink.

She was about to go back inside when she saw Cass with a man who could have been Anton. It was hard to tell because she could only see the back of him and even that was half in the shadows.

Ursula went over to check, but as she got closer she heard Cass talking: 'I asked you not to come. You need to go.'

The man laughed. 'I just wanted to see with my own eyes who these so-called models were that were so much better than your lovely nieces.'

'My other niece. The one you appear to have forgotten.'

Ursula froze, but then Anton touched her shoulder and broke the spell. 'Ursula, there you are.'

At the sound of his voice, Cass looked past Bernard Fry and stared at Anton first, and then Ursula. Bernard Fry turned around and suddenly, he and Ursula were eye to eye. It seemed to take him a while to recognise her. Then, he gave her a smile that sent a shiver straight through her. All those promises to herself about telling him to fuck off were meaningless now because all she could do was back away and run. Behind her, Cass and Anton were calling her name but she kept on running.

Anton finally caught up with her and took her arm. 'Come.'

'No. I can't be anywhere near that man. I need to go home.' She pulled away from him. She didn't want him. She wanted to curl up on the sofa with her mum and listen to funny stories from the office and pretend she hadn't come face to face with that despicable bastard who was her father.

'You're freezing. You can't get the bus home like that. I'll take you.'

He was right. She didn't even have her bag with her. She let him take her back to his building and they climbed a flight of stairs to a room with doors leading off it. They went through one of them and he sat her down on a leather chair then fetched his overcoat and put it over her shoulders. 'You're very upset.'

'It was seeing that man. He's my father. We don't speak.' She felt calmer now. Angry, but more with herself than anything for going to pieces like that.

Anton said nothing, but he was watching her. She looked beyond him and noticed how very ordered the room was. Hardly a thing out of place. Hardly a speck of dust. She pointed to a table that held a white model of a building. 'What's that?'

'That is my passion project. It's the house I want to build when I find the right land.'

In spite of everything that had happened, the idea of Anton being passionate about anything made her smile. 'I thought I was your passion project.'

He looked as if he was giving it some serious thought. 'Not yet. I'll take you home.'

She stood up so they were facing each other. He looked into her eyes and she thought he was going to kiss her but he just pulled the coat more closely around her. 'It's cold outside and we must walk to my car.' He went over to the desk, took out a red woollen scarf and wrapped it around her neck.

'What's this?'

He shrugged. 'It's a red scarf. I was going to surprise you and wear it in the morning, but you need it tonight, so...'

He'd done that for her? The sweetness of it made her

want that kiss. She pressed her mouth against his. They stood slightly apart, their lips still glued together, then he moved his away and touched her cheek. 'There is such beauty in you, Ursula.'

And in that moment, Ursula thought she might actually be falling in love with Anton Moller.

12

ONE SMALL ACT WAS ENOUGH

The hill was still heavy with cloud and the air had grown even colder. Ursula put her arm around Esteban for warmth. How strange that she should remember that first kiss in such vivid detail. The tenderness of it. The fragility of those first steps. Anton's, not hers. She wondered how long it would have been before he got round to kissing her if she hadn't instigated it. He was always a lot more patient than her. She was such an impetuous thing back then, pushing him into doing things at her pace. And the red scarf. She'd almost forgotten that. Whatever happened to that red scarf? Quietly disposed of when its purpose had been met, she supposed.

She'd received a tense apology from Cass when she'd gone to work the next day, and that week she had a pay rise. It wasn't spoken about again. Not until much later anyway. That was Cass's way. But it must have been hard for her, stuck between two opposing loyalties. It was obvious by the look on Bernard Fry's face that he hadn't known Ursula was working there, but it was bound to come out sooner or later. Although at the time, Ursula couldn't know the consequences of it coming out on that particular night.

Esteban let out a single bark. A figure that was obviously a man emerged from the still descending clouds. Suddenly feeling vulnerable up here on her own, Ursula grabbed the dog's collar. The figure stopped and turned to towards them. 'That you, Esteban?' It was the American, Howard.

Esteban was wriggling under her grip, itching to go to him, so she let go of his collar and crawled out of her shelter. 'Hello there. We stopped for a rest and a coffee.'

Howard came closer. 'A hot drink sounds pretty good right now. I don't suppose you have any left?'

'A little. If you don't mind sharing my cup. I think I'm fairly germ free.'

'I'm willing to take the risk. Thanks.'

She poured out the last of the coffee. 'I had some sandwiches but I'm afraid we ran out of those pretty quickly. Esteban has quite an appetite.'

'Not a problem. I ate at Megan's earlier. I was just heading back to the house, if you're going that way.'

'I was waiting for the cloud to lift, but it could be a while.'

He handed her back the empty cup. 'If I've learned one thing in all the years I've lived in this country, it's never wait for the cloud to lift.'

She laughed and felt herself relaxing a little. 'Good advice. Do you live in Wales then?'

'I live in London. I was rather guilty of generalising when I said this country, but I've been coming here for many years. You like my shelter?'

'Oh, it's yours? Yes, I do. I hope you don't mind me using it?'

'Not at all. Actually, it's not mine exactly. Gareth made it for me and anyone else who needs a little respite.'

'Megan's son?'

'Yeah. He's a good kid, although I am a little biased. We're related. Shall we go down before the rain starts up?' He let out a single whistle and Esteban stopped circling him and began to walk at his side.

'So you're related to Megan?'

'She's my wife's niece.'

'Oh I didn't know that. Your wife's not here with you?'

'No. Dilys couldn't make it this year. I'm taking lots of photos and sending them home. And you? What brings you here?'

'Andi. She's my oldest friend. We've known each other for … gosh, it must be forty-five years now.'

'Wow! So you know Pablo too?'

'I do, yes.' She'd been trying to read his expression, trying to work out how to phrase the answer but it was near to impossible to read this quiet American, so she stuck to a straightforward confirmation.

'Terrible business. I can see it's taking its toll on her. I hope you don't mind me saying that?'

'Not at all. You've seen a change in her then?'

'Yes. You would have noticed it yourself, I guess.'

Ursula had no answer. She'd just claimed to be Andi's oldest friend and Howard had rightly made the assumption that she would be close enough to notice the impact of Pablo's betrayal but the truth was, she wasn't. Not only had she not seen Andi for years, she'd hardly spoken to her since Anton's funeral. She'd been too tied up with herself, too intent on sticking to her routines. Too fixed on surviving. They'd made a promise to each other that night when they were high on the feeling of being young and invincible. They were never going to let anything or anyone come between them. She'd broken that promise more times than she cared to remember, and maybe Andi had too.

'Forty-five years. Late seventies then?' Howard must have got tired of waiting for her to speak. 'I would like to have known Andi back then. I bet she was even more gutsy.'

'Yes, she was. Absolutely fearless. She said you come every year.'

'That's right. Dilys was raised here. Before Am-nawr was opened we stayed elsewhere, but Dilys liked this place from our first visit. She liked how she could lock herself away for hours or find company when she was ready. She's a writer. Was a writer.'

They rounded the hill to face the house and saw the lake on the other side of it, glistening like steel through the gaps in the trees. Howard stopped to take a photo.

'Have you taken many photos for her?' She couldn't help thinking Dilys probably knew every inch of this place without the need for a photographic reminder.

'Hundreds.' He was gazing in the direction of the lake, but he wasn't really looking at it. He was obviously far, far away from here and she knew she'd lost him.

'I'll see you back at the house.' She didn't wait for an acknowledgement. The man needed to be alone with whatever was troubling him, and he wasn't listening anyway. She looked for Esteban and saw him sitting nearby, watching Howard. He must have decided she no longer needed his protection. And she didn't. She could see the bothy down below. Five minutes and she'd be there.

Brett was still toiling away at the crumbling bothy wall. In fact, there seemed to be less of it than there had been when she'd passed by earlier.

'Esteban not with you?' he said.

'He's not far behind. He's waiting for Howard.'

'So that's where Howard went. He's supposed to be giving me a hand.'

She sensed the irritation coming off him. 'I can help. Just tell me what you need doing.'

His face softened. 'You look frozen. Go in and get warmed up.'

She nodded, grateful he'd refused her offer. 'Okay, but I'll come back out when I've put on more layers.'

Esme was in the vegetable garden. Ursula couldn't see what she was doing but it didn't look to be a lot. She felt a pang of yearning for her own allotment. It was almost three. If she'd been back there, she'd have finished her afternoon coffee and would be selecting something for her evening meal now. Best not to think about it. It only set her on edge. She gave Esme a wide berth and took the longer path that led to the boot room next to the kitchen.

Inside, the house was quiet. She made herself a hot drink to take up to her room. As she got to the top of the stairs, she heard crying. Proper crying this time. Not like Charlie's. Human crying, low but constant. It was hard to tell which room it was coming from. Ursula stood still, listening, wondering if it was Andi and whether she should knock each door until she found out. She wanted to but there it was again, the reticence that always held her back, always kept her in check. Small acts of defiance, she reminded herself. But she'd already walked up that hill and one small act was enough for today, so she went to her room and closed the door behind her.

She got straight into bed and pulled the duvet up to her chin. Just ten minutes and then she'd go out to Brett. But she couldn't properly warm up. In the end, she fished a grey cashmere scarf out of the drawer. It belonged to Anton and had replaced the mysteriously vanished red one, so it was old. But it had been well looked after. Preserving things had been another of his passion projects. She wrapped it around her neck. It didn't smell of him anymore. It didn't smell of anything. Ursula preferred it that way.

13

NO TIME FOR PITY

The bang of the gong interrupted the sleep Ursula hadn't realised she'd fallen into. She jolted upright and woke at the same time. The room was dark and in her drowsy confusion, she had to fumble around for the bedside lamp that felt too bright when she switched it on. Her eyes were like wide saucers, growing ever wider as they grew accustomed to the light. It took a while to shake off the grogginess and by the time she got down to the kitchen, the other residents had taken their seats. There was only one other place setting left, opposite Andi at the head of the table. Pablo's place, she suspected. Not somewhere she'd normally choose, but choice didn't come into it.

'Feeling the chill?' said Don.

'What? Oh.' Her hand shot to her neck, she was still wearing Anton's scarf. 'I was cold when I got in from my walk. I fell asleep and forgot it was there. Sorry, Brett, I meant to come back to help you.'

'No worries. Howard gave me a hand. We've pretty much taken the wall apart, ready to rebuild.'

'How was the hill climb?' said Andi.

'Invigorating and cloudy.' Ursula nodded to Esteban who was stretched out on a rug close to the Aga. 'Esteban stopped me from getting lost on the way up.' She turned to Brett. 'He's a smart dog. Have you had him long?'

Brett shook his head. 'He's not mine.'

'He's Pablo's,' said Andi. 'He got him from a local farmer when he was a pup. I wasn't the only one he deserted.'

Of course. The name should have made it obvious.

'So I guess that makes us both free agents now. There's always a silver lining if you look hard enough.'

Yes, there was, but perhaps the others weren't so sure about that. They kept their heads down and an awkward silence hung over them. It was going to be as bad as last night.

Don suddenly tapped a fork against his glass and startled them all to attention. 'Tonight's offering is roasted spring veg with crumbled feta and chorizo, accompanied by a cheeky little Rioja from Bala's very own Bargain Booze. Tuck in.'

Esme prodded a potato with her knife. 'Where did they come from?'

'Ursula brought them from her allotment. Thank you, Ursula,' said Don.

Esme gave her another of those filthy glares. Ursula pretended not to notice and acknowledged Don's gratitude: 'It looks delicious.'

The rest of dinner passed without further incident and when it was finished, everyone dispersed to complete chores or relax for the evening. Andi opened another bottle of Don's cheeky Rioja. 'Let's find somewhere quiet so we can talk properly.'

Oddly, for the cosiest room in the house, the lounge's only occupant was Don who was sitting on the sofa gazing at the fire. He opened his arms out to them. 'Come and join me.'

'Not tonight, Don. We'll find somewhere else,' said Andi.

There was a flash of disappointment across his face that he tried unsuccessfully to disguise. 'No, no. You sit yourselves down. I'll go and watch a bit of telly.'

Ursula sat in the place he'd left. 'I feel bad throwing him out.'

'Don't. He doesn't mind. Anyway, it's my house. I'm allowed.' Andi grinned at her in the way she used to when they were girls, sharing secrets, gossip, and laughter.

'Does it bother you not having your own private space?'

'Not really. I'm used to it. Anyway, I do have my own private space upstairs.'

'Yes, I suppose there is always your room. I met Howard on my walk. He was telling me his wife loved the way you could choose both company and privacy here.'

'Ah yes, Dilys. You know Megan's her niece?'

'Yes, he said. I thought they seemed quite attached.'

'She worries about him. Probably too much, but she's very close to Dilys. Or at least she was. No one can get close to Dilys now. She has Alzheimer's. And Howard seems lost without her, wandering around on that hill day after day.'

'He's taking photos for her. I suppose he hopes they'll trigger something in her.'

Andi sighed. 'I think it's too late for that. Your scarf, was it Anton's?'

'How did you guess?'

'The colour. Anton was a devil for grey.' There was that cheeky grin again, the one that told her they were still sharing laughter, even after all these years. 'Did you find it hard to let go of his things?'

'I haven't got round to it yet.'

'Oh, Urs.'

Ursula laughed, even though she hadn't meant to but this wasn't how it was supposed to go. Andi wasn't supposed to be pitying her. It was the wrong way round. Ursula wanted to change the subject but she couldn't think of anything that would haul her back to safe ground. It would have to be something halfway then. Something uncomfortable but not impossible to talk about. 'When I was up on the hill, I was thinking about that night my father turned up at Talulah. Do you remember it?'

'I remember that man, your father, having a right go at Cass before storming off. I remember Cass in a blind panic and the two of us running up and down New Street looking for you. And all the time you were getting off with Anton in his office.'

'I was not getting off with him. I kissed him, and then he took me home.'

'Oh right, so that wasn't getting off with him then?'

Ursula made a face like she was weighing things up. She'd managed to steer it back to safe ground after all. 'I suppose you could call it that, if you were a facetious madam. I prefer to think of it as the start of my double life.'

Andi poured some more wine. She was smiling again. Perhaps she was happy to be on safe ground too. Perhaps she wasn't ready to be pitied either. 'Yes, that is a good way to describe it. We had some good times, didn't we?'

'Some bloody good times.' Ursula thought back to those days of music, dancing, and eccentric clothes. Days of silliness and sweetness and undying friendship. Promises that seemed so easy to keep. Undoubtedly, the very best days of her life. Shame she didn't know it at the time.

14

SECRET AGENT URSULA FRY – 1979

Ursula had one eye on the clock and one on the fabric she was running through the machine. It was only an interface so it didn't matter if the stitch line wasn't absolutely perfect, although Wanda would not be happy if she caught her. The clock ticked over to twelve-thirty, just as she was finishing off and almost together, she and Andi said: 'Lunchtime.'

When they reached New Street she looked up to Anton's office, knowing that he would be in the window watching for her. She waved to him. It was a little habit they'd got into whenever she wasn't meeting him. Andi waved too but she also stuck out her tongue. 'That man is obsessed with you.'

'No he isn't. He just loves me.'

'He's still obsessed with you.'

Ursula tutted. 'You sound like my mum. I need to go to Lewis's food hall. I'm buying cakes.'

'Why are you buying cakes? I didn't forget your birthday, did I?'

'Do you really not know? And there was me thinking you

were my mate. It's my one-year anniversary as your work colleague and best friend.'

'Work colleague? Is that what Anton calls us wage slaves? Hang on. A year? You're kidding me. Where has that time gone? I feel so old.'

'Well, you are a year older than me, so I can see why.'

Andi pretended to wince. 'Oh how bitchy. I'm not sure I want to be your best friend for another year if that's what I've got to look forward to. Shall we go out and celebrate tonight?'

'Can't. I'm going out with Anton. Anyway, I thought you were going out with that fella tonight. What was his name again?'

'No point reminding you because I've already dumped him. Too boring.' Andi got through so many boyfriends. She had a very low boredom threshold. Ursula was always surprised that she herself hadn't breached that threshold yet. Especially since she'd been going out with Anton who Andi swore was the dullest person she'd ever met. He was a bit dull, but Ursula didn't mind that. She didn't want to go out with someone showy and over the top. Someone like her dad. Besides, she had enough excitement in her life with Andi. When they were together, it mostly non-stop laughs. They shared secrets, anger, and sadness too, but mostly it was music and dancing and laughs. Being with Anton was a much calmer experience. They never larked about, or danced in sweaty nightclubs. They went out for dinner and drank in sophisticated bars. It was like she led two separate lives. Secret agent Ursula Fry, the girl with a double life. Perhaps that's what kept her under Andi's boredom threshold.

'Are we still going to the Holy City Zoo on Saturday?' said Andi.

'Yeah. If I can finish the dress I'm making, I'm gonna wear it. D'you know what you're wearing?'

'Probably something I've already got. I could do with some new stuff really. I should make something but it just gets in the way at home. Too many people and not enough space, especially since my sister fell out with her bloke and moved back in.'

'Come to mine. You can stay over the weekend. Come straight from work on Saturday. We can get ready together and spend all day Sunday in the sewing room.'

'You have a sewing room?'

'It's my mum's but she won't mind. She's been telling me to invite you over.'

'God, okay. In that case, we'd better go up to the haberdashery before we buy the cakes. Don't you see Anton on Sundays then?'

'No. He works on his passion project.' She rolled her eyes before Andi did. 'He's found somewhere to build his house.'

'How do I look?' Ursula stood in between her mum and the TV.

'Like you're going to a funeral. Where did you get that dress?'

'Anton bought it for me.'

Her mum felt the fabric. 'Well he has impeccable taste, I'll give him that. You look beautiful. A very beautiful mourner. Where's he taking you?'

'Dunno. A posh restaurant in town, I think.'

The doorbell rang. 'That might be him.' Ursula ran back to her room to get her bag.

Her mum looked at the time. 'It's exactly seven-thirty. Of course it's him. Shall I go?'

'No, I'm ready now. Don't wait up. Oh, I nearly forgot, Andi's coming to stay for the weekend. We're going to use the sewing room. That's okay, isn't it?'

'Of course it is. Have a good time, love. And don't go anywhere near a funeral directors. You might get mistaken for one of them.'

'Ha ha. Hilarious. You should be on the telly.' Ursula opened the door to Anton and saw that he was wearing a black polo shirt and black trousers. They were both in head to toe black. Maybe her mum had a point.

He frowned. 'I beg your pardon?'

'Nothing. Just having a joke with Mum. Let's go.'

They stepped into the lift. The doors closed and he turned to look her over. 'You wore the dress.'

'Yes, well I thought that was why you bought it for me.'

He leaned forward and kissed her. 'Stunning.'

It was the most romantic thing he'd said or done to her in all the time they'd been going out and it caught her off guard. The lift doors opened but she held on to him, not wanting the moment to end. He tugged her hand. 'We must go.'

She didn't bother to ask him where they were going. She liked the not knowing. It added some excitement to the evening.

It turned out to be an Italian restaurant called Lorenzo's. There were some faces in there that she recognised from TV. She pointed them out to Anton but he said he hardly ever watched TV. 'Well then what do you do in the evenings?' she asked.

He shrugged. 'I work, I read. I go out with you. Or I think about you.'

She hadn't expected that last bit. It made her feel quite pleased with herself. 'You think about me? All the time, some of the time, or most of the time?'

'Most of the time.' He smiled that awkward, shy smile of his, the one that snapped at her heartstrings like they were elastic bands.

'Do you think about me when you're in bed?'

'Sometimes.'

'Do you wish I was there with you?'

His eyes narrowed. 'Sometimes. You're joking with me now, Ursula. You're in a very jokey mood tonight.'

Maybe she was joking with him a little, but there was a good reason for her asking. They'd been going out for months and he'd never once tried anything more than a kiss with her. 'No, I just wondered what we've been waiting for. I mean, it's not as if we don't have somewhere to go, is it? There's your flat. And I'm on the pill.'

'You're on the pill?'

'Of course I am. Don't look so shocked, Anton. It is 1979 for God's sake.'

He looked around and lowered his voice. 'I just assumed you were...'

'What, a virgin? Are you?'

'No.'

'Well then.'

'Are you sleeping with anyone at the moment?' he said, his voice still low.

'Well my boyfriend isn't interested and I'm not a two-timer, so no.'

'I am interested. I was just waiting for the right moment.'

'When do you think that will be?'

'Soon.'

It seemed wrong that she should be the one pushing him into sex. It wasn't as if she was that bothered about it, or even that she was experienced. She'd only slept with two boys so far and neither of them were good enough to make her desperate to try again. It was just that she was beginning to think there was something wrong with her and Anton. Or maybe it was just Anton.

'I have to go to Sweden for a while. I don't know how long I'll be away for. It's family business.'

Now it was Ursula's turn to be surprised. He never spoke about his family. If she ever asked about them, he said very little. 'Is everything all right?'

'I don't know. But when I come back, things will be different. I promise.'

15

IT WAS LOVE, WASN'T IT? – 1979

Ursula was shattered. Normally when she'd been out clubbing with Andi she slept until lunchtime, but not today. They'd crashed in her single bed at around four that morning and didn't wake up until the alarm very rudely broke their sleep at nine. They'd set it early to give themselves plenty of time for sewing. It was Andi's first visit to the flat, her first time in the sewing room, and while Ursula was ready to crawl back into bed, Andi was wide awake and absolutely buzzing.

'I think what would work well for you would be something with some structure between the bust and the hips. Something like this.' Ursula's mum drew a sketch on her pad and turned it round to show Andi the top half of a bustier dress with a sweetheart neckline. 'You have such lovely curves, it's a shame to hide them. You could either have the skirt as a pencil line or more full and floaty but with a punkish twist.'

Andi did a happy little shrug. 'Or I could make one of each.'

Ursula's mum laughed. 'Yes you could. But you still need to decide which one to make first. The material you've bought lends itself more to a pencil line, so I'd suggest starting with that. You could make it strapless, like Marilyn Monroe used to wear. Take a look through the library. You should find some patterns in there with that sort of style. We can adapt it to suit you. Ursula, you help. You'll find them in the 1950s section. I'll put the kettle on. We'll need tea and biscuits to keep us going.'

When most people talked of libraries, they meant a place to store books, but not her mum. Ursula opened the door to the library which was actually a walk-in cupboard where the boiler lived. There'd been only two shelves when they first moved in, but more had been added to hold all the patterns her mum had collected over the years.

Andi gasped. 'It's that kind of library. Oh, Urs, you lucky, lucky cow.'

Ursula smiled. With a horrible father like hers, she'd never thought of herself as lucky, but actually, she was. She took down three boxes marked 1950s.

Andi took two of them from her. 'Do you think if I was on my very best behaviour, your mum might consider adopting me?'

Ursula snorted. 'You're not an orphan. You already have a mum.'

'Yeah. But she doesn't have a sewing room or a pattern library. And she can't sketch out a beautiful dress as easily as making a cup of tea.'

'I pity your poor mother. I bet she does all sorts of lovely things for you that you just take for granted,' said Ursula's mum. Neither of them had realised she'd come back in the room.

Andi covered her eyes with embarrassment, but when they came out of the library, Ursula's mum was smiling. 'I'll tell you what. If you're the best friend my daughter could have, in time, I might consider making you an honorary daughter. Would that be acceptable?'

Andi looked at Ursula who nodded her agreement. 'That's easy, so it's a deal, Mrs Fry.'

'Gillian. I only use Mrs Fry when I have to. Do you have a boyfriend, Andi?'

'Just dumped him. Too dull.'

Ursula began to sort through the boxes. 'She hates dull men. That's why she hates Anton.'

Andi slapped her arm. 'I don't hate Anton. I just think he's really boring. He's like an old man, the way he acts and dresses. Honestly, Urs, I don't know how you stay awake when you're out with him.'

'Well, he's gone away for a while, so I'll have plenty of time for excitement now.'

Her mum stopped what she was doing. 'Where's he gone?'

'Back to Sweden. Family business. He doesn't know how long he'll be. Could be ages.' Her mum and Andi both raised their eyebrows and Ursula just about resisted the urge to say: 'Yeah, who's boring now?'

Anton was back. She hadn't seen him yet, but he'd written to tell her when exactly he'd be returning and asked her to take the day off work. He'd been away for two months and during that time, he wrote to Ursula every week. They were strange letters that only ever talked about the difference between Gothenburg and Birmingham, or the progress of his own house. He never wrote a word about his family and the only time he mentioned the business that had taken him there, was to say that it was taking longer than he'd hoped. Except for his last letter which said the business had been concluded. He hadn't given her his address in Gothenburg so she couldn't write back to let him know she'd been able to book a day's holiday. Instead, she'd called his flat and left a message on his answerphone to say it was all on and she'd see him at eleven o'clock on Wednesday, as he'd asked.

And now it was almost eleven and she was at the window, watching for his car, feeling apprehensive. She wasn't sure how she felt about him anymore. Two months was a long time and she'd got used to him not being around. Her double life had become a single one and any gaps that had been left by him had been filled by Andi and her mum. Andi had become part of the family now. It was like having a sister, because she didn't count her father's other daughters as her sisters. Maybe she didn't need Anton anymore. Maybe she never needed him.

His car pulled up outside and he got out. She noticed the red scarf tucked into his grey coat, all neat and tidy. Too tidy. Too formal. Too much. Seeing him again had made her realise he wasn't right for her.

Within a few minutes he was at the door. Ursula was on the other side, her heart pounding. She didn't want to open it but she couldn't just hide in here until he went away. She'd have to let him in, even if it was to tell him they were over.

'Ursula.' His smile was the biggest, brightest smile she'd ever seen on him. It almost took her breath away. He put his hand on her chin and kissed her. Her lips tingled. Her whole body tingled. He might not be right for her but she wanted him. She wanted the irresistible wholesomeness of him. She grabbed his hand and pulled him along the hall to her room.

'But I was going to take you to my apartment,' he protested.

She pulled off his coat. 'I don't want to wait that long. Do you?'

Anton shook his head, his hands faltering as he unbuttoned her blouse. Ursula unzipped her jeans and let him unhook her bra and slip off her panties. He stood in front of her, taking in her naked body for the first time. Then he kissed her again. The gentleness of it made her insides throb. She couldn't wait another minute. She helped him out of his clothes and dragged him onto the bed. He pushed himself away and sat back on his knees. 'You have no patience, my love.' He pressed his finger against her lips to quieten her protests. 'Ach, this bed is so tiny. But, Ursula must have what Ursula wants.' He kissed her once more, and again and again, his lips grazing every inch of her, and Ursula began to realise just how inexperienced she was.

It wasn't until afterwards, as they were lying together in her bed that she remembered he'd called her his love. 'Am I really your love?' she said.

'Yes you are. Am I yours?'

She didn't know for sure. She only knew that when she was with him she wanted him. Was that love? 'I think so.'

'You only think so? Again, you disappoint me, Ursula.'

She sat up and looked at him properly. He was teasing her, wasn't he?

He met her eyes. 'Get dressed. We're going out.'

'Where to?'

'To see my other love.'

. . .

At first they drove towards town, but then he turned off and went through Moseley. Shortly after they passed a sign for Edgbaston, he stopped outside a large house that seemed to be all windows. 'We are here.'

'It's your house. Is it finished?' She'd seen the model in his office, but she hadn't imagined just how much it would resemble a great big box of concrete and glass.

'Not yet. There's still much work to do. Be careful not to slip on the mud.'

He held her hand and she felt a flush of heat surge though her. It was mad to think that a few hours ago she was going to end it. But that was before they'd made love. Proper love, not awkward clumsy sex. He'd shown her his true feelings. He loved her, and she loved him too. It *was* love, wasn't it? This need for him. This desire.

The inside of the house seemed twice as big as it had looked from the outside. That was probably because it was an empty space with bare brick walls, where there were walls. The ground floor had very few. In fact, part of it had no ceiling. It went all the way up to the roof. Ursula stood under this part and shouted out: 'Yoo hoo.' She was sure she heard it bounce back at her.

Anton frowned. 'What are you doing?'

'Listening for the echo. Is it supposed to be like this, with no ceiling and rooms?'

'Yes. You don't like it?'

'I didn't say that. I've just never seen anything like it before.'

'That's because you have no experience of these things. It's more common in Europe. When the interior is finished, you'll be able to visualise it more easily.'

'Do your parents live in a house like this?'

'No, nothing like this.'

'Will you bring them over to see it when it's done?'

'My father died. That was the family business. I have no one now.' The way he'd said it was so matter of fact she thought at first she'd misheard him.

'He died? Oh, Anton, I'm so sorry. Why didn't you say?'

'There was no point.' He looked out of the wall of glass that separated the high ceiling-free space and the garden. 'Is it possible that you could live here?'

'I suppose. Why do you ask?'

'Because I want to marry you.'

Ursula's mouth dropped open. Anton was full of surprises today. 'Was that a proposal? Did you just propose to me?'

'Yes.' He said it so quietly she almost didn't hear, but she noticed that his ears had turned as red as his scarf. And if there had been any doubt left in her mind at all, that one single thing determined what her answer would be.

16

STIRRING THINGS UP

It was almost nine o'clock by the time Ursula got up. Quite late by her standards. It must have been the talking into the early hours with Andi and the lack of sleep that followed. They'd spent all night reminiscing about the happy times, before Pablo arrived on the scene and before she'd married Anton. It was amazing how they'd found so much to talk about but, once they'd started, they were drowning in good memories. You'd think that would have been enough to send her to sleep with a warm feeling inside, but all she had in there was regret.

Charlie Big Potatoes was sitting on the kitchen table. He gave her an imperious look but eventually decided she was worth his attention and jumped down to greet her with a loud wail and a leg rub. The noise made Don look up from the sink where he'd been washing the dishes. 'Morning. Help yourself to breakfast. They're all out working on the bothy, except for Esme. I think she's out there staring at the vegetables and willing them to grow.'

'Is Andi working on it as well?'

'Yep.'

They wouldn't be resuming last night's conversation this morning then. Ursula put the kettle on and cut two slices of bread for the toaster. 'I'll go and help them too.'

'You don't have to. I mean, we all do our bit but it's not compulsory.'

'I like to be busy.' That was an understatement. She needed to be busy. It stopped her thinking about things that troubled her, although she wasn't so sure that was the case anymore. Lately, those things had a way of crossing through. Maybe she just hadn't been busy enough. Although it could just as easily be the lack of structure. Her mind drifted back to the allotment while she was waiting for the toast to pop up. She'd have already done a good few hours work by now if she was there.

Don was wiping his hands dry, his forehead wrinkled up like he was trying to solve a puzzle. 'I know what you mean. Helps to keep your mind occupied. Cooking's the thing for me. I'm always thinking of new things to try.'

'You're very good at it. Were you a chef before you came here?'

'Only an amateur one. My last job was a taxi driver in Aberystwyth.'

'That must have been busy.'

'Depended on the season. A lot of the time you were just waiting around for jobs.'

'I expect that can be a bit lonely.'

Even though she didn't think it was possible, Don screwed his forehead up even tighter until it looked almost painful, then he let it relax. 'It could be, but I ended up here because of it so I can't complain, can I? I picked Pablo up once when he'd had too many bevvies to drive home. It's a good hour and twenty, door to door, so we had plenty of time to talk. You know Pablo, he can talk. I suppose he sold the place to me. The next day he was back in Aber to pick up his car and he came to find me. Said they had a spare room going if I was interested. Been here ever since. Can't think of anywhere else I'd rather be. It's not the same since Pab left, mind.'

Ah, Pablo. The man everybody loved and the man who loved everybody equally. Perhaps too equally.

Esme was in the middle of the vegetable patch wearing her customary sour expression. Ursula couldn't help wondering what kind of life she'd led to make her so permanently angry. It was this thought alone that made her put on her veil smile and wish Esme a good morning. She received a blank stare and a nod in return. It was progress, she supposed.

Brett, Howard and Andi were in consultation over some boulders when she reached them. 'We're trying to work out which ones go where. It's been slow progress so far,' said Andi. 'We need an expert really, but that costs money.'

Anton would have worked it out easily. He had an eye for that sort of thing. That said, Anton would have pulled the whole thing down and replaced it with something stunningly modern in its place. Then he would have built a wall around it and kept it for himself. Ursula tried to imagine how he would have approached it. No, she couldn't. But she could think of it in a different way. She could imagine it through her mum's eye. 'I was thinking, how would Mum have done it?'

Andi thought for a minute, then smiled. 'She would have looked for shapes and patterns.'

'Your mum was a builder?' said Brett.

Ursula shook her head. 'She was a dressmaker. One of the best in her day.'

'And a designer,' added Andi.

'She would have said she was more of a magpie than a designer.'

Andi tutted and rolled her eyes. 'Yes, but we both know that wasn't true. We'll lay this wall out on the ground first. Look for patterns and shapes. Let's be more Gillian.'

Howard patted a bewildered looking Brett on the back. 'You heard her, man. Let's be more Gillian.'

They each picked up a rock from the pile that had previously been created and put them down in a clear space, then four more, and another four. It took a few more rounds before they found three that looked like they belonged together. They shuffled rocks this way and that, picked them up and re-placed them, and slowly, very slowly the missing wall began to appear. Esteban, who'd been keeping a distant eye on proceedings, didn't help when he decided it was more fun to pick up stones and add them to the mix. But by the time Esme came to tell them lunch was ready, at least a quarter of the wall had been laid out on the ground. They walked back to the house and all the talk was about how well it was going.

'Well you lot look happy,' said Don as they queued up to wash their hands.

'We've had a good morning,' said Andi.

Howard took his turn at the tap. 'You know, I actually had a great morning. I'd like to know more about Gillian.'

Andi sat down at the table. 'Gillian Fry could take one look at a person and work out exactly what style would suit them. Exactly where an extra stitch or a tuck was needed.

And then she'd just sketch something out without even blinking. The woman was a genius. Wouldn't you say, Urs?'

'So how come we've never heard of her,' said Esme, already bringing the mood down.

How come indeed? Her mum should have been celebrated. She should have been allowed to grow and fulfil her ambitions. 'For the same reason so many women get overlooked,' said Ursula. 'Men. Men with their money and power. She was treated badly by my father and his family. She had to leave her chosen profession and get an office job to support us.'

'That's really shit,' said Esme in an uncommon moment of empathy.

'Yes it was. She made lots of sacrifices in her life.'

'I still have that first dress she designed for me,' said Andi. 'The one the three of us made together. Do you remember it?'

'Your Marilyn Monroe dress. Funnily enough I was thinking about it last night.'

They'd carried on working through the afternoon until it was too dark to see properly. No one mentioned her mum again. She'd probably put them off with her rare flash of anger. Thinking of her father still did that to her. Most of the time she gave the impression of someone who floated through life, untouched by the kind of things that would crush a less spiritual soul. It was all crap really. Ursula wasn't at all spiritual and she hurt, she bled as much as the next person. Only a few people saw that in her and of those select few, only Andi was still around.

Don had produced another fine dinner. It made her realise just how long it had been since she'd cooked a proper meal. Six years probably. Not that she missed it. She had been a good cook though. She'd learned out of necessity. All those tiresome dinner parties for Anton's clients and friends. When she'd said yes to his highly inadequate proposal she'd had no idea what she'd let herself in for. And that wasn't just when it came to cooking. She should have listened to her gut instincts instead of giving in to lust. Because that's all it was. Carnal desire. Pure and simple. It certainly wasn't love. She didn't even know what love was. Until it hit her.

After dinner, the roaring fire in the lounge tempted her in. A long soak in the bath would have been nice, but one of the drawbacks of this place was that hot water and bathroom time were in short supply, so she'd have to bathe in the soothing warmth of the fire instead.

It wasn't long before Howard put his head around the door. 'I'm not disturbing you, am I?'

'Not at all.' She'd been expecting it to be Andi and had to resort, once again, to her veil smile to mask the disappointment.

They sat in silence watching the flames. It reminded her of when she and Samuel used to sit together in the evenings on the allotment. Samuel was one of those few people who saw through her. She didn't have to pretend with him. That was what made him such good company.

'I'm sorry I asked about your mother earlier.' He was still looking at the fire when he said it.

'It really wasn't a problem.' The veil smile was back again.

'I think I stirred things up. For you and Andi. That wasn't my intention.'

His eyes met hers. She thought of Samuel again and wished it were him she was talking to. 'We were very close, the three of us.' Most of the time anyway, but that was between only her and Andi.

'I got lucky with my parents. They had a very happy marriage. I can't imagine what it must have been like for you and your mother.'

She said nothing. What was there to say that would change anything? 'How is your wife? Andi said she's unwell.'

'Most days she's lost. Occasionally, she has a good day. I didn't want to leave her but the kids persuaded me to take a break. Have you ever been around someone with Alzheimer's?' She shook her head. 'You feel so damn useless.'

'So you came here to feel useful. The photos. Committing each step on the hill to memory so you can relate them back to her.'

'Sounds a little crazy, right?'

'It sounds like an act of love.'

'It won't bring her back to me though. I know it, but I still keep walking up that damn hill every day.'

She wanted to reach out and take hold of his hand. If it had been Samuel, she would have done, and God knows this man had a way about him that reminded her of Samuel in his later years. But this was Howard. She didn't know him and it wasn't appropriate. And besides, they were both so very vulnerable.

17

THE TIP OF THE ICEBERG

Mr Big Potatoes had been back at the windowsill with his early alarm call this morning, meaning Ursula was down in the kitchen by seven. Even so, she was still the last one up. She greeted everyone and got a couple of acknowledgements in return. But most were more interested in the good-looking young man who'd just come in from the boot room with the egg basket. 'That's eighteen in the car and five left in here for you, Don.'

Esme jumped up from the table. 'I'll take them.'

The young man's face creased into the kind of smile that made the world a brighter place to be in. 'Thanks, Esme.'

Every visible part of Esme body was glowing. It was a complete transformation. 'Do you want a drink?'

'Not today thanks. Mam's waiting for me. The hob's on the blink again.' He treated Ursula to one of those smiles. She noted the disappointment on Esme's face. 'Hi, Ursula. I'm Gareth, Megan's son and chief skivvy. Anyone need a lift into town?'

'Me! I would.' Esme's arm shot up in the air. Seconds later she was at Gareth's side, looking like an anxious little bird.

'Okay. I'll wait while you get your coat then, shall I? Anyone else?' said Gareth.

'You're about two hours too early for me, mate, but thanks for asking,' said Don.

Esme was back, wearing a jacket and a smile that made her look quite stunning. Ursula hadn't noticed until now how pretty she was. She reminded her of someone but she couldn't think who it was. She rarely watched TV or read the papers these days so it must be someone from the past. An old film star perhaps.

Gareth opened the boot room door for Esme. 'Just you and me then, Es. Mam said she'll message you with her shopping list, Andi.'

'Okay, I'll look out for it. I'm going to Barmouth today if you fancy keeping me company, Urs,' said Andi.

'I'd love to.' So this was why they'd hardly talked properly. Andi was saving it until they couldn't be interrupted by the others.

Andi drove a small Japanese car, not unlike Ursula's. She wasn't, as Ursula had assumed, the owner of the tatty old van she'd parked next to on the first day. 'I'll have to leave you to your own devices for an hour or so. I'm seeing a solicitor,' she said.

'To do with Pablo leaving?'

'Uh huh. There's a nice beach at Barmouth for a walk if you need something to pass the time. More shops, which is why I have a long shopping list. It's only about an hour's drive but we don't go there very often, so everybody wants me to bring something back that they can't get in Bala.'

'Is there an outdoor shop? I think I need a warmer coat.'

'Yes, there is. It will warm up eventually if you're staying until the summer kicks in properly.'

'I'm not sure how long I'll be staying yet. Does that matter?' The truth was, she was already longing to get back home. Not to the house. She'd be quite happy never to see that place again. But she was missing the allotments and her routine.

'No. The room's yours for as long as you want it, and if you go, you can come back and see me anytime. Wherever I might be.' Andi's face was rigid. She was trying to keep it together. She always came across as strong and defiant, but Ursula had been friends with her long enough to know there were times when even she was lost and frightened. She cursed herself then for forgetting the reason she'd come to Am-nawr. She was supposed to be saving her oldest friend and allotments and routines would just have to wait.

It took her a few minutes to grasp what Andi had meant by that last sentence and then she realised that it wasn't just Pab that was breaking Andi's heart, it was also the possibility that she might lose the house. 'Will you have to sell Am-nawr?'

'Not sure. I'm hoping the solicitor will tell me that. I haven't said anything to the others, by the way. I expect they're already asking themselves the same question but none of them has asked me.'

'They're afraid of the answer.'

Andi let out a muffled laugh. 'And so says Madam Ursula. Ever thought of doing palm readings on the side?'

'Hmm. That's not a bad idea. Would you like to have your

palm read by Madam Ursula, my dear? Tell you your future?' she said in a very bad continental accent.

Andi's mouth set itself in a straight line. 'The only future I'm interested in right now is whether that bastard is going to make my life even harder.'

Ursula was suddenly hit by an overwhelming feeling of hopelessness and she had to look at the unfolding scenery in case it showed on her face. This was embarrassing. She should be the strong one. But the only strength in evidence right now was coming from Andi, as was ever the case. She'd always been the weak one. 'I wish I could make things better for you,' she said when she'd finally pushed that pathetic feeling back in its box.

'You are. Just having you here is helping. The others don't really know me like you. And anyway, they feel as betrayed by Pab as I do. He brought them all here you see. They came because of him. And now he's dumped them.' Andi was doing what she always did, putting other people before herself. That was the trouble with being the strong one, you were always looking out for someone else. Up until he left her, Pablo had always come first but as he wasn't here, perhaps the residents were the next best thing.

'Andi, you've been with Pablo for over thirty years. Those people have known him for a few at the most. So no, they don't feel as betrayed as you do. They don't have the right to. You need to be thinking of your own survival, not theirs.'

Andi shook her head. 'Who is that I spy poking out from underneath all that sweet natured wholesomeness? Is that my old friend Ursula Fry? Are you still in there, Urs?'

'Just about. I meant to ask how the kids have taken it.'

'They're angry but not surprised. Not sure what that says about their parents' relationship. Don't want to think about it either. I've got enough emotional baggage as it is. On the plus side, Zak's talking to me now.'

'I didn't realise he wasn't. Did you fall out?'

'Not exactly but he's been distant for a year now.'

'Why?'

'Oh you know. Shit happens.'

Ursula looked out of the window. In the distance, the sea was coming into view. 'What kind of shit?'

'The kind I don't want to talk about right now.'

So that was it then. Conversation over. There were a few things that Andi didn't seem want to talk about right now. She told herself to be patient but, as Anton had once jokingly pointed out, patience was never her strong suit.

While Andi was with the solicitor, Ursula shopped for a warm waterproof coat and jumpers because she was already feeling the chill in draughty old Am-nawr. Anton's house might not have much going for it but at least it was always warm enough.

She was putting her shopping in the car when she got a message from Andi to say she was finished. They met in the harbour and went for a beach walk. It was long, flat and quiet. The ideal place for Andi to relay the solicitor's advice. 'The house is actually in my name. I bought it with my money. Pab used some of his for the repairs but he didn't have a lot. You know his views on money. It was only good for one thing.'

Ursula nodded but actually she hadn't really known because this was the first time Andi had mentioned it. She'd guessed though. Right from the start, Pab always seemed to be living beyond his means. Andi hadn't mentioned this rift with Zak before either. A year, she'd said. There was more to this, Ursula was sure of it. She had a strong feeling she'd only been shown the tip of the iceberg and there was plenty more emotional baggage to come.

'Anyway, the solicitor suggests waiting a few weeks, to see if he makes any demands. In the meantime she's going to put together a plan of action.' Andi stopped and looked out to the sea. 'I used to come here when I was a kid. It hasn't changed too much. You can still get donkey rides in the summer.'

'I bet it was wonderful. We hardly ever came to places like this. Only once to Cornwall with my nan, after we moved in with her. When my father lived with us, we went abroad. After he left, Mum couldn't even afford a week in Weston-Super-Mare.'

'Didn't you ever go with Anton?'

'You've got to be kidding. Anton didn't see the point in holidays. You know how often we travelled, but it was always for work purposes. No time for long beach walks.'

'I told you he was boring. I distinctly remember telling you that at least once a day before you married him.'

Ursula remembered that too. She also remembered Andi telling her not to marry him. In fact the only three women who'd ever had any influence on her had all said it. But she'd ignored them all. Then she recalled the other thing Anton had said about her when he'd told her she had no patience, 'Ursula must have what Ursula wants,' and she reminded herself again that wanting someone was not the same as loving them.

18

A HOUSE BUILT FOR SILENCE – 1980

An argument had started just before they'd got on the train but her mum had refused to keep it going in the carriage with the other passengers listening in. Ursula had to wait until they were on the platform to pick it up again. 'Why are you being so horrible about it? I actually think you don't like Anton.'

'Don't be silly. I don't dislike him. But he's very different to you, and I don't think you've really thought about how that's going to affect you if you marry.'

It had been like this from the day he'd proposed. Ursula had blurted the news out as soon as her mum got home, hardly able to keep it in. She'd been expecting celebrations when all she got was a stiff look and a suggestion that she was rushing into it. It was her father's fault. If he hadn't treated them so badly, her mum wouldn't see him in every man she came into contact with. 'He's nothing like him, you know.'

'Him? I take it you mean your father? I didn't say he was. Bernard was very charismatic.'

'Anton's charismatic.'

Her mum gave her a knowing smile, just to let her know she was being ridiculous. Ursula really didn't need telling, she knew it already. She loved Anton but even she had to admit he would never, ever be charismatic. Nor would he ever be exciting. Not in Andi's sense of the word anyway. Trying to change Andi's mind was also a lost cause. She was another one who was dead against it but that was probably because she was convinced Ursula had gone off the idea of them getting their own shop, which was absolute nonsense. All she was doing was getting married. Nothing else was going to change.

'You need to tell Cassandra.' It was her mum's parting shot before turning off.

'I will.'

'Today.'

Ursula tutted. 'I said I will.'

She knocked on the door to Cass's office. It was the third time she'd tried. The first time, she'd heard Cass's raised voice and had taken that to mean she was on the phone and the call wasn't going well, so she'd gone back upstairs for half an hour. The second knock had been met with a sharp: 'Not now,' so off she'd gone again. This time, the knock was answered by the door opening. Cass looked like the blood had been drained from her face. The only bit of colour came from her bloodshot eyes. The sight of her made Ursula want to run back upstairs again but it was too late for that now. She was getting married in six weeks and Cass needed to know. Admittedly, she should have told her earlier, but after all the flak she'd been receiving from her mum and Andi, Ursula had put it off for as long as possible. Stupid really because Cass didn't know Anton enough to have an opinion on him.

Cass folded her arms and let out a short but loud sigh. 'Well?'

'I just wanted to let you know I'm getting married.'

'You're getting married.'

'Yes,' she replied, even though it hadn't been a question. 'On 4th April.'

'4th April.' Again, not a question.

'Yep. I'd like two weeks off.'

'You know that's the week I was planning to launch the new collection.'

'I'm sorry, Cass. It's the only time Anton can fit it in.'

'Sounds like he's got his priorities in the right order then.'

'He's very busy.'

'I'll bet he is.'

'Is it okay then, the holiday?'

'No, but what choice do I have?'

Ursula backed away. 'Thanks. Sorry again.'

'For what it's worth, I think you're making a huge mistake.'

For fuck's sake. Could no one be happy for her? That was it. The very last and final straw. 'Well, for what it's worth, I don't.'

'Please yourself,' said Cass, right before she slammed the door shut.

Ursula gripped Anton's hand tightly, afraid she might trip up and ruin her brand-new coat if she didn't. He'd bought it for her while they were on their honeymoon and it had been so expensive, she was almost frightened to wear it. 'Can I open my eyes yet?'

'Absolutely not. Don't spoil the surprise.'

She shook her head but kept her eyes closed. 'It's not as if I haven't seen it before.'

'I know but not since it's been finished. Be patient. We're almost there. Take a step up.'

She tapped her toe around gingerly until she found the step. It was a bit silly really but she didn't want to ruin it for him. The wedding had been a quiet register office ceremony with very few guests. Her mum, Andi, and Wanda were there. Her nan, the only other member of what she considered family, had died four years ago. Cass had been invited but she'd opted to look after the shop instead. It was probably for the best. Even though her mum had said it was okay to invite her, it would have made things difficult. Anton's only guests were two friends from London who she'd never met. He hadn't even invited his work colleagues. It wasn't the kind of wedding she'd expected to have but it was okay. At least her dress had been beautiful, thanks to her mum who had actually cried at the ceremony. And the honeymoon had been really interesting. A lot of it had involved looking at buildings, but that was what you got for marrying an architect.

There was a sound behind her, the closing of a door, she thought. She listened for the other noises around her. Nothing. Silence. No more birdsong, or traffic, or anything. Just the sound of her own breathing. Anton let go of her hand but he was still very close. She could feel him next to her. 'You can open them now.'

She opened her eyes and was stunned by the brightness. The last time she'd been inside the house was the day Anton had proposed to her. It had seemed big then but now that it was finished, now that it was so white and polished and dazzling, it looked enormous. There was furniture in the room and there were paintings on the walls but it was the space between them that she noticed.

Anton was watching her intently. 'Do you like it?'

'Of course. It's absolutely beautiful.' She wasn't really lying. She didn't hate it. She didn't actually know how she felt about it but, as Anton had already joked on their honeymoon, she knew nothing about taste when it came to house building. 'It's very quiet.'

'I have built it for silence. The walls and windows, I could go into the technical details but you won't understand.'

'Try me.'

He shook his head. 'It would be a waste of time. It's beyond you.'

He was probably joking again but it still stung. He surveyed his work with an air of satisfaction that, hurt as she was, turned her on. When he showed her upstairs she was definitely going to tear his clothes off and jump on him. Not down here though, not with those enormous windows. Any passer-by could see. She pulled him towards the stairs. 'What will you do now you've finished your passion project?'

He reached out to her and she prepared herself for long, lingering kiss. It didn't come. Instead, he tidied a loose strand of hair that had fallen over her face. 'I will find another one.'

19

SPITEFUL, NASTY WORDS – 1981

'In the dishwasher, please.' Anton appeared as if from nowhere which was quite an amazing feat in a house with so few walls. Anyone else would have jumped out of their skin, but Ursula had got used it. He did it every morning at the exact moment she finished her breakfast, so the element of surprise had been lost ages ago. About a month after their wedding, if she had to pin it down.

'I was just going to.' She gave him the filthy look he deserved and slung her empty plate and cup into the machine. When they'd first moved in, the dishwasher had been the most exciting thing about her new home. As far as she was concerned anyway. But she'd soon grown tired of it. Or rather, she was tired of Anton reminding her to hide every dirty piece of tableware in it the second she'd taken her last bite. Absolutely nothing allowed to be left out in this house in case it messed up his precious clean lines. It was another of his little quirks she'd stopped finding sweet. In fact, it was bloody irritating.

In the short space of time it took her to close the dishwasher door, he'd moved to the chair she'd been sitting on and pushed it in so that it lined up with the others. Now he was looking at the spot on the table where her plate and cup had been. Wordlessly, she ran a cloth under the hot tap and wiped away all evidence that she'd been there. She counted the crumbs as she collected them in her hand. Three. Yesterday, it had been four. She was improving.

He held her coat out for her to slip her arms into, the one he'd bought her on their honeymoon last year. She took it from him. 'Oh, it's too nice for work, it'll only get messed up. I'll wear the other one.' Before he had a chance to complain, she was on her way upstairs to make the switch. She didn't hear his sigh in this house built for silence, but she could feel it which was bad enough.

'Mum's been asking about Christmas again.' Ursula waited until they were in the car to ask so he couldn't dash off on the pretence that he had some urgent business to deal with, which was what he'd done all the other times she'd asked. They'd gone to her mum's last year and had the cosy kind of Christmas they always did. Well, the kind Ursula and her mum always did. It had been torture for Anton. He hadn't said as much but it was obvious. Obvious and embarrassing, because it was also obvious to her mum. This year, she'd thought about inviting her mum to spend Christmas at their house. At least that way Anton could hide away upstairs when it got too much for him. There was one problem with that though. Their house wasn't in the least bit Christmassy. Anton with his clean lines again. Ursula could live with it, but she wasn't sure her mum could.

'I am afraid we have to be in Germany.' His expression was completely unreadable. He was always banging on about her and her bloody veil smile, but he was the master at bringing down the shutters.

'For Christmas? Are you having me on?'

'No. It's work. I must go there on the sixteenth for four weeks.'

'But it's Christmas. No one works over Christmas except doctors and nurses and people on the telly.'

'I must. I have a lot of work to do while I'm there. It's very important for the partnership. We will celebrate Christmas there.'

'We? I can't take four weeks off work. I can't even take a day off. This is our busiest time of the year. And the sixteenth is next week. Why are you only telling me this now?'

'I didn't know until now. I will go alone then. You can spend Christmas with Gillian. She will like that.'

'But I wanted us all to have Christmas together.' Ursula dug her nails into her palms. This had to be the crappiest way in history to get out of doing something you don't like.

'We will do that next year.'

'Unless you find some other excuse.' She folded her arms. She was so angry she was about to cry. And she didn't believe that rubbish about him only just finding out either.

Anton frowned, his eyes still on the traffic in front of them. 'Now you are behaving like a spoilt brat. You cannot always have everything you want, Ursula. You're not a child. Marriage is full of compromises, and the sooner you understand that the easier it will be for both of us.'

His words had hit her like a slap. She looked at him in astonishment. A spoilt brat? How could he say that to her, after all she'd been through with her father?

She jumped out of the car as soon as he pulled into the car park. She didn't want to be with him a minute longer. In fact, she was glad he wouldn't be here to spoil Christmas. She only wished she didn't have to wait until next week for him to go.

'I'll wash, you dry.' Ursula's mum plunged the glasses into the hot, soapy water. They'd given it a couple of hours after eating before tackling the mess that always came with Christmas dinner. There were dirty dishes and pans on every surface and Ursula loved the chaos of it. Although it had to be said, she was missing her dishwasher.

She'd come home the day Anton left for Germany, a bundle of confused emotions. One half of her had been upset at the thought of him being away for a whole month, and the other half was glad to see the back of him. Their argument had cut deeply, or rather his description of her had, and she'd hardly spoken to him for the rest of the week leading up to his departure. Pride made her keep it to herself and say nothing to her mum or Andi, but that didn't stop her going over and over it in her head and wondering whether she had been just a little bit childish in expecting him to refuse work just for her. Especially when it was so important to the business.

It hadn't taken long for her and her mum to fall back into their old routines and it was almost as though she'd never left. And being at home had its advantages. Especially going clubbing with Andi, something she never got to do when Anton was around. It was like being single again, without the added complication of getting off with men.

Andi was coming over later. She'd passed her driving test in October and had bought her brother's old Ford Escort off him. She was staying over. Amazingly, Cass had decided to close the shop until after new year, so they had some extra days off. Wanda told her the Frys were going away somewhere. That was as much as Wanda knew, and as much as Ursula wanted to know. Cass had only told them about the closure the day before Christmas Eve, so it had been too late to make arrangements to go to Germany. Not that Ursula wanted to go there anyway. She'd much rather be sitting in front of the telly with her mum and a box of Quality Street.

'Is Anton calling you today?' said her mum.

'Dunno. He gets carried away with work sometimes. He forgets.' That wasn't exactly correct; Anton hardly ever forgot anything. He hadn't called her at all since he'd left though. Probably because he thought it wasn't worth it if she wasn't talking to him.

'Are things all right between you two?'

'Yeah, fine. We're still adjusting to married life but that's normal, isn't it?' Ursula picked up a plate and ran the tea towel over it.

Her mum filled the space on the drainer with another plate. 'I've really enjoyed having you home. It's been very quiet without you blasting my ears with music all the time. I don't know how Anton copes.'

'Oh I don't put the radio on much these days. He needs quiet for work. It disturbs him. Honestly, you can literally hear a pin drop in that house.'

'Sounds awful. I know what to buy you for your birthday then. One of those new Walkman thingies like Andi has.'

'Oh you've seen that, have you?'

'Yes. She comes over from time to time to do some sewing and keep me company.'

'She never told me that.' And neither had her mum before now.

'Well, now that it's come up, there's something I do want to talk to you about. You probably know Andi's parents are moving away from Birmingham in the new year?'

'Yeah. She's been looking for a flat.'

'I've asked her if she wants to live here.'

'Here? But where will she sleep?'

'In your old room. That's all right, isn't it, love? You don't mind, do you? It's just that the extra money would be handy, and it would be company for me.'

'No it's fine. Honestly, it's fine.' Ursula picked up a dish and rubbed away at it. She wanted to cry but that would have made her look like an idiot. She didn't even know why she wanted to do it. Her mum was probably missing the company. And it was great that Andi was going to be looking out for her. So why was she being so stupid about it?

At that moment, the doorbell rang. Her mum put the last pan on the drainer and pulled the plug out of the sink. 'That'll be Andi. I'll let her in.'

Ursula could hear them whispering in the hall. No prizes for guessing what they were whispering about. She carried on with the drying up. After a while, Andi came in and took out a clean tea towel. Ursula noted that she'd gone straight to the right drawer, as if she'd done it a hundred times, although she couldn't remember her ever doing that before. That riled her a little bit. They carried on working away at the wet dishes until she couldn't stand it anymore. 'Why didn't you tell me you'd been visiting my mum on the sly?'

Andi stopped what she was doing. 'She asked me not to. She didn't want you to worry about her.'

'I thought you were going to get your own place.'

'I was, but I can only afford a shitty bedsit or a flat share. Gillian asked me last week if I wanted to move in. I haven't said yes. I wanted to see how you felt about it first. I won't do it if you don't like the idea.'

Ursula kept her mouth shut knowing that if any words came out, they'd be spiteful and nasty and she didn't want that.

'She's lonely, Urs. We both are.'

Her mum and Andi were filling the hole she'd left behind. Ursula was being squeezed out and it hurt. Her mouth opened and out they came, those bad words that she'd been trying so hard not to say: 'You should do it. I'm a married woman now. I've got my husband to think of. I can't spend all my time keeping you two happy.' She threw the tea towel down, went to the bathroom and stared at her sullen, bitter face in the mirror. And then it hit her. Anton was right. She was nothing but a spoilt brat.

20

A LITTLE HONEST ADVICE

Ursula stopped for a breather while Howard and Brett carried on piecing together the final layer of the bothy wall. They'd been plugging away at it for the last three days, a few hours here and there. Finding the right stones for the right holes had taken all her concentration at first. But like any jigsaw puzzle, the more you fit in, the easier it becomes and the harder it is to block out other distractions. Since her trip to Barmouth, more reminders of her past had insisted on providing those distractions.

This afternoon, the satisfaction of nearly finishing the wall was being marred by the memory of that Christmas Anton had spent in Germany and the subsequent fallout. Her second Christmas as a married woman, although, woman was probably stretching it a bit. She was twenty-two at the time but in reality, she'd been no more than a child. And if she hadn't been a child, then certainly the way she'd dealt with her mum and Andi's friendship had been childish. She'd understood that as soon as she'd said that hurtful thing to Andi, but it still didn't stop her being ruled by childish jealousy. When Anton returned she apologised to him for being unreasonable and threw herself into the marriage for no other reason than to spite her mum and Andi. It was a mistake, of course, because it opened the door for him to help her grow up. That was how he phrased it. She became his new passion project. But the biggest mistake of all was to let it drive a wedge between her and the only two people who could have stopped her from losing herself altogether.

'The last stone. Who wants to put it in?' said Brett.

'You've worked hardest on it. It should be you. Don't you agree, Ursula?' said Howard.

'Absolutely, but I think we should mark the occasion in some way. At least by getting the others up here to witness it.'

'Agreed. I'll go and round them up. Don't go away.' Howard went off at a pace towards the house. These last few days seemed to have brought him out of his shell. She wondered what he would do now that the job was done. Her too for that matter. For a short while this work had given her some much-needed structure and now it was over, she wasn't sure what would replace it. Then there was Brett. As far as she could tell, this bothy had occupied him since before she arrived.

'You'll have some time on your hands now,' she said.

'Nah. Starting on another repair job in Frongoch the day after tomorrow. Gareth's sorted it for me.'

'Have you been here long?'

'Coming up to a year now.'

'Andi said Pablo brought you here.'

'In a way. My grandad was mates with him from way back. He asked Pablo to take me in. Don't wanna go into the details but London wasn't working for me. I thought I was gonna hate it here but it turned out the opposite. I'm grateful to Pab for that. I don't know how he could have done that to Andi though. That was nasty. I just wanted you to know, what with you being her friend and everything, I'm on her side.'

Ursula smiled. 'Me too. Have you told Andi that?'

'Don't wanna bring him up. Can't stand to see her upset.' He nodded towards the house. 'Here they come.'

The cheers went up as Brett laid the last stone. Don produced a dusty bottle of prosecco that he'd found at the back of the larder and poured them all a drop into plastic cups that looked like they'd been found in the same place as the prosecco. 'To the bothy. May it stay standing for many more years to come.'

They knocked back their drinks like shots, realising as soon as it hit their tongues, why it had been left so long.

Esme stuck her head around the door. 'There's no furniture.'

Don winced as he drained the last few dregs of prosecco. 'All sorted, my lovely. Gareth's bringing some up this evening. I've asked him to collect a few bottles of wine on the way. Megan's coming too.'

'Sounds like quite a party you're planning there,' said Andi.

Don held his hands out. 'We've got a useable bothy. I'd say that was cause for a celebration, wouldn't you?'

Everybody looked at Andi. It was as if they were holding their breaths until they saw how she was going to react. They were all the same as Brett. None of them wanted to upset her.

'Yes, I would.' Andi smiled and straight away, everyone else was smiling too, the relief written large across their faces.

. . .

Gareth arrived just as it was getting dark. On the back of his truck was a small table with two chairs and a backless wooden bench that could be used as an emergency bed. They'd come from another old bothy up in the mountains that had fallen too far into disrepair. They carried the furniture into the boot room for the night so that Brett could finish off the inside tomorrow. Gareth had also brought with him six bottles of wine, two dozen cans of beer, and Megan.

As soon as she was inside, Megan grabbed hold of Howard. 'Any news on Dilys?'

His face lit up. 'Yes, she's much brighter today. The kids said she's responding to the photos I'm sending.' That explained his recent good mood then.

'That's promising then, isn't it?' Megan patted his arm. She was trying to reassure him. The trouble was she didn't look so reassured herself.

Don banged the gong, despite everyone being in the kitchen already. 'Right, you lovely lot. Coq au vin a la Donald is ready. Grab a seat and tuck in.'

What followed was a scramble for the best places at the table. For once, Esme chose not to sit by Andi but instead dived for the seat next to Gareth. It was clear the poor girl was smitten. It was less clear whether Gareth was equally smitten. Ursula took the only remaining chair, the one at the end of the table again. Megan and Howard were either side of her. The food was splashed onto plates, some of them had wine, some had beer. Almost all had something to say, much of it at the same time. It was a dinner party unlike any Ursula had been to. It was certainly not the kind of dinner party you'd find in a house built for silence. It occurred to her that before she'd come to Am-nawr, the thought of something like this would have terrified her. But she was actually enjoying herself.

Megan leaned in towards her. 'You're a widow then, Ursula.'

'That's right. And you, Megan?'

'Divorced and very happily unattached. I haven't got time for men, to be honest. Too much like hard work, if you ask me. Present company excepted, before you say anything, Howard.'

Howard grinned at her. 'I wouldn't dream of it, honey.'

Megan rolled her eyes. 'Hasn't he got a lovely way of speaking, Ursula? I could fall for that accent in a flash. If he wasn't my uncle and as old as my dad.'

Howard threw back his head and laughed. It was spontaneous and unexpected, and completely charming. He turned to Ursula, the creases around his eyes still showing the tracks of laughter. 'More wine?'

She pushed her glass towards him, already feeling a bit tipsy. He topped all three glasses up. Megan leaned back in her chair, glass in hand. 'How long you been a widow for?'

'Six years now.'

'Does it get any easier?' said Howard. She sensed he was asking for himself more than anything. Preparing himself for the inevitable.

'A little. Although, it doesn't really feel as if I've let him go.' She realised she hadn't given him the answer he was looking for. She should have said there were things you could put in place, ways to manage your days. Coping mechanisms. Just try not to let the ghost in the window frighten you. But then again, maybe she shouldn't have said that. Anyway, Howard would probably be overjoyed if Dilys came back to haunt him.

When the food ran out they moved into the lounge, as many of them as possible squeezing onto the two sofas. Ursula and Howard took neighbouring armchairs that had come from the other rooms.

'Where's Gareth?' said Esme.

'He's giving Brett a hand to find some more chairs,' said Megan.

Esme jumped up. 'I'll go and help.'

Megan grabbed her arm. 'No need, they'll be back in a minute. Come and tell me how you've been getting on with the vegetable garden.'

Esme hopped from one foot to the other, as if she was ready to take flight, but Megan still had hold of her arm. When Gareth appeared in the doorway, she stopped hopping. Brett was behind him. Both were empty-handed. Esme frowned. 'I thought you were looking for chairs.'

'No joy. I suppose we'll have to squeeze in with you lot.' Gareth glanced at Brett and in that slight exchange of looks, Ursula saw that Gareth was indeed smitten, but it wasn't with Esme.

Someone turned down the lights and the fire gave the room a warm and cosy flush. Don put some music on. Jazz. The soft kind that made good background noise but didn't detract from the conversation. Anton used to play something similar at their own dinner parties for that same reason. It was the only music he ever played. Everything had to have a function with him. If it didn't, it was worthless.

'You've gone quiet. Is everything okay?' Howard said it too softly for the others to hear.

'I was thinking about my husband. This music reminds me of him.'

'He liked jazz?'

'Liked isn't a word that featured too much in Anton's vocabulary. He was a very particular man. Earlier, when you asked if it gets any easier, I think it will. You seem to love Dilys very much. It will be hard for you when she passes away. So hard, you'll want to go with her. But eventually, you'll realise that's not possible. You'll find ways to get through to the next day and you'll learn how to live without her.'

He nodded. 'Thank you. I appreciate your honesty.'

'That's how it's been for me, anyway.'

'Have you learned how to live without Anton now?'

'Actually, I wasn't talking about Anton.'

'Oh, I'm sorry, I thought...'

She shook her head. 'I have lost someone who I cherished very much, but it wasn't my husband. Anton and I weren't close like you and Dilys. But oddly, it still feels like he's ruling my life. I still expect him to mysteriously appear at my side and tell me I've left a crumb on the worktop. Like I said, he was a very particular man.'

'If you don't mind me saying, he sounds quite difficult.'

'I got used to it.' A vision flashed up of Anton watching her from the office window and she wondered how he was managing without her while she was away. Considering how he felt about the place, he seemed to hate being there on his own. At least, he hated her not being there. Which, she supposed, wasn't the same thing.

21

AN INVITATION TO THE MUSEUM

Charlie Big Potatoes was no respecter of hangovers. Ursula put the pillow over her head to block out his persistent moaning but the cat would not be muted. If anything, he was getting louder. Anton would have told her to ignore him. In fact, Anton would have told her it was her own fault for pandering to him in the first place. And on that particular point she found herself agreeing with him. Nonetheless, she stumbled out of bed and opened the window to let both the cat and the cold in. Daylight hadn't found its way properly into the world yet and it was still half-dark out there. The hill was a shape, rather than a distinctive element, and the ones behind it were just blue-black shadows.

She opened the bedroom door wide enough for a skinny cat to slip through and took herself back to bed. But Charlie was only interested in following her. He edged his way down under the duvet and settled by her feet, his damp fur pressing up against the bare skin of her ankle. Ursula closed her eyes and tried to get back to sleep, but the spell was broken.

There were no other noises in the house, except for someone's distant snores. It sounded like even the early risers were having a lie in. Perhaps they were suffering as much as she was. But then a creak on the stairs let her know that at least one person had shaken off the effects of last night's party. It was enough to bring Charlie out of his hidey-hole under the duvet and on his way through the crack in the door. Ursula curled up into a ball and shut her eyes again.

'What do you think you are doing?'

She awoke with a start, her eyes flitting around the room, searching for the owner of that voice, even though he never came this close. She'd been dreaming, that's all. But it was enough to get her out of bed to peep through the curtains. The light had changed and the hill was clearer. She could see the different aspects of it now. The trees at the top where she'd sheltered with Esteban. The patches of bracken. The sheep. The man standing in the same spot where she'd seen him on that first day. Not Howard, as she'd been led to believe. This was a different shape that unfortunately, she knew well. Anton. She'd thought she'd left him behind, but that would have been too easy. Last night, she hadn't been honest with Howard when she said she hadn't been able to let him go. The truth was, she'd give anything to see the back of him. It was Anton who wouldn't let her go. He must have been watching her all this time and just when she'd started to feel a bit less anxious, just when she'd started to think she might even be enjoying herself he pops back up. Right on cue. *What do you think you are doing.*

Megan was at the kitchen table cradling an empty mug in her hands. 'You look like I feel.'

Ursula flopped down onto a chair. 'If you mean rough,

then I look exactly how I feel too. I don't think I've drunk that much in a long time.'

'Me neither. Doesn't do any lasting harm every now and then though, does it?' I'm having another tea. Do you want one?'

'Yes please. Did you stay over last night?'

'We both did. Me and Gareth. It's lucky Andi's got so many spare rooms.'

'Yes, I suppose it is.' Ursula suspected Gareth hadn't actually needed a spare room last night but that was none of her business.

'It was nice to see Howard having a good time. Dilys always liked a dance as well.'

'Did she?' Ursula frowned, not sure why Megan was bringing this up, and then a sudden flashback was all the explanation she needed. There had been music last night. And dancing. She may have insisted on dancing to 'Supernature'. She may also have insisted on dancing with Howard. 'Oh dear, I think I might have forced Howard to boogie.'

Megan laughed. 'He didn't need no forcing, he was way ahead of you on that one. It was a real tonic, I tell you. Gave me a boost anyway. I mean there's not much we can do about Auntie Dil now. It sounds awful but you can't stop it happening, can you? But we're all doing everything we can to keep Howard going without getting his hopes up too much. It would kill her to see how much he's suffering. They were proper devoted to each other and now she doesn't know who he is most of the time. It was lovely to see him let his hair down last night. Worth the hangover. Anyway, I'm in no fit state to drive this morning. Gareth's dropping me off. He's helping Brett with the furniture.' She stood up and went to the door. 'You won't say anything to Esme, will you?'

'About Gareth?'

'You've probably noticed she's got a crush on him.'

'It's not common knowledge then? He hasn't come out?'

'Only to a select few so far. I don't think he knew himself. Not properly anyway. Until Brett. They just clicked, I suppose. Only I saw you'd picked up on it last night.'

'I won't say anything. It's up to them to decide who knows what and when.'

'Thank you. I'm late, I must go. You're very perceptive, by the way. Very sensitive to others. I expect that can be a nuisance for you sometimes.'

A nuisance? Yes it could be on occasion. Megan had a point, but not one that she was prepared to debate this morning. Ursula set her expression to composed and serene. The veil was down again. And then she reminded herself that wasn't necessarily a good thing. She really should start that list of habits that needed breaking. Although perhaps there was another list that needed writing first. Ursula Moller's list of regrets. But she didn't think she'd ever have the stomach for that.

Andi found her in the lounge debating with herself whether to go outside. 'What are you up to?'

'Nothing much. Trying to make up my mind what to do today.'

'I've got something to show you.'

She took Ursula upstairs and unlocked the door to a room that could very well have been the one she'd heard someone crying in. 'Remember I told you I had somewhere private to go? This is it.'

Ursula followed her in and saw shelves filled with bales of

material, threads, and everything else a dressmaker needed. To one side of the room, underneath the shelves, was a table with two sewing machines. In the middle was a workbench and, in the corner, a mannequin that was an old friend. She checked the back of it and found what she was looking for. Chain stitched lines that had been sewn in a long time ago, charting the growth of one little girl. One a year, until she'd become taller than the dummy. Ursula traced her fingers along them, each one a symbol of her mother's love. 'It's hers. You kept it.'

'For you. I kept it for you. I have her pattern collection as well.'

'They must be antiques by now. I haven't made anything in years. Not sure I can remember how to.'

'It's been a year for me. Mostly I just come in here to be alone.'

'And to cry?'

'Yes. To cry. Yes.'

'About Pablo?'

'About lots of things.'

Was this going to be it, the moment Andi opened up? Ursula waited for her to say more but Andi's mouth was resolutely closed. She put her arms around her. 'What a pair we are. How did we get so lost?'

Andi shrugged. 'I suppose it's age. We get scared, don't we? Scared to let go of the past and just as scared to look forward. It leaves you stuck in limbo.'

'I don't know. I have friends who are in their seventies and they don't seem to be like that.'

'It must be the lives we've led then. Maybe the men we chose have helped make us this way.'

'You never wanted boring. You always chose excitement.'

'I know. I was an idiot.' Andi opened another door that turned out to be a walk-in cupboard with two rails of garments covered in protective plastic. 'My museum.' She took out a silver dress with a bustier bodice, a sweetheart neckline and a pencil line skirt. The first dress Ursula's mum had helped her make.

Ursula felt the fabric. 'I loved that dress on you. I was so envious that you had the figure to carry it off.'

'Really? You never said.'

'You were gorgeous. I always felt plain next to you.'

Andi's eyebrows shot up. 'Urs, you could have been a model. I always felt dowdy and fat next to you. You know what? We were both absolute stunners. We just didn't know it. What I wouldn't give for that figure and that face now. We were bloody beautiful. I was beautiful.'

'You still are.'

She put the dress back 'You're my best friend. I think you might be a bit biased.'

'Nonsense, my love.'

Andi smiled. 'You sound just like Gillian. That was very her.'

Ursula thumbed through the other outfits on the rails. A couple of them had belonged to her. She'd left them at the flat so that she'd have some going-out clothes when she went on her secret clubbing nights with Andi, before that became something else she stopped doing. 'I'm sorry I got so silly about you and Mum. I wasn't used to sharing her. And I was too immature to accept that it wasn't enough for her to wait for me to turn up for a couple of hours a week.'

'I understood. So did she. We got over it, didn't we?'

'Yes, but it wasted so much precious time.' She removed a pale blue A-Line dress from its cover. She and her mum had gone to London to get that fabric. 'There was supposed to have been a matching jacket.'

'She never finished it,' said Andi.

'She was waiting for a reason to.' Ursula put the dress to her nose to see if it smelled of her mum's scent. But how could it when she never wore it?

22

GOOD NEWS AND BAD NEWS – 1983

Ursula reached New Street and looked up to Anton's building. Before they'd married, he'd have been waiting on the corner, but not anymore. Nowadays, he stood in the window until he could see her before he left. She'd pointed that out to him recently. He'd just laughed and said his time was more important than hers. Well, it was an Anton laugh so not exactly a laugh, but the closest he was ever going to get to one. It was a bit annoying though, because Cass was very strict about lunch-hour times, whereas he was a partner in the firm so ten minutes here or there was no big deal for him.

She waved to him. He turned away without acknowledging her which ramped up her annoyance levels even more. Would it kill him to wave back? Or even a nod would do. Anything to suggest he'd actually seen her and was on his way.

It was almost fifteen minutes before he finally rocked up. She was not impressed. 'You're late. I've only got forty minutes left now.'

'I had to take a call.'

'You could have sent someone down to tell me.'

'Did you bring lunch?'

'No. I didn't have time. We'll have to buy sandwiches.'

A flicker of something flashed across his face. She'd noticed it before. In fact, it was becoming a regular occurrence lately. A little pattern that was building up whenever she questioned him or forgot something. She'd seen it enough times now to put a name to it. Irritation. But it wouldn't last long, because the news she had for him was going to change everything. 'We can get some from the sandwich shop on Temple Street and eat them in the churchyard.'

'It's a cathedral, not a church.'

She knew that, of course, but that was what she and Andi called it. And anyway, did it really matter? Whatever it was called, she was in a rush to get him there, so she ignored him.

Because it was a hot, sunny day, there were lots of lunchtime sunbathers in the churchyard. It looked like they'd have to sit on the grass but luckily, a couple were leaving a bench so they grabbed it and spread out their things. Straight away, Anton started eating his sandwiches.

'Aren't you going to ask me what the doctor said?' Ursula was almost bursting. She didn't know how she'd held it in so long. From the minute she'd left the doctor's that morning, all the way into town on the bus, she'd wanted to go straight up to his office and tell him. But she knew he wouldn't appreciate the interruption. His irritation would have been off the scale and she didn't want that. She wanted her memory of this moment to be a happy one.

'What did he say?'

'I'm pregnant.'

Anton put down his sandwich. 'That is definite?'

She nodded. 'The test result confirmed it.'

'So, we are to be parents.'

'Yes. Are you pleased?'

'I am shocked. Did you ask him how that was possible when you are on the pill?'

'He said it can happen sometimes when you take antibiotics like the ones I had for that ear and throat infection. And we did do it while I was on them.' She'd also forgotten to take her pill when the infection had been at its worst but she didn't want to mention that.

'Of course, I remember now.'

So did she. She'd been feeling really rough, which was why she'd said no. But instead of sympathy, all she'd got was that flicker of irritation, so she'd caved in. And now she was pregnant. It may not have been in Anton's annual plan but he only had himself to blame. Having children hadn't actually been in her plan either. Not yet anyway. She was too busy trying to be less self-centred and immature. According to Anton she had some way to go on that one, but if anything was going to make her grow up, it was becoming a mother.

'I'm going to invite Mum over on Sunday. You don't mind, do you?'

Anton patted her knee. 'Yes, invite her over. Will you ask Andi too?'

'No. I want Mum to be the first to hear the news. I can't wait to see her face.' She probably would have invited Andi if they'd been as close as they used to be, but things hadn't been the same since she'd moved in with her mum. They still got on, still went out together when Anton was on one of his trips away, but Andi had been like family. Until she'd become part of her mum's family, and then she became something else. To Ursula, anyway. And so had her mum. There was some distance between them now, but maybe this baby would change that.

'What's going on?' said her mum.

'What do you mean?' Ursula carried on stirring the gravy. She'd made a traditional Sunday lunch. She could have gone fancier but she knew her mum liked it, and a roast dinner with all the trimmings was one of the few things Anton liked about British cooking.

'Well, you've invited me to dinner and Anton's being pleasant. Something's up.'

'He's always pleasant.'

Her mum raised her eyebrows. 'The food's looking good. You're getting to be an excellent cook. Has Anton been giving you lessons?'

'God, no. He can't cook. But he did make me take a cookery course so we can entertain clients at home.'

'If he was so keen, maybe he should have done the course himself, or taken them to a restaurant.'

'Shh.' Ursula pointed upstairs to where Anton had retreated, all too aware how every single noise carried in this house. 'He's too busy and we don't go to a restaurant because the house is a way of showing off his work. You wouldn't believe how many contracts we've won, thanks to this house and my cooking.'

Her mum gave her a wry smile. 'You're right, my love, I wouldn't. Sounds like you make quite a team.'

'That's what a good marriage is all about. Working together to a common goal.' Anton had told her that and his parents had been very happily married apparently, so he was more qualified on the subject than she was.

'I thought it was about loving one another.'

Ursula snorted. 'What would you know?'

'Not a lot.' Her mum turned away. This wasn't how it was supposed to go. It was supposed to be nice and relaxed. Not the two of them trading insults while Anton hid upstairs.

She poured the gravy into the jug. 'We're ready.'

'Shall I call Anton?'

'No need. He'll hear.'

Anton was downstairs and fussing around her mum before Ursula had finished putting everything on the table. His brief escape had obviously been enough to revive him. Her mum was playing along with it. If you didn't know better, you'd be fooled into thinking they actually liked each other. He filled her mum's glass and then his own. 'So, Gillian, we have an announcement to make.'

Her mum had already noticed Ursula's glass of water. 'You're not... Oh Ursula. Are you really?' The sight of her eyes filling sent Ursula's emotions into a tailspin. She wanted to laugh and cry at the same time but all she could do was nod.

'How far on are you?'

'Twelve weeks.'

'Oh my love, I'm so happy for you.' She looked over to Anton. 'For you both. You must look after yourself properly now, Ursula. Anton, you need to take care of her. We don't do well with pregnancy in our family.'

The rest of the afternoon was spent talking of babies. When it was time to leave, her mum gave Ursula a big hug. 'I'm already looking forward to babysitting duties. Remember what I said now, no overdoing it.'

As soon as they closed the door, Anton said: 'I think Gillian is being a little overprotective. You cannot be wrapped in cotton wool.'

'It's because she lost two babies before me, and my nan lost even more. That's what she meant by not doing well with pregnancy. But I'm all right. I haven't even had proper morning sickness.'

'Lost? You mean miscarriages.'

'Yes. What about your family? Any history?'

'No. There are no defects there.'

Ursula winced. 'I don't appreciate you referring to me and my family as defects, Anton.'

'What? No, I didn't mean it like that. It's my English. Sometimes I choose the wrong word.' He gestured to the dirty dinner things. 'Come, we must clean up this mess.'

Ursula turned her back on him. In spite of the dodgy start, it had been going so well. But then he had to spoil it. And pretending it was his poor English was absolute tripe. His grasp of the language was better than hers.

He touched her arm. 'Ursula. Come.'

She moved it away. 'Fuck off. I'm going to take my mother's advice for once.'

She'd been asleep on the bed when the opening of the door woke her. Anton came in with a cup of tea that she knew would be horrible. Something she could honestly say he hadn't mastered during his half a lifetime in this country was a decent cuppa.

He sat down next to her and took her hand. 'You are calmer now?'

'You upset me.'

'It's your hormones. I read that they fluctuate wildly during pregnancy.'

'You've been reading about pregnancy?'

'I bought a book. It's fascinating. Also, I've been thinking about what Gillian said. You should leave your job.'

She sat up. 'Don't I get a say in it?'

'Of course. But if you really want this baby to survive we must shorten the odds. Gillian is right. You need to put the baby first.'

'That's not what she said.'

'That is what she meant. Don't you agree?'

'I suppose.'

'Then you will hand in your notice tomorrow?'

'All right.'

Andi was washing up the tea things in the sink. Ursula caught sight of her as she was on her way up from telling Cass. She stopped in the doorway, wondering if her mum had already divulged the stop press. 'I have good news and bad news. Which do you want to hear first?'

Andi turned, her hands dripping suds on the floor. 'I think I can guess the bad news.'

'I'm leaving.'

'Yep. Guessed it.'

'So if you knew, how come you haven't said anything to me about it all morning.'

'I dunno. Probably because I was waiting for you to tell me you were pregnant.'

'Surely you don't expect me to tell you before my mum?'

'No, but maybe before you told Cass. That would have been the kind of thing a best friend would have done.'

Ursula's cheeks burned. It was the anger. 'Right. Okay. Got yer. What else would a best friend do? Would they wheedle their way into your home and steal your mum?'

Andi let out a puff of air and shook her head slowly. 'You are so fucking puerile.'

'At least I'm not a devious cow.'

'I'm gonna let that one slide on account of you being with child. Congratulations on that, by the way. I suppose that's the end of us having our own shop now.'

So that was why she was so upset. Her stupid little pipedream was over. 'You can stick your congratulations up your fat arse.' Ursula stormed off back to the sewing room.

'Fuck off and take your bony little shrivelled up raisin of a derriere with you,' shouted Andi, loud enough for Ursula to hear, as well as everyone in the shop downstairs.

Ursula swallowed down the muesli that her teeth had been working away at. Even though it was ground down to a pulp, she still found it hard to stomach. Anton was insisting she ate more healthily. All part of his scheme to turn her into a tip-top baby machine, devoid of defects. He didn't know she waited until he went to work every morning before sneaking off to the newspaper shop for a Fry's Turkish Delight.

'We leave in ten minutes. I will tidy up while you get your things together,' he said, interrupting her Turkish Delight dreams. It was the only way she could get through the muesli without heaving.

Exactly ten minutes later, they left the house. Anton spent the journey into town emphasising the need for her not to increase her blood pressure. It was like living with a doctor these days. He pulled up at New Street station. 'You know where you're meeting Gillian?'

She climbed out of the car. 'Yes, all sorted. See you tonight.'

Her mum was waiting for her inside. The train to London was on the platform already. As soon as they sat down, her mum handed her a Turkish Delight. Ursula looked around guiltily, half-expecting Anton to swoop in and take it from her. 'Anton would have a fit if he knew. He's taking looking after me very seriously.'

'Well you can have a day off it today. We'll get the material and then find somewhere nice for lunch.'

The shop they went to was unlike anything Ursula had seen back home. The materials were displayed in swatch books. Once one was chosen, a bale of it was brought and rolled out on the table for closer inspection. Her mum chose a pale-blue silk that was perfect for a grandmother's christening outfit, and it went so well with her colouring.

'Can we see fabrics suitable for a christening gown?' She winked at Ursula. 'Your father insisted on you wearing one that had been in his family for generations so I couldn't make one for you. I always regretted that, so I thought we could make it together, the way we used to. It'll give you something to work on while you're waiting for the baby to arrive.'

Ursula tutted. 'You know I don't have a sewing machine.'

'Don't be silly. We can make it at mine.'

That would have been nice, like old times. Except Andi might be there and they hadn't really spoken since that row.

'Or I could come over to you,' said her mum. 'We'll work our way round things, just like we've always done.'

23

HER IMPERFECT LINEAGE – 1983

Ursula's mum was at the door. Last weekend, she'd brought her spare sewing machine and installed it in the room that was going to be the baby's so that they could make the christening gown together. Now that Ursula was twenty weeks, they were able to stop worrying and start making plans. In fact, aside from being a bit tired today, she'd practically sailed through her pregnancy so far. Naturally, Anton was taking the credit for that. It was true, he had been looking after her, but Ursula suspected the real reason was down to her father. She was tall like him, so maybe she'd inherited his sturdier body. It was probably the only time she was ever going to be grateful to him.

Anton gave her mum his customary greeting: 'Gillian.'

Her mum gave him hers: 'Anton.'

'I must go out this morning.'

'Oh dear, that's a shame.'

Ursula noticed that all too frequent flicker of irritation flash across his face. Her mum must have done too, judging by her triumphant expression. 'You shouldn't tease him like that. He doesn't understand your sense of humour,' she said, after he'd left.

Her mum gave her a wicked little grin. 'That's because he doesn't have one. God help that poor child. Where's he off to, anyway?'

'He's gone to pick up a new car. Apparently, a Volvo estate is the perfect family car.'

'Is that so? Planning ahead for an army of little Antons is he? Did you manage to finish the pleating and lace detail on the bodice?'

'Yep. I've attached the collar as well. Come and have a look.'

They went up to the nursery, its walls now painted in fresh lemon. Anton's one concession for the baby, although it had taken some persuading to make him deviate from plain white. On the table was the little ivory silk bodice. She'd stitched down three horizontal pleats that ran the full width of it and added a line of Venice lace above them to finish it off. She'd been so absorbed in it yesterday that she would have forgotten to eat if Anton hadn't called and reminded her. It was so good to be doing the thing she loved again. Since leaving Talulah, she'd felt so lost. But that wasn't just because she needed to be making something. A lot of it was down to the way things ended between her and Andi. It had been horrible after the row. They didn't speak to each other for the whole time she'd had to work her notice. It still upset Ursula to think about it. She missed Andi. Even the Andi who stole her mum. Even the Andi who told her to fuck off and take her skinny arse with her. And if Andi had said just one thing to her since the row, she'd have forgiven her. But she was too bloody stubborn, and Ursula was too proud to back down. But there was no point dwelling on it. As Anton had said, she'd have no time for friends when the baby was born.

Her mum examined the stitching of each pleat. 'This is excellent work, love. It looks lovely. I think we'll get it finished today.'

'I thought I'd make a bonnet with the leftover silk, if you don't mind me borrowing your sewing machine for a bit longer.'

'Keep it for as long as you like. Do you want to stitch the gown together, or shall I?'

'Will you do it? I like to watch you work.'

Her mum kissed the top of her head. 'Are you okay? You look tired.'

'Yeah. Never seem to be able to get enough sleep.'

'I was the same. You have a rest. I'll soon get this done.'

Ursula sat in a chair that Anton had brought up from downstairs. Her back was aching and she would have preferred a nice soft, squishy one like the sort her mum had at home but this being Anton's choice meant it was a design classic. Needless to say, it was entirely uncomfortable. She took her mind off the discomfort by watching her mum's hands swiftly and skilfully feeding the delicate material though the machine. Her thoughts began to wander and she saw herself as a child watching her mum and Cass, leaning over a table in a sewing room twice as big as the one in the flat, her mum suggesting this tweak and that. Cass nodding in agreement. The delight they shared over their creation. It must have been so hard to walk away from that. 'Can I ask you something?'

'Go on then.'

'Do you ever wish you were still doing this for a living.'

Her mum finished attaching a sleeve to the bodice and

cut the thread. 'Sometimes. But where would I have found a job that paid enough to keep us both? And to be truthful, I couldn't face it for a while after what happened.'

'With my father?'

'Yes. But it was what happened afterwards with Cassandra that ruined it for me. She was the only one in that family that stood up for me. Until they bought her off with that bloody shop. She was so desperate for it, she turned her back on us. I just thought, if that's what this business turns you into, I want none of it.'

'She took me on though. Maybe she regretted it.'

'Maybe she did. Guilt's a hard thing to live with.'

'Whenever I think of you and Cass when I was little, I always think of the two of you laughing. You were so close.'

'We were. That's why it felt like such a betrayal. Andi's not like Cassandra you know. She won't desert you. Things are bad between you now, but she'll be there when you need her. Just remember to do the same for her.'

Ursula yawned. She was so tired and the hypnotic rattle of the machine was making her eyelids heavy. She let them close with her mum's words still on her mind. She couldn't ever imagine a time when Andi would need her. In fact, she couldn't imagine Andi ever needing anyone. She was too invincible.

'All done.'

Ursula had to force her eyes open. Her mum was holding up the finished gown. She took in every tiny detail, the intricately pleated bodice, the darling little Peter Pan collar, the lace trimmed sleeves and tiny silk covered buttons at the back. 'Oh Mum, it's absolutely beautiful.'

'I've sewn something into the seam.'

She looked inside, beneath the lining. Attached to its seam was an embroidered label that read: *'Ursula Moller, 1983.'*

'You should have put your name in there.'

Her mum shook her head. 'No, my love. This is about you, not me. You can start your own christening tradition now. Bugger the Frys. Come on, we'll leave this here for now. Why don't you have a proper lie down? I'll make a cuppa and come and sit with you.'

Ursula lay down on her bed and stretched out. She was so desperate for rest and her back was really beginning to niggle her now. Perhaps if she had a good sleep she'd wake up feeling better.

Anton stood over the bed. 'I must go to work. I can't let the client down.'

Ursula propped herself up against the pillows. 'I wasn't asking you to stay.'

'We should have asked Gillian to come over.'

'It's too late now, she'll have gone to work. Just go.'

He sighed. 'Okay. You have the phone there, if necessary.'

She picked up the extension and put it to her ear. 'I have and it's working. I'll see you this afternoon.'

He left in the Volvo that he'd picked up two days ago, the same day Ursula's back pain had started. Yesterday, he'd called the private hospital she was booked in with and they'd said it was probably nothing, but she should go in for a precautionary check-up today. In the meantime, she'd been told to rest, which meant she'd been in stuck in bed, under Anton's supervision. Which also meant she was going out of her mind with boredom. He must have been worried about her because he'd bought magazines that would not normally pass his strict rules of acceptance. She laughed at herself. Honestly, if anyone was party to her innermost thoughts, they'd think he was a complete nightmare. He hadn't really banned them. He just banged on non-stop about them being utter trash and beneath her. So to save herself the earache, she stopped buying them.

The magazines kept her busy for an hour but not much more, and she really needed the loo. Apart from a pressure down below when she got out of bed too quickly, she was feeling fine. The bedrest must have put things right.

The pressure must have been caused by her full bladder because it seemed to take forever to empty. She filled the waiting time thinking about the christening gown and trying to imagine a baby in it. Not just this baby, but all the others that would come after it. Future generations of Mollers. Ursula Moller was about to start a whole new dynasty. The idea of it filled her with excitement. If she didn't have another look at that gown she knew she wouldn't be able to rest.

She went into the nursery where her mum had left it out on a little hanger. It was so sweet and beautiful, she almost cried. A lullaby that she remembered from childhood came into her head and she sang it as she laid the end of the gown across her arm and rocked it. This is what it would be like when she had a real baby in her arms.

It was the dampness between her legs that brought her to a stop. What, was she incontinent now? Is that what pregnancy did to you? Her mum had forgotten to mention that little detail. But suddenly it felt like more than dampness. Her pants were wet. Ursula pulled up her nightie and saw blood trickling down her legs. The ache in her back was there again, but this time it was growing and moving across the whole of her. The life was being squeezed out of her and she could hardly stand or breathe. She dropped the gown and grabbed her belly. The pain eased long enough for her to get back to the bedroom but then it came again, even more brutal than before.

Anton's number rang and rang. She tried it again in case she'd misdialled. Still no answer. There was blood on her feet. It was thick and dark, like jelly. Something terrible was happening and she was going to have to deal with it all on her own. She clicked off and called the only place she could think of where someone would pick up straight away.

'Talulah.'

'Auntie Cass. Help me.'

Lights were flashing above Ursula and there was talking, lots of talking. Someone she didn't know was using her name but she couldn't understand what they were saying. It was the pain and the fear making her stupid and deaf. The trolley stopped and she realised the lights weren't flashing, it was just that they'd been moving so fast along a corridor. She didn't know where she was but it wasn't the private hospital. Anton would be annoyed about that. She'd have to explain it wasn't her fault. If only he'd answered the phone. Cass had called the ambulance. Ursula could have done that herself, but she wasn't thinking straight. It was the blood. Another surge of pain took control of her and she screamed. The baby was gone. Nothing could stop her losing it now. And nothing could stop her screaming and howling and crying.

And then Cass was there, holding her hand. 'It's okay, I'm here with you, my darling.'

'What's happening?'

'They're taking you into theatre. Your mum and Anton are on the way.'

'The baby's dead.'

Cass didn't answer. Ursula was moving again. The trolley turned around and she was going feet first through some double doors. She looked around for Cass but instead she saw Andi running towards her. And then the doors closed behind her and the flashing lights were back as they rushed along the corridor towards the theatre.

After her body had forced out the last remains of the baby, they cleaned her up and took her to a room of her own, away from the main ward. Anton was in there, waiting for her. He kissed her hand and stroked her cheek but said nothing. It occurred to her this was the most tender he'd been since before they were married. 'I tried to call you. You didn't answer.' She knew it wouldn't have made any difference if he had answered but she needed someone to be angry at.

'The client wanted to meet me at the site. If I had known you were that unwell, I would have stayed at home.' And there it was, that look that made everything her fault. He was blaming her for not knowing she was about to lose the baby. Her and her imperfect lineage.

'I wasn't unwell. The baby was. He was, what did you call it? Defective. Your son was a defect.'

'My son?'

'You didn't ask them. I thought you might at least have asked them. It was a boy.' She thought of her mum jokingly referring to him planning an army of little Antons and tears began to leak out of her. 'We were going to have a son.'

'You're distraught. It's understandable.' He sounded so clinical, so devoid of emotion.

'Yes, I am. And what about you, Anton? Are you distraught? Or are you as cold and unfeeling as you seem?'

He let go of her hand and sat back in his seat. 'Naturally, I am distressed. But we will get over it.'

No, she didn't think she would but he'd never understand that. He just didn't have it in him. 'Where's Mum? I want to see her.'

'Gillian is outside. I'll get her.'

'What about Andi and Cass?'

'Only Gillian was here when I arrived.'

24

SHE WOULD NEVER CRY AGAIN – 1984

Anton was doing something noisy in one of the other bedrooms, Ursula had no idea what. She could get out of bed and look but that would have taken some effort. Besides, she was on the phone.

'Shall I come over today?' said her mum.

'No need, Anton's here.' The call had been going on for about ten minutes and she'd had enough. Everything was too much these days. Especially when she knew what was bound to be coming next.

And out it came, precisely as she'd predicted, the inevitable 'are you going to pull yourself together' question: 'Does that mean you're going to get out of bed?'

'I dunno. Later maybe.'

'It's been six months now, love.'

She knew that. She'd been counting every single day since it happened. Not that any of them mattered. Autumn, winter, Christmas and the new year had come and gone in one long stretch of nothingness. Only one date mattered to her and that was the day she'd expected her son to be born, 16th February. But it had passed without commemoration. It was as if he'd been packed away in a neat little box marked 'Unmentionable'. Or, 'Forgettable'. Ursula wasn't sure which, but she did know there would never be a time when she'd put him into either of them. The absence of any acknowledgement of the day had been almost as bad as the reminder of what she'd lost and it took her to a new low. The sorrow filled her up. It was immeasurable and interminable. Two weeks later, she'd crawled into bed and stayed there for hours, days, weeks, months, only getting out when absolutely necessary. As time went on, the necessary got less and less. Six months. Not since the day she lost her child, but since the day she lost the desire to live.

'Do you think you should see someone? They have people who can help you these days.'

'Help me with what?'

'Your grief. They'll help you let it go.'

Her grief? She almost laughed. Why would she want to let it go when it was all she had left of her little boy? 'I'm all right as I am. Stop worrying. I've got to go. Anton wants to talk to me about something.' It was a lie. Anton didn't want to talk to her. It had been months since he'd done anything with her other than feed her. He'd even stopped sleeping in the same bed. The smell of her was disgusting, apparently.

Something clattered against the door and made her jump. His footsteps on the stairs were heavy, like he was carrying something. He was in the garage now. She heard the car door slam and curiosity finally dragged her out of bed. The room spun as she stood up, one of the disadvantages of spending all your time lying down. Ursula steadied herself against the wall and waited for the room to right itself.

As soon as she was out of the bedroom, she could see there was only one door open, the one to the baby's room. He must have been in there, moving things around, changing things. Something piercing suddenly caught her lungs and left her gasping for breath. She closed her eyes and swallowed. The air burned her windpipe as it came in, as if it was unused to being there. She opened her eyes again and leaned over the landing banister to ease the discomfort. From here she could see down to the dining area. From here, she could throw herself into oblivion.

Another noise, the garage door closing, brought her back to her senses. She turned away and took slow steps towards the nursery. The first thing she saw was the sewing machine on the floor. Anton must have been dismantling the table it had been on. Ursula pushed the door further open, the memories of the last time she'd been in here still raw. Her feet stepped onto a clear plastic sheet that was covering the wooden floor. They moved awkwardly, like there were new to walking, and came to a stop at the place where she'd first seen the blood running down her legs. The splashes had been scrubbed off the floor now but if she looked very, very closely, she could see a patch that was lighter than the rest. Over scrubbing, probably. Their son had left his mark whether Anton liked it or not.

The pretty lemon walls were back to white. For a few short months, this had been on the way to becoming a nursery for a living, breathing baby and now it was as sterile as an operating theatre. Just like every other room in this house. She touched one of the walls and came away with white fingertips. It was still wet. Aside from the sewing machine, the furniture was gone. And so was the christening gown.

She felt Anton behind her and swung round. 'You've got rid of him.'

His expression reminded her of that first time she saw him, her first day at Talulah. Curiosity. He'd probably seen her as a strange creature then. He probably still did. 'I have simply redecorated. Is Gillian coming to see you?'

'No. I told her not to.'

'Then I will take the machine to her.'

'What have you done with his christening gown? Have you got rid of that as well?'

'Of course not.' He went into the room he'd been sleeping in and brought it back.

She seized it from him, sobbing and weeping. He gave her a look. A new one. Pity? Disdain? Contempt. Yes, contempt. He picked up the sewing machine. 'I'll be back in time for lunch. Take a shower.'

From the window, she watched him drive away. How easy it was for him to redecorate and move on. She lay the gown across her arm and tried to sing, but she couldn't remember the words to the lullaby. Anyway, it didn't feel right. She couldn't imagine a baby in it anymore, just as she could no longer imagine a baby in this room. She went back out, already needing the safety of her bed. But then she remembered the look he'd given her. They couldn't go on like this. Something had to change. Perhaps he knew that already and that was why he'd painted the room. He was trying to bring her to her senses. He'd done it to help her. She could see that now. Ursula closed the door on the newly painted room. The next time they could start fresh with a new colour and things would be different. There was a spot of blood on the gown. She'd have to ask her mum how to get that out.

.   .   .

By the time Anton returned, she'd showered and brushed her teeth, tidied her hair and put on clean clothes. The bed linen had been changed and she was making lunch. They sat opposite each other at the table to eat it, the sound of cutlery scraping against the plates and creating an echo in the open space above them. It was obvious he wasn't going to be the first to hold out an olive branch so it was up to her. 'I'm sorry,' she said.

He put down his knife and fork. 'We must never do this again.'

'Agreed. Next time we'll be more prepared. I'll take extra care and if it happens again, we'll be stronger.'

He shook his head. 'You misunderstand me, Ursula. There will not be a next time. I do not want children. I would make a bad father. I was prepared to go along with it this time because I had no choice, but now I'm telling you. There will be no more pregnancies.'

A bubble of laughter came from somewhere within Ursula. Anton glared at her as if she was mad. She was of course. Mad with grief. But not so mad that she couldn't see he meant it. He really didn't want children. Despair was threatening to wash over her again. All hope was gone, just when she thought she'd seen a tiny spark of it shining in the distance.

Her eyes were already full with tears before she reached the top of the stairs but she forced them to stop. She locked herself in the bathroom, washed her face and waited for the red blotches to die down. She wouldn't give him the satisfaction of knowing she'd been crying again. She would never give him that satisfaction because she would never cry again. Not unless he changed his mind.

Before going back down she fetched the christening gown from her wardrobe. Anton was still at the table. She threw the gown at him. 'You may as well get rid of this then, seeing as we won't be needing it.'

25

JUST REMEMBER

'What are you thinking about?' said Andi.

Ursula put her mum's unfinished dress back on the rail. 'I was thinking about Mum. I wish I'd told her the truth about why we never had children. Maybe if I had, she'd have stopped waiting for them to arrive.'

'Urs, I really don't think she was that fussed about grand-kids. She just wanted you to be happy. That was what kept her up at night, worrying about whether you were happy or not.'

'Did she tell you that?'

'Uh huh. She'd bend my ear about it all the time. Hey, shall we play dressing up? You do remember? Don't tell me you've forgotten.'

She had. But then it came back to her. A game they used to play, back when Ursula still lived at home and Andi was a weekend visitor. The three them, her mum included, would dress up for Sunday tea, the flashier the better. 'I remember. What would we wear though?'

Andi stretched her arm out along the rail of clothes. 'Take your pick.'

An oversize blousy shirt in cobalt blue caught her eye. Underneath it was a pair of striped satin straight leg trousers. More years ago than she cared to do the maths on, it had been a favourite outfit. 'Now this I do remember. What are you choosing?'

'Well, unlike you, my figure is not what it used to be, so there's no way I'm going to squeeze into my New Romantic outfits. It'll have to be one of my nineties creations. I think ... this.' She pulled out a red check dress with a corseted bodice and a full skirt. It was typical Andi style back then, very Vivienne Westwood. 'It's got a jacket too. I made it for an industry thing. It wasn't long after I'd had Jet so I was still quite heavy.'

Ursula was disappointed to find that her outfit was looser than it used to be. Andi was disappointed too, but for the opposite reason. 'Can't believe I'm even fatter than I was after childbirth.'

'You're not fat.'

'You said I had a fat arse once, or have you forgotten that too?'

'I'm sorry, that was nasty of me. I was angry. Anyway you got me back. A bony little shrivelled up raisin of a derriere, I believe it was. Much more original than me.'

Andi giggled. 'Yes I suppose it was. Make-up, we need make-up. Back in a tick.'

She returned with what looked like a toolbox full of make-up. 'I'll do you first.'

'Don't go too mad. I haven't worn make-up in years.'

'Don't worry I won't, although I suppose that's not really in the spirit of the game. Close your eyes. Open them again. Bloody hell, Urs, have you never considered having those eyebrows threaded? They're like two albino caterpillars. Mascara alert. Coming in. And now a bit of blush. You're done. What do you think?'

Ursula looked in the mirror, amazed at the difference a bit of cosmetic trickery could make. 'Where did you learn to do that?'

'I used to help with the make-up when we were busy at the shows. You like, madame?'

'I love. I mean I still look like an old woman, but at least I only look my age now.'

Andi made herself up and joined Ursula in front of the full length mirror. 'Yep. Still got it. We are smokin' baby. I could go to a club right now.'

'Yeah, me too.'

'Where do you fancy, the Rum Runner or the Holy City Zoo?'

'Got to be the Zoo.' They caught each other's eye and burst out laughing.

The laughter was interrupted by the sound of the gong downstairs. Andi hooked her arm in Ursula's. 'Well it might not be the Zoo, darling, but shall we?'

If it had been possible to capture the astonishment they were met with when they strolled into the kitchen arm in arm, Ursula would have done so. Because this was a memory she would like to keep coming back to. Everyone was there today, even Howard, but only Don seemed to be unphased by their appearance. He swirled a tea towel in the air and gave them a flamboyant bow. 'Well now, what do we have here? Ladies, we are honoured that you've graced our humble kitchen with your presence.'

Andi stuck her hand out. 'Too kind, sir. Too kind.'

He obliged her with a kiss for it. 'A seat at the head of the table for milady,' he said, running ahead to pull it out. 'And if I may assist the other fine lady? Your hand, ma'am.'

Ursula couldn't speak she was giggling so much, so she gave him her hand and let him lead her to the table. Howard jumped up and pulled out a chair. 'Allow me.'

Don flapped the tea towel at Howard. 'Fie, sir. Would you have my honour in a bread basket? I challenge you to a duel. Choose your weapon. I shall take my trusty whisk.'

'Then I shall take the soup spoon. Prepare to die, sir.' Howard put his hands on his hips and stuck his nose in the air.

'You scoundrel. Take that.' Don thrust the whisk at Howard and the duel began.

The kitchen was in uproar. The only person who wasn't laughing was Esme. 'Lunch is getting cold,' she said flatly.

Don slapped Howard on the back. 'In that case I declare a draw. Let's eat.'

'Why are you wearing those clothes?' said Esme.

'We've been playing dressing up,' said Andi.

Esme sent Ursula her first scowl of the meal. 'I thought that was a kid's game.'

'Why should kids have all the fun?' Andi's eyes were twinkling. She had a glow about her that had nothing to do with the make-up. Perhaps she didn't need to have a long tearful conversation about Pablo and what he'd done. Perhaps all she needed was to be herself again.

'Well I think you both look ravishing. Don't you agree, Howard?' said Don.

'I do indeed,' said Howard.

'So do I.' Brett turned to Andi. 'It's about time you had some fun. Sorry. Just saying though. No offence or anything.'

. . .

Andi had some errands to run in Bala and Ursula was going with her so a change of clothes was needed after lunch. Don suggested they kept their fancy outfits on but they pointed out they might look a bit overdressed for the Co-Op. They kept the make-up though and, vain as it was, Ursula spent the drive down glancing at herself in the wing mirror.

'It suits you,' said Andi.

'You're very clever. I look like a clown when I put it on.'

'I suppose Anton told you that, did he?'

'Not in so many words.' She looked in the mirror again and saw herself, how many years ago was it? Too many to pin down. The first time he'd said something, anyway. She'd been getting ready to go to a cocktail party. Some people he wanted to impress, so he'd bought her yet another simple black dress to wear. She was sitting at the dressing table when he came in. She'd already done her eyes and was about to apply some blusher to her cheeks. He took the brush out of her hand. 'We are going to a sophisticated party, not a nightclub. Wash it all off. And put your hair up. You can at least try to look the part for one evening.' And of course she did just that, because Anton knew best. He always knew best. At least that's what she thought at the time.

'I could teach you,' said Andi.

'What?'

'How to apply it. The make-up. It's not hard. As Brett might say, it's about time you had some fun.'

'He doesn't agree with what Pablo did to you. He told me that specifically. I think he wants you to know he's on your side but he can't find a way to say it. I think they're all on your side. Especially Don.'

Andi pulled into a car park by the lake. 'Why especially Don? Has he said something too?'

'He doesn't have to. It's plain to see he dotes on you.'

'He's a good friend, that's all. And I've had my fill of men, thanks all the same. All the ones I've ever been involved with have turned out to be shits.'

'Don could be the trend bucker.'

Andi flashed her palm at Ursula. 'I'd rather not find out that he isn't. I like his company too much. Talking of which, what's going on with you and Howard? I've noticed you giving him sneaky side glances, and I haven't seen him this cheerful in a long time.'

'He reminds me of someone I used to know, that's all. I can't speak for him but perhaps he's cheerful because his wife's responding to his photos.'

'Perhaps. He's leaving on Saturday. Did you know?'

'No, he hasn't said.'

'It was planned. He has to get back to Dilys.'

They took the lake path into the town centre. The lake was quite spectacular but she was too distracted to fully appreciate it. Of course, Howard had to go back to Dilys. He was only here for a break. Ursula knew that but it didn't stop her feeling disappointed.

'Talking of going away, Zak called me this morning. He's asked me to go and see him. Do you mind if I do? It's just that I think he wants to talk to me about something and given everything that's gone on, I can't really say no.'

'Of course not, you must go.' Ursula stopped on the pretence of taking in the lake but really, she was composing herself, pushing down the uneasiness that had just bubbled up to the surface. Andi was leaving her here. Howard going too. She'd be on her own with Don, Brett and, more worryingly, the dreaded Esme. She found herself trying to remember what she'd be doing on the allotment right now but to her dismay, she couldn't. She'd been away too long. She needed to get back. That was why Anton had appeared again, to let her know he was tired of waiting for her. Yes that was it. She'd go home to the safety of her little patch and her daily structure, and to the ghost who lived behind the closed door. Because Andi didn't really need her, she was coping just fine.

Andi slipped her arm through Ursula's. 'It'll only be for the weekend and maybe when I come back, we'll talk properly. I'm just not very good at it. It's stuck here inside me and I can't get it out. But having you here, it's helping. Even if you don't think it is.'

'It's all right. I'm not going anywhere.' Ursula wanted to jump in her car and not stop until she hit Birmingham, but she was thinking about the day she lost the baby. Andi running towards her, arms outstretched. It was clearer now than it had ever been. Andi's face was streaked with mascara. She was crying. She was crying for her. And then she thought of her mum's words: 'She'll be there when you need her. Just remember to do the same for her.'

26

HOT AIR AND BRAVADO

Before she left, Andi had given her the key to the sewing room so that she could go in there if she felt like it. Ursula didn't feel like it. Too many ghosts of a different kind. It was bearable while Andi was with her. It had even been fun to dress up and act like they were girls again. But those girls who wore outrageous outfits to go out dancing were long gone. That was the saddest thing of all. Sadder even than her mum's unfinished dress.

Ursula was in her room trying to make up her mind what to do today. It was easier back in Birmingham because every day was the same. Get up, get ready, go to the allotment and stay there until dark. Nice and simple. Organised. Structured. Contained. No room for random memories. No empty spaces for the regrets to inch in. But the only structure here was mealtimes and if she missed them, so what? There was nothing to hang on to. Even before her self-imposed daily regime, her life had been subjected to one kind of structure or another. She was so used to it that she hardly noticed it was there and it was only now, in this big, brooding house, that she felt lost without it. That could be why her mind was taking her down the dark alleys of time and playing tricks on her.

Anton was on the hill again. Ursula had never believed in ghosts, but that didn't stop Anton. When had anything ever stopped Anton? Especially when he was trying to teach her a lesson. It was too far away to see his face but she knew it would be full of cold but righteous indignation. Well she was sick of it. Six years was long enough to atone for her sins. She was going to go up that bloody hill, to that very spot, and tell him so.

The air was full of a fine mist that drenched her face but she was warm. Too warm in fact. It was the new coat and the pace she was going at. If she'd been in a different frame of mind, she'd have stopped at the bothy for a look at Brett's finishing touches, but she needed to stay focussed if she wanted to keep her courage and do what she hadn't been able to do at home. On and up she went, along the same path she'd taken before, until she came to a right fork that led to the other side of the hill, the one that faced the house.

It wasn't long before the path became no more than a straggly line in the bracken. Ursula trudged on through rain sodden ferns that refused to part, her jeans made heavy by their watery offload. She stumbled on stones and splashed through tiny streams of water spilling downwards. And then there it was, the place Anton had chosen for his haunting. He wasn't there. Gone back to some white-walled minimalist Hades that was his resting place, no doubt.

'I know you're here, I can feel you. You have to stop this, Anton.' She'd shouted it out at the top of her voice, but the speed of her ascent and the worthlessness of it had caught up with her and the effort it required was the undoing of her.

She sank to her knees and all the hot air and bravado began to slide away. 'I'm sorry. I didn't mean it. Please, just let me go.'

Up ahead, a figure appeared from behind some trees. Was it him, was it Anton? Or was it the one person who might be able to save her again? 'Samuel?'

'Ursula. Ursula, it's me, Howard. Are you okay?'

Howard. It was Howard all along. How stupid of her. 'Yes. I thought you were someone else. Sorry.'

'Let me help you. It gets a little boggy around there.' He held out his hand for her and led her up to firmer ground where Esteban was waiting for them. 'I was just on my way down. I only stopped because Esteban refused to go. You must have taken a wrong turn and come up the harder way.'

'No wrong turn, it was deliberate.'

He frowned. He was trying to work out what she was about, but she'd pre-empted his possible question and the veil was already in place while she composed herself. 'I'm ready to go back down now though. Perhaps we can go together.'

'Sure. What do you say, Esteban, can we go now?' The dog ran ahead of them. Howard looked down at his hand and seemed surprised that it was still holding hers. He let go of it and his mouth skewed into a half-smile. 'I guess that means Esteban's ready too.'

'I expect you know I'm leaving tomorrow,' he said, as they picked up the track that took them past the bothy.

'Andi told me. You'll be glad to get back to Dilys.'

'Yes. Although it's not really Dilys anymore. Not my Dilys anyway.'

'Tell me about your Dilys.'

He puffed out his cheeks, as if there was so much to tell it would take a whole lifetime, and a short walk wouldn't even cover the colour of her eyes. 'She is the most remarkable woman I have ever known. She's beautiful and hilarious. Such a wicked sense of humour. Even now she still comes out with the funniest things. When I first met her I couldn't understand a word she said, but the way she said it just melted my heart. There's something quite captivating about the Welsh accent, don't you think? It got me, anyway. She was in Philly on a year's visa. We fell in love.'

'You didn't stay over there?'

'For a while after we got married. But when we had kids, she wanted to come home, and I would have followed her anywhere. We ended up in London. Not quite home, but we spend a lot of time here.' He sighed. 'Spent a lot of time here, I should say. We lived in London, but this was her real home.'

'And where's home for you?'

'Wherever Dilys is.' He looked like he had all the weight of the world on his shoulders. Or perhaps he was just wondering if anywhere would feel like home after Dilys was gone. Ursula wanted to tell him how lucky he was to love and have been loved so deeply. A love like that touched so few people. But he probably knew that already. Just as he knew Dilys would never spend time here again. 'She still thinks she lives here, you know.'

Ursula touched his arm. It felt like the right thing to do this time, now that he'd shared more of himself. 'That's a beautiful thought to hold onto, isn't it? There must be some comfort in knowing that in her head she's walking by that wonderful lake or climbing these hills. She might not seem it on the outside but somewhere inside, she's as free and happy as the girl she once was.'

Howard stopped. His eyes met hers and she was momentarily unsettled by it. But then he looked towards the house and the lake beyond it. 'Hmm. I hadn't thought of it like that, but I guess there are worse places for your head to be at.'

They carried on until they reached the bothy. 'Have you seen inside?' he asked.

'Not yet.' She went in for a look. It was quite welcoming now the furniture was in there and a basket of logs and kindling had been left next to the fire. She noticed a small wooden cupboard, very similar to the one she had in her allotment shed. Inside it was a large bottle of water, tea, coffee and powdered milk. On top of it was a camping stove. All it needed was a tin of biscuits to make her feel at home.

'Cosy, huh?' said Howard. 'Almost one. Are you coming in for lunch?'

As they reached the door that took them into the boot room, Ursula glanced back at the hill. Anton had taken up his usual station there. Her attempt at confronting him had been a waste of time because she was never going to be rid of him. She suddenly saw her future laid out before her and she only just managed to stifle a scream.

As it was Howard's last night, Megan and Gareth came for dinner. But even the extra guests couldn't make up for the lack of Andi. And it wasn't just Ursula who felt it. At different points during the meal, Andi's name was on everyone's lips. Especially Megan's: 'Does anyone know why she went off at such short notice?'

'Zak said he needed to talk to her,' said Don.

'There you go then. It's all a bit fishy, isn't it? He's been refusing to have anything to do with her for the last year, and all of a sudden he wants to talk.' Megan addressed them all, but she was looking at Ursula when she said it.

Andi hadn't painted it quite so badly when they spoke about it on the way to Barmouth, but Ursula recalled how she'd sensed Andi wasn't telling the whole story. All the same, she felt the need to defend her old friend from this gossip. 'I'm sure there's nothing to worry about.'

'Well you'd know, Ursula, wouldn't you?' There was something in the way Megan said it. She was either fishing or being sarcastic. Ursula couldn't work out which but Megan was right, she should know. In fact, there was a lot about Andi she should know. Why she and Zak had fallen out for one thing. What had actually happened with Pablo was another. But she'd have to wait until Andi was ready to tell her, because one thing she did know was that she didn't want to hear it from anyone but her.

'I meant to say, you and Don were a riot yesterday, Uncle Howard.' In one sentence, Gareth had closed his mother down and sent them off on a completely different tangent. Ursula wasn't sure what he did for a living but whatever it was, it was the Foreign Office's loss, because that young man would have made a very credible diplomat.

'I'm not with you,' said Howard.

'Didn't Brett show you? Oh my God, Brett, what were you thinking, man? I tell you what, you two could be Tik Tok sensations.' He handed his phone to Howard. 'Press play. Here, let me do it.'

'Is that what I think it is?' said Don, over the sound of the phone's tinny laughter. 'Brett, you little bugger. I had no idea you were filming us.'

Brett's face turned pink. 'I only sent it to Gareth. Not because I was laughing at you or anything.'

'And I only showed Mam,' added Gareth. 'It won't go no further, I promise.'

'Well, not quite,' said Megan, setting her mouth on a downward curve. 'I did send it to your kids, Howard. I thought it would be nice for them to see you more like your old self. They loved it. So don't expect an apology because you won't get one.'

It was getting late. Megan and Gareth had left a while ago. As far as she knew, the others had gone to bed, but Ursula was too keyed up to sleep. Thoughts of Anton and her future life were battling with worries about Andi and Zak. She went into the kitchen to make a milky drink that might trick her mind into readying itself for sleep. The light was off but the kitchen wasn't completely dark. The day's rain had emptied the clouds out and the starlit clear-as-glass sky bathed the room in a dim half-light. Through the window, she noticed Howard further out into the garden. She threw on her coat and boots and went out to him.

As she got closer, she saw that his head was turned up to the sky. He tilted it slightly towards her. 'Will you look at the size of that moon.'

She looked up and saw it, full and fat, surrounded by stars glistening like diamonds on black velvet.

'There's the plough, and see that bright one over there? That's Mars And that one's Jupiter.'

'You know a lot about astronomy.'

'Not really. I have an app. I like to pick out the planets from the stars but you don't get skies like this in the city.'

'No, you don't. It's quite special. I've seen the Northern Lights. In Norway. Tromso.'

'Now that must have been special. Were you there for a holiday?'

'No, work. My husband's work. We spent a month there. Fortunately it was late autumn, so I saw them several times.'

She saw him blink. He was thinking about what she'd just said, turning it over in his head. He'd probably worked out what hadn't felt quite right about her words and, at this moment, he was probably wondering whether she'd meant to say she and Anton had seen them several times. Now he was probably wondering if it would be rude to ask. She saved him the turmoil: 'His work was his life. Most nights, I was left to my own devices. But actually, seeing them on your own is quite a spiritual and uplifting experience. I can recommend it.'

They turned back to the sky and then, out of the blue, he said: 'Thank you, Ursula.'

'For what?'

'For talking to me. For making me dance. For making me laugh again.'

She thought about putting her hand on his arm again but she stopped herself. Because she wanted it far too much. And because she couldn't be sure what might happen next. So she kept her hands in her pockets. 'It was nothing.'

'No,' he said. 'No, it wasn't.'

27

TODAY WAS NOT THE DAY

Anton and Mr Big Potatoes were both in their usual places this morning. Ursula opened the window to let the cat in and made a point of ignoring her husband. He might be insisting on spooking her but she wasn't going to make it easy for him. Howard was gone. She'd heard him leave earlier. She hadn't gone down to see him off, choosing instead to hide away up here. They'd said goodbye last night and she'd left him gazing at the stars, no doubt wishing Dilys was with him. After that, she'd headed straight to bed to wrestle with her own thoughts. Thoughts like why she was dragging her husband's ghost around with her, and why she was falling for a man she hardly knew. A man who belonged to someone else. But then, that wouldn't be the first time, would it?

Charlie was straight at the door, probably ravenous and on the hunt for food. So Ursula was on her own again. Back under the duvet, she checked her phone for the first time in days and saw that she'd had a couple of messages from Clyde, updates on the allotment and asking how she was getting on. Feeling bad for not picking them up sooner, she sent him a quick reply and promised to be in touch soon. Then she pulled herself out of bed and got ready to face the day.

From the top of the stairs, it was easy to catch Megan's voice drifting up from the kitchen. She must have come to collect eggs for the café. Ursula didn't feel ready for another conversation about Andi and Zak so she had two choices for a shelter, her bedroom or the sewing room. She chose the sewing room but only because she couldn't bear another spell of avoiding Anton, or lying in bed, wallowing in her own remorse.

The sewing room was still and quiet. She breathed in the smell of uncut material, thread, and paper patterns all mixed up together. The happiest memories from her childhood and teenage years were in rooms like this and even now, that smell was the smell of home. So since when did sewing rooms become such scary places? The answer to that was easy. Since she began to associate them with loss and hopelessness. The last thing she'd made was her son's christening gown. She'd been unable to sew another stitch since he was wrenched from her body in such an untimely and savage way.

Propped up against one of the sewing machines was an envelope addressed to her. Andi had left her a note:

'Urs,

You found it then? I've got a mission for you while I'm away. I've left some fabric on the table. Do me a favour and run up a tablecloth and napkins. The measurements are in with the fabric. Shouldn't take long, unless you want to go to town on it. It's for a special day. When you see the material, you'll know which one.'

Back soon x'

· ·   ·

Run up a tablecloth. She made it sound so simple. Ursula unfolded the material, a white cotton linen mix embroidered with holly designs and occasional poinsettias. A Christmas tablecloth then. She laid it out and set it against the rulers that were built into one end and one side of the table. This she managed without too much trouble, but the act of smoothing the fabric out was enough to bring on a dryness in her mouth. She ignored it and picked up a yardstick and tailor's chalk that had been left out for her. It set off a tremor that started in her chest and found its way to her hands. Ursula put the chalk down. Today was not the day to begin again. She decided to go for a walk into town and along the lake as far as the path would take her.

The rooms downstairs were empty but she could hear Don outside. It was only when she stepped out the back door that she saw he was with Esme in the vegetable garden. They were shouting. Actually, it was Don that was shouting. Esme was making angry, incomprehensible noises while she was pulling up lettuces and throwing them at him. It was enough to make Ursula turn tail and head in the opposite direction to the front of the house.

She hadn't even reached the road when Don caught up with her. 'I'm going into town if you need a lift.'

'Thank you but I'm planning a walk. I was just coming to tell you I'll sort myself out for lunch but...'

'You saw me and Esme. I try not to let her piss me off but sometimes I could cheerfully strangle her. I'll apologise to her when we've both cooled off but if I go back now, it'll make things worse.'

'Would you like me to check she's all right?' she said, desperately hoping the answer would come back as no.

'Would you? I've properly upset her. And all over a bit of salad. I just said I was getting some for lunch from the Co-Op and she flipped because I wasn't using the stuff she'd grown. She just won't have it that it's inedible.'

Esme was huddled on a bench by the vegetable garden, sniffing into a piece of disintegrating toilet paper. Ursula took a packet of tissues out of her coat pocket and held them out for her. She snatched them off her without looking up.

'Mind if I sit down?'

'Do what you like, it's a free country.' Esme blew her nose on a fresh tissue. 'I suppose you've come to gloat?'

'Actually, I came to ask if you were okay.'

'Yeah, I'm good, yeah. Andi's left me here with a house full of wankers and bitches and the chief wanker has just told me I'm a shit gardener.'

Ursula sighed. It was no wonder Esme had no friends. 'So I suppose that makes me a bitch then, does it?'

'Not just you. Megan as well.'

'I see. What is it that makes us bitches, Esme? What have we done to you?'

'Megan just is.'

'And me?'

'Well, you're just so fucking perfect, aren't you? People like you have everything handed to you on a plate. Easy life. Easy everything.'

'Not really.' Ursula could have said more but her life was none of Esme's business and besides, Esme wasn't listening.

'Everyone thinks you're so nice. Especially Andi. Her best friend ever, that's what she calls you. We haven't had a look in since you got here. And I suppose you've got the best allotment ever. I don't suppose people would rather get a bag of salad from the Co-Op than eat the lettuce you've grown especially for them with your own bare hands.'

Ursula was certain now that Esme wasn't quite normal. If there was such a thing as normal, that is. Because one person's definition of it is another person's definition of crazy, or repressed. Or cold and unfeeling. Normality was a flexible concept. But from where Ursula was standing, Esme was very possibly on the outer reaches of it. She tried to think of something to say that might make her sound a bit less threatening which, in itself, was ironic. 'When I first started my allotment, I was hopeless. Everything died, except the potatoes. The other allotment holders showed me how and what to plant, when to plant and when not to. That's how I learned. I'm not an expert. I still get things wrong, but I can pass on some of that advice if you want to hear it.'

Esme stared straight ahead. 'It's my passion project.'

'I beg your pardon?'

'It's my passion project.' She looked Ursula up and down like she was a piece of dog dirt. 'Pablo said everyone should have one.'

Ursula started to back away. 'That's not true, Esme. It's not true at all.'

28

AN UNEXPECTED OFFER – 1985

'I have left a list of jobs on my desk. I would like you to do them for me today, if you have time,' said Anton.

'I'll make a start as soon as I've cleared the breakfast things.' Of course she had time. There wasn't a day in the week when Ursula didn't have time. At least that would be the case if Anton's lists weren't there to occupy her. The jobs were nothing more than mundane tasks that anyone could do. She knew that but she played along with it, because she understood why the lists were so important. It was 10th February. In six days, their son might have been a year old. She needed to be occupied. The lists were Anton's way of helping. This was how they lived now. This was how she survived from one day to the next.

He kissed her cheek. 'I think that maybe you're neglecting yourself again.'

'No, I'm not, I promise. I'm showering every day and I'm eating properly.'

He cast his eyes over her. 'Perhaps a trip to the hairdresser then. We have that open evening coming up. You'll want to look your best for that. And a new dress. Something sophisti-cated to give the right impression.'

She put on a smile. 'I'll add it to the list, shall I?'

He kissed her again. 'I think my wife is poking fun at me.'

'And I think my husband is going to be late for work if he doesn't stop giving me jobs.'

'I am never late but yes, I will go.' He smoothed her hair down with his palm and gave her another sweet, tender kiss. He was more like the Anton she'd fallen in love with now. Things were getting back on track. Except for his determina-tion not to have a baby. On that he was immovable. For the moment at least. Ursula hadn't completely given up on it yet.

She loaded up the dishwasher and wiped the table. It was already spotless but Anton was bound to find something with his eagle eyes. With that done, she went upstairs to start on today's list. The room that had once been the nursery was now his office. He'd changed its purpose not long after he'd painted it. She'd hated him for it at first, actually hated him, but eventually she saw the sense in it. She could come in here now without having to fight the urge to break down. She'd already vowed to herself that she would never to cry again until Anton changed his mind about children. But making a vow and keeping it were two different things and there'd been a couple of times when she'd only just managed to stop herself from crying a bucketload of tears.

The last time she'd felt that way was the day he'd brought home the model he'd shown her the night she ran away from her father, the one of the house he'd wanted to build. This house. His passion project. It was the reminder of that night, the way he'd been so sweet. The red scarf that had meant so much to her. She could have wept for the loss of the people they once were. But then he'd set the model down in his new office and something hardened inside her. She hadn't had so much as a damp eye since. So it had worked. She was better.

The only thing that was stopping a full recovery was her reluctance to go back to work. Ursula couldn't face sewing again. She'd thought about it. She'd even bought some material for a simple skirt. But as soon as she'd rolled the fabric out, memories of the christening gown came flooding back and suddenly she was reliving that awful, awful day all over again. And then she was shaking violently and vomiting. And then she was wanting to die again. So it was more than reluctance. It was fear. Fear that going back to Talulah might be the downfall of her.

On top of that, she hadn't spoken to Andi since the day she left work. She thought she'd seen her that day at the hospital but everything had been so confused, and Anton had said neither her nor Cass had been there when he'd arrived. She could have asked her mum, but that would have meant bringing up that day again and she didn't want that. It was too painful for both of them. Cass could have told her, but she was another person Ursula had hidden away from. It was better not to mull on these things. Better not to look back. Anton had said that to her so many times since the day she decided to pull herself together, and he was right. Looking back didn't help you to survive. Neither did looking forward.

The first job on the list was to dust the model. She rolled her eyes fondly. Him and his bloody model. She lifted its roof off carefully. If she dropped it and anything broke, she'd never hear the end of it. The inside was like a doll's house without any furniture or dolls. Just empty white boxes within a larger empty white box, but it was Anton's pride and joy. Or at least a miniature replica of his pride and joy. He'd worked on projects all over Europe as well as this country, but this house was his obsession. Yes, that was a good description of it now that she thought about it. Everything in this house, down to the pans they used for cooking, was part of his design. Except for her, of course. But even she was changing to look more like one of his designs – her hair, clothes, speech. Even the way she carried herself. All turning her into Mrs Anton Moller. It was easier that way. Ursula Fry couldn't have coped with the life she led now, and she certainly couldn't have coped with losing the baby.

Anton was very particular about dusting his pride and joy. He had a special set of brushes to fit every crevice and woe betide her if she used the wrong one. She lifted off the top floor as carefully as she'd lifted the roof, and selected a soft medium-sized brush. She'd only managed a couple of brush strokes when the doorbell rang.

Ursula looked out of the window which was perfectly placed to see everything in front of the house. It fell a few feet short of the main door, but unless the caller had pinned themselves to it, you could usually see who was there. To her complete shock, Andi was looking up at her. Ursula took a backwards step, her first instinct being to hide. The doorbell rang again. This was stupid. She needed to get a grip of herself. It was just Andi. The worst that could happen was that she'd call her a skinny arse cow. She went downstairs, her heart pumping. Andi was here. She'd come to see her. She didn't know whether to be excited or terrified.

She opened the door and there was Andi, bundled up in an oversize tweed coat. Her hair was now a mass of curls, fixed on top of her head with a red wrap. She looked fantastic. Ursula felt old, older than her years.

Andi smiled at her but it was a nervous smile. 'You gonna let me in then?'

Ursula stood back to give her room. 'You want tea or coffee, or something?'

'Tea would be good, ta.' She followed Ursula into the kitchen. 'It's quiet in here.'

'I can put the radio on.'

'I'll do it. Where is it?'

'In that cupboard. Probably at the back.'

Andi found the radio and switched it on. Two very serious people were in conversation. 'Well this isn't exactly Radio One, is it?' She pressed buttons and turned dials until Bananarama came on. 'That's better.' She threw her coat on the back of a chair and took the one next to it. 'How are you, Urs?'

'Okay.'

'I'm sorry about the baby.'

What kind of thing was that to say? Now, after all this time. After everyone else had stopped mentioning it. After Ursula had stopped allowing herself to think about it. 'Taken you a while to tell me that.'

'I didn't think you wanted to see me. I tried, but–'

'So why now?'

'Talulah's closing down. I thought you might want to know. We finished our last dress this week. The shop'll officially close next week.'

The nugget of anger that just taken hold of Ursula fizzled out. Talulah was closing. How could this be? 'But what will you do?'

'Wanda's retiring. Cass got me a job with someone she knows in London. I'm leaving, Urs. I've told Gillian. She's been really good about it. I expect she'll be glad to have the flat back to herself again.'

Ursula slumped down on a chair. This wasn't right. How could Cass let this happen? 'I suppose Cass got a better offer.'

'No, she's gutted about it. I don't think sales have been that great and we've had less and less orders coming through.'

'She doesn't need to worry about that. The Frys have bankrolled her for years.'

'Not anymore. She's broke. Well, broke for her. Probably not broke for you and me. Okay, probably not broke for me. You're all right now.'

'My baby died. How can I be all right?' There, she'd said what she'd been holding back for so long. Her baby had died. Some people, the so-called experts, would have said it was too early to call him a real baby and that he didn't actually die, but he was real to her. And she felt his death as much as if he'd been full term.

'I'm sorry, I didn't think. That was a really stupid thing for me to say. Of course you're not all right. Any moron can see that.'

'What do you mean?'

'Well look at you. You're so thin. And those clothes. What is that, classic M&S?'

'Classic designer actually.'

Andi whistled. 'Well, Westwood it ain't.'

In spite of her heart feeling like it was being ripped out, Ursula laughed. 'Special fogies collection.'

Andi grinned. 'What's your favourite song this week?'

This week? Ursula didn't even have a favourite song this year. Or even last year. There was a reason that radio had been in the cupboard. 'I haven't been listening to much lately.'

'No kidding. What are you gonna do, Urs? You can't go back to Talulah now, but you can't carry on like this, in this fucking clinic.'

'My house is not a clinic.'

'It looks like one. Where's the colour? And what's with the echo?'

'What echo?' she said, even though she knew perfectly well there was one.

'This one.' Andi sent it up to the top of the house.

'Oh that. It's just because the ceiling's so high. It's part of the design.'

'Well it's creepy.' She lay on the floor. 'Get down here. Let's see if it carries this far down.'

Ursula lay next to her and they made hooting sounds, giggling as the hoots came back to them. She'd missed this. She'd been an idiot to let it go. 'I didn't think you wanted to speak to me either. That's why I haven't tried to make it up with you.'

'But I came to see you that day at the hospital.'

'Did you? I wasn't sure if I'd imagined it. And when Anton said he hadn't seen you, I thought I'd got confused.'

'But he did see us. Cass anyway. In the car park. We were leaving because Gillian had arrived and, you know how it is with her and Cass. But Cass got out the car and spoke to him.'

'Are you sure? It's just that–'

'Come to London with me, Urs.'

'What, just walk away?'

'Yeah.'

Her and Andi starting a new life in London? Was that possible? She could get a job, she supposed. Not sewing but in a shop, or a bar, or as a typist. Was it so stupid? 'But what about Anton?'

'Leave him.'

Leave him? Could she really do that after everything he'd done to take care of her? She couldn't even remember to keep herself clean and healthy without him reminding her. And what would he do if she went? He loved her. It was true he irritated her sometimes with his silly particular ways. And yes, she suspected he kept things from her, like seeing Cass at the hospital. But he probably had his reasons and she still loved him. Not just that. She needed him too. 'I can't.'

'Okay,' said Andi, as if all she'd done was ask her if she wanted another cup of tea. It was just like her first day at Talulah when she'd dropped an insight bomb and then asked about favourite songs. That was Andi all over, and that was why she loved her. But she'd managed to live without Andi for a while now. She hadn't managed to live without Anton.

29

TOO LATE – 1985

'Andi came to see me today.'

Anton looked up from his reading. 'Oh.' He went back to his book, a new one about Bauhaus, as if he hadn't already read everything there was to know about it. But even though he'd probably read the same thing in a hundred other books, it was obviously far more interesting than Ursula's announcement.

'She's leaving. Going to London.'

'Probably for the best,' he said, his eyes still on the page.

'What do you mean?'

'There will be more opportunity for her. There's nothing here now that the business is closing.'

'You knew. How did you know?'

He marked his page and closed the book. 'It's common knowledge in the business community.'

'Why would the business community be interested in a little shop like Talulah?'

'It's not the shop but the money behind it. It's the Frys we're interested in.'

Yes, that made sense. They often entertained 'the business community' and from what Ursula could see of them, they were snidey, gossipy haters of both the little people and the big people. She should have realised they'd be taking an active interest in Cass's ruin. No doubt they'd be hoping it was a signal that the Frys were in trouble. But that didn't answer another question that she was burning to ask. 'If you knew, why didn't you tell me?'

'We discussed it a month ago.'

'We did not.'

'Yes we did. At Lorenzo's. With Simon and Cecily.' He reached over and kissed her. 'Perhaps you were too busy flirting with the waiter to hear.'

'How dare you. I was not flirting.' It was true, she definitely wasn't flirting but she was enjoying the waiter flirting with her, and Simon and Cecily were very, very boring. Perhaps she had missed the change in conversation from taxation to Talulah. Unlikely, but not impossible. She also wanted to ask him about seeing Cass at the hospital, but that could wait because this conversation was moving in a direction they hadn't been in for some time, and she was finally ready to go there with him. 'He was flirting with me.'

Anton moved closer and ran his finger along her leg. 'I can't blame him for that. I would do the same if I were him.'

'You, flirting? I'd like to see that.'

He pulled her to him. 'This is me flirting.'

Ursula woke up before the alarm. Anton still had his arms around her. She snuggled up to him, delighting in the feel of him next to her. They'd made love last night for the first time since she'd been pregnant. She'd cried when she came. Out of happiness, not sorrow. She'd explained that to him. She was happy that they were back together again. Properly together as lovers should be, because a marriage was nothing if you weren't lovers too.

She turned around to face him and opened his eyes with a kiss. 'Hello.'

He smiled. 'Good morning. What time is it?'

She traced her fingers across his chest. 'Time to be lovers again.'

Anton was singing in the shower. Something Swedish she thought. It was one of those once-in-a-lifetime events that she should treasure. Her husband was not a singer for two reasons. One, it wasn't in his nature. Two, he had an awful voice. Awful voice or not, she didn't care. Because Anton was singing, and she was feeling happy. Everything was going to be okay.

He kissed her again when he came down for breakfast. She'd done boiled eggs, ham and rye bread. A favourite from his childhood. 'Are the eggs all right?' she said. It had taken a long time to learn the art of boiling them so that they were neither too soft nor too hard.

'Very good.' Coming from him, that was high praise. 'You still have the list from yesterday?'

'Yes. Andi stayed for most of the day so I didn't get round to it. I don't think I'll get much done today either. I'm going up town. I thought I'd look for that new dress. Your little house will have to put up with the dust for a bit longer.'

'My poor house.' He laughed. He really was in an unusually good mood.

'You never said, did you find a new passion project when you finished the house?'

'No need. I already had one.'

'Really? What was that?'

'You, my darling. You are my greatest creation yet. You are this close to perfection.' He held his finger and thumb an inch apart and winked. He actually winked. Another first.

She slapped the back of her hand against his chest. 'Cheeky sod.'

Ursula turned into Ethel Street. She'd gone the back way to avoid passing Anton's office. Last night and this morning had been so lovely, she'd decided not to mention she was going to Talulah. Andi and Wanda wouldn't be there, but it wasn't them she was hoping to see. It was Cass she was here for, and the shop itself. She needed to see them both before it was too late.

Her heart broke when she saw the big closing down sale notice plastered across the windows. It broke a little bit more when she opened the door and found only two sad looking rails of clothes. There was no one manning the till. It hadn't occurred to her that the shop would look any different to the last time she'd been here, and the reality was a shock.

Ursula went through to the back. At least the office looked the same, although that too was unoccupied. Every step on the stairs creaked as she took them. She'd once seen an old film about a ghost ship and she couldn't help thinking about it as she walked along the top floor, checking every room for signs of life and wandering why there were none. And then she came to the sewing room and stopped. Her heart was like a drum and she felt sick, but she had to go in there. If only to prove to herself there was a faint possibility that one day, she would sew again. She pushed the door open. The sight made her gasp. There was nothing left of it. It had been completely gutted.

Footsteps on the stairs brought her back out to the landing. They sounded too heavy for Cass but she called out anyway: 'Cass, is that you?'

At first she didn't recognise the man in the car coat, jumper and slacks. She couldn't remember seeing him without his trademark suit and tie. Selective memory perhaps.

Her father's eyebrows knitted together as he looked her up and down. 'Ursula. You're looking well. A little thin. Are you eating properly?'

It struck her as a bizarre thing to say, although perhaps in his mind it was a perfectly natural follow on from the last thing he'd said to her. Right before he'd walked out on them: 'Be a good girl.'

'I came to see Cass,' she said, in case he thought she might be here for him.

'She'll be back soon. Would you like to wait?'

'Not if it means waiting with you.'

He gave her a smile that was so like her own it was unnerving. 'I can stay in the office. I'm tidying up the paperwork.'

She shook her head and tried to pass him.

'I hear you married Anton Moller.'

Ursula stopped in her tracks. 'You know Anton?'

'He designed the house I live in now. Did an excellent job too. You made a good choice. Well done.'

If she'd thought it was impossible to feel any more hate

for this man, he'd just proved her wrong. 'I don't need your praise. Tell Cass I called.'

He moved aside to let her past. 'This is your mother's fault, you know. None of it would be happening if she'd agreed to let me have you.'

'Have me?'

'You'd have been part of my family. I could have given you everything your sisters have.'

She looked him up and down with the contempt he deserved. 'We're all just possessions to you, aren't we? This may be hard for you to understand, Bernard, but I would hate to be a part of your family. You and your sort disgust me. And by the way, I have no sisters. It's always been me and Mum. And that's how I like it.'

Her heart was racing but she she refused to leave the shop at anything faster than walking pace. That's not to say she didn't want to run away again but she wasn't going to let that man get the better of her. When she got to the corner of New Street, her head automatically turned towards the window where Anton worked. He was there, looking down at her. How did he do that? It was as if he knew she'd be there. She took the flight of steps up to his practice two at a time and waived away his secretary's protestations as she stormed into his office. She was out of breath and her heart was still running too quickly when the words came out: 'Why didn't you tell me you'd designed my father's house?'

His sigh was heavy and pointed and yes, there was that flash of irritation back again. 'It was before I met you. When I realised the connection and what he had done, I decided you wouldn't want to know.'

'Uh huh, I see.' Her voice was normal again now but the rest of her was still pumping. She was walking in circles in front of his desk, trying to work out whether that seemed plausible. 'Tell me something else then. Did you see Cass and Andi at the hospital the day I lost the baby?'

A new look now. Bafflement? Or was it just put on? 'I don't believe so.'

'You don't believe so. Right. So you didn't speak to Cass then, in the car park, say?'

'No. Where did you get this from? Ah, of course. It was Andi. She's wrong. Or lying. I don't know which. Can we discuss this tonight? I have a meeting that I must go to.'

She nodded, not quite listening. Andi lying? No, she wouldn't do that.

'Can I get you some tea?' said his secretary after he'd left for the meeting.

'No thank you. Just let him know I've gone.'

She caught the train at Moor Street. Andi was leaving today but she hadn't said what time. If she hurried she might just catch her. What she would do if she did catch her wasn't quite clear yet, but there was every chance it would involve a new life in London.

Panic began to set in when she couldn't see Andi's car out the front but she carried on up and rang the bell to her mum's flat. The panic subsided when she heard someone coming to the door. But it was her mum, not Andi. 'Hello, love, did you forget your key?'

'It's at home. I only decided to come at the last minute. Is Andi here?'

'She left a couple of hours ago. I took a day's holiday to see her off.'

'Did she give you her new address?'

'She doesn't have one yet. Someone she knows from school lives in a squat there. She's staying with them until she can find somewhere. I told her it's not a good idea but she's set on it. Why, what is it?'

Too late. She was too late. Every part of her was sinking now. 'I just. I just. Oh, Mum. So much has been happening. I thought I was getting better but now I'm so confused. I don't know what I'm doing anymore.'

Her mum grabbed her shoulders and ushered her in. 'Let's see if we can work it out together. Tell me everything.'

'Well I can see why you were upset,' said her mum. 'Cassandra and Andi were definitely at the hospital. They left shortly after I arrived. Anton turned up about fifteen minutes after they'd gone, so there is a chance they might have bumped into one another. But if Anton's saying he didn't and you don't believe him, I suppose you'll have to ask Cassandra'.

'I was going to ask her that when I went to see her but I couldn't hang around while that man was there. Especially after he said that about you.'

'Well, it was actually the truth. Bernard did want to buy me off and take you to live with him and that horrible woman, who plainly wasn't happy about it, by the way. She would have been vile to you. I wasn't going to have that. Also, we wouldn't have been able to see each other. I wasn't having that either.'

'I'm glad you said no. What was the price for me? How much did he think I was worth?'

'It doesn't matter. If it had been a million pounds I'd have still said no. It wasn't, but it would have been enough for me open up my own Talulah with money to spare. As for Anton designing his house, I can see why he didn't tell you. Mind you, it was stupid because it was bound to come out eventually. What are you going to do?'

Ursula shrugged. 'Well I can't run off to London.'

'Yes you can. If you want to.'

Not without Andi she couldn't. Although twenty-four hours ago, she didn't even think she could do it with Andi.

'Or you can come back here.'

That was tempting, but not for now. She'd made up her mind to go back home and talk to Anton. Maybe she'd try calling Cass as well. She had her home number. And if she was still unhappy when Andi eventually sent her address, she'd definitely follow her to London. 'I think I should talk things over with Anton. If that doesn't work, I know I have you to fall back on.'

'That sounds like a very sensible plan. I'll give you a lift back.'

'Will you be all right on your own now that me and Andi have gone?' said Ursula when they were in the car.

'I think so. I'm even planning a little holiday when the weather warms up.'

'Alone?'

'No, with a friend.'

'Oh, a friend from work?'

'No. Someone I used to know when I was younger. We both worked at Fry's for a while. We bumped into each other again a couple of years ago.'

'That's nice. What's her name?'

'Solly.'

'Solly? As in–'

'Solomon.'

Ursula's mouth fell open. 'Mum, are you saying you've got a boyfriend?'

'More of a man friend really. Is that all right? I've been waiting for the right time to tell you.'

'It's the best news I've had in ages. Go on holiday with him, Mum. Have a great time. If anyone should, it's you.'

'Thanks, love. He's divorced as well. He's got three kids, a bit older than you. I haven't met them yet but he says they're very pleased he's got someone. You can still come home if you want to though. There'll always be room for you.' Her mum pulled up at the house. 'Just a thought. It might be an idea for you to make proper plans regardless of whether you stay or go. Think about what you really want to do.'

'I will. And maybe I can meet Solly soon.'

Ursula waved her mum off and turned towards the house, instinctively looking up at Anton's office window. It was getting dark but he wasn't back yet. She let herself in, thinking about what she could make quickly for dinner. The light on the answerphone was flashing. He'd left a message to say he'd be back late and not to wait up. So much for discussing later then.

Anton was already in the bathroom when she woke up. He must have crept into bed while she'd been asleep last night, and crept out again this morning. She got up and went down to make breakfast. It was another half hour before he came down carrying his suitcase. 'You're going away?' she said.

'Yes. That was what the meeting was about yesterday. It should have been a colleague but he was taken ill, so I must go in his place.'

'Where? How long for?'

'Canada. A fortnight, I think. It depends. It's a great opportunity, I can't turn it down. I have left you a very long list. You will be all right?'

'Yes. I will.' February 16th was just a few days off but she had plenty to occupy her. She was going to make a list of her own. It was time to make plans.

30

ALWAYS THAT INCH AWAY

A car drove towards Ursula and tooted as it got closer. It was almost on top of her before she realised it was Don, on the way back from his controversial shopping trip. She raised a hand to acknowledge him, not wanting to give any indication that something was wrong. But something was most definitely wrong. Passion project. Those were the exact words Esme had used. Pablo's theory, she'd said. Ursula knew she was reading too much into it but why now, in this place? And why Pablo? It was Anton's philosophy, not his. Anton, the man who wouldn't know passion if he lived to be a hundred. Two hundred. Three hundred. Four. But cold and unfeeling as he was, at least Anton meant it. At least he knew how to dig in and work and craft on his so-called passion projects. Something that feckless shit, Pablo, would never understand. So where did Pablo get the idea from? He would have stolen it, of course. It wouldn't be the first time he'd taken something that wasn't his.

Through the gaps in the trees, she saw the lake, dark and shimmering, with a sheen on it like pewter. She was surprised Anton wasn't there standing, Christ-like, on it. But no. It seemed he reserved his hauntings for terra firma.

Another car was coming her way. It slowed down almost to a stop. She screwed her eyes up, squinting to see if she could make out the driver in case it was one of the few people she knew here. The driver pointed to the side of the road. She realised then he was asking her to move out of the way. She was almost in the middle. Ursula mouthed an embarrassed apology, swerved over to the verge, and told herself to stop being ridiculous. It was just two words, one common phrase, and it was only because Anton's ghost was in her head that she was connecting things that had no business being connected.

You are this close to perfection, he'd said, and she'd assumed he was joking. Sometimes Ursula thought she really wasn't very bright at all. Because looking back on her life, as she'd been forced to do lately, all she could see was misunderstandings and missed opportunities. Take her father for instance. She'd misunderstood him completely. *This is your mother's fault. None of it would be happening if she'd agreed to let me have you.* He wasn't talking about the way things were between them. He wasn't even talking about how he'd left them without a penny and made sure it stayed that way. He was talking about Talulah, and Cass. By taking Ursula on, she'd gone against him and he'd made her pay for it. It took Ursula fifteen years to work that one out and, even then, she'd needed it spelled out to her.

The part of the lake where she'd walked with Andi a few days ago was upon her. She took the same path but she was going so quickly, she swallowed it up too fast. She stopped at a café a few yards off the path, took an outside table and ordered coffee. Not that she wanted a drink, but it was a good spot to sit and view the long stretch of water disappearing into distant mountains and clouds. It would have been quite peaceful if episodes from her life weren't jumping around her head in a tangled mess. They came to a halt at that first day in 1978 and, once again, she saw Anton watching her. She wondered if, even then, he'd been considering whether she could be his greatest creation yet. *You are this close to perfection.* If only she hadn't stopped to breathe.

She never did get round to having things out with him. Neither did she get round to leaving him. It took months for Andi to get in touch and by then, Ursula was too wrapped up in being Mrs Anton Moller. She'd spent the fortnight he was in Canada trying to come up with a plan, only to conclude she couldn't think of anything other than to learn to drive. And even that had been her mum's suggestion to give her some independence. It turned out she was good at it, passing her test first time which made her feel like she'd accomplished something on her own. She didn't realise it then, but that one thing was enough to stop her losing herself completely, which was probably why her mum suggested it.

As it happened, she hadn't needed to worry because Anton had already made a plan for her. When he came back, he said there was no point in her trying to find a job because he'd won the Canada project so they'd be away for at least a year. After that there was time spent in Norway, France, Germany. Wherever he travelled, she went with him. She became the perfect professional wife, entertaining clients, looking good on his arm, seeing to his every need. Anton's second passion project had turned out just right for him. Although he wouldn't have said that because she was never quite perfect enough. Always that inch away.

'Too good for my place then, are you?' Megan stood over

her, hands on hips. 'Only joking. They do a good coffee here. Anyway, I've closed up for the day. Fancied a bit of fresh air. Mind if I sit with you?'

'Not at all.' Ursula dragged herself away from her thoughts, glad of the respite, even if it was Megan doing the dragging.

'Don popped in earlier. Got his knickers in a twist because Esme went off on one over a bit of salad. He doesn't want to upset Andi, you see. I told him not to worry. Did you have any luck with her? He said he'd left you to pick up the pieces.'

'I'm not sure. I offered to help with the vegetable garden.' She thought it best not to mention that Esme had called them both bitches.

Megan rolled her eyes. 'Her passion project? That was brave of you. Oh, have I said something wrong?'

'Not really, it's just that phrase...'

'Passion project? Bugger, I've said it again, haven't I? Pablo was always banging on about it. Late onset midlife crisis, if you ask me. That and running off with a woman half his age. If anyone needs a bit less passion, it's him.'

Yet another revelation. Andi hadn't mentioned the woman was a lot younger than him. 'He was a bit of a...' Ursula was searching for the right word. Something that wouldn't betray Andi too much.

'Arsehole. Not that I'd say that to Andi, you understand. Poor woman's suffered enough. But as it's just you and me, let's be honest, the man's an arsehole. What I don't get though is why they all love him so much. It's like a cult. The cult of Pablo.'

'I suppose they all think he saved them in some way.'

Megan let out a loud snort. 'More fool them then. If you

ask me, the only reason he brought them here was to feed his ego. And that goes for his family too. Do you know what Amnawr means in English? This will do for now. That's Pablo all over, that is. Use it and lose it. Sorry. I'm in a bad mood today.'

'Something's wrong,' said Ursula.

'You do that a lot, don't you? Notice things.'

'I suppose so. Does it bother you? You said before it must be a nuisance for me.'

'Not exactly. It's just that I notice things as well. I find it a nuisance sometimes because it gets me thinking. For instance, I notice the way you try to be as quiet and invisible as possible, like you're frightened to take up space.'

'I hadn't realised it was that obvious. I got into the habit a long time ago and I can't seem to get myself out of it. It was my husband you see. He liked quiet.'

'Sorry if this comes out the wrong way, Ursula, but he sounds like a right barrel of laughs.'

Ursula's face broke into a much welcome smile. 'Thank you, Megan. I needed that.'

'It's Dilys. She's got pneumonia. Happens a lot with that illness apparently. They're saying it's only a matter of time. That's why I'm in a bad mood. At least Howard's with her.'

'I'm so sorry.'

She dabbed her eyes with her fingers. 'I always think you can break any habit if you try hard enough. Unless you don't want to, of course.'

31

LOOK IT IN THE EYE

Unless you don't want to. Megan's words were still nagging away at her, making it sound so easy. If only it were that simple. Of course she wanted to be free of all those annoying habits that ruled her. Of course she did. But wanting something didn't make it happen, even if you tried really hard. Those habits ruled her for a reason.

She reached Am-nawr and her heart sank a little. What she wouldn't give to be back at the allotment right now. Don was tackling the dusty hall with the vacuum when she got in. 'Trying to get it nice and shipshape before Andi gets back.'

'I'll give you a hand.'

'I'm finished now but thank you for the offer. And for speaking to Esme. She seems to have calmed down. What about you though? You looked a bit upset when I passed you on the road. Did she have a go at you?'

'Not really. I've just got a lot on my mind at the moment. It's sort of crept up on me out of the blue.'

'This place has a way of doing that to you. Most of us came here to forget our past, only to find ourselves remembering it all the more. It does go eventually, I promise. Peace will come.'

Ursula wanted to tell him it wasn't the same for her. She'd come here for Andi. But she remembered what Esme had said about them not getting a look in since she arrived and she wondered if that's how Don felt too, so she changed the subject: 'I bumped into Megan. Did she tell you about Dilys?'

'Yes. I've let Andi and the others know.'

'I'll try Andi later. I haven't wanted to bother her while she's with Zak.'

'Yeah, I expect they've got a lot of catching up to do.' He picked up the vacuum and turned towards the kitchen.

'Do you know why they stopped talking?' She blurted it out before he had a chance to walk away.

'Best ask her that.'

Ursula stood in the hall, wondering if she'd crossed a line. Don was normally so easy going, if you didn't count his run-ins with Esme. It could be that he was coming to terms with the news about Dilys. Then again, it could be that he was just very defensive when it came to Andi. Either way, it didn't feel right to follow him with more questions, so she turned the other way and went into the library.

The library had two bookcases that held a mish-mash assortment of books, in no particular order. Anton would have been appalled at the lack of structure. But then he would also have been appalled at the lack of serious content on display. The only books in their house had been weighty tomes, mostly related to architecture or business. Needless to say, she never read them.

On one side of the room was an ancient computer, one of those big heavy things that was browning with age. This was where she'd seen Andi doing her accounts. Behind it was a wall of framed photos, mostly of Am-nawr through its stages of reclamation. When Andi and Pablo had first come here with the kids they'd lived in a caravan while they brought this wreck of a house back to life. They'd poured everything into it. Dare she say it was their passion project? Strange then that it should feel so lonely.

There were pictures of Jet and Zak, looking like archetypal hippy kids. They hadn't wanted to leave the big city to come here but they settled in eventually. There was Jet as a teenager, sticking her tongue out at the camera to reveal a piercing. So like Andi. And Zak. Shy, a little awkward and very sweet. That's how Ursula remembered him. It was hard to imagine that boy refusing to speak to his mum for a year. The last time she'd seen either of the kids was Anton's funeral. They were all grown up by then and she'd hardly had time to say more than a few words to them. A lot of the photos were of Pablo. Pablo with a saw in his hand. Pablo hammering at a wall. Pablo digging what looked like the vegetable garden. On and on they went. There were very few of Andi.

On the next wall was a noticeboard with more photos pinned to it. Group photos mainly. She recognised Don and Esme in them but couldn't see Brett. Megan was in there with her arm around an older woman. Howard was on the other side. Was this Dilys? There were other faces she didn't recognise. One in particular caught her eye. A young woman, slim with blonde hair pulled up to a top knot on her head, wearing a boiler suit splashed with paint. The photo had been taken in Ursula's room, the murals on the wall only half done. She must be the artist. It was a striking image, not least because of the way the woman was gazing straight at the camera. As if she had nothing to hide. As if she'd already laid her soul bare to the photographer. It was too much to witness, like you were spying on an intimate moment. Ursula's mind was racing again. She needed the comfort of talking to someone who knew her, someone she didn't need to be guarded with. She called Clyde.

He answered almost immediately. 'Good timing. I'm at your allotment.'

'How's it looking?'

'Good as ever. What about you and your friend?'

'Things aren't quite as straightforward here as I thought they'd be. I'm not sure I'm handling them too well.'

There was a moment's silence at the end of the line then: 'Want to talk about it?'

'Not yet. It's too jumbled up. I'm seeing things that aren't here and not seeing things that are here. At least I think they're here. I can't tell. Reality seems to be playing tricks on me at the moment. I may be moving towards something though. I just wish I could see what it was.' She brought herself to a stop. The words had fallen out of her like a runaway train, making no sense whatsoever.

Clyde's sharp intake of breath told her she'd said too much. He was one of the dearest, kindest people she knew but he was of a generation that weren't used to sharing their innermost thoughts. So was she, but this place and this yearning for her normal life had got the better of her. 'Let it come, Ursula. Don't hide from it, that only makes it harder. Look it in the eye and learn from it. And remember, you're stronger than you think you are. Samuel always said that about you. If you need me, call me. Anytime, day or night. If I have to, I'll drop everything and come to you.'

Oh the darling, darling man. How lucky she was to have

him for a friend. 'Don't drop Colonel, whatever you do' she laughed.

'No chance. I'd have to be able to pick that damn fool dog up to do that. I'll bring him with me. He's missing his biscuits.'

'Give him a big sloppy kiss from me. I promise I'll call you if I need you. And, Clyde, thank you.' As she cut the call, she was smiling at the thought of Clyde and Colonel riding to her rescue. She wouldn't ask him to come but it was good to know he would. Besides, he'd already given her all she needed to keep going. His advice had been to face whatever was coming and learn from it. And if she was moving towards something, or even if something was moving towards her, she could only do that on her own. Whether she had the strength in her to do it was the question. Clyde seemed to think so. Samuel too from the sound of it. Ursula wasn't so sure.

32

SOMETHING MOMENTOUS

Ursula ate breakfast with Don and Brett. It had just been the three of them last night at dinner. Esme had taken herself, a large bag of crisps, and a packet of chocolate Hobnobs off to sleep in the bothy. It was probably too much to hope that the isolation might bring about a period of reflection but on the upside, the evening had been far more agreeable without her. They'd had a very pleasant and relaxed meal and without Esme here to spoil it, the mood had carried over to breakfast.

'I messaged Howard this morning. Just to let him know we're all thinking of him and Dilys,' said Don. 'I told him not to worry about replying. How long you got left on this job then, Brett?'

'Nearly done, but I might have another one lined up after. Could be permanent.'

Don patted him on the back. 'That's brilliant, that is. I told you all that hard work would pay off, didn't I?'

'Yeah,' said Brett, blushing. 'I hope so anyway. Keep your fingers crossed for me.'

Ursula held her fingers up. 'I'm crossing mine now.'

'Maybe you'll be my lucky charm, Ursula.' Brett looked at his phone. 'Better go, my lift's here.'

Don gave him a bag of food. 'Here, I've made you some lunch. Go get 'em boy.'

'You look after him,' said Ursula, after Brett had gone.

'Someone's got to, I suppose. It's been the making of him coming here. One of the few good things Pablo did.' He clapped his hands together. 'Right, I'd better crack on. I've promised myself a walk before I start my jobs. Care to join me?'

'Thanks but I have my own job to do. It might take a while so I'm starting early.' She'd woken up this morning with her mind on one thing. Breaking habits. The phone call with Clyde had set her thinking, and maybe it had given her a tiny injection of confidence too. She was thinking that if she dug really deep, she'd find the strength to make one change, and if she could do that, perhaps more would follow. So this morning, she was going to break a habit. Or, as she liked to think of it, look a fear in the eye.

Charlie Big Potatoes caught up with her on the stairs and slipped through her legs as she opened the door to Andi's sewing room. Ursula shooed him off the table where the fabric was still laid out. He gave her a haughty flick of the tail then curled up on one of the chairs, closed his eyes, and dozed straight off.

Her hands started trembling as soon as she began to mark out the measurements. By the time she picked up the scissors, they were shaking so much there was no way she'd be able to cut a straight line. Ursula closed her eyes and took one long breath, then another until the shaking stopped. She might just get through this. But then she saw herself with the christening gown in her arms, the blood running down her legs, and she couldn't breathe.

It was Charlie's miaow that brought her back. He was rubbing himself against her, weaving this way and that around her. Ursula loosened her grip on the scissors and saw that her fingers were marked with vivid red indentations. She wanted to put the scissors down but if she did that, she might not pick them up again. Slowly, she slipped the fabric between the open blades and, even more slowly, began to cut. Every snip brought with it another image of blood and terror and lost babies. She needed something to stop them. And then as if from nowhere a wobbly voice was singing 'Supernature'. It took her a moment to realise the voice was hers.

At last she reached the end. Every part of her was still trembling. Her face was damp with sweat, and her top was stuck to her back, but she'd managed to cut a line. It would never have passed muster with her mum or Wanda but she'd done it. Finger by finger she let go of the scissors and lay down on the floor. Charlie jumped on top of her and pushed his head against her face. Ursula closed her eyes and saw her mum smiling back at her.

She must have been there ten minutes or so before there was a soft knock at the door. 'Okay if I come in?' said Don.

'Yes, it's not locked.'

'I heard you singing. I thought you might like a coffee. Oh, there you are. Taking a break?'

Ursula hadn't realised she'd been singing so loudly. She sat up. 'I'm building myself up to the next phase.'

'You're making the Christmas tablecloth. Andi makes a new one every year. It's a bit of a tradition. You must be good if she's asked you to do it.'

'I was, once. A lifetime ago. I'm not sure it'll be as good as Andi's.'

'If she's asked you to make it, she must be confident you'll do it justice. Very important the Christmas tablecloth tradition. I'll leave you to it. By the way, what I said about Pablo earlier, I just wanted to say, it's not that I'm not grateful to him for bringing me here.'

'I understand. Can I ask a question about the photos in the library? There's a young woman in one of them. I think she's the artist who painted my room.'

'Claudette. Yes she is. Was that your question?'

'Who took the photo of her?'

'Ooh, not sure. I think it might have been Pablo.'

Ursula snipped the final thread. Her back ached and she had to lie down on the floor again to stretch it out. When she used to do this sort of thing all the time, a tablecloth and napkins would have taken a couple of hours at the most. But it had taken all day to put together something that was halfway decent. In Andi's collection of ribbons and bindings, she'd found a reel of dark green satin that was a perfect match to the embroidered holly leaves. It made a lovely edging for the tablecloth, and she was proud of it. How strange it was after all these years to be proud of her work. How unfamiliar. But there was more to it than simply making a tablecloth. Something momentous had happened today. She'd followed Clyde's advice, faced a fear and learned from it. And the thing she'd learned was that hidden away deep down inside was the strength that might just help her face her biggest fear.

She shut her eyes hoping to see her mum again but all she saw was darkness. She was fine with that. Anything was better than blood and death. Her mum would have approved of this room and, if she'd been here now, she'd have been patting Ursula on the back, just as Don had done with Brett this morning. Her mind treated her to a flashback she hadn't had in years. A happy one this time. A little reward for her good work. Her mum and Cass together, working on a design. She'd tried to ring Cass after Anton had gone off to Canada, but there was never any answer. She'd gone back to the shop but it was closed up. She'd even visited Cass's house. Again, there was no one there. She'd just disappeared. Until the day she came back, that is. And by then, Ursula had almost forgotten about that conversation in the hospital car park.

33

SOMETIMES YOU NEED A REMINDER

Andi was back, bringing with her more bags than she'd taken. Zak lived in Hebden Bridge now which was close enough to Manchester to warrant a day's shopping, and she seemed to have made the most of it. But she'd brought more than that. There was a visible difference in her. She seemed just that little bit more alive, just that little bit more like the Andi of old.

Ursula had decided against calling her in the end. Better not to pull her away from precious moments with Zak. But she'd sent her a message with a photo of the tablecloth and napkins: *'Job done.'*

A reply had come back: *'Proud of you, mate. Tell me more tomorrow. I'll be home by lunchtime.'*

So now they were sitting in the kitchen, Andi, Don, and Ursula, having lunch. Brett was working and they weren't sure where Esme was. They hadn't seen her since the other night when she'd gone off to the bothy.

'Have you looked in on her?' said Andi.

'I've tried,' said Don. 'I've been up there four or five times but she hasn't been around. I know she's sleeping there though. There's empty pop bottles, crisp packets, that kind of thing. And a sleeping bag. Every time I go up there, I leave proper food and it's been eaten when I go back. I've seen her from a distance but I reckon she's deliberately avoiding me.'

Andi didn't say anything but it was obvious she was mulling it all over.

'If you ask me, she's going out of her way to pick fights over nothing. She really kicked off over me buying a bit of salad.' Don turned to Ursula as if looking for back up. 'Ursula managed to calm her down, but then she took herself off up the hill and hasn't been back since. She's getting worse, Andi.'

'Noted.' Andi picked at the sleeve of her cardigan, her sparkle already beginning to dim.

'How's Zak? I was thinking about the last time I last saw him. Must have been Anton's funeral.' Ursula was trying to steer them towards what she was hoping would be a more agreeable topic.

'I suppose it was. He's absolutely fine. More than fine, actually. His girlfriend's pregnant. He's about to become a dad. And I'm going to be a grandmother.' She looked at Ursula with an expression that was much too serious for such good news.

'Oh that's wonderful. It is wonderful, isn't it? You are happy about it, aren't you?' said Ursula.

'Yeah, I'm over the moon.'

Ursula threw her arms around her. 'I'm really happy for you, mate. Really happy.'

'Thanks, Urs. Let's go up to the sewing room. I'm dying to see the tablecloth.'

· · ·

Ursula stood over Andi. She couldn't keep her hands still, she was so fidgety and jittery. How mad was that? All she was doing was showing her a tablecloth that had taken more out of her than it bloody well should have done.

'It's gorgeous. I love the ribbon border. It must have been hard,' said Andi.

'It's just a tablecloth.'

'Yes it is, but that's not what I meant, Urs.'

'I know. Yes, it was hard. I'm glad you asked me to do it though. Did I ever tell you Anton used to leave me lists of jobs to do?'

'I don't think so.'

'They started after I lost the baby. I used to think they were to help me get through the day. Something to distract me from the misery. They probably were, in the first place.'

'That isn't why I asked you to make the tablecloth.'

'I didn't think that for one minute. You were giving me something to overcome. Helping me build strength.'

'And Anton wasn't?'

'No. Andi, I don't want you to think you can't talk about Zak's baby to me. When I said I was really happy for you, I meant it. It's not your fault I didn't have children.'

Andi took her hand. 'I thought that was how you'd feel but I needed to hear it. Do you think you've overcome your sewing phobia now?'

'Not completely, but I'm getting there.'

''Good, because I've got something for you. I picked up some material in Manchester. I thought we could help each other get our sewing mojos back. This one's for me. And this one's for you.' She gave Ursula a parcel wrapped in brown paper.

Hidden inside the paper was a beautiful lightweight silk,

with abstract off-kilter squares within squares in purples, blues, lavenders, oranges, yellows and whites. They reminded Ursula of a scarf that had belonged to her mum. An Italian designer, Schiaparelli. Solly had bought it for her on their honeymoon. It suited her colouring perfectly. And the one physical attribute Ursula had inherited from her mum was her colouring. 'It's fabulous.'

'That's what I thought when I saw it. So you.'

'It's been a long time since anything like this has been 'so me', but it's good timing. I'm trying to break a few bad habits.'

'Good. Ditching the grey is well overdue.' Andi spread a deep teal-green smooth satin crepe across the table. 'What do you think of mine?'

'Oh it's so you, darling.' She laughed but she could already feel the pressure building up inside her. 'This is a bit different to running up a tablecloth.'

Andi put her arm around her. 'I'll be here with you this time. What do you say? We could make them for Christmas. It's ages away and you'll probably have gone home by then but you can come back. We do great Christmases here. Well, we used to. No idea what this one's going to be like. You'll come though, won't you?'

'I suppose so, yes.' How could she say no when Andi was practically begging her?

'Marvellous.' The twinkle had returned to Andi's eyes. 'To the pattern library, before you change your mind.'

They'd been searching through the collection of patterns for over an hour. It was taking so long because the discovery of each one was accompanied by a reminiscence or two, and they were in no rush to return to the present. But eventually the present came knocking at the door. 'Go away, we're busy,' said Andi.

'It's Don. Mind if I step in for a minute?'

'God bless him,' whispered Andi. 'All right, but only for a minute.'

He came in and closed the door behind him 'It's Esme. She must have seen that you're back. She's outside, wanting to talk to you. Well, demanding really.'

'Is she now? Well you can tell her I will talk to her when I'm good and ready. And I am certainly not in the mood to talk to her now. Can you do that for me, Don?'

'Er yes, I think so.'

'Good man. And if you fancy making a cuppa for me and Urs, I'd be ever so grateful.'

'Leave it with me. Assuming I survive the backlash, your tea will arrive in due course.'

Ursula waited for him to go. If there was ever a time to ask about Esme, it was now. 'Andi, just say if I'm prying, but is there a connection between you and Esme?'

'Not exactly.'

'Then I don't understand why you put up with her. Sorry, I know I'm not being very tolerant, especially when she's obviously got problems. It's just that I've tried to find one redeeming feature in her and I can't.'

'She's Pab's daughter. Hardly a redeeming feature, I know, but that's why I put up with her.'

Of course she was. How had she not realised that before? Esme even looked like him. That time she'd smiled at Gareth, when Ursula had been racking her brains trying to think who she reminded her of. It was Pablo. The blindingly obvious had been staring her in the face all the time. 'But how?'

'How do you think? Sorry, Urs, I didn't mean to snap. All I

can tell you is I knew nothing about her until she turned up on the doorstep twenty months ago claiming to be his. He could have denied it but instead he invited her to stay. And then all hell broke loose.'

A lightbulb switched on in Ursula's head. The rift with Zak. It was all beginning to make sense now. 'Is that why Zak stopped talking to you?'

She nodded. 'He was angry with Pablo and just as angry with me for not throwing the pair of them out. I was being a doormat apparently. But Pab said it had been a one-night stand, a stupid mistake. He laid it on thick about how the poor girl had had a tough life. He reckoned she'd been in and out of care and he owed it to her to give her a home. I felt sorry for her, so I said she could stay. Zak had a big fight with us over it and then he walked out and moved in with his girl-friend. They left Bala not long after. Wouldn't even tell us where he'd gone.'

'But he's okay with you now?'

'Sort of. He won't come here while Esme's here though. She was vile to him. I think she's jealous of him, because he had Pablo growing up. She's obsessed with Pab. Followed him around like a lost puppy. Pab thought it was funny. I told him he needed to do something about her, so what does he do? He fucks off, and now I'm stuck with her. I made the wrong choices, Urs, and it cost me my son. We were so close, me and Zak, but there's a distance there that's like a huge chasm and I don't know if I'll ever be able to close it.'

'And Jet? What about her?'

'Oh she hasn't bothered to come here in years. Keeps well out of it. She's fine with me. She hasn't got a lot of time for Pab though. Not that he noticed. He was too busy trying to screw a woman who's practically a child.'

'Was it Claudette? The woman.'

'Who told you, Don?'

Ursula shook her head. 'I only asked him her name after I saw the photo in the library. I took an educated guess on the rest.'

'Madam Ursula strikes again. She's young enough to be Zak's girlfriend, you know. I thought he was just being nice to her because he was missing the kids and because he felt sorry for her with her so-called mental health problems. But they were carrying on right under my nose. Probably longer than that. He brought her here just like he brought the others so, for all I know, they could have been at it for ages. And the only mental health issue I witnessed while she was here was an inability to keep her fucking clothes on. She was always parading around half-naked, even in the middle of winter. And believe me, it's really fucking cold here in winter.'

Ursula turned away from the patterns. She couldn't face them anymore. That nostalgic bubble they'd been lost in had burst. This was all such a mess. So much chaos and disruption, and it was all down to one man. 'Something else I don't understand. Why do you keep her photo on the wall downstairs and why leave the bedroom as it is? Isn't that just a constant reminder?'

'Yes, it is. And that's why they're still there.'

Ursula lay in bed, too restless to sleep. This room had lost its appeal recently. In fact, there was a definite menace to the summery meadow now. A reminder from Claudette that she'd ripped the heart out of this house. But Claudette had only painted it. It was Andi who'd decided to keep the room as it was. That should have surprised Ursula, but it didn't.

She wasn't so very different. She'd hadn't changed a thing in her house since Anton died. Sometimes, you want a reminder. More than that. Sometimes, you need one.

Sick of tossing and turning, she got up and looked out the window. It was too dark to see anything, but she felt him out there, watching her every move. Just as he'd always done. She turned away. She wasn't giving Anton the space in her head tonight. It had already been reserved by a very different kind of man.

34

THE MAN WHO LOVES YOU – 1992

'You're back! I thought you weren't due home until next week. Why didn't you tell me?' Ursula's mum pulled her in for a hug.

'We came back early. I wanted to surprise you.'

'Well you've done that all right. It's a lovely, lovely surprise. Come in. Sol, get the kettle on. The prodigal daughter's returned.'

Solly appeared in the hall, all smiles. 'Marvellous, marvellous. And you look so well. Doesn't she look well, Gillian?'

Her mum stepped back and looked her up and down. 'She does. Still dressing like a funeral director though. What happened to that little girl who loved colour?'

'She grew up and became an architect's wife.'

'Hmm, not sure you can blame the entire profession of architects for your husband's terrible taste in clothes. What do you say, Sol?'

'Oh no, I'm not getting involved. Tea, is it?' Sol retreated to the kitchen. They were still living in her mum's flat. His previous flat had been above his tailor's shop. When they'd first got married, they'd considered buying a house together but, in the end, he paid off the mortgage on her flat instead.

'So how was Norway? Tell me all about it,' said her mum.

'It was great, So beautiful. We saw the Northern Lights.' Well, she supposed Anton might have seen them too, but not with her. He'd been working day and night. But she'd been treated to the sight of them four or five times while they were in Tromso and, actually, she'd been glad to have seen them on her own because he didn't appreciate that sort of thing. He'd have explained the science behind them and made her feel stupid and childish for thinking they were magical.

'Tea for my two lovely ladies.' Solly came in with a tray of tea and Jaffa Cakes, her favourite. They always had them in now because Sol loved them. A little too much in her mum's opinion, but she indulged him. It was coming up to their fourth anniversary but it felt like they'd always been together. They just fitted each other so well. He kissed the top of each of their heads. 'I'm leaving you to have a chat. I've got some work to do.'

'Work?' asked Ursula, after he'd closed the door.

'Just a jacket he's altering. He brings work home with him now and then. We like to sew together. It's nice,' said her mum. 'And I expect he wanted to give us some time on our own. He's had some good news but he probably thought it was best coming from me. His daughter, Gail, she's having a baby.'

'Oh. So you'll be a grandmother.'

'I suppose so. A step-grandmother anyway. Would that bother you?'

'Of course not.' She plastered a smile across her face. 'I'm really happy for you. For both of you. To be honest, it's a relief. With us not wanting kids, I felt a bit guilty because, you know, we're depriving you of grandchildren, aren't we?'

'Ursula, love, I've never thought like that. If you really don't want children that's fine with me, and it would have been fine if I'd still been on my own. If you really don't want them, that is. I just wasn't sure if you couldn't have them, after–'

'No, all fine there. It just made me realise I'd had a lucky escape, that's all.'

Her mum nodded, her eyes searching Ursula's. 'That's all right then. And you're happy?'

'Why wouldn't I be? I have a great life travelling with Anton. I wouldn't have got to see the Northern Lights if I'd been stuck at home with kids, would I?'

'I suppose not. As long as you are happy. Oh, I have some other news for you. Andi's moved again. Did she tell you?'

'No, but I've got a pile of post to go through when I get back. There might be a letter in there. Where is she now?'

'Leyton. She's moved in with someone. Spanish name. Hang on.' Her mum grabbed a letter from the sideboard and scanned it. 'Pablo. I think she's serious about this one. She's given me the address in case we want to visit.'

'Will you?'

'We'll see. Depends on whether Solly can spare the time. He's quite busy at the moment. Unless you want to come? We could do a day trip on the train.'

'Maybe.' Ursula was thinking of the last time they took a day trip to London. The talk then was of babies. 'I'll check with Anton when I get back. Anyway, I'd better go. I need to get something for tonight's dinner.'

She'd lied about needing to go shopping. It could have waited but she'd had to get away. It was the other lie, the really big one, that made it impossible to stay. Of course she wanted children. She'd wanted them from the moment she found she was carrying her little boy and through every contraction that rejected him. And even more so after she'd come to her senses again. In the years since Anton told her there'd be no more pregnancies, she'd tried to reason with him, but he would not be reasoned with. And now this news about Solly's daughter. She had nothing against Gail. She seemed like a really nice person. But this. This was too much. And keeping up the pretence that she was happy childless was killing her.

The garage door was open when she pulled up on the drive. Anton was in there, cleaning the Volvo. She'd expected him to get rid of it after she lost the baby but no, he'd kept it like a prized possession, spending his free time keeping it pristine. She sometimes thought it was deliberate, to remind her of how she'd lost the one thing most precious to her. To show her that her most precious thing meant so little to him.

She stood on the drive watching him pouring his love and attention into this big hulk of metal, another of his passion projects, his babies. Yes, Anton had his babies. They just weren't made of flesh and blood. They were cold, hard things with no soul, no ability to love you back. That suited him, but what about her? What did she have?

'How are Gillian and Solly?' He was hard at work trying to eradicate a mark on the bonnet and hardly glanced her way.

'I want a baby.'

The announcement made him stop and look up at her. 'We have discussed this. I have explained why I don't want children.'

'We haven't discussed it. You've just told me. But I want a baby, Anton. I really want children.'

The ripple of irritation was back, the look of annoyance that came every time she took a step out of her mould. 'How much do you want them? Enough to ruin our marriage? Enough to divorce me?'

'What?' She felt a sudden rush of something hot in her belly. It was pushing up and making its way to her windpipe. 'Are you saying you want a divorce?'

'No, but I think you are.'

'Don't be so stupid. I never said that. I said I want children.'

'And I do not. So if you want them that badly, you must divorce me and find someone who can give you what you want.'

'You can give them to me. You just don't want to.'

'Not anymore.' He was talking in riddles, trying to twist things round and confuse her. She didn't know what game he was playing this time but she didn't want to be a part of it. She turned away and went inside.

There was a neat bundle of letters waiting for her on the table in the hall. All bills or rubbish. Nothing from Andi. She went upstairs to use the bathroom. That encounter had made her feel sick. He did that to her. Always managed to find something to lob at her when she was least expecting it. In Tromso, he'd accused her of throwing herself at one of the Norwegian team when all she'd done was ask the man to teach her a few words of the language. That was why they'd had to come home early, because she'd damaged his professional reputation.

Anton was moving about downstairs. Probably putting the shopping away. God forbid the house might look a little lived in. Had he really suggested a divorce? It sounded like it to her. And maybe if she wanted children she should leave him because time was marching on, and if he wasn't going to change his mind... She re-ran the conversation in her head, word for word, just to be sure. Yes, he had suggested it, although it had actually sounded more like a threat. But out of all that strange exchange, one thing stood out. What the hell had he meant by it?

She found him in the kitchen, wiping the worktop where she'd left the shopping bag. As expected, the shopping was gone. 'You said, not anymore. What's that supposed to mean?'

'I can't give you children anymore. I had a vasectomy.'

'You did what?'

'My first trip to Canada. I took the opportunity.'

'You took the opportunity? Without even talking to me?' It was so ridiculous, she laughed. 'You know, Anton, we've been married for twelve years and I have no idea who you are.'

He put his hands on her hips and looked straight into her eyes. 'I am the man who took care of you when you were suicidal with grief. I am the man who refuses to see you go through that again. And I am the man who loves you and will always love you. Whatever you do.'

She pulled herself free and ran for her car before he could tell her she was being emotional and childish. She should go to her mum and Solly and let them look after her, but if she did that, she'd have to admit she wanted children. She'd have to tell them she'd been lying. And what she really wanted was to be somewhere no one would expect her to be. A place where she could be alone.

She drove into town and out again towards the north side of the city, through Erdington, and Wylde Green and on until she reached Sutton Park. Before her father turned his back on them, before they'd moved across town, her mum brought her here every week. Sometimes, Ursula would ride her bike here with the friends she lost when she moved away. It had been hard for her to make friends like that again. Until Andi. Andi. She wanted so much to see her again. To talk and laugh and dance like they used to. And then just like that she knew where she needed to be. Tomorrow, she'd get the address from her mum and go to London.

35

TO LONDON AGAIN – 1992

Thanks to Solly, she'd managed to get Andi's address without too much explanation. Her mum had been pushing for more, but Solly had stepped in and suggested they should just let Ursula say as much as she wanted to. So Ursula didn't let on that she'd spent the night in her car, although the state of her might have led them to guess that. The other thing she kept to herself was that she wanted a baby so much now, it was almost a craving. And she certainly didn't tell them Anton had asked her if she wanted a divorce. Mainly because she still couldn't believe he'd said it. Although the more she thought about it, the more it made sense. They were incompatible. Poles apart. It was obvious to her now. Except they loved each other and loving each other topped everything. Didn't it?

As she'd hoped, Anton had gone to work by the time she arrived home. She showered and put on clean clothes, then tried Andi's contact number. It turned out to be the place she worked. A man informed her it was a bit early for Andi and she should try later. 'Can I leave a message? Can you tell her

Ursula said she's coming to see her and I'll call again when I get to London?'

'Yeah, sure,' he said, then put the phone down, leaving her doubtful the message would be passed on.

She packed a suitcase and called a taxi to take her to New Street. On her way out the door she scribbled on the back of Anton's latest list: *'Going to Andi's.'*

Halfway through the train journey, she wondered why she'd told Anton where she was going. Force of habit maybe. Yes that was probably it. Because she was so used to accounting for her day to day movements, the lists, the phone calls to check up on her. She'd done it without thinking. It was past midday. He would have already called home. Another thing he'd started after she lost the baby that had become a part of her daily regime.

At Euston, Ursula found a phone box and called Andi's work again. A woman picked it up this time. 'Andi? Yeah, hang on.'

'I don't have much change left,' she said, as someone else came on the line.

'Urs, is that you?'

Ursula shoved her last ten pence in the slot. 'Yes, I'm by Euston. I've run out of coins.'

'Okay, this is what I want you to do. Go down to the underground and get the Northern Line for one stop to Camden Town. Got it?'

'Northern line to Camden Town.'

'I'll meet you there.'

Back inside the station, Ursula fell in with the hordes of people jostling to get onto the escalator taking them down to the underground. One stop hardly seemed worth it. She could have walked it if she knew where she was going.

At Camden, she scanned a sea of faces, so many of them and none looking like Andi. It had been seven years since they'd last laid eyes on each other. Ursula had been busy travelling with Anton, and Andi had been so hard to pin down, moving from one house to another, one job to the next. What if they didn't recognise each other anymore? But then she saw her. Andi was here. Different but the same. It was going to be okay.

She launched herself at Ursula. 'I can't believe you came to see me.' Her hair was long and straight now with a fringe that nearly touched her eyelashes. She was wearing a faded black T-shirt under a black biker jacket, a blue tartan mini skirt, above the knee socks and heavy, clompy shoes. She looked unbelievably amazing and standing next to her, Ursula felt dowdy and frumpish.

'Did they mind you coming out for me?'

'Nah, all fine. They're pretty relaxed. Are you here for today or you staying longer?'

'Longer. I've left.'

'Left?'

'Done a runner.'

Andi screwed up her face until the penny dropped. 'Right. Where are you staying?'

Ursula shrugged. 'Haven't worked that out yet.'

'You can stay at mine, if you don't mind sleeping on the settee. I warn you though, it's a bit of a shithole.'

Andi lived over a bakery on the corner of Leyton High Road. The name of the other road had been painted over but all Ursula needed to know was that the door to upstairs was on this nameless road.

'We're on the top floor. The bathroom's on the first floor. Just here.' Andi pushed open a door to a grimy bathroom that looked like it hadn't been cleaned in months. Probably longer. 'There's a separate toilet here as well.' She pushed at another door but it didn't give. 'Someone must be in there. We share it with the other flat.'

'Oh right. How many live in that one?'

'Er, two I think. I haven't met them. Then there's me and Pab. To be honest I usually wash in the kitchen and just use the shower in the bathroom.'

Ursula could see why but she didn't say anything. She didn't want to sound like she was judging.

They climbed the next flight of stairs which led straight to a door. 'Home sweet home.' Andi pushed it open to reveal a room that was divided by a screen wall that stopped two-thirds of the way up. To the right of it was a kitchen diner with a Formica table and some basic cheap cupboards painted orange. You had to go through a gap in the screen to get to it. The rest of the room was the living room. There was a sash window in the kitchen and two in the living room that looked out onto the High Road and rattled as a bus went past.

The furniture was old. There was a sideboard just like one Ursula's nan used to have, and the settee and armchair were more than a decade out of date. An electric fire in a wooden surround was switched on, its two bars just giving out enough heat to raise the temperature a notch above chilly. The only parts of the room that hinted they were in the present day were the posters on the walls of bands Ursula had never heard of and a big, shiny stereo with huge speakers.

Andi opened a door that Ursula hadn't noticed before.

'The bedroom's through here. It's a mess at the moment. It's full of Pab's decks and stuff. He's a DJ.'

'Wow! Exciting.'

'I suppose. If you're into that kind of thing.'

Ursula sat down on the settee. 'Since when did you stop being into that kind of thing?'

Andi sat next to her. 'Since when did you start running away from home?'

'I asked first.'

'Yeah, but I asked the more important question.'

Ursula sighed. 'Smart arse. We had a row. Well, the closest me and Anton will ever get to a row. I want a baby and he doesn't. He said if I want someone who's going to give me kids, I should divorce him.'

'He said that? Shit. Does he want a divorce then?'

'No, but he thinks I do.'

'Do you?'

'I haven't made up my mind yet. He had a vasectomy without telling me.'

'Jesus, Urs. Look, I'm just gonna say this, right. Don't be angry at me or anything but don't you think you might be better off with someone else?'

'Maybe. I need to think about it. Listen, Andi, you must not tell Mum this. I told her I don't want kids. If this came out she'd be worrying about me all the time. Solly's daughter's having a baby, and I don't want her feeling bad about enjoying that because Anton refuses to have them. Promise me you won't say anything.'

'Cross my heart. I'll take it with me to the grave. And you can stay as long as you want. If you want a job, I can ask at work. The guy I'm working for, you spoke to him this morning, he's just on the verge of making it big. He might have room for someone with your skills.'

'I can't sew anymore.'

Andi laughed. 'You'll soon get back to where you were.'

'No, I can't. I really can't. It's a mental thing. I haven't been able to do it since the baby.'

'Oh, Urs, I didn't realise. It's okay, mate. We'll find a way out of this crap.' She put her arm around Ursula, and Ursula rested her head on Andi's shoulder.

Suddenly the door burst open and a man came in from the stairway. He wasn't particularly tall but tall enough, with black, wavy hair and huge brown eyes. He was so good-looking Ursula had to stop herself from staring at him. He glanced from Andi to Ursula and his mouth split into a big wide grin. 'Hello, hello. Have I just walked in on something?'

Andi let out a loud tut. 'Fuck off, Pab. We're having a private moment here.'

36

WICKED AND LECHEROUS – 1992

Beauty is only skin deep. It was an old saying that Ursula's nan had been fond of repeating if ever she'd caught her spending too much time in front of the mirror. It had been quite infuriating for Ursula in those teenage years because her beauty was the only thing she'd had going for her. Especially in the friendless years of senior school when only the older boys were interested in her. But after ten days of living with Pablo, Ursula was beginning to see what her nan had been getting at. Because while he was definitely the most beautiful man she'd ever seen, Pablo was also the most selfish, arrogant prick she'd ever met. He really did love himself. But when everyone else was in love with you, perhaps you couldn't help thinking you were a god. She guessed it was the good looks and charm that sucked people in but Ursula was immune to that sort of thing, thanks to her father.

Unusually, her father had been on her mind a lot lately. She didn't normally give him the space but she'd been a bit aimless since leaving Birmingham. Andi was at work, and without Anton and his lists to keep her going, Ursula had little else to do except wander around London, visiting museums and galleries, and thinking. Perhaps it was Pablo triggering him in her thoughts. To some extent they were similar. But Pablo's faults were minuscule when you held them up against her father's. That man was so far off the Richter scale of selfishness, arrogance, and downright nastiness that she didn't even bother comparing him to anyone else.

She'd never understood how someone as decent and as level-headed as her mum could have fallen for Bernard Fry when there were good men like Solly in the world. But seeing Andi with Pablo had opened her eyes. Andi took the piss out of him relentlessly, she complained about him doing nothing around the flat and about him spending all his money on himself. You name it, she had a go at him about it. But she still worshipped him. In the last ten days they'd argued at least three times about something Pablo had done or hadn't done and each time, she'd caved in. It just didn't seem like Andi at all.

Ursula left the station and walked up the High Road. All she'd done that afternoon was ride on the tube and sit on the steps in Trafalgar Square watching the tourists. She'd gone out at the same time as Andi that morning while Pab was still in bed. He generally didn't get up until the afternoon because he worked at night. They'd tiptoed around the flat, whispering as they got ready, trying not to wake him. Not that he'd extended the courtesy the other way when he'd come in at dawn, clattering around, drunk or high, waking them both up. Andi was having a big meeting with her boss today to try to convince him to include one of her designs in his next collection. Pab knew that but it didn't stop him banging on about what a great set he'd had when all they wanted to do was sleep.

She let herself into the flat with the spare key that had been cut for her. Andi was going to be back a bit later tonight so Ursula had offered to cook dinner. She'd stopped at a good supermarket in the West End for ingredients and wine. She wanted to cook something nice for her friend, but given the limited cooking facilities, she was going for a simple and easy to cook pasta.

The stereo was on, another tune Ursula didn't recognise, and a half-empty mug of coffee had been left on the floor by the armchair. Other than that, the flat seemed empty, but she shouted: 'I'm back,' all the same. No one answered but she knew Pab couldn't be far away. She took out the ingredients and a bottle of wine and started preparing dinner.

She was in the middle of chopping the vegetables when Pablo came in. He didn't notice her until he got to the gap in the screen. 'Fuck! You scared the life out of me.' He had a towel wrapped around his lower half. He must have been taking a shower.

'Sorry. I'm making dinner.'

He came over to the table where she was working. 'What you making?'

'Beef ragu.'

'Nice.' He stood right next to her, his bare skin almost touching her, and he reached around for the wine bottle. 'Good wine as well. You've got expensive tastes, Ursula.'

'Not really. I just wanted to spoil Andi. It's an important day for her today.'

'Oh yeah. Shame I won't be here. I've got a big night tonight. Could get an Ibiza contract out of it.' He opened the bottle and poured himself a glass. 'You want some?'

She shook her head. 'I'll wait, thanks.'

'You know your problem, Ursula? You're a real knockout but you're uptight. You wanna let your hair down occasionally.' He grabbed her arm. 'You should come out dancing. I know you like dancing. Andi's told me all about you and her. Right couple of ravers, weren't yer?' He wiggled his hips and the towel shifted slightly.

She pulled her arm away. 'You're losing your towel.'

'Whoops.' He was laughing as he went into the bedroom. She noticed he'd left the door open again. He kept doing this when Andi wasn't here. One time, he left it wide open and was walking around the bedroom stark naked, even though he knew she could see him.

He came out in just his underpants, turned the stereo up, and stood there for a while, drinking wine and scratching his arse, watching her chop onions. She kept her eyes on the table and carried on working away with the knife.

When he came out of the bedroom again, he was fully dressed. He moved closer to her, so close his aftershave tickled her nostrils. Then he leaned across her to pour another glass of wine, before drinking it in one go and dropping a flyer on the table. 'This is where I'm playing tonight. Tell Andi to bring you down. You'll love it.'

'Will do,' she said, as he went out the door with his cases of records.

She listened for the downstairs door slamming, then rushed over to the front windows. He was on the other side of the road, loading the cases into his car. He looked up. Ursula stepped back but it was too late, his grin told her he'd seen her. It was a wicked and lecherous grin that made her shiver. She closed her eyes and made herself small against the wall. She saw Anton smiling at her, the way he used to when he realised she was teasing him, and she wondered if he was missing her.

She chanced another look outside. Pablo's car was gone, but she could still smell him. His aftershave was clinging to her. She went to find a clean top and wondered how much longer she'd be able to stay here.

37

I HAVE COME – 1992

Andi scraped the last trace of ragu off the plate and licked the fork clean. 'Urs, that was delicious. No one's cooked a proper meal for me since I left Gillian's.'

'Thanks. I thought about doing a paella for Pablo but it's a bit complicated. And in any case, it didn't matter because he's not here.'

'Why for Pab?'

'Because it's Spanish.'

'Ah, like Pablo.' Andi was grinning.

'Yes. What?'

'Darling, I've got more Spanish blood than Pab. He's from Catford and so are his parents. Pablo's not even his real name. It's all bullshit to make him sound more exciting. The punters love it. They think he's some hotshot Balearic DJ.'

'You are kidding? So what is his name then?'

'Steven. Pablo's real name is Steve. Don't tell him I told you though. He likes to keep it under wraps. Have we used all the wine up?'

'We've got another bottle yet. Oh, I meant to say, he left a flyer for the club where he's playing tonight in case we want to go.'

'It's not a club, it's some poxy warehouse miles away. Bollocks to that. After the day I've had, I just want to fill my belly and get drunk.' Andi hadn't said much about the meeting when she got home which probably meant it hadn't gone as well as she'd hoped.

Ursula poured out some more wine. 'Was it really bad then?'

'Not exactly but it wasn't great. I thought I was going to get on in this place but I get the impression I'm treading on too many toes. There's too much attention on bruised egos and not enough on the designs and the craftsmanship. You know, sometimes I wish I could be back in Talulah with you and Wanda. And Cass. I miss it. I miss Brum.'

'You could always come home.'

'I would you know. But Pab won't leave London, and I can't leave him. Yes, he is a big-headed twat who pretends to be someone he's not, but this is the real thing. I love him. Plus, he's not boring.'

'Ooh, that was below the belt.' Ursula slapped an outraged expression on her face that crumbled as she laughed. But really, she was thinking there are worse crimes than being boring.

Ursula was dreaming she was back in her kitchen making paella, when she was woken by a small, sharp sting to her face. It came again while she was still coming round. The third time it happened, she opened her eyes. The room was lit up orange by the electric fire, but she was sure she'd switched it off before she'd gone to bed. Something was soaring in the air towards her, a tiny missile, the size of a fly. She batted it away and sat up. More of them slid off her chest into her lap.

'Pistachio?' Pablo was in the armchair, cracking open the nuts and lobbing empty shells at her.

She swatted away another one. 'What time is it?'

'Dunno. You didn't come, Ursula. I was going to show you how to have a good time and everything, and you let me down. Big time.'

Jesus Christ, the man was a child. A pathetic dickhead. How could she have been scared of him? 'Fuck off, Pab.' She pulled the blanket over her head. 'Just go to bed.'

It was Sunday morning. Andi and Pablo were still in bed. Last night Andi had taken her to a club where he was doing a set. They'd danced and got a bit drunk. It had been fun, but she'd felt old in there. Pablo had been up on stage, playing to the crowd, loving it and loving himself even more. The young girls had flocked around him, all wanting a piece of him. Andi had said they always did that, it was nothing. Maybe it was, but Ursula had seen the way he'd enjoyed it and she disliked him even more because of it. He was nothing like Anton. Boring, safe Anton. There were many things about her husband that drove her mad, but he would never have done anything like that.

It had been four days since the night Pablo had woken her with his pistachio torpedoes and he was still behaving like a prize prick. Ursula couldn't stick it any longer. This flat was too small for three people to live in. Especially when one of them was Pablo. Buckingham Palace would have been too small when one of them was Pablo. So she'd made a decision.

She was going back to Birmingham. Later, she'd find a phone box and call her mum to see if her old bedroom was still on offer. First though, she had to tell Andi she was leaving.

Andi came out of the bedroom wearing one of Pablo's T-shirts and her pants. 'Morning.' She went over to the window. 'Ugh, sunshine. I'm too hungover for sunshine.'

Probably too hungover to hear about Ursula's decision as well. It would have to wait a while. Ursula filled the kettle. 'I'll make some tea.'

'My saviour. Oh, bloody hell. Am I seeing things, or is that Anton down there?'

Ursula ran over to the window. Anton was out there, standing on the pavement on the other side of the road. She grabbed her coat. 'Sorry, you'll have to make your own tea.'

He watched her crossing over, his hands in his coat pockets. He looked so out of place, this neat, tidy man on this dirty, scruffy street.

'Have you been here long?' she said when she reached him.

'One hour and thirty-three minutes.' Always precise, always exact, always direct. So very unlike that overgrown schoolboy, Pablo.

'You could have tried the door.'

'I did. There was no bell and no one answered my knock.'

'Ah. It's hard to hear on the top floor. There's a reasonable café further up the road that opens on Sundays.'

'Then we should go there and let Andi take a rest.' He nodded to one of the top floor windows where Andi was standing guard.

Ursula waved to her and started walking in the direction of the café.

'Is it as bad up there as it looks from the outside?' he said.

'It's not to your taste, that's for sure.'

They ordered coffees and found a quiet corner. Anton put his elbows on the table and leaned towards her. 'So, I have come. Was I wrong to do that?'

She shifted in her seat. 'That depends on why you're here.'

'I have come for you. I cannot function without you, Ursula.'

She smiled, amused by the fact that he had no inkling of how funny he could be. 'Is that your way of saying you've missed me?'

'Yes. I want you to come home.'

'Why should I, Anton? You can't give me what I want. You made sure of that without telling me.'

'In hindsight, I should have told you but after you lost the baby, you were unreachable. I was angry about what had happened to you. I only want to protect you, Ursula. But our life is so much more than children.'

'My life is empty. I don't have a career like you. I have nothing.'

'Then we must fill it.'

'With cleaning and cooking? What joy is there in that?'

'We will find something that gives you joy. I love you. You must know that. You do still love me, don't you?'

'I ... I don't know.'

'But why else did you tell me where to find you? The note. If you didn't want me to come for you, why did you tell me you were with Andi?'

Was that why she'd told him? Was it really that simple? Perhaps it was. Perhaps she never really wanted to leave him. But no, that couldn't be right. What about the cruel way he'd denied her a child?

'Will you come home with me?' He held his hand out for her.

She looked at it knowing that taking it would only lead her back to the same hollow existence that had become her life.

'We will be happy again, Ursula.'

She didn't know if that was possible. Not the kind of happiness she was looking for anyway. Anton closed his hand around hers. 'Please.'

'Okay. But I can't promise I'll stay.'

She'd told Anton to wait in the café for her, mainly because she didn't want him to meet Pablo. Pablo was coming out of the bathroom as she passed it on her way up to the flat. 'Where is he? Do I need to get dressed?'

She looked at him in his boxers, and had to work hard to hide her disgust. 'Don't put yourself out on our account. We're not stopping.'

Andi was standing in front of the fire, her arms folded. She'd put some jeans on. 'You're going, aren't you?'

'I'm giving him another chance. I'm sorry, Andi. I'll pack my things.'

It didn't take long to fill her case, seeing as she'd been living out of it for the past few weeks. 'I'll write to you. Let you know how things are.'

Andi caught her sleeve. 'Are you sure about this?'

Pablo flopped down into the armchair still in his boxers, half of their contents on display and for a split second, Ursula considered asking Andi the same question. Instead she put her arms around her best friend and kissed her. 'Look after yourself, mate. You know where to find me if you need me.'

38

TWO VERY DIFFERENT DISCLOSURES

'I was thinking about that first flat you had in Leyton last night,' said Ursula.

'What a dump that was. Remember that disgusting bathroom? It was always so cold as well. Even in Summer. That bloody fire used to cost me a fortune. What about these two? We could mash them up.' Andi showed her a pattern with a sheath dress that finished at the knee and another one of a dress with a close-fitting, cowl-necked bodice that gave way to a looser flowing midi skirt.

'What kind of mash-up are you thinking of?'

'The bodice from the sheath and the skirt from the other one.' Andi began to sketch out a style.

'That could work. Do you think if we added a tuck detail to the waist it would make the skirt fall into an asymmetric finish?'

'Can you draw it for me?'

Ursula's initial sketch was a disaster. The second marginally better. She tutted, annoyed with herself, because it wasn't that hard. She used to do this without even thinking about it. She tried it again.

Andi turned the drawing round to get a better look. 'Yeah, definitely with that silk. It would be lovely. The tuck could drape into that asymmetric finish at the front.' She added a few touches to demonstrate.

'I like the look of that.' Ursula was smiling to herself: this was how it might have been if they'd ended up having that shop together.

'See, it's not that hard.'

'Yes it bloody well is, but I'm not giving up yet.'

'I should hope so. How am I gonna get my mojo back if you give up that easily? No pressure but there's a lot riding on this dress. Let me work out how that tuck's going to affect the pattern.' Andi drew some shapes and jotted down a few notes. 'Okay, I think I've got it. Right, let's measure you up, missus.'

Ursula stood up straight while Andi ran the tape measure around her and jotted down the numbers. 'Your measurements have hardly changed.'

She knew that of course. Her dress size hadn't changed in all the time she'd been with Anton. That's what happens when you live with a control freak who's obsessed with perfection. 'Surely you don't remember my measurements from all those years ago?'

'That would be pretty amazing, wouldn't it? No. I've still got my old sewing journal. Yet another museum piece. I've also got Gillian's measurements in there, and my mum's. And my sister's from when I made her wedding dress. That was a nightmare never to be repeated. World's worst client. Let's put the pattern together.'

Ursula took out parts of one pattern and then the other

while Andi marked out the new shape needed for the changes to the skirt. Next, they pinned them to that gorgeously colourful silk. 'Do you want to do the cutting out?' said Andi.

Ursula remembered the state she'd got herself into just cutting out a simple tablecloth. 'You do the first one.'

Andi cut out the trickiest piece quickly and easily, then handed the scissors to her. 'Your turn. Don't worry, we've got some spare fabric.'

Ursula bent over the table and glancing at her hands, noted they were hardly shaking at all. The first cut was made. She stopped for a second to steady herself, then took another snip. The silk was a dream to cut. The blades slid through it like they were slicing through water. Very like the silk they'd used for the christening gown. The thought of it suddenly brought her up sharp.

You're doing fine,' said Andi.

Yes she was. She just had to keep those bad memories tucked away and press on.

The first piece was done. She moved straight on to the next, not daring to stop in case she let the demons back in. That was the secret. You had to keep busy so they didn't have room to settle. That had been the secret for a long time now.

The final piece came free. She'd done it. Oh the ridiculous sense of excitement and relief. Ursula felt giddy with it. She lay down on the floor looking up at a very confused Andi. 'Trust me, it helps,' she said.

'In that case, move over.' Andi laid down next to her. 'I don't remember this being a thing at Talulah.'

'It's a new tradition I've recently started.' She reached over for Andi's hand. 'Thank you. Believe it or not, I am enjoying this.'

'Me too. You know, you could cut yourself some slack now and then.'

Ursula was transported back to that flat in Leyton, Pablo telling her she was uptight. She'd often wondered if they discussed her and her weaknesses.

'Anton's not here anymore. You could indulge yourself a bit. No one's going to tell you you're a bad person for having an extra slice of chocolate cake.'

Ah, so that was what she meant. Nothing to do with her being uptight at all. 'That would make sense, if Anton wasn't still here.'

'What?' Andi was giving her a funny look. Sod it, she hadn't meant for that to come out and now that she'd said it there was no going back.

'Anton's haunting me. Back at the house, he haunts his office. Here, he stands on the hill behind the house.'

Andi rolled over and supported herself on her elbows. 'Urs, you know ghosts don't exist, don't you?'

'Yes, I do, but try telling that to Anton.'

'Does he speak to you?' She was making the kind of face that Ursula had known would be there if she let the secret out. She wanted to slap herself for letting her guard down.

'No. He just watches me through the office window when I come and go, or from that hill. I do know how mad this sounds, by the way, which is why you're the only person I've told. Although Howard did see me up on the hill one time, screaming at Anton to show himself.'

'You should have explained it to him. He did something to do with psychology before he retired. He might have a plausible explanation.'

No need to ask Howard, or anyone else. She already knew what the explanation was. So did Anton.

Andi was still giving her that look. Ursula was almost glad when the door swung open and Esme appeared on the other side. It was the first time she'd been back inside the house since she'd taken herself off to the bothy, in spite of Andi's return.

Andi scrambled to her feet. 'Esme, this is my private room. I expect you to respect that.'

'He's in Spain. I thought you should know.'

'Who?' said Andi.

'Who d'you think? Pablo.' Esme's face was a picture of smug triumph. Ursula hadn't thought it was possible to dislike her any more than she already did, but now she realised there was so much more to Esme to find distasteful.

'And you know this, how?'

'I messaged him. I told him we all missed him and you still loved him.'

Andi's hands balled into fists. She pushed them into the pockets of her dress. 'You had no right to say that, Esme. My feelings towards Pab are nobody's business but my own.'

'But it's true. Anyone can see you want him back.'

'Actually no, I don't. And I'd like you to stop interfering in my personal affairs.'

'Oh.' Esme's elation dissolved. But then, quick as a flash, it was back: 'Probably just as well because he said he loved Claudette now. And they've started a new life in Spain.'

'Esme, why don't you just fuck right off?' Andi grabbed hold of the door and slammed it so hard the room rattled.

'I think that told her,' said Ursula.

'I fucking hope so.' Andi's face was white. Ursula was waiting for it to crumble but it didn't happen. There was a steeliness about her instead. A kind of simmering rage.

Perhaps she was building up to something. An outpouring maybe.

'Do you want to have that talk now?'

Andi shook her head sharply. 'Not ready yet.'

'Okay. Do you think he calls himself Pablo over there?'

She turned to Ursula, her face instantly softening. 'Nah, they'd see right through him.'

'Back to Steven then. Or Steve.'

'Yep.' Her mouth spread into its trademark mischievous grin. 'Not sure how well that will go down with Claudette though, what with her being another pretentious bullshitter.'

Ursula gave Andi a tight hug. 'You all right, mate?'

'Yeah. Let's go out tonight.'

'Paint the town red?'

She laughed and sniffed at the same time. 'Rein it in, babe. This is Bala we're talking about.'

39

ONLY A PATCH OF LAND

Dilys had died. The news came in that afternoon. What with that and Esme's outburst, Andi seemed to have forgotten all about Anton and his hauntings. Ursula hoped that was the case, anyway. At dinner, Brett slipped out another news bulletin. He and Gareth were a couple. It was official. No one was surprised. Although Esme wasn't there. She was still holed up in the bothy. It seemed only right after that to invite Don and Brett to the pub.

No one wanted to miss out on a drink so they walked into Bala. On the way in, Don confessed that he'd invited Megan along: 'I thought she might need cheering up, what with Dilys passing.' It was a nice thought and perhaps it wasn't just Megan who needed cheering up. None of them seemed to be in the happiest of moods.

They took the lake walk so they could watch the sun setting and have a minute's silence to remember Dilys. Since she didn't know Dilys, Ursula spent the time remembering other sunsets with Samuel. And then she realised she hadn't thought about him or the allotment for a few days. The others were already back on the path into town. She caught up, still wondering how she could have forgotten to think about them. As compensation now, she made herself think about how she'd be outside Samuel's shed watching the same sun go down, if she were there at this moment.

Megan and Gareth came into the pub while Don and Brett were at the bar getting the first round. 'How are you doing?' said Andi.

Megan looked weary with grief. 'You know, getting on with it. I said to Gareth, it's a release really. I just wish it felt like one. We should have a date for the funeral tomorrow.'

'I'd like to go,' said Andi.

'Thank you. Howard will appreciate that. Don's thinking of going as well.' She looked up at Don as he came back with a tray of drinks. 'Aren't you, Don? Thinking of going to the funeral.'

'I am, Megan.' He put a glass of white wine down in front of her. 'Here, my love, get that down you. Gareth looking after you, is he?'

'He is. And so is Brett. I'm so glad my Gare's got someone nice.' She blew her nose. 'Sorry, I'm a right drama queen at the moment. Slightest thing and I'm off. But the good news is they've come out about it now, and everybody's been happy for them.' She waved to Gareth and Brett who were still at the bar. 'Well, everybody except you know who.'

'Oh, they told Esme?' said Ursula.

'Yesterday. They went up to the bothy together and told her. Needless to say she was her usual nasty piece of work. Still, I hear she got her comeuppance today, Andi.'

Don shuffled sheepishly on his seat. 'Sorry, Andi, I might have mentioned it.'

'Might have mentioned it? He couldn't wait to tell me.

Proper old gossip is our Donald. Slammed the door on her, he said. The house shook apparently.' Megan raised her glass. 'Good for you, lady. It's been a long time coming if you ask me. What are you gonna do about her?'

'I haven't decided yet, but that explains why she was in such a spiteful mood.' Andi caught Ursula's eye. Clearly that was all she was prepared to tell the others at this point. Although, there was a chance Don had heard everything. And even if not, Ursula didn't rule out the possibility that Esme had told him Pablo's whereabouts too.

To Ursula's relief, Anton was not watching her from the hill when she drew the curtains that morning. Perhaps telling Andi was all she'd needed to banish him. Mr Big Potatoes was however on his usual spot on the windowsill. She let him in and he rubbed himself gratefully against her. There was something very soothing about it, and she needed soothing this morning. She'd been thinking about that flat in Leyton again. How Anton had stood outside all that time, waiting for her to notice him. It had touched her, but it wasn't the reason she'd gone back with him. The reason was fear. She could see that now that she'd been revisiting her past in such vivid detail. Pablo had been right in a way when he'd said she was uptight, but she would have called it something else. Conditioned. She'd become conditioned to Anton's regime, to his likes and dislikes. So, of course, she went back with him and, of course, she never left him again because anything outside of that carefully constructed stronghold frightened her. That's not to say she didn't think about it now and again, but the fear set in and instead she made do with minor disobediences. Small acts of defiance that rattled him much more

than they should have done. And that was how she managed
to carve out a tolerable life.

Through the window she saw Andi walking towards the
hill. It looked like she was going to the bothy. Ursula went
down to the kitchen. There was no one in there and she ate
breakfast alone, then went outside. Andi was on her way
back and she stopped at the vegetable garden to wait for her.
A closer inspection of Esme's salad leaves explained why Don
had preferred the shop-bought variety. Not only were they
thin and straggly, they'd been left to bolt: if you let them
flower, the leaves become bitter.

Andi had reached her on the path. 'It needs an overhaul.'

'Yes, it does.'

'It's Pab's really. He started it with the kids when we first
came here. Esme claimed it after he left. I've been up to see
her. Told her to shape up or ship out. She's moving back in.'

'You're giving her another chance.'

She nodded. 'A last chance. I might be a soft cow but I'm
not a complete walkover. I've said I want the bothy put back
to the way it was before she took up residence. It's in a
disgusting state, after Brett worked so hard to make it habit-
able as well. I'm so pissed off about it, I nearly threw her out
there and then. If you want to have a go at the garden, just
say.'

'Maybe. I'll think about it.'

'Okay. Coffee? And then we can get on with that dress.'

It had been a good day. All morning, she and Andi had
worked together on the dress and she'd managed it without
getting the shakes. After lunch, they'd popped to Bala and
stopped off at Megan's café. They were back now and Ursula

was in the lounge looking at a photo Clyde had sent her of Colonel waiting at her shed door for biscuits. She sent him a message to ask how things were. A minute later he was calling her. 'That dog's vexing me something bad. You'd better come back soon, Ursula, before he drives me crazy. How you doing? You good now?'

'I think so. I don't know when I'm coming back yet though. How are things there?'

'Same as usual. Nothing changes much here. There's a committee meeting tonight. They got an update from the council, so we might know more about what's happening with those allotments. It's a busy night. I got a big dominoes match as well. I'll have to shoot straight off.'

'Will you have time to message me if there's any news?'

'Sure. No problem.'

A crashing cymbal-like sound announced that dinner was ready. 'Sorry, Clyde, the dinner gong's just gone. I've got to go.'

He started to laugh. 'You got a dinner gong? What kind of a place they got you in, woman?'

Ursula was chuckling to herself all the way to the kitchen, and her good mood was only slightly spoiled by Esme's usual filthy look. At least the others were their usual selves. In fact, it was as if they'd decided the best way to get through the meal was to pretend Esme wasn't there, and the chat went on without any deliberate attempts to include her.

After dinner, Ursula helped Andi wash up. She showed Andi the photo of Colonel waiting at her shed door and before she knew it, she was talking about her allotment and all the things she grew on there. She noticed Andi was smiling at her. 'What?'

'Nothing. It's just that you've gone all glowy. You must really love that place.'

'Well, you know, it's good to be growing things. To feel like you've nurtured something. It's given me some...' She was going to say purpose but she stopped herself. She was already feeling a bit silly.

She was saved by her phone pinging in her back pocket. Clyde had sent her a message. She opened it up and read that the council had given up on the car park idea for those four abandoned allotments, including Samuel's. It was up to the committee to decide what to do next, but it looked like they were going to tidy them up, ready to be let out again.

'Everything okay?' said Andi.

'It's just an update on a friend's allotment. Nothing to worry about.' She slipped the phone back into her pocket. It was only a patch of land. Nothing more. She just had to keep reminding herself of that.

40

MR SAMUEL SWEETING – 1995

Ursula put her head round the door to Anton's office. 'I've left a tuna salad for your lunch.'

Anton looked up from his work. 'You're going out?'

'Yes. I did say last night.'

'Ah yes. This allotment.' There was a hint of amusement in the way he said it. Roughly translated, that meant the idea was so hilarious he was practically wetting himself. 'You will be back in plenty of time for tonight.' As usual, it reached her not as a question but a directive.

'Yes. I'm only going to talk to someone about it. It won't take long. I'll probably stop off at Mum's as well.'

The office phone rang, giving her the opportunity to leave before he found something to keep her there. She closed the front door and almost made it to the car without looking up. But look up she did and there he was, at the window. She ducked into the driver's seat and drove away.

It had been three years since he'd come for her in Leyton and since then, she'd tried to find something to fill the empty hole inside of her. But nothing had done it. Anton had offered to build her a sewing room in the garden. She told him she'd gone off sewing, although she hadn't been able to bring herself to explain why. She'd broached the idea of getting a job, but he pointed out that if she was working, he'd have to travel alone and sometimes he could be away for months. She'd tried evening classes. Volunteering. Exercising. But nothing gave her the meaning she was looking for. Anton's solution to all of this was to make his lists longer. He'd begun to base himself in his home office two or three days a week. She'd brushed up on the skills she'd learned at secretarial college and had picked up some of his admin work. It didn't make her life any more fulfilling but it kept her busy.

She'd spotted the poster about allotments in a supermarket in Selly Oak. It wasn't where she normally shopped so it was quite by chance. There were plots available at a site that was a shortish drive, or a longish walk, from her house. Ursula had fond memories of summer holidays spent with her grandad on his allotment when she was little. Not that she remembered anything practical about those times but it couldn't be that hard to grow a few veg, could it? She'd called the number the next day, when Anton was working in town, and made an appointment to meet someone for a look around.

She parked in front of the allotment and waited at the gate where she'd been told someone would meet her. Someone called Samuel Sweeting. In the near distance, she could see the figure of a man coming towards her. As he got nearer, she began to fill in his details. Tall and straight, broad shoulders, a little on the heavy side, black, middle-aged.

'I tek it you're Ursula,' he said when he got to the gate.

'I am. You must be Samuel.' She held out her hand.

He looked at it and frowned. She realised at once she'd greeted him as if he was one of Anton's clients. She'd forgotten how to behave when meeting real people. But then he gave her a warm smile and shook it with such strength, she thought her hand was going to shatter.

He let her through the gate and took her along a path that seemed to circle the site. 'You do much gardening, Ursula?'

'No, not really. I used to help my grandad on his allotment though.' She'd stretched the truth but she was too embarrassed to say she was a complete novice.

'You don't have a garden at home?'

'Yes, but it's my husband's domain.'

'Ah, he's the gardener.'

That wasn't what she meant. Anton's contribution to the garden was to employ a man to keep it perfectly tidy and weed free. He only ever went in there to inspect it, give instructions on it, or show it to clients. 'Do you have many plots left?'

'Three. This is the best one.' He stopped at a plot that was just off the main path. 'Belonged to an old couple who gave it up last month. It's been well cared for. The shed needs a lick a paint but it's sound. You do much painting, Ursula?' He gave her a cheeky grin that she couldn't help thinking was a little flirty.

'Take a wild guess, Samuel.'

He laughed, a big, deep belly laugh that took her by surprise. 'We got plenty here can help. We're very community minded in this place, yer know. What do you think? You wanna give it a go?'

Ursula looked at the shed with its peeling paint. There was room in front of it for a chair to sit and be alone, or maybe have a conversation with the other allotment holders.

One that had nothing to do with that other place that took up all of her time and gave her nothing in return. It didn't really matter if she didn't grow as much as a single carrot. All that mattered was that this place would be hers. 'Yes, I think I do.'

'You've done what?' said her mum.

'I've put my name down for an allotment.'

'What does Anton think of that?'

'I haven't told him yet, although he didn't seem too impressed when I said I was going to look at it.'

'In that case make sure you do it. Small acts of defiance keep you strong, my love.'

'You make it sound like I'm in a war zone.'

'I've got a letter for you from Andi.'

Ursula rolled her eyes. 'I don't know why she sends them here.'

'Yes you do.' Her mum was referring to Andi's theory that Anton was intercepting her letters. This had come about because Andi claimed some of them weren't reaching Ursula. That included the one she'd sent with her address in Leyton, before Ursula had gone there. Since Anton hadn't contacted Ursula's mum the whole time she'd been in Leyton, that was the only explanation they could come up with. When she'd asked him how he'd got the address, he'd said that his company had ways of finding these things out. It was true, they did, but Andi and her mum still clung to their belief.

'Honestly, you two and your ridiculous notions.' Ursula snatched up the letter. It was mostly full of the usual updates about work and Pablo, until she got to the end:

· · ·

'One last thing. I guess you can tell this is hard for me to write, Urs, because I've rambled on for two pages about nothing before getting to the real reason for the letter. It's hard because I think this is going to make you sad and I don't want to do that to you.

I'm having a baby. Pab is so happy about it. I am too, but I know what this news will mean for you and I'm scared of what it might do to our friendship. I really hope you'll still want to be my best mate, Urs.

Call me. If you don't, I'll understand.'

Ursula folded the letter and put it in her bag. 'She's having a baby. Isn't that great?'

'Yes, it is.' Her mum already knew. Her lack of surprise had given her away. 'Are you going to call her?'

'Tomorrow. I need to go home and get ready for a boring function. Anton's won an award so we can't get out of it. I'll have more time to talk properly tomorrow.'

All of last night, Ursula's mind had been on Andi. She'd sat through endless small talk and countless speeches, smiling, nodding and clapping when required, but she hadn't really been in the room. Andi was having a baby and that was all she could think of. There were so many things she wanted to know. How far gone was she? Was her bump showing? Was she taking care of herself? Was Pab taking care of her? How would she, the woman who'd been denied babies, react when this one came into the world, and would it mean she couldn't be friends with Andi anymore?

Anton pushed his breakfast things over to her to put in the dishwasher. When they'd first married, he'd done that

kind of thing himself. Made a point of it in fact, to show her
how it should be done. Somewhere along the way, it had
become her role. She couldn't remember when. His new
award was on the table next to him. He picked it up. 'I'll take
this into the office. What did you think of my acceptance
speech?'

He did this every now and then. She sometimes
wondered if it was to see if she'd been listening. Usually, she
memorised a couple of sentences that she could quote when
tested but this morning, she couldn't remember a single one.
So she just smiled and said: 'It went down very well.'

'Ah, the veil has returned. You're hiding something from
me. That you were not listening, perhaps? Maybe the speech
was too complicated for you.'

She searched his face for the hint of a smile but there was
none. He meant it. He actually thought she was stupid. Now
she had something else to mask. Her hurt. 'No. Sorry, I had a
headache. I couldn't concentrate.' She gathered the breakfast
things together and put them away. Her back was turned but
she knew he was watching her, trying to work out what was
going on in her head. But as he'd quite rightly observed, the
veil had come down and not even Anton could see through
that.

He left without any further discussion on the subject. She
waited for an hour and then rang Andi. She was in a different
flat now. One with a phone. 'Congratulations. I'm so happy
for you.' She was too mixed up to know if she really was
happy but she was going through the motions, saying the sort
of thing other people would say.

'You don't mind?'

'Don't be daft. When's it due?'

'September.'

'But that's only a couple of months away.'

'Yeah. I should have told you earlier, but I was worried how you'd take it.'

'Don't be worried. Just look after yourself. Don't take any chances.'

'Urs, I'm fine. The baby's fine. Pab's looking after me. What about you and me though, are we fine? Are we still mates?'

'Yes of course we are. Absolutely. Definitely.'

Ursula was back at the gates to the allotment, waiting to be met. Her application had been accepted and today she was coming to get the keys to the gate and be shown to her plot. It had been more than a month since Andi's letter. She'd left it a while before telling Anton the news. He'd been pleased for them. She hadn't expected that. He'd been less pleased when she told him she was taking the allotment. He'd thrown all kinds of arguments at her to make her change her mind. It would be too much for her. It would interfere with their busy lives. It wasn't the right sort of hobby for an architect's wife, and so on. If Andi hadn't been pregnant, Ursula might have caved in but, for once, she was determined. If this allotment was her small act of defiance, then so be it. Because she needed something.

Samuel Sweeting strolled down the path towards her and greeted her once more with a warm smile. 'Ursula! You're back.' He opened the gate and handed her some keys. 'Come in.'

'Thank you. Which plot did I get?'

'The best one of course. There was a lot a competition but I held them all off.'

'Really?'

He laughed that big, hearty laugh. 'No, sweet lady. I cannot lie. No one else was interested.'

She shook her head, her eyes and lips already creasing. 'You're a real comedian, Mr Sweeting.'

'Not according to my wife, I'm not. She doesn't know I save all the best jokes for here.'

41

THE SERENITY OF SUNSET – 1995

The council leaflet had been very specific about the colour of sheds. Mid-green or nothing. But on this site, the definition of mid-green had multiple variations. The one Ursula had picked was called shades of sage. She'd been in a rebellious mood when she'd chosen the colour, if only because it wouldn't have been allowed anywhere near the garden at home. But now that she'd finished painting it, her conviction was beginning to wobble. The paint wasn't dry yet but it was definitely coming out lighter than expected, and that was enough to make her worry she'd get an angry visit from the allotment committee. She stepped back from the shed, chewing on her lip. Mid-green it was not.

'Good afternoon, Ursula. We've come to admire your fine shed.' It was Samuel and his friend, Clyde, the two of them standing with their arms folded, grinning like a pair of Cheshire cats. Clyde was from Jamaica originally, just like Samuel. He was quieter than Samuel but they liked to laugh at the same things, one of those things being Ursula. She didn't mind. It was funny and gentle teasing. Light relief from the lack of humour at home.

'Has it passed scrutiny?' she asked, aware they could be here in their official capacity as members of the committee.

'Well I'm not sure, what do you think, Clyde?'

Clyde pushed his straw trilby back and scratched his head. 'I don't know Samuel, I think we need a second opinion.'

Samuel called over to Marcie in the next plot. 'Marcie. What do you think of this shed? Is it up to scratch?'

Marcie stopped what she was doing and leaned on the tool she was doing it with. A hoe, Ursula thought it was called. 'It's lovely. You've done a very good job, Ursula. Leave her alone you pair. You should be making yourselves useful giving her a hand instead of winding her up.'

Samuel shook his head. 'But that's not so much fun, Marcie.'

'I suppose she's got a point, Samuel,' said Clyde. 'You got some tools in that fine shed, Ursula, or do we need to get our own?'

'Better bring your own. I don't want you messing up my fine shed while the paint's wet,' she said. It was enough to set their laughter off again as they went off towards Clyde's plot.

'You're settling in well. Do you think you'll stick it?' said Marcie.

'I hope so.'

'So do I. Oh here they come, Morecombe and Wise. They'll sort you out. There's not much they don't know about growing fruit and veg. When they're not larking about, that is.'

Clyde crouched down to inspect some straggly vegetation on Ursula's plot. 'Your ears burning, Samuel?'

'On fire, Clyde. Somebody call the fire brigade. If only some nice lady would mek a cuppa to cool us down.'

Marcie rolled her eyes. 'I'll get the kettle on.'

The two men began tidying up the rows of plants, pulling out weeds and digging up vegetables. Before long, Ursula had a selection of beetroots, potatoes and carrots that had been planted by the previous tenants. Marcie announced tea was up and called them over. While they drank it and ate biscuits in the sunshine, the three old hands bombarded Ursula with instructions on what to plant, what to harvest and what to discard. Marcie fetched a pad and pen for Ursula to jot down key points and make a list of equipment she needed to buy. She was making lists. It might be the one thing about this allotment Anton would approve of.

Samuel held his hand out for the list. 'Let me see. Hmm. Don't forget your camping stove, cups and a water container.'

'Tea and coffee,' said Clyde.

'And a biscuit tin,' said Marcie. 'We get through a lot of biscuits.'

Ursula added them to the list. She'd get them tomorrow while she was shopping for a gift for Andi's baby. She'd had a girl. Jet, they'd called her. She was going to see them next week with her mum. Not that she really wanted to. But once again, she was doing what was expected of her.

Ursula and her mum got off the tube at Leyton and walked up the High Road, but they turned off before they reached Andi's old flat. From outside, the new place looked like a house but it had been split into two flats. A bleary-eyed Pablo opened the door to them. It was midday. If he wasn't the father of a newborn baby, he'd have still been in bed.

Andi looked exhausted, but stunning. Motherhood agreed with her. She picked up a tiny bundle from the Moses basket. 'This is Jet.' The baby had a mass of black hair, a mini version of Pab.

'Oh she's just beautiful. Will you look at that hair,' said Ursula's mum.

'Do you want to hold her?' said Andi.

'I'd love to.' Her mum took the baby in her arms and rocked her. Jet made a little noise and yawned.

Pab hopped around nervously behind them. 'You've got the knack. She's a nightmare usually.' He seemed different. Not so full of himself.

'She'll grow out of it. Ursula hardly ever slept till she was six months old.'

Andi looked at Ursula, as if she'd only just realised she was there. 'Do you want to hold her, Urs?'

She shook her head. 'I might drop her.'

'No you won't. Sit down and I'll hand her to you,' said her mum.

'Okay.' She wanted to be sick but she couldn't let them see it.

'Here you go, love. Cradle her head in your arm. That's it. There you are.'

Everyone in the room was watching her, waiting for her reaction. A shiver caught hold of her and she held the tiny bundle tighter in case she really did drop her. It made the baby wriggle and stretch out her arms.

'She wants a feed.' Pab was moving in on them, anxious to take his daughter off the uptight childless woman.

Andi's arm flew out to stop him, not realising it was exactly what Ursula wanted. 'She's good for a bit. She's just waking up.'

The baby opened her eyes, deep blue and unfathomable, willing Ursula to look at them. It was pointless resisting. And even though she knew Jet couldn't really see her, it felt like she was looking straight into her. But it was all right. Bearable.

'You okay?' Andi's voice was hardly more than a whisper.

Ursula held her finger out for Jet to wrap her tiny fist around. 'Yes I am. I really am.'

She didn't linger at home after she got back. Anton was in Edinburgh on a site visit and wouldn't be returning until tomorrow. She drove straight to the allotments. It was early evening, not her normal time. He liked to have her home when he'd finished work, but he wasn't here so she could do what she liked. Most people had gone by the time she got there and the place had an extra calmness about it.

She made herself a hot drink on her new camping stove, sat outside on her new garden chair, and let the tension she'd been carrying all day slip away. The sun was going down behind her. She got up and walked along the path that cut through a hedge, certain she'd get the best view of it from there. The hedge partially hid four more plots from the main site, one of which was Samuel's.

To her surprise he was there, sitting on a colonial style wicker chair in front of his shed. 'Ursula?'

She took the smaller path that led to his plot. 'What are you doing here, shouldn't you be home now?'

'I like watching the sun go down.'

'Me too.'

'You want to sit with me?' He brought another chair out from his shed for her.

She sat down and was treated to the sight of a gloriously red sun floating just above the far trees. 'Do you often stay here until this time?'

He nodded. 'I like the stillness, the solitude.'

'Oh, would you rather be alone? I can go.'

'We can enjoy it together. Look, it's almost gone.'

They sat quietly, neither saying a word, just listening to the sound of descending night and watching the fireball in the sky sink below the trees and hedges. It was peaceful and serene. Like everything had slowed down And right then, Ursula knew she truly was going to be all right.

42

HER GREATEST ACT OF DEFIANCE – 1997

Anton pushed his used breakfast plate across the table. 'I will be late tonight. We're meeting a new client for dinner. The list is in my office.'

Ursula arranged her expression into her veil face. She was about to deliver some news which, in her experience, was best delivered passively. 'I'm not sure I'll have time for your list today. I have my own list.'

'What do you mean?'

'We've been away for a month. I've got a lot to catch up on at the allotment. I'll need to put a full day in to get it back to where it was before we went away.'

A twitch appeared on his left eye and crept along the rest of that side of his face. This was a new development. 'There is urgent work that needs to be done here.'

'Perhaps you could ask your secretary to do it.'

'Perhaps you could re-prioritise your hobby.'

'No, I don't think so.' Her voice was small and self-conscious under the spotlight of his glare. It was another new occurrence, this menacing glare. It was taking all her willpower not to give in to it. They'd been in Germany until yesterday. A field trip. Much of the time Ursula had been alone in their rented apartment, and when she wasn't alone, she was either waiting on Anton, pandering to him, or entertaining for him. Lately she'd come to think she'd accidentally slipped into a past decade where she was the good little wife whose sole purpose was to see to his every need. She'd done all of it without a word of dissent, if only to avoid situations like this. But she was desperate to get back to her allotment now. She wanted to check on her crops and sit outside her little shed sharing tea, biscuits and chatter with her friends. And if she was honest, those days alone with nothing to do but anticipate Anton's return had woken something in her. She didn't know what else to call it, she just knew she was sick and tired of being that good little wife.

Anton pulled on his jacket and knocked non-existent fluff off the shoulders. She thought he was going to leave without saying another word and that for once, she'd got away with it. But, as he reached the front door, he stopped. 'This ridiculous obsession of yours has gone too far.'

'We agreed I could find something fulfilling when you came to fetch me in Leyton.'

'This cannot be fulfilling.'

'It is for me. It's my passion project.' She surprised herself with that one. Him too, but it didn't take long for his surprise to turn into something darker. His words had been thrown back at him and he was incensed. She was met with an expression of cold, hard rage that made her want to run into a corner and hide.

'Once again you disappoint me, Ursula.'

She felt herself shrinking, but then she thought of her mum and those small acts of defiance and she pulled herself up and looked him in the eye. It was enough to make him leave, slamming the door behind him, the sound of it echoing through the house and bruising her ears. She gasped and realised she'd been holding her breath.

In spite of being neglected for a month her plot was quite tidy and very little work needed to be done. If she wanted to she could just spend half a day here and then start on Anton's list. But this morning had been a victory. If she went back on it now, the next one would be even harder to achieve. Besides, she'd stopped off at a supermarket on the way here to buy food and wine. So she was going to bloody well stay.

It had only taken a few months to become part of this community. They'd been so friendly and helpful. Especially Samuel, Clyde, and Marcie and her husband, Gordon. For the first time since Talulah, Ursula felt like she belonged somewhere. But it was more than that; she could do what she wanted here. No one was going to judge her on what she was wearing or tell her how to fill her time, and she could paint and furnish the shed however she liked without being criticised for having terrible taste. Keeping this allotment going was her greatest act of defiance. Not her passion project. She'd only said that to get at Anton. She never thought of it as that because that phrase belonged to him, and she didn't want him anywhere near this place.

Weeding was her priority; she didn't want them sucking the goodness out of the soil and depriving her plants. When she first started this allotment, she'd found it hard to tell the young weeds from seedlings but after nearly two years, she'd become good it. At the beginning, she'd only wanted to grow fruit and vegetables. Flowers held too many unhappy associations. First there was the house she'd lived in when she was little. There'd been lots of flowers in that garden. Her father had liked flowers. Every weekend in the summer, he wandered around the borders, cutting the best ones to put into a big glass vase in the hall. The actual gardening was left to the gardener. Until her father had walked out on them. Her mum had to let the gardener go then and the flowers were left to their own devices. It hadn't occurred to Ursula before but he she now wondered if her father had another garden at his other house. The one where he kept his mistress. And if he did, did he also cut flowers every weekend and arrange them in another big glass vase, in another hallway? Probably. The man was all show. She wondered too if he'd been a better father to those other children. He was probably a grandfather now. She wouldn't know. The last time she'd seen or heard anything of him was that day at Talulah, and she was happy to keep it that way.

The garden at home was another reason she didn't want flowers. In Anton's garden, flowers were strictly ornamental. Weeds were obliterated as soon as they poked through. Every tree, every bush, every plant was carefully monitored in case it dared to shoot off in an unsanctioned direction, and the lawn was so neat and clean you really could eat your dinner off it. Not that such a thing would be allowed. Far too messy. There'd been a time when she'd found his need to control funny. Endearing even. These days she hadn't quite settled on her feelings towards it. Some days she pitied him for it. Some days she hated him for it. Some days she hated herself for allowing him to do it.

It had been Samuel who'd persuaded her to plant companion flowers to attract pollinators and lure pests away. She was glad she'd given in to him because she loved the straggly sweet peas that lived alongside the brassicas and leafy greens. She was grateful to the pretty nasturtiums every time they lured a fat slug or snail from the cucumbers. And she could sit all day watching the butterflies, bees and hover-flies crowding the English lavender.

At eleven she went up to the gates because her mum was stopping by for an hour. She was retired now and often came over to the allotment when Ursula wasn't travelling. Ursula suspected she preferred it to visiting the house.

She was already there, waiting on the other side of the gate. They took a slow walk back, her mum stopping to admire the other plots every now and then. 'Lovely day to be outside. I expect you've got a lot to do, haven't you?'

'Not really. I think my friends have been keeping it tidy for me. I've got lots of crops ready though. Plenty for you to take home. Have a sit down. I'll make us some tea.'

This year, Ursula had installed a bench by the lavender. It was in the middle of the plot but still close enough to the main path to catch passers-by who wanted to stop for a chat.

'Did you enjoy Germany?' said her mum.

'It was okay. Glad to be back.' Many people, her mum included, assumed she led an exciting and glamorous life, travelling to different parts of the world with her successful husband. But when it came down to it, she was just doing the same things she did at home without the added joy of her allotment.

'Well, I've got some news. Prepare yourself. Andi's coming home. They're leaving London.'

'Oh wow. That is news. Did she say why?'

'No. I expect they're finding it hard now they've got the two kids. She'll get more support here from her family. And us too.'

.   .   .

Her mum stayed for a picnic lunch and didn't leave until mid-afternoon. A couple of hours later, the diehards who worked during the day but couldn't keep away were beginning to arrive. Samuel was one of the first. He spent so much time here, you'd never think he had a family. He stopped in front of her plot, that big warm smile of his reminding her of the other reason she'd been so desperate to be here. 'Ursula, you're back.'

'I am. Thanks for looking after things for me.'

'It wasn't just me. Clyde can't stand a messy patch. Are you back for a while?'

'I hope so.'

'Good. I'll be seeing you.' He never asked her about her trips away. She liked that about him.

She carried on pottering until she had nothing left to do outside. Next, she swept and dusted the shed, and then there really was nothing left to do. The sun was low now and she thought how nice it would be to sit and watch it go down. She did that occasionally with Samuel, if Anton was away without her and, as he wasn't going to be home until late, she could do that now. A thought made her turn back from the path and she grabbed the wine and the remaining food before slipping through the gap in the hedge.

Samuel was sitting in his chair. He gestured to the seat he'd already put out next to him. 'You come to share the sunset, Ursula?'

'If you don't mind. I brought food. And wine.'

He raised his eyebrows. 'Wine? You some fancy woman, yer know.'

She laughed. 'Sorry. Don't you like wine?'

'I can tek it, but I prefer rum. You got some glasses in that bag of yours?'

She shook her head. 'No. I thought we could use mugs.'

'I can do better than that.' He fetched two tumblers from his shed. 'Me and Clyde like a tot when we're listening to the cricket. What else you got in there?'

'Some bread, cheese, and meats. Fancy meats, I'm afraid.'

He let out one of his booming laughs. 'Priscilla would be scandalised if she knew I was eating fancy meats with a fancy woman.'

'Who's Priscilla?'

'Me wife. Look now, the sun's leaving us.'

They stopped talking and watched the day close. Then they drank the wine and ate the bread, cheese and fancy meats while the darkness descended.

'How you getting home?' he said.

'I'll walk. Can't drive now.'

'I'll walk you home.'

'There's no need.' She stood up too quickly and the alcohol went straight to her head.

'I'll walk you anyway,' he said.

On the way to her house, he talked about his plans for next year's plantings, suggesting things she might like to try growing. When they reached the house he let out a long whistle. She laughed. 'Fancy house?'

He nodded. 'Goodnight, Ursula.'

She loved the way he spoke her name as if he was singing it. She looked up at him, the want in her almost too much. 'Goodnight, Samuel.'

She turned and saw Anton in his office window. He was at the top of stairs when she closed the front door. She didn't want to look at him but not doing so would give too much away. 'I thought you were going to be late.'

'Who was that?'

'A friend from the allotments. Some of us stopped for a drink this evening. I left my car. He walked me back to make sure I got home safely.'

The menacing glare was back again. Perhaps he'd seen the longing in her. Panic made her blurt out the first thing that came into her head: 'Andi's coming back to Birmingham.'

He gave her another look she hadn't seen in a long time. Disgust. Then he went back into his office and closed the door.

43

A LACK OF COURAGE

What would have happened if she had kissed Samuel that night? Knowing Samuel, he'd have told her in the gentlest possible way that it wasn't right. He was loyal and kind like that. Loyal to Priscilla. Kind to Ursula. In all the years they were friends, there was never a day when he wasn't kind to her. Never a day when he wasn't loyal to Priscilla either. '*Ursula*.' She could still hear him saying her name, still feel that same thrill when he said it. She looked up to the lone figure on the hill, back yet again. Why couldn't it be Samuel?

That night changed her and Anton. It didn't matter that nothing had happened. In his mind it had, and that was enough. Not enough to set her free though. The clients and partners liked her and that made her a valuable asset. Anton always said marriage was a partnership. This development with Samuel just altered the partnership. A frost crept over their marriage after that night. She might have been able to recover it if she'd given up the allotment. God knows he insisted often enough. But how could she give up her sanctuary? And how could she give up seeing the only man she'd ever truly loved? Even if he didn't love her back. She hadn't realised the full extent of her feelings for Samuel at the time. Only that she hungered for him with a capacity she never knew she had. But that hunger was as responsible for the change in her marriage as much as Anton was. She wanted it. She took power from it. Even so, she still wasn't brave enough to walk away.

Andi and Don had left for Dilys's funeral in London. Ursula had promised to look after things at Am-nawr while they were away. She'd also agreed to help Esme rescue the vegetable patch. It wasn't the most enticing prospect but the alternative was too much time on her hands and that never worked out well.

She was back to measuring her day by her home schedule again. It was ten-thirty so she'd have already put in a few hours tidying up her plot by now. Here in Am-nawr, she'd been waiting for ages for Esme to get up and make a start. Esteban, the Welsh collie with a Spanish name, was keeping her company. Yet another poor soul who'd been abandoned by Pablo, the fake Spaniard. This place seemed to be littered with them. She checked the time again. Enough of this wait-ing. 'Sod it. Let's make a start, Esteban.'

A quick survey of the brassicas was enough to confirm they'd been decimated by caterpillars and needed to come out. The carrots were in a better state. There weren't many but they looked edible and ready to harvest. She lifted a couple of potatoes and found them to be in decent shape but the lettuces had all either bolted or had too much slug damage to be of use. She'd have to dig out some of the weeds before she could see what else was in there. She began by taking up the cabbages and cauliflowers, hoping to find one or two that could be saved.

The sound of footsteps on the path made her stop and look up. It was Esme, out of bed at last. 'What are you doing?' The belligerent sulk that seemed to be a permanent fixture was already set on her face.

Ursula shoved the spade in the ground and left it there. 'I'm taking these out. They've been ruined by caterpillars.'

'How do you know that?'

'You see all these holes? That's where they've eaten through it. And this stuff on the leaves, it's caterpillar excrement.'

'Excrement? You mean shit.' Esme snorted. 'Caterpillars don't shit.'

'All animals shit in one way or another, Esme. It's an essential part of being alive. Are you going to help?'

'Nah, I don't think so.'

'I thought you'd promised Andi.'

'Yeah well she's not here, is she? Anyway, Pab said not to bother. He said I can go and live with him in Spain. No point hanging around here. You all hate me.'

That much was probably true. Ursula thought about trying to reassure her it wasn't the case but she'd probably only end up getting more abuse. And anyway, she was sick of everyone expecting her to lie down and take any old crap with a placid smile. 'You know, Esme, people might be nicer to you if were nicer to them.'

Esme's top lip puckered and curled up. 'Why don't you just fuck off back to the hole you crawled out of, you sad old hag. You know nothing about me and the things I have to put up with.' With that she flew off back inside the house, but not before kicking a stray cabbage in Ursula's direction.

Esteban dodged it and ran to Ursula with a whimper. She

bent down and stroked him. 'It's all right, mate. She won't hurt you. I won't let her.'

The radiator in the library was cold and with no other visible means of heat in here, Ursula was feeling the chill, despite it being early summer. She'd put on an extra jumper as well as Anton's scarf but the gloomy weather had settled in her bones. She'd made good headway on the vegetable garden yesterday but heavy rain had set in, making it impossible to work on it this morning. Consequently, she was roaming around the house looking for things to stem her mind's aimless drifting from one unsettling memory to another.

The library was in the front of the house. It gave her the opportunity to hide away from Anton, but she'd forgotten there were ghosts in here too. Everywhere she looked, Pablo was grinning at her from one of his many places in the photo montage. This room was a shrine to him. She wondered how long it would be before Andi stopped torturing herself with them. The thought sent her hand to her neck and the scarf, and she reminded herself of that phrase about people and glass houses.

Her eyes landed on a rare picture of Andi with Zak and Jet. Andi was a good mother. As far as Ursula could tell, anyway. And actually, Pab had been a decent father too when the kids were young, although her experience in that area was limited. They'd left London because he'd got into some kind of trouble and not, as her mum had thought, because they were struggling with parenthood. Ursula never got to the bottom of what that trouble was. Andi had been sketchy on the details. She'd always assumed it was something illegal, or that he'd got mixed up with the kind of people you needed to get away from in a hurry. Knowing what she knew now, she considered the possibility that it might have been to do with Esme. Maybe she was putting two and two together, but Esme was about the right age.

When they came back to Birmingham, Andi and Pab found a house in Perry Barr, on the north of the city, close to Andi's sister. Pab started working for her brother-in-law who was a landscape gardener. It didn't pay a lot but it allowed him to look after the kids while Andi set up her own business in the flat above Solly's shop.

It wasn't long after the move that Pab started tormenting Ursula again. For Andi's sake, she tried to ignore it but it was as if he could sense the dread coming off her. It was a game to him. A challenge too. She was his prey and every chance he got, he trapped and taunted her.

To everyone else he was the fun-loving, nice guy who didn't take anything seriously. Even her mum liked him, despite seeing through him from the off. 'He'll do the dirty on her one day, if he hasn't already.' That was her assessment of Pablo, and she was right. Just how many times he'd done the dirty was anybody's guess. It could have been once, twice, or a hundred. You never knew with a man like him. Naturally, neither of them ever said anything to Andi. Maybe they should have done.

Most surprising of all was that Anton tolerated him. On the rare family occasions he attended, Pablo was the one he sought out for company. That might have been where Pablo had picked up the idea of a passion project. Anton might have planted the seed of this place in his head, because Pab was in awe of their house. That was probably why Anton enjoyed his company. Because when it came to his work, her husband was not immune to flattery. He had an ego the size of a planet in that regard. In fact, the reason they went to so many events was because they enabled Anton to strut around like a prize cockerel. Thinking about it, he and Pab were a match made in heaven. They should have married each other.

In the absence of anything else to do, Ursula went up to the sewing room where her dress was waiting to be finished. Once again the pattern made her think of that gorgeous Italian scarf Solly had given to her mum. But it was just a trinket compared to the love he'd given her. Their happiness was a joyous thing to witness and no one deserved it more than her mum. Ursula didn't need that kind of love anymore. She'd lived so long without it, she wasn't sure she'd recognise it anyway. A healthy dose of happiness would be enough. But maybe happiness was another thing that needed to be earned. In which case, she'd be waiting for a long time before it came her way.

The sewing machine was already set up. The skirt and bodice had been tacked together and ordinarily it wouldn't have been a difficult job to run it through the machine. But Andi wasn't here, and that made all the difference.

The cupboard door was open. Her mum's unfinished christening outfit was at the front of the rail. So stylish and unique. So very beautiful. Her mum in a nutshell. It was impossible to put into words just how much Ursula missed her. She closed the door. There had to be a way of finding something other than this dreary trudge through time. If only she knew how to find it. She went over to the sewing machine. She would start small. Another small act of defiance. Only this time, she was defying the voice inside her.

.   .   .

The rain stopped while she was working on the dress. It had been another shaky start but she'd managed to produce something passable. She put the dress on the mannequin and sent a photo of it to Andi. Clyde rang as she was locking the door. She picked up his call as she went into her bedroom and dropped the key onto the bedside table. He was outside somewhere, she could hear the sound of traffic in the background. 'I'm on my way to the allotments to meet some of the committee. They want to take a proper look at those plots before they decide what to do next. We got another meeting about it tonight. Thought you'd want to hear.'

'Thanks. Will you let me know what happens?'

'Sure.'

Ursula ended the call, her mind on the probable outcome of the committee's visit. A creak in the floorboards behind her made her swivel round. She was half-expecting to see Anton gloating but instead she caught a glimpse of Esme's back. She went back out on the landing. Esme had gone. From the bottom of the stairs, Charlie Big Potatoes let out another loud and desperate miaow that sent her rushing down to him, only to realise he was just looking for food.

By the time she'd finished giving Charlie, Esteban, and the other cats an impromptu lunch and fed herself, a weak sun had broken through the clouds. She pulled on her outdoor boots and went out to the vegetable garden. Encouraged by her success in the sewing room, she was set on finishing the digging today. The rain had loosened up the soil, making it easier to dig. The weeds were coming up fairly easily but were revealing absolutely nothing underneath except more weeds. The garden's only redeeming feature was the potato crop which was healthy and plentiful.

Esteban growled. It was because Esme was on the path. 'Found any more shit today, Ursula?'

'Not yet. I'll be sure to tell you if I do.'

'Yeah, you do that.' Esme was laughing to herself as she went back inside. Ursula wanted to go after her and ask what was so funny but there was a darkness about that young woman that rattled her more than it should. She despised her cowardice, but it took a lot of courage to walk away from a lifetime of being a certain way and she simply didn't have it.

Samuel didn't have that kind of courage either. The more she got to know him, the more she came to understand that the allotment was his hiding place, just like it was for her. It wasn't the same for Clyde. All the different aspects of his life seemed to flow seamlessly into one another. It wasn't unusual to see Clyde's late wife Carmen with him, or his kids and later his grandchildren. Or even a friend from his club.

Samuel had a son and three daughters. And of course, he had Priscilla. But they seemed to exist on the outer reaches of his life. He spent all his spare time at the allotment. Ursula asked him once why that was and he didn't have an answer for her. But she'd worked out her own theory from the little he'd told her. Samuel was afraid of doing things badly. The fear of being a bad father or a bad husband paralysed him. So he hid behind the thing he was good at. Ironically, that made him a bad father and a bad husband. But it also made him an excellent friend.

Unlike Carmen, Priscilla never came to the allotment. Well, only once and that wasn't really to see the allotment. Or Samuel. Ursula never told Samuel she loved him. It would have betrayed their friendship which was sacred to her. But Priscilla looked in her eye and saw it. She knew.

44

THE MEASURE OF HER – 2000

Anton was in Miami for a week. He hadn't required her to go with him this time. There was every chance this was the start of another new development in their marriage. There'd been a couple since that night Samuel had seen her home. The first had been the sex. Or the lack of it. Anton had stopped having sex with her. They hadn't had it once in the last three years. That didn't actually bother Ursula. It had been good in the early days but, if she was honest, it had become boring and stale by the time he'd decided to take it away. The second development had seen him move to working almost entirely from home. He might not have wanted her anymore, but he still wanted to monitor her every move. And now this. A trip away without her. Did he think he was punishing her? Did he actually think she'd have wanted to go? If she'd have been Andi she'd have told him: 'Newsflash! I'm happy to see the back of you.' But she wasn't Andi. So she packed his bag neatly, drove him to the airport, and promised to do all the jobs on his extremely long list.

From his chair, Samuel nudged her arm. 'There he is. Mr Fox.'

She leaned forward to get a better look. On the furthest plot, a fox's head poked out from under a hedge. Samuel had promised he'd come and they'd been waiting for over an hour. 'How do you know it's a mister?'

'Because him such a big handsome boy. Much like meself.'

Ursula laughed. 'I had no idea you held yourself in such high regard.'

'Not just me. When I was a young buck, all the girls wanted a piece of me. Priscilla had to fight them off just to get a look in.'

'Poor Priscilla. It must have been awful for her.'

'Not Priscilla. She a tough little woman. One o' them pocket rockets, you know what I'm saying?' His laugh sent the fox dashing off to find a quieter place to hunt.

'Tell me about Priscilla. How did you meet her?' She was curious about the woman Samuel seemed to hide from and yet still have the greatest affection for.

'It was at a house party, back in Kingston. I saw her bottom first, jiggling around the floor. It was the most heavenly bottom I'd ever seen. Like a beautiful round peach. I went right up to her and told her. She called me a fool. But all night, she kept on jiggling that bottom and fluttering them big eyes at me. I knew she wanted more. She was some woman.' He shook his head and smiled. 'She still calls me a fool.'

She thought of Anton who had never called her a fool but made it clear in so many other ways that she was one. 'My husband's away all week, so I'll be spending longer here.'

He nodded. 'I won't be here tomorrow. The pastor's

coming round. If I'm not there, Priscilla says she'll divorce me.'

'Oh. Is it...? Sorry, I shouldn't pry.' Even so, her heart was fluttering with excitement.

'It's our boy. He's got in with some troublemekkers. The pastor's coming to talk to him.'

'Have you talked to him yourself?'

'He don't listen to me. Come now, Ursula. Let's have some quiet and watch the sun going down. Maybe Mr Fox will come back.'

Knowing she wasn't going to see Samuel today, Ursula was in no rush to go to the allotment. She spent the morning tackling Anton's list and doing some food shopping. It was while she was in the middle of the supermarket that her mobile phone rang. Anton had quickly embraced this new fad, but she'd only just had one forced upon her by him. Most likely so he could keep tabs on her. But it wasn't Anton calling this time. It was her mum. 'Ursula, can you come over?'

Ursula looked at the trolley, half full with shopping. 'Is it urgent?'

'Kind of. Cassandra's here. Will you come? Oh, and don't mention this to anyone. Not even Anton.'

She left the trolley in the aisle and drove straight over. Andi pulled up just as she got out of the car. She waited for her to catch up. 'Mum called you too?'

'Well, it is a momentous occasion, Cass's return. Two momentous occasions if you count Gillian letting her into the flat.'

Cass was sitting next to her mum on the sofa. They were turned slightly towards each other, holding hands. It shot

Ursula straight back to those times when seeing them with their heads together was a daily occurrence. Except that this time, they both looked as if they'd been through the wringer. Especially Cass. Her eyes were red raw. And then another thought occurred to Ursula. Perhaps Cass was here to tell them Bernard Fry was dead.

Andi was already opening her arms for Cass to fall into. 'Talk about a shock.'

Cass stood up and hugged her. 'Gill's been telling me how well you're doing. I always knew you had it in you.' She held out her hand to Ursula. 'Hello, Ursula.'

'Is he dead? My father, he's dead isn't he?'

Cass frowned. 'No. Still going strong as far as I know. I haven't spoken to him since I left Birmingham. You're wondering why I'm here after so long away? It's simple really. I wanted to come home.'

'But where have you been?' said Ursula. 'I looked for you at the shop and at your house. I tried calling you, but you just disappeared.'

'Did you? I'm sorry I didn't tell you but I had to get away. I went abroad. Various places. I met someone and we travelled together until I realised I'd never be happy unless I made amends with Gill.' Cass glanced at Ursula's mum. There was every chance the two of them would burst into tears at any moment. She turned back to Ursula. 'You haven't told Anton I'm here, have you?'

'No. He's in America anyway.'

'I'd rather you didn't. I don't want my family knowing I'm back. You know Anton moves in the same circles. I can't risk him dropping it out.'

'I've never seen any of the Frys at anything I've attended.' Ursula saw Cass's reaction and was annoyed with herself for being so defensive. So what if Anton shielded her from them? That didn't mean he didn't bump into them occasionally on a professional basis. And it wouldn't be the first time she'd kept secrets from him. Her feelings for Samuel in particular. Anyway, she suspected there were many things he didn't tell her. Like where he went for sex. 'I won't mention it and he hardly ever comes here anymore.'

'Make sure he doesn't then, love,' said her mum. 'Because Cass is staying with us for a while.' Then, before Ursula could ask if she was sure, she added: 'It's been a difficult few hours for both of us but we've made our peace.'

'I don't get it though,' said Andi. 'Why are you so scared of your family finding out where you are?'

Cass shook her head. 'I'm not scared, I just don't want anything to do with them. I'm not like them, Andi. I can't use people and throw them away when a better offer comes along. I did that once and lived to regret it. And when I tried to put it right, Bernard destroyed me. I won't let him do that again.'

Ursula remembered the last time she'd seen her father. He'd said something like none of it would have happened if her mum had agreed to let him have her. She'd been the reason Talulah closed down. 'It was because you took me on.'

Cass gave her a weak smile. 'The shop was just ticking over with financial support from the family firm but when he found out you were working there, he withdrew it. That New Romantic collection helped me struggle on for a while but the next one didn't do so well and I went under.' It all made sense now. All those fraught phone calls and the mood swings. She must have been under such pressure.

'But I'd left by then.'

'Yes, but the damage had already been done. Besides, I

thought you'd be coming back. I kept a place for you. To be honest, it was a relief in a way to let it go. It was never the same without Gill.'

Ursula's mum sighed. 'I suppose it was my fault for making you take Ursula on. But I don't regret it, Cass. It got you away from them and it brought us back together again. Although I have to say, you took your bloody time.'

'I was building up the courage. You have no idea how frightening you are,' said Cass.

'That is true,' said Solly. Everyone turned to look at him. He pulled his mouth into a downward smile and shrugged, and suddenly they were all laughing.

'I'm not telling Pab,' said Andi as they walked back to their cars. 'He doesn't know Cass anyway but he might say something to Anton.'

'Good thinking. Things must be bad if she's worried Anton will say something.'

'Bit over the top, I thought. Still, it's nice to see the two old mates back together again.'

'Yeah. I really thought their friendship was broken beyond repair.'

'I guess some friendships can never be truly broken.'

'Do you think ours is like that?'

Andi frowned. 'You have to ask? Fucking hell, Urs. What are you like? I gotta go. I've got a wedding dress to finish before Saturday.'

Ursula got in the car and headed for the allotment. Maybe she shouldn't have asked but it was the mention of Pab. If anyone was going to break their friendship it was him. And if she really didn't want it broken she'd have to say nothing to Andi and just hope he grew bored of trying to get a rise out of her.

She parked up and went straight into her shed. There wasn't really any work needed to be done so she made some tea and sat on the bench. It was a glorious August afternoon. There were children running around and the place had a holiday feel to it. Ursula sat back, enjoying the sunshine. On a day like this there was no better place to be.

She noticed a woman standing by the gate, small, dark-skinned and immaculately dressed. Ursula waited for a while, to see if anyone came for her and when they didn't, she went to offer help. 'Hello. Are you waiting for someone? Would you like me to get them?'

The woman lifted her chin. 'I'm looking for Ursula.'

'I'm Ursula. Can I help you?'

'No. I just wanted to see you for meself.' She looked Ursula over, as if she was examining every inch of her and with one last piercing stare, she walked away.

Ursula watched her go, not realising Clyde was by her side. 'Was that Priscilla Sweeting?'

'Yes, I think it was.'

'What did she want?'

'I don't know.' It was a lie, but she was too ashamed to tell Clyde that Priscilla had come to see her, to get the measure of her. And there was no doubt in Ursula's mind that she had done exactly that.

45

GRIEF AND YEARNING – 2002

'This move is very inconvenient. Your presence would have been helpful.' Anton took his suitcase out of the boot. Ursula could tell by the way he wrenched at it that he was more than a notch above irritated.

'I'll be sure to pass on your sentiments to Mum and Solly.' Years ago, he'd have given her a pained smile and asked if she was teasing him. All she got today was a blank look and a short sigh. 'It's only a fortnight. Your team will give you all the support you need.'

'I'll call when I get to Stockholm. Keep your phone on.'

'Don't I always?'

She waited until he was out of sight before getting back into the Volvo, the family car for a family that almost was. Every time she sat in it she was reminded of that fact and she hated every square inch of it. Their son would have been nineteen now. At university, probably. She allowed herself a moment to let the grief settle. It never went away. Not really. But some days it was more active than others. Although lately she was beginning to ask herself if it really was grief she was experiencing and not just a plain old yearning for the things she couldn't have. Maybe the two were the same thing.

She drove home, swapped cars and went on to her mum's flat. She and Solly were moving to Eastbourne today. Cass was going with them. After two years of sleeping in Ursula's old room, she was moving into her own place near them. Although he didn't know it, the move had been planned to coincide with Anton's trip. It had been fairly easy keeping Cass's return a secret which just went to show how separate their lives had become.

The removals men were closing up the van as she arrived. Solly and Cass went shortly after them, leaving Ursula and her mum to have a quiet moment alone in their old home.

'I'll miss this place. It meant such a lot to have somewhere of our own,' said her mum.

'I'll miss it too. Will you have a sewing room in the new house?'

'I haven't decided yet. I've left everything with Andi for now. I didn't think Anton would want them cluttering up his nice, neat house.'

'True. Are you ready to go?'

'I think so.' She pressed her palm against the door as she locked it up for the last time. 'Goodbye, old friend.'

Ursula touched the door too. That feeling was upon her again. Grief and yearning.

Her mum was watching her. 'You'll be all right without me here, won't you, love?'

Ursula's face creased into a frowny smile. 'Of course I will.'

'You've got to keep fighting, Ursula. Keep some control. Small acts–'

'Of defiance. Yes, I know.' She rolled her eyes. She might have cried if she hadn't given that up long ago.

After a chaotic but lovely week in Eastbourne, Ursula was on the way home. Anton wasn't due back for another six days and the thought of all that freedom gave her a happy buzz. She'd promised to call in on Andi first so she took a detour to the north of the city. It could have waited for another day but Andi had mentioned Pablo would be out and any opportunity to miss him was one to be seized upon.

To her dismay it was Pab who answered the door. Zak was on his shoulders and Jet was hanging onto his leg. 'Say hello to Auntie Ursula, kids.'

'Hello Auntie Ursula,' they said, almost together.

Ursula fixed a smile on to hide the anxiety that came every time he was around. 'I've brought presents. Who wants a present from the seaside?'

The kids screamed with delight. Pablo put Zak down. 'All right, calm down. If they're full of E numbers, Ursula, you are dead.'

'No E numbers, just things that make a lot of noise.' She gave the children a bag each. It was a mistake because they ran off with their prizes, leaving her alone with Pablo.

He leaned in, too closely as always, and closed the door behind her. 'In that case, I am definitely going to kill you.'

She stiffened, despite willing herself not to. 'I thought you were out today.'

The kids were calling her and she tried to follow them but he moved so that she couldn't get past. 'Change of plan. Couldn't miss seeing you, could I?'

'Is Andi here?' No matter how much she tried to force a smile this time, it wouldn't come.

'She's gone to get wine. Apparently you're staying tonight.'

'Not as far as I know.'

'Try telling her that.' He was right up close to her now. There was hardly a breath between them.

The front door swung open and they both turned to see Andi, her eyes flitting from Pablo to Ursula, and back to Pablo again.

He sprang into action, grabbing the shopping bags off her. 'I was just telling Ursula she's staying the night.'

'Yeah, I thought you might want some company.' Andi smiled but she wasn't entirely happy. Ursula could tell.

'I'm all right. Really.' She had no desire whatsoever to spend the night under the same roof as Pab. But then she caught a look in Andi's eyes and she realised the suggestion hadn't been for her benefit. 'Okay, why not?'

'Great. Pab's going to the pub later, so it'll be just you and me.'

That at least, was something to be grateful for.

He stuck around for an uncomfortable dinner and then left. Ursula put the kids to bed while Andi cleared up. She read them a story and stayed with them until they fell asleep. When she got back downstairs, Andi handed her a glass of wine and they settled on the sofa. Ursula was expecting her to ask about that moment in the hall but she said something else: 'I think Pab's having an affair.'

It didn't come as a complete shock. In fact, she'd have been surprised if it was the first time. Not that she was ever going to say that to Andi. 'What makes you think that?'

'You can read the signs, can't you?'

Yes, you could. It was the disinterest in you and anything related to you. The door closing for certain phone calls. The extra time taken in the bathroom. Coming home smelling freshly showered but with the smell of stale sex lingering on his underpants. All pieces of the same puzzle. 'What are you going to do about it?'

'I don't know.' A tear slid out of Andi's right eye and ran down her cheek. 'Do you think he's going to leave me?'

'I don't know, mate. I'm not close enough to him. Have you asked him?'

The tear had reached Andi's jawline now and she swept it away with the back of her hand. 'I'm scared of what the answer will be.'

'Anton's having an affair. Well, he's having sex with someone other than me.'

'Anton? But he's so–'

'Boring?'

'Fixated on you. Are you sure?'

Ursula shrugged. 'I can read the signs too. And he's not very good at hiding them. Although that might be deliberate.'

Andi looked shocked. She was probably used to Pab doing all he could to hide his cheating. It must be hard to understand why Anton was going out of his way to make it obvious. 'Do you think he's trying to make you jealous?'

'Maybe. It's a punishment for something. Well, it would be if I cared.'

'Urs, are you saying you don't love him anymore?'

'I'm not certain I ever really did love him. I thought I did, but I was so young and naïve.' It was the first time she'd admitted that to anyone, including herself, but it was another of those things she'd been considering lately. And she couldn't help thinking it had a lot to do with grief and yearning. Particularly yearning.

'Will you leave him then?'

'Where would I go? Anyway, I can't.'

'Yes you can. Hey, we could run away together with the kids. We'll leave those two bastards behind.'

Ursula laughed. 'Okay. Let me know when you get to that point.'

'You said he's punishing you for something. Can you tell me what?'

'He thinks I'm in love with someone else.'

'It's not, it's not Pab, is it?'

'What?' Her mouth fell open. It was the shock of what she'd just heard, what Andi was accusing her of. 'Absolutely not. How could you even think I'd do that to you? I don't even like... I have never felt that way about Pab. Never. And I never will.'

'Sorry. It's just that he talks about you a lot. And when you said... I'm sorry. I was way out of order. Of course you wouldn't do that.'

Ursula was too angry to answer. If she hadn't had so much wine, she'd have got in her car and left. But she was stuck here with her supposed best friend. She'd like to have told Andi what she really thought of Pablo, and that far from screwing him, she wouldn't touch the creep with a ten-foot barge pole. But she knew if she did say those things she'd regret it when she sobered up. So she ignored her indignation and put her arm around Andi. 'We've both had too much to drink. Perhaps we should call it a night and go to bed.'

Andi made up a sofa bed in the lounge for her and said goodnight. Ursula pulled the quilt up to her neck. She was still angry but the drive from Eastbourne and the wine had worn her out and she went straight to sleep.

It felt like she'd only just shut her eyes when the creak of the door forced them open again. The light from the hall framed Pab's silhouette in the doorway. She lay completely still while he stayed there watching her. He was swaying a little. Drunk, probably. It was a good fifteen minutes before the door closed and the room was back in darkness. Even so, she waited a beat or two before breathing, in case her eyes were playing tricks on her and he still was in the room. Finally sure he was gone, she tried to relax enough to doze back off. But then she remembered something Andi had said: '*He talks about you a lot,*' and there was no chance in hell she was going to sleep again in this house.

Pab was still in bed when she got up and Andi was behaving as if nothing had happened last night. Ursula took the hint and didn't mention it either, but she left as soon as she was washed and dressed.

She only stayed at home long enough to dump her case and get changed, and then she was straight out to the allotments. Marcie and Gordon were on their plot when she got there. 'We're not stopping long,' said Gordon. 'Just come to get the week's veg before the rain comes in.'

'Oh I haven't seen the forecast. Is it going to be bad?'

'Bad enough.'

She made a start on pulling up her own vegetables for the week ahead, before it got too unpleasant. The air hung heavily around her and she could feel the nearness of the rain. She ought to go home, but where was home? Certainly not that prison she lived in. She couldn't even go to her mum's anymore. And now that Andi's house was off-limits, this was the only place she could think of that felt anything like it.

The first spots came down. Marcie and Gordon packed up their things and waved goodbye. Ursula carried on until it was too wet to do anything other than retreat to the shed. She put the camping stove on and warmed her hands while she waited for the kettle to boil. Great globs of sleety rain fell from the broody sky and lashed at the window. There wasn't another soul around. But then she saw a tall, broad figure coming through the gate and along the path. She opened the door and called to him: 'Samuel.'

He ran to her. His big frame crowding her in the small shed. 'We are two mad fools to come out in this.'

Mad or lonely. She opened up a fold out chair. 'Here, take a seat. I'm making coffee.' She made his strong, sweet and milky, the way he liked it.

He wrapped his long, thick fingers around the mug. 'I don't think we'll get a lot done today, Ursula.'

'Did you forget to check the forecast as well?'

'No. I knew it was going to be bad, but it was here or church. What about you?'

'Here or home. Or my friend's home. But that's not too welcoming right now.'

'You want to tell me?' It's not like we got anything else to do.'

And that was the cue she needed to tell him all about Pablo and Andi. 'I don't know why she stands him. She could do much better.'

'Maybe she don't want to.'

'Yeah, that would be it. He's like a drug to her. But I'm no better. My marriage is hardly the best example.'

'Ursula, my friend, I wish I could take it away from you.'

'Take what?''

'The sadness. I see it weighing you down and I wish I could take that burden from you.'

Was it really that obvious? She concentrated on the coffee swirling around the inside her mug. 'I lost a baby. A boy. A miscarriage they call it, don't they? I always think that sounds like he was some kind of easily forgotten malfunction. I've tried to leave him in the past, but... Perhaps if we'd had more children he would have been easier to let go.'

Samuel held her hand. She felt a sensation in her breast that made her breathless. 'Priscilla and me, we lost a son. He died when he was three. I would never let him go'.

'I didn't realise. It must have been so hard for you both.'

'We dealt with it in our own ways. Priscilla went to church. My way was different. I'm not a great talker when it comes to my boy, but I feel it. When I'm watching the sun go down, I know he's with me. I got four kids alive but he's as real as them. Just because your boy didn't get born, there is nothing wrong in keeping him with you. Never forget that, Ursula. And if that Spanish fella comes bothering you again, you tell me. Me and Clyde will see to him.'

46

SADNESS AND REGRET

Something had set Esteban's tail off. He let out a happy yelp and ran past Ursula to the source of his pleasure. Gareth knelt down and ruffled the dog's fur. 'You've made good progress there. Don't suppose you know where Brett is, do you?'

Ursula took a breather from the potato crop. She'd been so lost in her memories that she hadn't noticed she'd lifted quite a pile of them. 'Somewhere in Frongoch, he said. Not sure where exactly.'

'I know the place. I thought I'd go over and say hello, like.'

'How did the funeral go?'

'As well as you'd expect. Mam was well cut up. We all were really. She was lovely, Auntie Dilys. We just got back. Can't stand London. Horrible place.'

Ursula smiled. 'Too busy?'

'Too everything. Give me Bala any day. Shall I take Esteban with me? Give him a run out.'

'I don't think you've got much choice. By the look of it,

he'll be gutted if you leave him behind. Do you think your mum might want some company?'

'She's not here. She's coming back with the others tomorrow.'

'Oh, I thought you said...' But Gareth was already walking away and Esteban was on his heels, ready to go whether he was invited or not. Megan hadn't come home with him then? She must have misheard him.

Ursula went back to the potatoes. Only a small area left and then she'd be done. The sense of achievement that finishing the dress had given her was in her sights again and she worked quickly and methodically, thinking only of what she needed to do. And then it was finished, and she could relax. As much as it was possible to relax in this house anyway.

Back in the kitchen, she made a hot drink and took it out to the bench to watch the sun go down. It was more like watching the night take hold because there wasn't really any sun to speak of, but she sat there all the same and thought of those happy evenings with Samuel. She pictured him sitting in that old wicker chair telling her so many things. Like how every piece of earth was teeming with life. How glorious the sun was in Jamaica. She pictured him asking if that Spanish fella had been bothering her again, his fists clenched. Asking her if there was anything he could do to take her sadness from her. Of course, there was something he could have done. But she would never have asked him to do it.

Her phone rang in her pocket. It was Clyde: 'Am I disturbing you?'

'No, I'm having a cuppa on a damp bench after digging up a neglected vegetable garden.'

'Sounds right up your street. The decision's been made.

We're going to clear those allotments and put them back up to be let.'

'Oh.'

'I'm going to do it. I've got a friend who'll help me. We'll be respectful.'

She felt she should say something but a searing pain was blasting through her, as if it were snapping her in two.

'Samuel would have wanted it, Ursula.'

'Yes, yes he would.' She pressed her hand against the place where the pain was worst.

'I know it means a lot to you.'

'It's only a bit of land, Clyde.' But it wasn't though, was it? The pain was still there, sharp and ferocious. 'I have to go.'

'I understand. Call me whenever you want.'

'Thank you.' She cut the call and told herself again, it's only a bit of land. It was just that it was Samuel's land, and she had so little left of him. This pain was crippling her. She pushed herself up and went inside.

The beginning of night had caught up with the house and it was in darkness. Ursula switched on the lights as she went through the kitchen, the hall, and upstairs. She needed to lie down. But as she reached the landing, she noticed the sewing room door was open. She'd definitely locked it this morning. She remembered doing it and putting the key on the bedside table while speaking to Clyde. But afterwards, she'd been distracted by Esme on the landing and then Charlie. She'd left the key there instead of putting it away. Esme must have taken it. But why? And to leave the door open like that. As if she wanted Ursula to know she'd been in there. Just like Anton and his heavy hints about his women.

She didn't want to go in there to see what fresh hell was waiting for her. Because she was sure there would be some.

But she had no choice, she had to face it. That was what you did with bullies. Her mum had told her that, back when the girls at her private school had turned on her after her father left. They were bad enough, but the other bullies at her new school were worse. They saw her posh manners and fancy clothes and tore her apart. She hadn't been able to deal with it back then. But she was older and wiser now and if she'd learned anything from living with Anton, it was how to cope with bullies. Because he was a bully, in his way. So was Pablo. And so was Esme. They all saw her as an easy target and they swooped in. Just like those girls at school.

As soon as she pushed the door open, an earthy, pungent smell caught the back of her throat. Ursula's hand fumbled around the wall for the light switch and, when she found it, the hell she'd been expecting was revealed. Her dress was no longer on the dummy. It had been laid out on the table and someone had scattered droppings across its beautiful, flowing silk skirt. Some of the droppings had been left to sit on top of the fabric and some had been crushed into it. Not only that, Esme had also crushed and smeared them across the bodice.

A scream came out of her. She reeled backwards, crashed against the door and stumbled out onto the landing, then flew downstairs and out of the house. The dark shadow of the hill was in front of her. She ran towards it, towards Anton. He was up there. Waiting to reap his own revenge. Waiting to get her. Just like Esme. The pain was all over her now. Her chest. Her sides. Her gut. Her legs. Everywhere hurt. She had to stop running before she got too far up, too far into the darkness, but she couldn't go back into that house. She needed somewhere else to hide.

The ground around the bothy was muddy and she slipped and slid in her haste to get inside but somehow managed to remain upright. It was empty. She'd been afraid Esme would be here and she'd have to face her in this state. Ursula felt her way to the bench and sat down before her legs buckled. And then came the unexpected tears. Not fierce and heavy but silent and steady. She was crying. My God, she was crying.

The rain started up again, a gentle patter at first that became faster and louder. The door suddenly opened and the outline of a tall, broad man in a big coat filled the doorway. For a heartbeat, she thought of Samuel and that rainy day in her shed when they'd swapped sorrow stories. But then the outline switched on his phone's torch and shone it on her. 'Ursula.' It wasn't Samuel's joyful melodic voice that she would have given anything to hear again. It was sadder, more reserved. It was Howard.

He used his torch to find a battery operated light that gave the room a dull shadowy hue and left no place for Ursula to hide. 'You've been crying. What's happened?'

'So many things,' she said, the tears still falling.

He sat next to her and put his arm around her. 'Is this okay?'

She nodded. Yes, it was okay. It was more than okay.

'You wanna talk?'

'No. This is enough.' She rested her head on his shoulder. She shouldn't be doing this. Not with him. He had his own mountain of heartache to deal with. All the same, she left it there and they sat in the semi-dark, the sound of rain shutting everything else out, until she felt his body trembling next to her. He was sobbing. Ursula had never seen a man cry so uncontrollably. It was heartbreaking. In spite of her inner voice screaming to keep away, she pulled him to her and held him.

'My apologies,' he said. 'I just...'

'It's all right.' She brushed away his tears, saw his response and realised she should have listened to herself. 'I didn't mean to do that. I'm sorry.'

His eyes met hers and his brow creased into deep furrows as he stroked the side of her face. This was wrong, it was so wrong, but she didn't want to stop him. The softness of his touch, the tenderness of it, was too sweet. Her lips moved towards his. He met them with his own, gentle and tentative. And then there was no space between them as they embraced, tears splashing on one kiss after another. They undressed each other, the cold air pricking their skin. He sat on the edge of the bench. She settled on his lap, cradling his head in her hands, letting him caress her breasts and neck. It had been so very long and yet it felt so natural, so wanted.

'This isn't right,' he said.

No it wasn't. He wasn't Samuel and she wasn't Dilys, but they both needed to feel something other than sadness and regret.

47

AN ILLUSION OF BEAUTY

The bench held no comfort for old bones like theirs, but Ursula and Howard found softness in each other's bodies as they clung together, wrapped in blankets that had been left for resting walkers. They'd managed to light the fire so, while they weren't particularly comfortable, they were at least warm. They'd hardly spoken since they'd given in to their needs and even though there was nothing to separate them, each was lost in their own private thoughts. Ursula couldn't speak for him but she imagined he was thinking about Dilys. She was thinking about Samuel's allotment and Esme's spiteful desecration of the dress, and was trying to decide whether the news about the first had influenced her reaction to the second. She was also feeling bad for leaving it to contaminate Andi's sewing room. She'd have to clean it up as soon as it was light. Not now though. It was too dark out there and she didn't want to go back in that house yet.

Howard got up and went over to the window. 'I thought I heard something out there. Probably just a sheep.' He'd wrapped a blanket, toga-like, around him. He had a good body. Soft around the middle, but strong arms and legs and a solid chest.

He gave up trying to see out and sat on the end of the bench. 'I'm sorry. You were upset and I took advantage of it.'

She sat up too, careful to leave some space between them. 'I could say the same thing.'

'When I said it wasn't right, I didn't mean–'

'It wasn't right. I don't regret it though.' She let that settle in her head, the idea of not regretting something she'd done. The thought of it was refreshing, optimistic even.

'Me neither. But my wife has just died. I should regret it. I'm ashamed of myself.'

'How long has it been?'

'Since we last made love? Five or six years. Not long after she was diagnosed.'

'It's been a lot longer for me.'

'Really? You wouldn't think so.' He gave her a pained expression. 'Sorry, I didn't mean to imply... Oh God, I'm an asshole.'

She reached across for his hand. 'No you're not. And thank you. I'd forgotten that part of me. It's nice to know it still exists.'

He smiled and nodded. 'I guess we should put some clothes on.'

'Are you going?'

'No, not until daylight. I messaged Gareth to let him know I might sleep here tonight, so I won't be missed. I came back with him. I needed to get away from London for a few days. It's kinda stupid but this place is where I feel closest to Dilys.'

'It's not stupid at all.' She was the same with the allotment and Samuel.

'Also, I was hoping to run into you. Although not in that way, I should add.'

'Oh, why?'

'I don't know how to explain it but there's something about you. A kind of aura. I'm not a spiritual person at all, but you have this effect on me. Whenever I talk to you I feel peaceful. Like things will be okay. You're a beautiful person, Ursula. I don't mean the way you look, although you are a very beautiful woman. I'm talking about what's on the inside. You have real beauty inside of you. I'm sorry if that sounds corny, but it's true.'

It wasn't the first time she'd been told that. Anton had said the same thing years ago, back when she'd mistaken his stiffness for shyness. But Anton had wanted to keep that part of her to himself, giving nothing in return. Howard wasn't like that. 'I feel the same peace whenever I'm with you. I thought it was because you reminded me of the man I loved, but I was selling you short. You're a good man, Howard. That's why so many people care about you.'

The sound of the dawn chorus woke her although, in truth, she hadn't slept that much. She'd been trying to work out what Howard and Anton had meant when they'd said she had beauty inside of her. She'd seen it in other people like her mum, Solly, Samuel, and Howard but she preferred to call it goodness. Perhaps goodness was beauty in its purest form. But she'd never thought of herself as good. She was too selfish for that. Otherwise, why would she have coveted Priscilla's husband? Why would she have had sex with Howard when he was desperately grieving Dilys? And why did she stay with Anton rather than take a risk on life without him? No. There was no goodness in her, and no beauty either. It was all just superficial nonsense. An illusion to protect her from real feelings.

Howard was sleeping behind her. The bench wasn't wide enough for them to lie any way other than side by side, like two spoons. His arm was around her waist. Perhaps in his dreams he was lying with Dilys. The fire had gone out hours ago but the blankets and the heat of his body kept her warm. She heard a whistling noise through the cracks in the door and window. A bird of prey. A buzzard, she thought, if she'd remembered Andi's teachings correctly. She wondered if Anton was still up there on the hill, full of disgust at her depravity. Depravity, secrets and lies. Those had been his words when they'd had their first proper row. You'd have thought it would have been when she was younger, but back then she'd have done almost anything to avoid his displeasure. It had to wait until she was older and more hardened. And for something catastrophic to happen.

48

SOMETHING CATASTROPHIC – 2007

They were in the middle of a dinner party when Ursula's phone rang. She'd forgotten to turn it to silent again. Anton flashed her a look that told her she'd be hearing more about this after their guests had gone. For him it was the height of rudeness to have phones ringing at the dinner table when they were entertaining. She let it ring out. A minute later, it rang again. He gave her another look. Ursula turned away from him to one of the guests, a pompous man who was looking for someone to design a new office block. 'Excuse me, I'll just switch that off.'

She went over to the drawer where she kept the phone which was refusing to stop ringing. It was Solly. He never called, it was always her mum. She picked it up and shot past the dinner table before Anton had a chance to say anything.

'Ursula, I'm calling about Gillian.' Solly didn't sound like his usual self. Something was definitely wrong.

'What is it, what's happened?'

'She's had an accident. The car. She's...' He was sobbing now, unable to get the words out.

'She's what? Solly, tell me. She's what?'

'She's dead.'

Ursula opened her mouth but her brain wasn't connecting so nothing came out. The room suddenly became airless and bright. She was floating in a bright, airless space. Someone's arms were beneath her. They were Anton's. He was holding her up. She wasn't floating at all, she was fainting and he'd caught her before she hit the ground.

Andi was driving them to the hospital. Although how she managed to keep her mind on the road was anybody's guess. Anton would have been best to do it but he was over the limit and Ursula had refused to wait until morning.

The journey was a blur. The hospital was a blur. Everything was surrounded in a fog that was affecting Ursula's senses. Anton went to find someone to talk to about what had happened while she and Andi were led into the room where her mum's body lay. There were some cuts on her face but nothing that looked like it could have killed her. Solly and Cass were either side of the bed, weeping. Andi who had held it together all the way here was crying as well now. Ursula wanted to cry too, but she was coated in a hard shell that was refusing to crack.

Anton came in. She searched his face for reassurance that she wasn't some kind of degenerate who couldn't weep for her dead mother, but his attention was on her mum's lifeless body. Then his eyes met hers and she saw the compassion she'd been looking for. Love too. But it was all too brief, because now he was looking beyond her, at the woman whose tears for her oldest friend were limitless. Cass was beyond noticing Anton was in the room but the sight of her jolted him. He turned back to Ursula and the compassion was gone.

Solly got up and helped Ursula into his seat. She took her mum's hand. It wasn't frozen She'd expected it to be frozen. Perhaps they'd made a mistake. But no. She was kidding herself. Her mum was dead. She was gone forever.

There were so many people at the funeral that Ursula didn't know. Local people who'd befriended her mum and Solly in the five years they'd been living in Eastbourne. Old friends from Birmingham too, and all of Solly's family. Andi had clung to Pab throughout the ceremony, her heart so obviously broken by the loss. Cass was virtually catatonic and Ursula wasn't much better. Andi and Anton had gone home the day after their dash to the hospital, but she'd stayed with Solly, the two of them moving around the house like robots forcing themselves to get through to the next day.

For most of the reception, Pab and Anton were huddled in a corner like two plotting conspirators. Andi was trying to bring Cass out of herself with little success, and Ursula did the one thing she was good at. She talked to all the people she didn't know. Sometimes it was social chit chat and sometimes it was a story about her mum that she'd never heard. Funny stories, charming stories, and stories about a woman who'd spent her life defying the odds in small ways.

When most of the guests had gone, she found a quiet place in the garden to sit and breathe and think about how she was never going to see her mum again, never going to hear her laugh, or tell her to keep going with her small acts of defiance.

'Mind if I join you?'

She looked up and saw Solly standing over her. She moved along to make room for him. He sat down and wrapped his hand around hers. 'How are you doing, my lovely?'

She shrugged. 'Badly, I think. I can't seem to let the grief out. I can feel it here inside, but it won't come out. I bet they all think I'm a hard bitch. Not one tear.'

'Who cares what anyone else thinks? It's got nothing to do with them. We all deal with it in our own way.'

'Will you look after Cass? She needs someone.'

'Of course. Gillian would expect nothing else.'

'And yourself. You'll look after yourself, won't you?'

He put his arm around her and kissed her head. 'Don't you worry about me and Cass. We're a couple of old troopers. We'll get by. But you will come and see us, won't you? I know I'm not really your dad but you're as precious to me as any of my girls.'

'Yes I will. You're precious to me too, Solly. As far as dads go, you're the best.'

'Well I don't suppose I've got much competition there, have I? Listen, love, that grief will come out. Probably when you're least expecting it. It might be a while but it will. I guarantee it.'

Anton appeared at the kitchen window. Wherever they went, he found a window to watch her from. He'd be wanting to go back to Birmingham as soon as possible. She didn't want that. She wanted to stay here, amongst her mum's things, but she knew that wasn't going to help. She was in limbo, drifting between longing and reality. Anton would pull her back to reality whether she liked it or not. Samuel would too. But his way would be kinder.

Solly nodded at the window. 'He likes to be in control, doesn't he?'

'Yes, I suppose he does.'

'You know what Gillian would say? Keep resisting.'

'Small acts of defiance.'

'Exactly. Anytime it gets too much, I want you to remember this will always be your home. She used to say you were a fighter in your own quiet way, you know.' He squeezed her shoulders. 'One other thing Gill used to say was that it was about time you started liking yourself a bit more, Ursula. She was always telling me you don't love yourself enough.'

Anton had travelled to Eastbourne in the Volvo. She should have known it wouldn't have occurred to him that it reminded her of death. Then again, perhaps it had occurred to him. It was hard to tell with Anton. In all the time they'd been together, she'd never really understood him. Most likely, he'd never understood her either. They were two polar opposites who'd entered into a contract that had somehow become a business partnership rather than a loving marriage. But she had seen love in his eyes the night her mum died. She knew from that one look that he did still love her. It was a shame he was incapable of showing it. She detested that about him. And yet she knew she couldn't leave him. Not yet. Because she needed him now more than ever with his control and his structure. It was the only thing stopping her from finding some way to be with her mum again.

It had been a clear sunny day when they left Eastbourne but as soon as they got close to Birmingham, the grey skies appeared, as if the city had been waiting for her to darken its mood. They'd driven home hardly speaking, except for

Anton outlining his timetable for the week and the events he expected her to take part in. He couldn't even allow her a moment of grief before ramming his bloody schedules down her throat.

They passed through a rain shower that lifted by the time they reached the house. Its white exterior glistened in a sudden burst of sunshine. It always looked at its best in these conditions. He stood in front of it like an artist admiring his own painting. She unlocked the door, in no mood to join him, and went upstairs to get changed into her allotment clothes.

'You're going to the allotment?' He sounded quite astounded.

'Yes. It's been neglected for a few weeks.'

'Then another day won't matter.'

'I need something to do, Anton.'

'I have things for you to do here.'

'I don't want that right now. I need to be there.'

'To be with him, you mean.'

She took a sharp intake of breath. 'There is no him. I only have friends there. Nothing else.'

He shook his head, his eyes narrowing into small slits. 'Don't lie to me. You don't have the intellect for it. I know how you spend your nights there when I'm away. Yes, Ursula, I know all about you and Samuel Sweeting.'

'You're talking absolute rubbish, Anton. If you've had me watched, you'd know that.'

'If that's true it can only be because he doesn't want you. And who can blame him? You were beautiful once, but that was a long time ago. You've lost your unique selling point, my dear. Your beauty was the only thing that was interesting about you.'

The words sliced into her and, just as they always did, made her shrink. Maybe she was ugly, dull, and stupid. And maybe Samuel thought so too. Maybe she should just stop fooling herself and give in. But Samuel wasn't like that, and if she gave in now, she was going against everything her mum had wanted for her. She summoned up the courage to open the front door. 'There is nothing going on between Samuel and me. He's just a friend, like all the other friends I have there. I go there because I like being with them. Because they treat me with dignity and respect and not like some child who needs to be constantly monitored for bad behaviour.'

He pushed the door shut and grabbed her arm. 'Lies, all lies. You're full of them. Depravity, secrets, and lies.'

'Depravity? Will you just listen to yourself? I'm going out to see my friends, and if you can't handle that then tough.'

'Why didn't you tell me about Cassandra?'

'Because it was none of your business.' She opened the door again and this time, he didn't try to stop her.

She drove away, the sound of her heartbeat filling her ears. She might well be ugly, dull, and stupid but she was also a fighter. Hadn't her mum said so? Yes, she needed Anton right now, but she'd just realised it wasn't for the same reason she'd needed him before. It wasn't the lists, the structure, the control. It was the fight against all of that, the fight against him that would save her this time.

49

TOLERANCE LOST

Howard woke her with his movements. She must have gone back to sleep while she was thinking about the start of her resistance period. Another stage in her long and disastrous marriage that had been sparked off by that first row. Depravity, secrets and lies. The way he'd come out with it like some Victorian patriarch was as laughable then as it was now. Especially considering he wasn't above secrets and lies himself. She wasn't sure about the depravity though, unless you counted spying on your wife as depraved. It had taken ages for her to shake off the paranoia. Every time she saw a new face, she'd wonder if it belonged to a private detective.

More arguments followed after that fight. Only a few a year, but each one left another crack in their relationship that neither of them cared enough to repair. Once in a while, she'd bring up his affairs. He denied them. Told her she was a fantasist. But he carried on leaving the signs for her, as if he wanted her to know just how ugly, uninteresting and brainless he found her. She already knew that but Anton enjoyed hammering home the message.

Howard sat up and stretched his back and arms. 'Hell, I'm stiff.'

'Yes, it's not exactly the Hilton here, is it? Do you want some coffee? There's a bottle of water and some instant.'

He arched his back. 'Sounds great.'

She lit the camping stove and put the kettle on. 'How are you feeling?'

'Physically?'

She shook her head.

'Oh, the other stuff. I still feel like I did a bad thing but I think it's helped me. I'm hoping it's helped you too?'

'I think so. It's too soon to tell. But even if it doesn't, I'll remember it as a beautiful moment when two lost souls gave each other hope.'

He smiled. 'I like that. Mind if I adopt it?'

'Take it. I give it to you as my gift.'

'Do you wanna talk about what happened to bring you here last night?'

'I had some upsetting news from home. Something's changing that means a lot to me. Then Esme did an awful thing to hurt me and I suppose I just flipped and ran. And you? Was it really to get away from London or to see me?'

'Yes and no. I came back to do a terrible thing.'

'To join Dilys?'

Howard sighed. 'Yes. Another selfish act on my part. It would have destroyed our kids. I realised that while I was up on the hill, so I went to Am-nawr to find you. I thought if there was one person who could make me see the point of going on, it was you. You weren't there and I couldn't face anyone else, so I came here.'

Ursula poured boiled water into the mugs and gave him one. 'I could tell you Dilys would have wanted you to go on, or that your kids and your niece obviously love you very much. But you already know that. And anyway, that's what those other people want. And, dear as they are to you, the point of going on has to come from inside of you. For me, the point has always been resistance. There have been times in my life when I've wanted to give in. Days when I've wanted to be closer to the people I've lost than to the ones I'm with. But then someone at my allotment will stop by to say hello, an old friend will do a kind thing to heal me, or a good man will stand in the dark and point out the planets for my benefit, and I'll know I must resist those thoughts at all cost. Because there are still people in this world that bring me joy and love, and the people I've lost haven't really left me. If you stop and wait and listen occasionally, you'll feel them with you.'

Howard smiled. 'I think you may have oversold me there. I pointed out the planets for my benefit. It made me happy to share it with you.'

'And that is exactly my point.' She bumped her shoulder against his. 'Anyway, who said that was you? You think you're the only man I've stargazed with?'

He laughed. 'Oh, that was a killer blow. Just when I was starting to feel a little better about myself.'

She stretched out her hand. 'This is the hand of a friend, Howard. It will always be there for you, no matter what happens. But for now, you need to go and see Gareth. There's no phone signal here. He'll be worried about you.'

'You're right. And you, what will you do?'

'I need to go back down the hill. I have some cleaning up to do.'

. . .

Her phone pinged when she reached the vegetable garden. It was a message from Andi saying they'd set out early and should be back by eleven which meant she had a couple of hours to sort out the sewing room and decide how she was going to explain what had happened to the dress.

Charlie Big Potatoes was on the back step. As soon as he saw her, he made a beeline for her legs. She picked him up and let him push his nose against hers. She could have added the joy of a four-legged friend to the list of reasons for resistance, but that was a very recent addition. In the kitchen, she filled a bowl with cat food and put it down. The smaller cats appeared, their thin squeaky calls a sharp contrast to those of Mr Big Potatoes. Ursula fed them too and the only cat noises she could hear then were a chorus of steady purrs.

There was a note on the table:

'Ursula. Esteban's with me. Will be back around twelve.
Brett.'

Unusual that he was coming back at that time. It occurred to her that it might have something to do with the goings on upstairs. She had, after all, left the sewing room door wide open when she'd fled yesterday.

The sewing room door was closed. Ursula held her breath and pushed it open. The smell had changed. Disinfectant laced with a more muted hint of that strange, earthy scent. Someone had been cleaning up, and they'd removed the dress. She flung the window open, then went down to the kitchen and came back armed with a bowl of hot soapy water and an assortment of cleaning products. She scrubbed the table and floor, and every surface was sanitised but there was still a faint lingering odour. Unless it was coming from her.

It wasn't until she'd taken a long shower that she felt properly clean. She dried her hair and put fresh clothes on, and was just thinking about what to tell Andi when she heard Don's car pull up outside.

Andi was in the hall before Ursula got there. They met at the foot of the stairs and Andi greeted her with a firm hug. 'I'm so sorry. Where is she?'

So she knew then. There was no need to worry about an explanation. Ursula pulled away. 'I don't know. I haven't seen her since yesterday afternoon.'

Don brought the bags in and seconds later, Megan came crashing through the door. 'Nasty, filthy little cow. I told you she wasn't right in the head, Andi. Didn't I tell you?'

Andi nodded. 'Megan, would you mind putting the kettle on? I'm desperate for a cuppa.'

Don grabbed Megan's arm. 'Good idea. I'll give you a hand, Megan.'

And then Ursula was alone with Andi. 'It's okay.'

'No, Urs, it isn't.'

'I shouldn't have left the key for her to find.'

Andi frowned. 'Stop it. This is not your fault. I'm going to take a look.'

Ursula trailed behind her. 'I think Brett got rid of the dress and cleaned up. I've had another go at it this morning.'

They stopped outside the sewing room. Ursula unlocked the door and gave Andi the key. Andi stepped in and went straight to the cupboard that held her museum pieces. Satisfied they hadn't been defiled, she walked around the room, checking every nook, cranny and surface. 'I've never seen it so shiny. I don't think it was this clean when Pab first built it for me.'

'I wanted to make sure there were no traces. There might still be a whiff of it'.

Andi sniffed the air. 'I'll get a diffuser. Can you check she's not hiding in her room?'

Ursula went along the landing and gave Esme's door a quick tap before going in. The curtains were closed and it was in darkness but as far as she could tell, Esme wasn't here. She switched the light on. No, Esme definitely wasn't here. The room itself was a mess. Dirty plates and cups were scattered about the floor and a heap of clothes had been piled onto a chair. She spotted a framed photo of Esme and an older woman on the chest of drawers. Her mother, possibly. There were other photos, mostly old ones like the ones in the library. Pablo was in them all.

'She's not here then?' Andi was in the doorway, eyeing the photos. 'She must have pinched them from downstairs. I thought there were some missing.' She took her phone from the bag that was still slung across her body, stabbed at it a couple of times and put it to her ear. The sound of ringing stopped. Andi pressed again and the ringing restarted. It stopped again, even more quickly.

Ursula went over to the window and opened the curtains. This room was in the back of the house like hers. She could see the hill and Anton.

Andi called Esme again. This time it was answered. 'Where are you? You've got half an hour to get your disgusting little arse back here. Otherwise, I'm going to take everything you own into the garden and set fire to it.' Andi's voice was clipped and sharp. You could sense the quiet fury coming off her. She was a woman who'd reached the end of her tolerance. Ursula knew how that felt. She'd been there herself. Only once, but once was enough.

50

EVEN AT THE END – 2017

'The list–'

'Yes, Anton, I know. The list is on your desk.' Ursula cocked her head to one side and grinned. They were having a rare good week. Probably because there was a big business event coming up and he wanted her to give her best performance as the dutiful, loving wife.

He treated her to a pained smile. Anyone who didn't know him as well as she did might have assumed he was constipated, but this was what passed for reasonably happy in Anton's world. 'I'll be back by two o'clock.'

'Will you want lunch?'

'No. The client is insisting on brunch.' He raised his eyebrows to show his disapproval. Anton wasn't a fan of brunch. It interfered with his daily structure.

'How terrible for you. You have my utmost sympathy.'

He grimaced and laughed at her joke. Moments like this were rare and Ursula chose not to spoil it by telling him she was going to the allotment later.

As soon as he drove off she went straight up to the office,

in a hurry to finish the list and get away. Samuel and Clyde were planning the allotments' summer show and she'd promised to give them a hand.

Naturally the first task on the list was dusting that bloody model, his doll's house, his miniature prison. She took it apart as methodically as she always did and applied gentle strokes of the brush. It was yellowing a little, she thought. 'Showing your age, old chap. I wonder which of us will cave in first.'

Next, she tackled the stack of invoices he'd left out for her to record and file. For a minimalist devotee, Anton was surprisingly keen on paper records. Ursula's job was to enter the details into a separate spreadsheet and file them in his specially made cabinets. This she did meticulously because she knew he'd check to make sure she'd done it properly. Ursula suspected his secretary did exactly the same job with exactly the same invoices in his office in New Street. He probably checked those as well. Although he probably had more faith in the secretary.

Number three on the list was to go through his inbox and move into a folder any new invoices that needed his approval before being sent out. Yet another boring and pointless job he'd invented to keep her home. Ursula clicked on the email icon but, instead of opening the general inbox, a message popped up asking whether he really wanted to delete a mail. It was unusual for him to leave a job half done like that. She closed the window, leaving the mail undeleted, and made a note to remind him to look at it when he got back.

She was about to click close on the email when she noticed the title: *'Let's do brunch.'* It must have been from the client he was meeting, although it sounded too informal for that. Especially as there was a smiley face after the words, like the sender knew him well enough to tease him about his dislike of brunch. Maybe it was from the latest lover. She'd never given his other women much thought before now, but they hadn't invaded her home before. And yes, this was only an email and it wasn't technically in her home, but it was close enough to make Ursula read it.

'Hi Anton,

Sorry I had to cancel Friday. Mum had another relapse and Dad wanted us all to be there for her. She's recovered now but I think the sooner we get this project concluded the better. Dad's really keen to get her into the new house as quickly as possible. I know it's asking a lot of you to prioritise us, but you're the only one he trusts to design something he'll like. You know how exacting he can be.

Can you do 11.00 tomorrow at the usual place? Bring the plans.

We really enjoyed seeing you both last month, by the way. You must come again. For a weekend next time.

Susannah'

Whoever this Susannah was, she probably wasn't his lover. But they had a usual place, so more like a friend who happens to be a client. Ursula read it again and stopped at the same sentence that had pulled her up the first time: 'We really enjoyed seeing you both last month.' There'd been a conference in London last month, or so he'd led her to believe. It sounded like he'd spent part of it with this Susannah and at least two others. The lover would be one of them. It must be serious if he was introducing her to clients and friends. Ursula looked for more clues, caught the sender's full name, and saw all she needed to know. Susannah Fry-Weatherall. Anton was building another house for Bernard Fry, but this was more than business. He was friends with them. She remembered Cass's nervousness about Anton knowing she was back. It was no wonder.

Ursula printed off two copies of the email. Anton would only delete it when he got home and make out she'd imagined it. She put one copy in the glove compartment of her car ready to take to her allotment shed, the one place she could hide anything from him.

Back in his office, she looked at the list. Another twelve jobs before she reached the end of it. She took a pen, a red one, and scored lines from the left top corner to the bottom right and did the same the other way. Then she turned it over and wrote on the back of it. Something for him to find after he came up here to lick his wounds. Something that made quite it clear what she wished for him. She looked around the room, looked at the lighter patch on the floor where she'd once left traces of her baby, and promised herself this was the last time she would do Anton's bidding. Then she went downstairs to wait.

A little before two, the Volvo came into the drive. Ursula sat at the table, stiff and upright, while Anton drove it into the garage, closed the door and came into the house. He frowned slightly at the sight of her sitting there, watching him for once. She pushed the email across the table. 'You forgot to delete this.'

He scanned it and said nothing, but if you knew him as well as she did, it was just possible to spot the signals of disquiet. The blinking for one thing, and the tiny beads of sweat on his forehead for another.

'You also forgot to mention you were designing another

house for Bernard Fry. Or that you were friends with him and this woman, who I assume is my half-sister.'

'It's just business.'

'It's never just business when it comes to that family, and well you know, Anton.'

'You're being ridiculous. I can't turn business down just because you have a problem with your father. Besides, it shouldn't really matter now that Gillian is dead. He is willing to bury the hatchet. I don't see why you can't do the same.' He'd found his voice and what a spiteful, bitter voice it was. What a ruthless, self-serving, conscienceless man she was married to.

'The trouble with you, Anton, is that you're entirely devoid of empathy. You're cold and empty. You always have been, and I have no idea why I've been prepared to live with it for so long. The truth is I despise you, and ordinarily I have no interest in what you do or who you do it with. But you've crossed a line. If it was your intention to drive me away, then you've succeeded.'

'Now you are being melodramatic. Sit down and let us talk this through.'

'No. I'm going out now to see my friends, and to make arrangements.'

'What arrangements?'

'To leave you.'

She went for the door but Anton got there first, blocking her way. 'Don't be a fool. You can't exist without me. You can't even dress without me telling you what to wear.'

She jolted to a sudden halt, knowing there was some truth in his outburst, and she almost gave in. But then he came towards her with an expression that said he'd won, yet again. He'd seen the doubt in her and was moving in to take advantage.

'I won't allow it.' His voice was softer now, the sort you used to placate an empty-headed pet.

How dare he assume she was nothing without him? And how dare he assume she was his to control. A violent fury rose in her and without realising what she was doing, she ran at him and pushed him. He fell away much more easily than she'd expected and landed on his backside.

Ursula stepped over him and walked outside. The whole of her body was shaking and she had to hold onto the car while she let the air in and out of her lungs. Each breath came out with a laugh. She was free. She could hardly believe how easy it had been. Habit made her look up to the office window. He was there already. Watching. Always watching. Even at the end.

She was greeted at the allotment by Clyde, eager for her to meet his new friend, a gangly mass of long black fur called Colonel. 'My daughter got him for the kids but the fool girl didn't think about the effort you have to put in with a dog, so he's come to live with me until she works out what to do with him.'

Samuel came sauntering along the path towards them. Clyde pushed back his hat in acknowledgement. 'I'm introducing me new lodger to Ursula.'

Ursula tickled Colonel behind the ears, amazed at how calm she felt after what had just happened. 'He's very sweet.'

Samuel scratched his head. 'Him still a youth. When him full grown, he'll be a giant.'

Clyde nodded in agreement. 'I told that girl she was crazy

to get him, but she wouldn't listen. I'll be back in ten minutes. Come on, Colonel.'

'I'll get the kettle on and find a biscuit for Colonel,' Ursula called after him. Clyde did a thumbs up as he strolled away, the dog trotting along with him. It was nice to see him smiling again. He hadn't been doing that much lately. 'Did his daughter really get Colonel for herself?'

'That's what she told Clyde. I have my doubts but it don't matter. Him needed someone to care for since Carmen passed.' Samuel put his hand on her shoulder. 'You look different today, Ursula.'

'I'm leaving Anton. I might have to go away for a while to sort myself out.'

'You must do what you have to do. We'll be here when you get back. Me and Clyde. And Colonel. That dog's going nowhere.'

She was in no rush to get home and knowing she'd be away for a while, Ursula stayed until late at the allotment, watching the sunset with Samuel. Earlier, she'd called Solly to ask if she could stay with him and Cass. They were living together now. Not as man and wife, but as two old friends looking out for each other. So it was all arranged. Tomorrow morning, she'd pack her things and go.

The house was in darkness when she pulled in but she could see Anton's outline in the office window. She wondered whether he'd been there all afternoon and evening waiting for her. Unlikely. He probably heard her car pull into the drive.

When she got inside, she turned on the lights and

listened. It was eerily quiet, even by this house's standards. She went upstairs to make up the bed in the spare room.

The door to his office was half open. He was in there in the darkness, sulking. Ursula walked past it to the linen cupboard and took out the spare bedding. On her way back, the duvet pushed against the door and knocked it further open. It caught on something and came to a stop. 'Anton?' Her voice cut through the silence. She tightened her grip on the bundle in her arms and peered into the darkness. 'Anton?' She switched the light on, looked behind the door and dropped the bedding. It was him, curled up on the floor like a foetus. She touched his wrist to find a pulse, but she already knew there was none to find. Ursula could tell by his eyes, wide open and vacant. Anton was dead.

51

PABLO THE LIAR

Ursula shuddered. It was her fault. Anton was dead and it was all her fault.

Andi was standing next to her. 'Urs, what's the matter?'

'Nothing. Is Esme nearby?'

'There's a bunch of skanky individuals she hangs out with in town. She's with them. Did she do anything to hurt you?' Andi was scrutinising her now, trying to work out why she was so spooked.

Ursula shook her head. Some things you had to keep to yourself. 'No, nothing like that. I think she'd already gone out when I found it. It shook me up, that's all. I should have stayed and dealt with it but I ran away.'

'Understandable. Brett and Gareth sorted it. Where did you stay last night?'

'The bothy.'

Andi nodded. 'Shall we go and get that tea before the big showdown?'

Don and Megan were huddled over the kitchen table in quiet discussion. They stopped when Andi and Ursula walked in. Andi took her bag off and dropped it on the table. 'It's not too bad. The boys and Ursula have done a good job of cleaning it.'

Don jumped up. 'I'll get you that tea. And toast. How about a round of toast?' He hovered, waiting for an answer. None came. 'I'll make some. I don't know about you lot but I'm hungry.'

Megan leaned across the table towards Andi. 'What are you going to do about her?'

Andi's phone alerted her to a message. She glanced at it. 'Something I should have done months ago.'

The plate of toast lay largely untouched, except for a few slices that Don had eaten. Only his self-conscious nibbling and the gulps of hot tea sliding down their throats broke the silence. The kitchen door opened. Esme was here, her face like a thunderous cloud. 'You better not have touched any of my stuff.'

Andi got up, her breathing long and slow. 'You violated my private space and you violated my friend. You're lucky I didn't put a match to it straight away.'

Esme snorted. 'It was a joke, that's all. Anyway, she was horrible to me so she deserved it.'

Andi crossed the kitchen and stood in front of her. 'You're not welcome here anymore. Go and pack up your things.'

Esme twisted her head this way and that. 'I'm not going anywhere. You can't make me.'

Megan stood up and folded her arms. 'I'll tell you what, Esme, I'll do it. You got some bin liners, Don? I reckon it'd take me ten minutes, tops.'

Don took a roll of bin bags out from a drawer. 'It will if I help.'

'Don't you dare touch anything.' Esme tried to push Andi

out of the way but Andi refused to budge. All the same, she looked small and unprotected next to the young and spiteful woman and Ursula ran to her side. Don and Megan did the same.

Esme looked at them all, one by one. 'You lot make me sick.'

'Just go and pack before I do something you're gonna regret,' said Andi.

Esme turned back to Ursula. 'This is all your fault, Miss Perfect. Not so perfect now though, are you? Did she tell you she was screwing Howard last night, Megan? No? Thought not.'

'Shut it, you lying little bitch.' Megan's fingers were twitching, as if they really wanted to do some damage to Esme.

'It's true, I saw them. Disgusting it was. I'm amazed they waited for Dilys to die. Probably been at it ever since she got here.' She looked as if she was really enjoying herself now. She was so like Pablo, it was uncanny.

'Enough!' Andi thrust her hand in front of Esme's face. 'You're lucky I haven't called the police to report you for malicious damage. Now get your crap together. Your ride's on its way.'

'What ride?'

'The one you've been waiting for. Your father's coming to collect you.'

'Pab? He's come all the way from Spain for me?' A smile spread across Esme's face. All of a sudden she was a child who'd just been given everything she wanted. Her dad was coming for her. Ursula understood that feeling. She might have wanted it once herself. Not when she was Esme's age though. But the smile had given Esme away and allowed

Ursula to see what Andi had known all along. All of this vindictiveness was about one thing, or rather one person. Pablo.

'No,' said Andi. 'Crouch End. He's never been to Spain. Not even for a package holiday.'

Esme's smile slipped. 'But he told me–'

'He lied. That's what he does, Esme. He's a big, fat, fucking liar. Get used to it.' Andi moved out of Esme's way. The others shuffled back with her. 'The clock's ticking and he won't be staying, so you'd better get a move on.'

Esme slid past them and snatched the bin liners out of Don's hand. Andi followed her out. Don tutted. 'I'll go and keep an eye.'

'Good idea, Don. I wouldn't trust her not to lay one on Andi.' Megan scanned the dirty pots and dishes that Brett and Gareth had left from last night. 'We'll clear up down here.'

'Right. I'll go up then, shall I?' He shook his head. 'It's some business, this.'

'It is,' said Ursula. She picked up the plate of cold toast and emptied it into the bin. So Pablo was on his way? She hadn't seen him since Anton's funeral, and before that not since just after her mum died when they'd moved here under another cloud that Andi had never fully explained.

Megan filled the sink and started to wash up. Ursula picked up a tea towel and waited, not for clean crockery but for the inevitable question that she was obviously building herself up to ask.

'Is it true?' she said, eventually.

Ursula picked up a cup and started to dry it, trying to work out what to say. It was, after all, no one's business but hers and Howard's.

'I think you've just answered my question.' Megan looked at her and Ursula saw she was on the brink of tears.

'You should talk to Howard.'

'I'm talking to you.'

Before they could say any more, the door to the boot room opened and Brett and Gareth burst in with Esteban at their heels. 'Sorry we're a bit late. The job took longer than I thought it would,' said Brett. 'You all right, Ursula?'

'I'm fine. Thank you for clearing things up last night. It must have been horrible for you to find it.'

Brett shrugged. 'Actually, Gareth did it.'

Gareth grinned at her. 'Don't worry about it. I've spent most of my life farming. A bit of goat shit doesn't bother me, does it, Mam? So what's happening then?'

Megan cleared her throat. 'The great leader's coming to take her away. He's been in Crouch End, apparently. Not Spain. Another fantasy. Andi and Don are upstairs supervising the packing. Brett, love, will you go and help. That Esme's a vicious cow and if she starts, I don't fancy either Andi or Don's chances. Neither of them are exactly spring chickens, are they?'

Gareth frowned. 'You all right, Mam?'

Megan wiped her damp hands on her trouser legs. 'Stop fretting, Gareth. It's not all about me, is it? Have you seen Howard?'

'Not seen him as such, but we've had a call. He seems all right. A bit brighter.'

'Does he?' Megan eyes shot to Ursula, then back to Gareth. 'I'm gonna head home. You stay here and look after Andi.'

Gareth watched her go then plunged his hands into the

water and carried on with the washing up. 'Mam seems upset.'

'Esme said something.'

'Ah right. Well if there's one thing you can rely on Esme for it's to say something that's gonna set your world on fire. Was it about me?'

'No, nothing like that.'

'About Howard then? Was it about last night?'

Ursula swivelled round to face him.

Gareth gave her a little smile. 'We guessed you were in the bothy and thought you probably wanted to be left in peace. When Esme came in mouthing off about what she'd seen, we told her what we'd found and then we told her to piss off back to her seedy mates. Don't worry about Mam. She'll get over it. She just needs a bit of time to process things. It's how she deals with stuff. For what it's worth, I don't think there was anything wrong with you and Howard comforting each other. You gotta do what you gotta do, haven't you?'

Esme was kicking off about something upstairs. Gareth went to investigate and lend some weight in case things got nasty while Ursula put the clean dishes away. Four supervisors was a bit over the top. Esme was only one person, but it wasn't only about physically protecting Andi. It was about standing together. Safety in numbers. Maybe she should go up there too because Pab was on his way and safety in numbers sounded very appealing right now. But then she heard the outside door open in the boot room and felt the shift in the atmosphere just as easily as she felt a change in the wind, or the rain coming. It was too late. Footsteps on the tiled floor made their way towards the kitchen and there he was. Pablo the liar. Pablo the cheat. Pablo the thief. Pablo the would-be rapist.

52

THE TASTE OF HIM – 2017

According to the doctor, a massive heart attack had killed Anton not long after Ursula had left him that afternoon. She told the doctor it was impossible because she'd seen him at the window when she came back, but apparently she'd been mistaken. At first, she let herself believe the doctor was right and it had been a trick of the light, or rather the lack of it. But she'd seen him there again. In fact, she saw him at the window every time she left the house. Earlier, he'd watched her get into the funeral car with Solly and Cass. He'd even watched his physical self being driven away in the hearse. Ursula had thought about asking Solly and Cass if they saw him too, but she was afraid they'd think she'd lost her mind. Besides, she knew the answer would be no. She was the only one he was haunting.

Bernard Fry and his daughters were at the funeral. His hair was white now but otherwise he looked well enough. The wife wasn't with him. Perhaps she was too frail. Ursula took selfish comfort from knowing he might soon be losing the woman he'd cast her and her mum aside for. She hoped he was feeling the pain of it and that he was living each day in fear of it. It was cruel of her, but she could be cruel too. She'd only lately realised that.

With the service finished, people came over to offer their sympathies. She accepted their condolences, listened to them heaping praise on Anton, and thanked them for coming. She was playing her role to the end. She owed him that much. But always in the back of her mind was the thought that it was the last time she'd have to do this. Freedom had come at last. Just not in the way she'd expected it. And it had come at a price.

The Fry family were talking to a woman who looked a bit like Cass when she'd been younger. A relative? Anton's last lover? She could even be both. Ursula's stomach clenched when she realised Fry and his daughters were coming towards her. She sent an icy stare their way and slowly moved her head from side to side. One of the daughters picked up on it and turned them around.

'Thank God for that,' Cass whispered into her ear.

Ursula looped her arm through Cass's. 'Do you know who that woman is they were talking to?'

'Afraid not. Why?'

'It's not important. I just need to speak to some friends, then we can go.'

She found Samuel, Clyde, Marcie and Gordon in a huddle away from the other mourners. They were here for her, not Anton. 'Thank you so much for being here. I really appreciate it. Will you come back to the house? If you can spare the time.'

'Ursula, love, we're all retired. Spare time's the one thing we've got lots of. Of course we'll come,' said Marcie.

There were fewer people at the reception than the funeral

but still enough to fill the downstairs. Thankfully, the Frys were among those who'd decided not to come. Anton hadn't been at the window when the car brought them back. Just as well, he'd have hated all these people polluting his passion project with their dirty feet and loud noise.

Andi was in the dining area, making sure plates were piled high and glasses were topped up. She'd come straight from Wales that morning and they'd hardly had time to speak. She saw Ursula and pulled her in for a hug. 'How you doing, mate?'

'I'm okay. Where's the rest of the family?'

'The kids are in the garden, I think. Not sure about Pab. Probably talking to an investment banker about some get-rich-quick scheme. Sorry. I can call him off if it's embarrassing.'

'Don't worry about it. I don't think I'll ever see these people again after today anyway. I'd better go and mingle.'

Samuel was on the stairs, probably looking for the bathroom. She excused herself from talking to Anton's partners and followed him up. The main bathroom door was shut so she guessed he'd found it. She went to go back down but then she noticed the door to Anton's office was ajar. It had been closed since the night they'd taken his body away. Ursula pushed it further open, expecting to see him frozen in time at the window. Someone was in there, but it wasn't Anton.

Pablo had his back to the door and didn't hear her going in. If he had, he probably wouldn't have pocketed something from Anton's desk.

'Put that back,' she said, sounding calmer and braver than she actually was.

He swung around, a smarmy grin on his face. 'Put what back?'

'Whatever it was you took. I imagine it was Anton's watch, as it's the most valuable thing in here.'

He put his hands up. 'Don't know what you're talking about, babe.'

'Look, Pab, I don't want to make a scene but I will if I have to. Put the watch back.'

'Only joking, Urs. Here. Take it.' He held his jacket out for her to dip into the pocket. He was toying with her again. Intimidating her. It would have been easiest to run away and forget the watch but it had meant something to Anton. He'd kept it for years, and she couldn't allow Pablo to steal it as if it were no more than something to be pawned for pocket money. She reached for his jacket.

He grabbed her wrist. She tried to pull away but he held on, so she let her arm go limp and forced a smile. 'Stop being so silly, Pab.'

'Stop being so silly, Pab,' he said in a ridiculous, high-pitched voice. 'You know, Urs, sometimes you sound like an old school ma'am.'

He was too close again. His breath smelled of whisky and cheese. She felt her stomach churn. 'I'd like you to go.'

'And what else would you like?'

'Just go.'

'Spoilsport.' He lunged and almost fell onto her. The weight of him sent her flying backwards and suddenly she was being pressed against the wall. He rubbed himself against her, his erection pressing into her groin.

Ursula wanted to scream but his mouth was on hers, his tongue pushing between her teeth, the vile taste of him invading her. She pushed and wriggled and squirmed to get free but he had her pinned down. She was trapped. Then, out of nowhere, a hand grabbed Pablo and jerked him backwards and before he could fight back, a fist smashed into his face, sending him flying across the room. It was Samuel. He'd saved her.

Pablo was rolling around on the floor, nursing a bloodied face. Samuel stood over him, ready to throw another punch. 'You want to call the police, Ursula?'

Yes she did, but she knew it would break Andi's heart. If she believed her, that is. Andi had a massive blind spot when it came to Pablo. Either way, it would spell the end of their friendship and Ursula couldn't bear that. 'No. Not this time. But if he ever tries it again, I will.'

Samuel took a step away from Pablo. 'You gonna get up now, mister, and you gonna leave this house. And if you ever go near this good lady again, you will have more than this old fella coming after you. Yer get me?'

Pablo scrambled up and inched past him out onto the landing. 'Anton was right about you two all along then.'

Samuel went for him but Pab was too quick. He shot down the stairs, pushed through the crowd, and was straight out the door. He was gone but the foul taste of him was still there on Ursula's tongue.

53

A WAY THROUGH THE MESS

Pablo was wearing Anton's watch. He never did give it back. But then Ursula hadn't seen him since he took it. She wondered what he'd said to Andi about it, because the inscription on the back made it obvious who it belonged to: *'To Anton with love, Ursula.'* It had been a birthday present, back when she still believed they loved each other. She knew how he'd explained his running away to Andi because Andi had in turn explained it to her. It had all got too much for him, the loss of his great friend, Anton. He'd just had to get away. So much so, he didn't turn up until a week later. According to Andi, it was the first time he'd disappeared like that. It wasn't the last. She never mentioned the watch and neither did Ursula, even though they could both see how the gift of it might look.

'Made it here at last then, Ursula? Thought you'd never come.' Pablo held his arms out as if he was calling her to him.

Ursula stayed where she was, the full width of the kitchen safely between them. 'I see you still have the watch you stole.'

He looked at it as if he'd only just realised it was there. 'Stole? You're misremembering, Urs. You gave it to me after the funeral. I didn't want to take it but you insisted. As a token of Anton's affection for me, I think you said. I hear you've been upsetting, Esme.'

'Your secret daughter.'

'Not that secret.'

'She's a nasty little bully. Quite a chip off the old block.'

He made a show of wincing. 'You haven't changed. Still need the right man to loosen you up. I'd love to oblige but you've passed the best-before date, old girl.'

'I can't tell you how relieved I am that you won't be trying to rape me again.' She was trying to decide the fastest way to get to the safety of the others but he was already striding across the room and even though she was telling herself to run, her legs weren't listening.

'That's quite an accusation, Ursula. You wanna watch what you're saying.' He was almost on top of her now. Her legs finally woke up and she stepped back, realising too late that she was pressed against the worktop. He leaned in and even though she knew it wasn't there, she caught the smell of whisky and cheese on his breath. All the times he'd been too close and too threatening flashed before her eyes and stopped at that last time. The one moment he'd been building up to, until Samuel spoiled it for him. But Samuel wasn't here anymore, and Pablo was coming closer, puckering his lips up for a kiss. This time she'd have to save herself. She filled her mouth and spat in his face. It was enough to make him jump back and give her the space to dart around him. But she wasn't quick enough and he seized hold of her.

'Get your hands off her.' Andi was standing in the doorway.

Pablo let go of her. He rolled his eyes at Andi. 'Sorry, babe, I just lost it. Fatherly instincts cut in. You shouldn't have said those nasty things about Esme, Ursula. She can't help the way she is.'

Andi's face was a blank. 'Esme's waiting for you by the front door. We'll help you carry her stuff out. Then the pair of you can fuck off.'

'Charming. Don't I even get a cup of tea?'

'No you fucking don't. They're waiting for you.'

Don and the boys were in the hall with Esme. The reception they gave Pab was frosty and judging by his face, not what he'd been expecting. The only one pleased to see him was Esme who threw herself at him, conveniently forgetting that he'd lied to her about being in Spain.

They threw Esme's things into Pab's car. Esme got in without saying a word but she was still grinning from ear to ear. She'd got what she'd wished for. Pab had come to take her away. Ursula wondered how long it would be before she realised what a hollow wish it was.

Pab was trying to regain his position as a top bloke. He tried to talk to Brett about his grandad but Brett closed him down with no more than a few grunts and nods. Even Esteban moved away when he tried to pat him.

Andi took hold of Esteban's collar and pulled him to her. 'Time for you to go.'

'See you soon, babe.' Pab gave her a smile that Ursula had seen so many times before. In the past she'd watched Andi melt under it, but that didn't look like it was going to happen today.

Andi returned it with a hard stare. 'Let's hope not.'

Pab shook his head and held his hand out to Don. 'Look after her, mate. She's precious.'

Don pushed his hands in his pockets so that Pab's hand was left mid-air. 'We'll all look after her. That's what people who care for you do, you see. They don't do the dirty on you and leave you broken-hearted and broke. But you wouldn't know that, would you, Pab? Because there's only one person you care about.'

Pab put his palms up in front of him. 'Whoa, steady on there, cowboy.'

Don put his arm around Andi. 'I think you'd better leave, don't you?'

Pab made a sound that came out like a puff of amused air. Nobody said another word to him as he got in the car. He switched on the engine and loud music blasted out all the way down to the road. And then the sight and sound of him was gone.

Ursula looked at Andi, trying to work out what she was thinking about the scene in the kitchen, but Andi had her eye on Don. Don slipped his arm off her shoulder. 'Sorry about that. I got a bit carried away.'

Andi was still looking at him, frowning. 'How did you know I was broke?'

Don shoved his hands back in his pockets. 'Doesn't take a genius. It'll be all right, Andi. We'll work it out.'

She gave him a peck on the cheek and went inside, unaware he'd just turned a bright shade of red. They followed her in and all stood in the hall as if uncertain what to do next. Andi made the first move. 'I'm going for a lie down.'

'Yeah, I'd better go and check on Mam and Howard,' said Gareth.

'I'll make some lunch,' said Don. 'Want to give me a hand, Ursula?'

. . .

Don sounded the gong. They waited a while but Andi didn't come down. 'She's probably sleeping. I'll put some by for her,' he said. He was a good friend to her. They all were. Except for Ursula, because she was starting to doubt her own credentials in that regard. She couldn't stop thinking about the way Andi had looked at her and Pab earlier. She'd given them that look before and a few hours later, she'd asked Ursula if she was in love with him. Ursula had kept the truth a secret to protect Andi but lately, she'd been wondering if the only person she'd been protecting was herself.

Lunch was over and Andi was still in her room. Don gave up waiting for her and announced he was going into town to get some groceries. Brett still had a couple of hours work to do so he went with him.

Ursula fed the lunch scraps to Esteban and started clearing up. So much had happened today that her being with Howard seemed like weeks ago. And yet it was only this morning that she'd walked back from the bothy feeling something other than guilt, regret, and fear. Yes, fear. She could see it now. She'd been paralysed by it, and all because she'd been afraid of losing the few people left who she truly loved.

But then Andi had called and asked if Pab was with her and that fear had made her walk away from her nice safe routines and places. She'd had to come because as much as she tried to hide from it, she knew what that question meant. Andi believed she'd taken Pab from her. She was going to lose her oldest and dearest friend, the greatest and worst of all her fears. And that was why Ursula was here in Am-nawr. Not to save Andi, but to save herself.

Andi came into the kitchen looking red-eyed and worn out. Ursula doubted she'd slept a wink. 'Where is everybody?'

'Don's gone to get groceries and Brett's gone back to work. He's left some lunch out for you.'

'I'm not hungry. Fancy a walk up the hill? I'm ready to talk now.' And there it was. The look that spelled the end of their friendship. Ursula had always believed Pab would be the one to break their bond at some point in the future, but she'd realised something today. That bond had been at breaking point for a long time. She'd just been postponing the inevitable.

Esteban ran back and forth ahead of them as they left the garden and climbed up the hill, past the bothy. 'Tell me about you and Pab,' said Andi.

'There is no me and Pab. There never has been. I don't even like him.' She was being honest at last. There was nothing to lose now that she was sure their friendship was over.

'The watch?'

'He stole it on the day of Anton's funeral.'

Andi stopped walking and looked straight at Ursula. 'Is that when he tried to rape you?'

She had heard then. 'Yes. It was in Anton's office. I can't say for sure if he'd have gone through with it. My friend, Samuel, stopped him before it went that far.'

'When he came back a week later, he had a scab on his face, like a cut, and there was still some bruising. Was that Samuel?'

Ursula nodded.

'There's more isn't there? Urs, I need to know everything.'

.   .   .

They were sitting in Gareth's shelter at the top of the hill. Esteban lay just outside of it, keeping a steady watch on Andi, waiting for signs to jump up and lick away her tears again. But Andi looked like she was done with crying. 'You should have told me.'

'I didn't think you'd believe me. You were so in love with him.'

'You should still have told me.'

'Yes. I should, but I was scared.'

'Of him?'

'Yes. And scared of losing you.'

Andi looked Ursula up and down and she was suddenly reminded of Priscilla Sweeting that time she came to get the measure of her. 'We'd have found a way back, Urs. We always do.'

It was pointless telling her she didn't want to risk it. Andi probably wouldn't understand. She'd always had much less at stake than Ursula. But now that Ursula was about to lose her, she could ask a question she'd always wanted to ask. 'We've never really talked about you and Pab. I mean you knew all about me and Anton, but the only time you ever confided in me about Pab was that night you asked if I was having an affair with him. Why is that?'

Andi reached out to stroke Esteban. She was quiet for so long that Ursula thought she wasn't going answer. 'You remember I said Zak called me a doormat? It's true. I've forgiven Pab more times than I can remember. I've stood by and let him ruin our lives over and over again. And, every time, I've cleared up his crap and pretended it wasn't happening. That's why I couldn't talk to you about it. Because if I told you, I'd have to admit it was real, and I couldn't face that hurt and shame.'

'But it was me, Andi. You could have told me anything.'

Andi winced. 'So could you. But you didn't, did you? Seems neither of us is great at sharing when it comes to Pab. There's another reason I didn't tell you. I thought the two of you had a thing. Obviously I know now that wasn't true but he made it look that way. He's cruel like that. We could go to the police about what he did to you.'

Ursula shook her head. 'It's too late. There's no evidence and my star witness is dead. Do you think he might have done it to other women?'

'I hope not. The others all seemed to be willing participants but I can't say for sure. I can say you're the only one he was infatuated by. You know, I feel like I've enabled it by letting him get away with so much.'

Ursula slipped her fingers between Andi's. Maybe there was a way through this mess that meant they could still be friends. 'I feel the same. I should have done something about it at the time.'

Andi screwed up her face and shook her head furiously. 'Will you listen to us, blaming no one but ourselves. Let's not do this, Urs. This is not our fault. We're not the guilty parties here.' She pushed herself up. 'We should get back down the hill before Don sends out a search party. I hope he remembered to buy alcohol.'

Ursula scrambled up and caught up with her. 'How long have you known he was in Crouch End?'

'Only since I saw Jet when I was in London. He turned up at her flat last week.' Her mouth broke into her usual cheeky grin. 'My girl told him where to shove Crouch End.'

They walked back down the hill. Andi stopped at the bothy and stuck her head around the door. 'By the way, how was the sex?'

'Enlightening.'

Andi tipped her head back and laughed. They were friends again. Things were going to be all right. For now, anyway.

54

THE RIGHT TO BE BRAVE

Don had banked up the fire so much it was roaring and their faces were red with the heat. If she'd been back in Birmingham, Ursula would have switched the heating off months ago but this house never seemed to warm up. It was just the three of them tonight. They'd worked their way through two bottles of wine and were now opening a knock-off Bailey's that Don had picked up because it was on special. They were testing it for Christmas. Ursula was coming to realise that Christmas at Am-nawr was a big thing with a very long preparatory build up.

He poured them each a glass. 'I think we deserve this, ladies. We've had quite a day. I don't think I've had this much excitement since... Well, I don't think I've ever had this much excitement, full stop. There you go.'

'I'm not sure I'd call it excitement,' said Andi. 'But it's definitely been one hell of a day.'

Don picked up his drink. 'Okay then. We've had one hell of a day, and the cult of Pablo has been broken.'

'The what?' said Andi.

'Megan thinks it's like we've been living in a cult. The cult of Pablo,' he said.

'She does,' confirmed Ursula.

'Oh!' Andi lifted her eyebrows. 'Maybe she's right. Well, cult no more. The king is dead. Long live the queen.'

'The queen,' said Don and Ursula together, then all three knocked back their drinks in one go before coughing their guts up.

'That was a bit unwise,' said Don.

Ursula's eyes were watering. 'Perhaps stick to the real thing for Christmas, Don. I think this one might be too much of a health risk.'

'In that case we'd better finish the bottle off.' Andi held out her glass for more. She saw Ursula frown and tutted. 'Urs, you're sixty-four, if you don't take a risk now you never will. After all the shit you've put up with over the years, I think you've earned the right to be brave.'

'Maybe, but there's brave and there's stupid,' said Ursula.

Andi grabbed the bottle. 'Let's be stupid then. We can be brave tomorrow.'

Ursula let Andi fill her glass and wondered if Anton could see her. For all she knew, he could have other spying points besides the hill, other places to watch and wait for the confession he'd been hanging around for. Because that could be the only reason he was still here. Would it be stupid to do it now? Just come out with it. Or would it be brave? She'd been brave once already today and it had turned out okay. Perhaps she didn't have to wait for tomorrow to try again. 'I killed my husband.'

Don choked on his drink. Andi tutted at both of them. 'Ignore her, he died of a heart attack.'

'But if I hadn't told him I was leaving. We had a fight. I pushed him. If I hadn't walked out and left him–'

'He'd have died anyway. You stood up to him. That wasn't a bad thing. And it isn't the reason Anton's dead.'

'Then why is he haunting me?'

'He's haunting you?' said Don. 'You mean like a ghost? We could do that Ouija thing and ask him.'

Andi let out a loud and heavy sigh. 'We are not doing the Ouija thing. It's not a ghost. It's you, Urs. It has to be you. Something is making you think you're seeing him.'

'Maybe it's because you think you killed him,' said Don. 'That would do it.'

Once again, Charlie Big Potatoes proved he was no respecter of people's private space. Ursula rolled out of bed and let him in through the window. 'They have doors for this kind of thing, you know.' She looked out to the hill. It seemed the confession hadn't done the trick. But then, she hadn't told them the full story. Maybe he was waiting for that. Bloody Anton. Always the fucking pedant. She stuck two fingers up at him. 'Yes, Anton, I did get spectacularly drunk last night, so there.'

She crawled back into bed and let Charlie snuggle in under the duvet, but she was awake now and thinking about everything that had happened in the last two days. She reminded herself of the wonderful release she'd experienced in the bothy when she and Howard had lost themselves in each other. After that she'd felt something she hadn't felt in a long time. Strength. She'd needed it too. It had helped her stand up to Pablo and be honest with Andi. She'd like to have that feeling again without having to rely on someone else for it like she always did. All her life she'd had one crutch or another – her mum, Andi, Anton, Samuel, and maybe Howard too. She needed to learn how to stand on her own two feet. And she needed to set Andi free to let her rebuild her own life. But she couldn't do that here.

Charlie's sharp teeth bit into her big toe. She pulled back the duvet and glared at him. He gave her an innocent look in return. 'Don't give me that. You know what you've done. Come on, you monster, let's get breakfast.'

She saw Andi in the library as she went past. She was taking the photos off the wall. Ursula went in to help her. 'Making a change?'

'It's been a long time coming.'

She put her arm around Andi. 'I need to go home.'

'I know.'

'I have to face him.'

'The man who's been dead six years?'

'Yes. I'm trying to be brave. And you need some space to concentrate on yourself. You can't do that while I'm here.'

Andi laid her head against Ursula's shoulder. 'I'm gonna miss you, mate.'

'I'm not far away. If you need me, I'll come,' she said. And this time, she meant it.

Am-nawr's driveway seemed to go on forever this morning. It had been a sad farewell to everyone, including her four-legged friends. Ursula had given Mr Big Potatoes and Esteban an extra-long cuddle. Charlie had dug his claws into her when he'd had enough, but Esteban had been far more polite.

As she drove onto the main road, she saw Howard

walking towards her. She pulled over and waited for him. 'I'm stopping off in Bala if you want a lift.'

'I was actually coming to see you. Gareth told me you were leaving.'

'It's time I went home.'

'Me too. I'm going back tomorrow. I wanted to ask about friendship. You said the other day.'

She held out her hand. 'This is the hand of a friend.'

'I'd like to take it. As a friend.'

'Then you have it.' She gave him her phone. 'Send yourself a message from this, then we'll have each other's numbers.'

He did just that and handed it back to her. 'I talked to Megan. I'm sorry it came out the way it did.'

'That's okay. I don't like secrets anyway. I'll speak to you soon. Take care of yourself, Howard.'

Megan was alone in the café. By the look of it, she'd only just opened up. 'That's you going home then, is it?'

'For now, yes.'

'You want coffee?'

Ursula shook her head. 'I'm not stopping. I just wanted to see you before I went.'

Megan nodded. 'You're all right, Gareth and Howard have talked me to death over it. God knows why but they seem to think that will help me process it. Gareth's very keen on me processing things lately.'

'We didn't intend to disrespect Dilys. We were both upset and it just happened. It helped us.'

'That's nice.'

'Is it?'

Megan shrugged. 'You coming back for Christmas?'

'Andi's asked me to.'

'Make sure you do then. You never know, I might have processed by then. Take a scone with you for the journey. And some coffee. On the house.'

Her first stop was the allotments. She just reached her shed when a deep bark told her that Colonel was on his way. He lumbered up to her, his tail wagging, and she crouched down to hug him.

'Do I get one of those?' said Clyde.

'You certainly do.' She threw her arms around him. 'It's good to see you again. My allotment looks great. I'm not stopping long. I just wanted to see how things were going with Samuel's plot.'

'We haven't touched it yet. Thought you might want to see it again first. Come and see us before you go. Come on, Colonel.'

Samuel's plot was even more overgrown now that they were in the beginnings of summer. Ursula sat in the old garden chair and closed her eyes. A warm breeze touched her cheeks and she let herself believe it was his way of telling her he'd been waiting for her to come back to him. She recalled another day like this, not so long ago, and a tear appeared from nowhere and trickled down her cheek.

55

NOT SO LONG AGO – 2021

Samuel was on his way out the gate as Ursula pulled up at the allotments. He didn't usually get here this early in the morning. She nearly always did. Mainly because she liked to get out as soon as she'd had breakfast. Sometimes before, if the house was feeling especially oppressive. Not that there were many days when it didn't feel like it was suffocating her. Most mornings she woke up hating it and vowing to sell it, but something always stopped her. Or rather, Anton was stopping her. You'd think he'd give her a break now that he was dead, but no, he was still appearing at the window, making his disapproval known. That day he died, when she'd left him, very much alive, she'd tasted freedom for all of, what, six hours? What a heady six hours that was, before she crashed back down to reality.

'Good morning, Ursula.' Samuel smiled and banished all thoughts of Anton.

'Good morning. You're early.'

'Who wouldn't want to be early on such a glorious day?

I'm going to the café up the road for some breakfast. You want to come?'

She considered it for a moment, but she knew the café Samuel went to and the last time she ate there, it had upset her stomach. Even so, it would be nice to just sit with him and have a cup of tea. But today was Wednesday. Not one of her usual café days which meant going there would send her whole day off kilter. 'No thanks, I've already eaten.'

'I'll see you later then.'

'By the way, does Priscilla know you're sneaking off there?' she shouted after him. He winked and tapped the side of his nose.

She walked the long way round to her allotment so she could check Clyde's plot over. He was due back from visiting his son in Bristol tomorrow and she wanted to make sure it was looking its best for him. The plot needed no attention. Samuel had probably been there before her. So she carried on round, stopping to say hello to the other early birds along the way.

The morning was spent doing very little other than chatting with Marcie and Gordon. Marcie had been troubled with health problems in the last two years and it meant they came less often these days, so Ursula liked to spend time with them when they were here. The old timers like her, Samuel, and Clyde kept things tidy when they weren't here which made it easier for them to manage.

Samuel came back with a carrier bag of what looked like snacks and a bottle of rum while the three of them were having tea and biscuits. 'Got your lunch sorted, have you?' laughed Marcie.

He chuckled. 'Damn right. The sun is shining and it's the

test match. Don't bother coming over because this face is gonna be one big do-not-disturb sign.'

'Not even to say tara-a-bit when we go?' said Marcie.

'That's the only exception. Otherwise...' He pulled a long face that must have been his do-not-disturb face.

Ursula cracked up at the sight of it. 'That's us told then.'

The sun was close to going down and Marcie and Gordon had gone. On the way in this morning, Ursula had picked up a bottle of wine and some cheese and meats from the supermarket. Fancy meats, as she and Samuel liked to call them. It was a little joke between them that went back to the first time she'd shared them with him. It must have been twenty-five years ago. That's how long they'd been friends.

The allotments on other side of the hedge looked a bit sad these days. Samuel's was as lush and well maintained as always, but the rest had been left to go to seed when their owners gave them up. It was out of the committee's hands unfortunately. The council were planning to reclaim this patch of land and use it to extend the neighbouring leisure centre's car park. They were fighting it but until a decision was made, no one wanted the pitches. Except Samuel, who was refusing to budge.

He grinned when he saw her coming along the path with her bag of goodies. 'You brought me some fancy supper, Ursula?'

'I have indeed. Is that okay, or do you need to get home?'

'I have all the time in the world. Come. Sit with me.'

She put two plastic wine glasses on the ground and filled them up. 'Did you win the cricket?'

'Not yet, but we will.'

'Do you want your fancy supper yet?'

'Later.' He rubbed his chest. 'Too many bad things today.'

'You've got indigestion? Serves you right, Samuel Sweeting.'

He laughed. 'What, you don't feel sorry for me?'

'Not one bit. Well perhaps a little bit. Shall we just sit here quietly?'

He nodded and looked up at the moon taking the sun's place in the sky. 'My boy is close tonight, Ursula.'

She squeezed his hand. 'Do you want to be alone with him?'

He nodded again. 'I'll see you in the morning.'

She left him in his chair, looking up at the sky, smiling.

The first thing Ursula did when she got to the allotments that morning was go through the hedge to look for Samuel. He wasn't there. She'd had this feeling he'd still be sitting in his chair looking at the sky so it was a relief to see that he must have gone home.

She was about to turn around when his shed door opened and out he came with a toothbrush and a mug. The moment he saw her, Samuel froze. Ursula marched down the path. The shed door was still open. He pushed it shut but not before she spotted a camp bed inside. 'What's going on?'

'Priscilla don't want me in the house no more.'

'She threw you out? Why didn't you tell me? You could have stayed at my house.'

He shook his head. 'It wouldn't be right, Ursula.'

'But we're friends.' She stopped herself. 'Or is that the problem?'

'It's one of the problems.'

'Okay. But you can't sleep here, a man of your age.'

'Clyde will be back later.'

'You'll stay with him?'

He nodded. 'Until Priscilla comes round.'

'Do you want something to eat?'

'All tekken care of.' He pushed the shed door open to reveal eggs sizzling in a frying pan on the camping stove.

She rolled her eyes. 'I'll come back later to make sure you haven't set fire to the place.'

'Remember the test match.'

'Do not disturb. I know,' she said as walked back down the path.

She popped her head through the gap in the hedge a couple of times to make sure he was all right. The first time, he shooed her away because the cricket had just started. The second time she looked, he was asleep in his chair, the radio on in the background. Spending the night on the camp bed must have taken it out of him. She'd called Clyde earlier and let him know what was going on. He promised to come straight over as soon as he was back. It was lunchtime now. Ursula had brought enough food for both of them and as he hadn't been back out to the café, Samuel was probably hungry.

He was still asleep in his chair. She stopped on the path wondering whether to disturb him or come back later. But then a robin landed on his hand and Samuel didn't move. Ursula dropped the food and ran down the path, calling out to him but his head stayed bowed. She fell at his feet and touched his wrist, his neck, his heart. No pulse. No beat. She put her hand against his face. It was already too cool for a hot summer's day. Samuel's eyes were closed, as if he really was sleeping. But he was gone. She'd lost the only man she'd ever loved.

56

SECRETS AND LIES

Tears, twice in a week. It was a record. When she'd been young, there was always something to cry about. In fact, throughout her life, there'd been much to turn any normal person into a sobbing wreck. But Ursula wasn't a normal person. She had been once, before Anton had groomed her into this cold, unfeeling thing. But then again, she wasn't being entirely fair on Anton. She had to take some responsibility for the person she was now. She was the one who vowed never to cry again. It had been the only way to deal with the savage grief and anger that was crushing her. She hadn't realised it would take deep roots that clung to each new loss, making them harder to recover from. If she had, she might never have vowed it.

She wiped her eyes. The tears had been few and quiet, not the kind that wrenched at your guts and left you exhausted. But they were enough to register an acceptance that changes were happening. They'd begun in Bala, these changes, but there'd be more to come.

At Samuel's funeral, she'd been the anchor that Clyde,

Marcie, and Gordon had held on to. At the front of the congregation, Samuel's children wept for him. Priscilla sat in the middle of them, stern and stone-faced. The only dry eyes in that church belonged to her and Ursula. Afterwards, as she led the procession out, Priscilla had stopped and looked Ursula in the eye. Getting the measure of her again. Letting her know that she knew Ursula would have stolen Samuel from under her nose, given the chance. Ursula stayed away from the reception. Clyde and the others didn't try to talk her into it. They must have known it too.

She rushed along the path towards the car park, She couldn't face Clyde now that she'd admitted to herself just how bad and selfish a person she was. No better than Pablo really. Perhaps he saw that in her and that was why he'd been so obsessed with her. But she couldn't escape that easily. Clyde was waiting by her car. 'You okay, Ursula?'

She shook her head. Time to be brave again. Time to be truthful. 'I wanted Samuel for myself. I was glad Priscilla threw him out because I thought at last I could show him how much I loved him.'

Clyde pushed his hat back and scratched his head. 'He already knew that. You didn't have to show him any more than you already did.'

'But I wanted him. I wanted him so much and I shouldn't have done. He wasn't mine to have.'

'Him and Priscilla lost their way a long time before you showed up. He was Priscilla's husband and he would never stop being that. But he did love you, Ursula. I promise you that. Every day he saw you was another day worth living for Samuel, and I thank you for that.'

She was crying again, big, fat tears rolling down her cheeks. Clyde held on to her. 'Hush now, honey. You got to stop beating yourself up over this. It would break Samuel's heart. You got to be happy. For him. And for yourself.'

Anton was back in his usual place. He'd arrived home before she had, but then he hadn't stopped off at the allotments and had a good cry on Clyde's shoulder, had he? Any lightness she'd felt after her tears was already slipping away. She left her case in the car and climbed the stairs, her heart sinking a little bit more with each step.

Ursula stood in front of the office door. It had been closed on the day Pablo assaulted her and had stayed that way ever since. She swallowed down the dreadful taste that was coming up from her throat and turned the handle.

Anton was not at the window, or anywhere else in the room. As she'd noted before, he liked to keep his distance. Dust covered everything. Six years' worth of cobwebs dangled from the ceiling, the corners and the shelves. The spiders had set up home in the model that was now a discoloured, webby mess. Anton would be appalled. No wonder he was haunting her.

She'd made a promise to herself on the way back. If she could clean this room up, she was going to call in on that estate agents by the allotments. It was a big ask but she was feeling stronger again after talking to Clyde.

She started on the cobwebs, setting the spiders free through the window as she went along sucking their webs away with the vacuum. The dust went the same way, once she cleared the shelves of Anton's awards. Next, her eyes fell on the model. She felt surprisingly sorry for the old thing and despite her dislike of it, took it apart to clean it. It didn't look so bad once it had been restored to its almost former glory, although she wasn't sure what to do with it now because she didn't want it. Perhaps she'd ask the estate agent if the buyers would like it.

The awards were cluttering up the desk. More things she didn't know what to do with. When it boiled down to it, they were all just lumps of plastic and glass. Worthless symbols of a life spent chasing accolades above all else. She wondered if these were the last things Anton saw before he'd collapsed and whether he'd looked at them and thought, yes, it had all been worth it. Or had he realised, as he gasped for his dying breath, that his life had been wasted? Tomorrow, she'd get some boxes and take them to the tip. Today, she'd clear out the filing cabinets.

One by one, she emptied the cabinets. The papers she'd once so diligently filed were slung into the recycling bin, along with all the other meaningless papers. She was nearly done now, just one cabinet to go. The top two drawers of the final cabinet came open as easily as the others but the bottom was locked. She searched the desk drawers for the key, methodically emptying them as she went along, until she came across a piece of paper with red diagonal lines slashing through Anton's handwriting. It was his last list. He must have put it in there before he collapsed. Probably to use against her when she came back. Instinctively, she glanced at the empty window, then slapped the list on the desk and carried on with her search.

The next drawer held nothing but a box of business cards, they went into the recycling too and she pushed the drawer shut. A noise from inside made her open it again. A small pot, the kind you kept trinkets in, had slid to the front. The box must have been keeping it in place at the very back of the drawer. The pot was bright blue with a picture of the

Statue of Liberty on its lid and *'New York, New York'* around the sides. It was cheap, gaudy, and the most un-Anton like object you could imagine being in his possession. Inside it was a key. She tried it in the cabinet drawer. It worked.

The drawer held three boxes. In the first, she was surprised to find the red scarf he'd once bought just because she'd said it would suit him. She opened the second box and gasped. Their baby's christening gown. 'Oh, Anton.' Ursula lifted it out of the tissue it was wrapped in. The red dot of blood was still there but faded now. She looked for the embroidered label on the inside: *'Ursula Moller, 1983.'*

She felt something on her shoulder and swivelled around. There was nothing to see, but he was here. She could feel the change in the atmosphere. She put the gown away and turned her attention to the last box. It was a collection of old photos. There were some of her, one standing outside this house when it was still unfinished. She recalled he'd taken it the day he'd asked her to marry him. One of her pregnant, the bump hardly showing but she recognised the dress she'd bought especially for her pregnancy. An older photo was of a family. The boy, a teenager, was obviously Anton. But there was another child. A girl, younger than him. He'd never said anything about a sister. In fact, when his father died, he'd said there was no one left. Perhaps something had happened to her. Perhaps that was why Anton was the way he was.

All that was left in the box now was an envelope. Inside was a letter and more photos. The letter was more of a note really. Just a few words:

'Anton, This has to stop.'

She'd seen that writing before, but she couldn't think where. And then she looked at the photos and she knew exactly who it belonged to. Twelve photos. Six of Cass, smiling, laughing, blowing a kiss, pulling those funny faces she used to pull to make Ursula laugh when she was little. The final six were of Cass and Anton together. The first two were of them in some kind of beach bar, him with his arm around her, looking so relaxed and happy she almost didn't recognise him. The last four were taken in New York. She could tell that because of the backdrops. In one they were dressed in evening wear. He was standing behind her, his arms wrapped around her waist, his chin resting on the top of her head. They were looking straight at the camera and they were so in love. You could just tell. On the wall behind them was a banner that read: 'A *New York welcome to 1982.*' That would have made it New Year's Eve 1981. Ursula and Anton's second as a married couple. Except they hadn't been together because Anton had told her he had to be in Germany, all through Christmas and the new year. He'd made her feel bad for not dropping everything and going with him when all the time he'd planned to go to New York with Cass. Cass of all people. How could they?

Ursula looked at the photos again of the two of them at the beach bar. Anton looked younger than when he was with her, and that wasn't just because he was happy. They'd been taken before she met him. He'd been with Cass before he'd been with her. Their marriage had been a non-starter from the beginning because Anton had never loved her. It was Cass he'd wanted. Not her. She staggered backwards and fell onto the desk. Lies. All of it. Everything about her and Anton was secrets and lies. Her rage was like a physical thing, bubbling to the surface, bursting to get out. She let it out with a great roar. 'Are you still with me, Anton? Are you watching me finding your dirty little secrets? I hope you are because I've got something for you.' She grabbed hold of the biggest and heaviest of his awards, a rock-shaped thing, and landed it right in the middle of his precious model. The roof splintered and broke in two. She picked the rock up again and smashed it down again, again and again, until there was nothing left but yellowing rubble.

Ursula sank to her knees, screaming and wailing. All those lost and lonely years she'd endured had all been for nothing. 'I hate you. Do you hear me? I never loved you. I only ever loved Samuel.'

Her heart was splintering into a hundred-thousand shards as all the lost opportunities and all the regrets raced through her mind. What was it about her that was so bad, so very terrible, that she should deserve this? And then she noticed Anton's last list on the floor next to her. It had fallen off the desk, the back of it facing upwards, her words in bold red capitals revealing just how bad she was and reminding her of the real reason why Anton was haunting her:

'GO TO HELL AND TAKE YOUR LIST WITH YOU.'

57

FINALLY LEARNING

She woke with a start, her eyes instantly wide open. It was morning but you wouldn't know it, such was the darkness inside and outside the house. She'd slept on the bare mattress without undressing, exhausted after an orgy of destruction that had started with Anton's model and had progressed onto his collection of Bauhaus books and anything else that could be torn or broken. Ursula rolled over, sat on the edge of the bed, and checked the time on her phone. Not even five o'clock. Two tiny pieces of paper fell from her hair. There were more of them on the floor arranged into a thin, straggly trail of red-inked particles leading out to the landing. Anton's last list. She followed it all the way back to the office.

Yesterday's carnage was waiting for her, piled up in the middle of the room like a bonfire ready to be set alight. She tried to recall if that's what the intention had been but last night, she'd been consumed by a madness that she'd never seen in herself before. Thankfully, sense had prevailed and she hadn't sent the place up in flames. The house was worth too much to her for that. Financially anyway. No other reason. Besides, she might endanger her own life and she didn't want that. She was intending to live for many years to come, and she was intending to make them good years too.

There was a diagonal crack in the window that ran all the way from one corner to the other. She didn't remember doing that, just as she didn't remember leaving the paper trail, although something had caused her to wake so suddenly this morning. There'd been a sound, like ice breaking, that she thought had been a dream. Then again, she had been throwing those bloody awards around like frisbees. With little success, because they seemed to be completely indestructible. Unlike the window which she'd have to get fixed.

Her stomach rumbled loudly and it occurred to her that she hadn't eaten since yesterday's breakfast. She remembered the scone Megan had given her was still in the car. That would have to do since there was no food or drink in the house. She turned back towards the doorway and caught sight of a flash of red under the desk. Anton's scarf had been cut to shreds. And then, to her horror, she saw fragments of ivory silk. The christening gown. Had she done that? Had she really been that crazed?

The coffee that Megan had also given her was heated up in the microwave. She drank it and ate the scone while sitting on the sofa with a scrap of silk on her knee. She should be angry with herself for doing something so destructive and brutal but all she felt was relief. It was just an old dress that before yesterday she'd thought long gone. A relic from another life. It wasn't her child she'd damaged. He never came into this world. That was okay. Things like that happened and it was sad, but she'd been holding onto him for too long now. It was time to let go. And it was time to face the truth about Anton.

Cass opened the door. Ursula had called ahead so she'd been expecting her. 'Solly's taking a nap. I thought a walk would be good. There's a nice café on the beach.'

'How is Solly?'

'Soldiering on. He gets tired very easily. I catch him talking to himself sometimes. I haven't said anything to him about it but I think he's talking to Gill.'

Ursula smiled. 'Maybe he can see her. I've been seeing Anton for the last six years.' He'd been there again this morning when she left the house, or at least his outline had. The rest of him had faded a little. She was taking it as a good sign.

'I think I'd rather see Gill than Anton,' said Cass. 'You said you'd found something you wanted to show me?'

'Some photos and a note. I'll show you when we get to the café.'

They went straight there. Ursula put the envelope on the table. 'You might want to look at them on your own. I'll order some drinks.'

Cass peered inside the envelope and her face drained of all colour. 'Where did you find them?'

'Locked away in Anton's office. I'll give you a few minutes.'

She took her time at the counter. When she got back to the table she sat opposite Cass. The photos were set out in a line between them. 'You both look so in love.'

'We were. I'm sorry, my darling, I know that's not what you wanted to hear.' Cass picked up one of the beach bar photos. 'This was in Corfu. 1977, I think it was. It's all so long

ago now. We met through Bernard. He'd taken him on to
design his new house. He was younger than me but that
didn't seem to matter to him. We had a lot of fun.'

'Fun? With Anton?'

She smiled. 'He was different then. They were happy
times. But then things got serious and everything changed. He
asked me to marry him. I made the mistake of telling Bernard
and my brother, being the kind of person he was, laughed in
my face. He told me it was a well-known fact Anton was a
social climber who was only interested in me for the money
and connections. I always struggled with self-confidence, so it
didn't take much to convince me. I broke it off a month before
you came to work at Talulah, but Anton wouldn't accept it. He
kept calling me and watching out for me from his office
window. When I came into work in the mornings he'd be
waiting on the corner, begging me to take him back.'

'I thought he was doing those things for me.'

'I'm sure he was, later. I think sometimes Anton saw you
in me and me in you. He was forever caught between us,
never knowing which one to choose.'

'Why didn't you tell me? You could have stopped me
before things went too far.'

'I hardly knew you at the time. You weren't the little girl I
remembered, and Gill had made it clear I was to stay out of
your life. I thought he was doing it to make me jealous and
he'd tire of you, or you'd get bored with him. You were such a
bright, lively young thing, I couldn't imagine you sticking
with him for long. By the time I'd realised how wrong I'd
been to let him go, it was too late. I went to see him and told
him I still loved him but he said he was with you now and he
was going to marry you. I was heartbroken and so angry with

you both. And I suppose I thought you'd be divorced within a couple of years and I could wait it out.'

'But the photos in New York, they were after we were married.'

'I'm sorry, that was unforgivable of me. He came to me not long after your wedding saying he'd made a dreadful mistake. I still loved him and to my shame, we picked up where we'd left off. I went with him to New York that Christmas and he promised me he was going to tell you. I honestly thought you'd be better off for it. But he didn't tell you, he just carried on flip-flopping between the two of us. After about three months, I said I wasn't prepared to put up with it any longer.'

'Is that when you sent the note?'

'No, the note was later. Just like the first-time round, he'd refused to accept it. I did my best to avoid him but it was hard. When you were pregnant, before you told me, he came over to my house and threw it in my face. He knew how much I wanted children. That's when I wrote the note. I sent it to his office so there'd be no chance of you coming across it. But I don't think that was what stopped him. I think it was losing the baby. It hit him hard. I saw him in the hospital car park on the day of your miscarriage. I had to tell him what had happened. His reaction. I'd never seen him so raw and exposed.'

'It was the shock I expect. He soon recovered from it,' said Ursula. She was bitter. Even now. But if anyone had a right to be, it was her.

Cass shook her head. 'No, I don't think he did. I think it did something to him. Days before we closed the door on Talulah, he came in to gloat. He'd changed so much from the person I loved, he actually frightened me. I knew then that I needed to get away.'

'So that's why you left Birmingham. That's why you didn't want Anton to know you were back.'

'Yes. Although it was also a chance to get away from Bernard. Gillian did the right thing in leaving him.'

Ursula frowned. 'But I thought he left us.'

'Sort of. You know he had two families on the go? When Gill found out, he would have been perfectly happy to carry on the arrangement but she had too much self-respect for that. She told him she didn't want him. It cost her. She lost everything. Except for the thing most dear to her. You. She was a strong woman. I've often wished I could be more like her.'

'Me too.' So yet again, Ursula was being presented with another new fact about the courageous and remarkable woman she'd been privileged to call her mother. She really wanted to be that kind of woman too. Hopefully, it wasn't too late.

Cass smiled. 'You're not entirely unlike her. I'm glad you know at last. It's been heavy on my mind for such a long time. Not just the fear that you or Gill would find out and it would be the end of us again, but the guilt. It feels like I've been drowning in guilt nearly all my adult life. I know I have no right to ask for your forgiveness, but it would mean so much to me.'

Ursula looked at the photos and then at Cass. They looked alike, the two of them, especially now that Cass's hair was white. She could see how Anton might have seen an opportunity to have the next best thing when he couldn't be with the woman he really wanted. And Cass had loved Anton much more than she'd been able to. It was no different to her being in love with Samuel. She and Cass had more than looks in common. Hadn't she been living most of her adult life drowning in fear and guilt too? Perhaps this was her chance to let it all go and do something good that would atone for wanting to steal Priscilla's husband, and for sending her own husband to hell. 'I forgive you.'

Cass clutched Ursula's hands. She was crying. 'Thank you, my darling. Thank you.'

Ursula was crying too. She didn't seem to be able to stop herself lately. People were looking at them. She should have been embarrassed but the only emotion she felt was immense relief. And perhaps a little bit of happiness. Yes, there was every possibility she was feeling a little bit happy at last. She bundled the photos back into the envelope. 'Let's go and see Solly, Auntie Cass.'

'I'm glad Anton found love with you, Cass. Even if it was only for a short while, because I couldn't give it to him,' she said as they walked along the front, arm in arm.

'He came to see me after Gill died to apologise for the way he'd behaved.'

'Then he must have really loved you. He never once said sorry to me in all the years we were together.'

'He said something else too. He told me he'd been right to stay with you because you needed him most.'

Ursula snorted. 'Typical. Anton the silent martyr.'

Cass laughed. 'I told him he'd got it the wrong way round. I told him he'd chosen the person he needed most.'

Solly was sitting on the garden bench. They waved at him through the window but Ursula wasn't sure he'd seen them.

'His eyesight's not the best these days,' said Cass. 'Why don't you go out to see him?'

His eyesight may have been on the wane, but he recognised her as soon as he saw her walking towards him. 'Come and sit with me, lovely. It's been too long.'

She nudged up against him. 'How's mum?'

He turned to her in surprise then smiled. 'Cass giving away all my secrets, is she?'

'I see Anton too.'

Solly pretended to shudder. 'You want to stop that, lovely.'

She laughed a light, happy, tinkling laugh that she hadn't heard in a long, long time. 'I think I will be very soon. When you talk to Mum again, say hello from me. And tell her, I'm finally learning to love myself.'

58

URSULA MOLLER'S LIST OF REGRETS

Ursula sat at the dining table with a notepad, a cafetiere, and a slice of chocolate cake. She'd been shopping that morning and had treated herself. She took a photo of the cake and sent it to Andi: *'I'm on my second slice.'* That would please her.

While she'd been in Bala, Don had shown her how to get music on something called Spotify. It was amazing. You could play whatever you wanted on your phone. She selected some tunes that she and Andi used to love and turned them up loud. She could do that now Anton had disappeared. He wasn't at the window when she'd returned from her stay in Eastbourne and he hadn't been back.

She'd been thinking about Anton a lot since talking to Cass. Reassessing their life together, now that she'd seen a different side to him. And she'd come to understand that they had loved each other, just not enough. In choosing one another, they'd settled for something or someone second best. Anton probably knew he'd done that but he must have seen it in Ursula the night he saw her with Samuel. That was why he took it so badly.

It didn't hurt to think of herself as his second best, but it hurt to think of all those wasted years of longing. She'd longed for a child, and she'd longed for Samuel, but before that, even before Anton, there had always been something. A father. A friend. Acceptance. Love. Anton could never have filled all those gaps. No one person could, or should. But perhaps if they hadn't ruined things by marrying, they'd have been friends. Perhaps he would have been a much-loved uncle. Because she had liked him back then, that funny, odd man with his old fashioned, not quite British, not quite foreign ways. She had liked him very much. Yes, they would have made great friends.

She looked all the way up to the high ceiling. This house was beautiful but it wasn't right for her. Tomorrow, she'd be stopping off at that estate agents by the allotments. 'I'm sorry, Anton, but I've been here too long. It's time for me to leave.'

From her seat, she could see the carnage that she'd brought down from his office and dumped in the garden, ready for the other thing she'd purchased this morning, an incinerator bin. She was intending to have a bonfire later. But first she had a list to write. It had been a long time coming but she was finally ready to write it, and it would be the last list she was ever going to need. It seemed only right that such an important list should have a heading so she gave it one:

'Ursula Moller's List of Regrets.'

She tapped the pen against her chin while trying to decide where to start. And then she realised the best place to start was the beginning. 1978. If only she hadn't stopped…

Three hours had passed by the time she reached the final regret. It was quite a big one. She wished, she hadn't let her life be ruled by guilt and fear after Anton died. Because doing that had led to so many more regrets for the way the last six years had turned out. If she had only faced those two things at the time, she might have found the courage to tell Andi about Pablo. She might have reported him to the police too. It was all speculation but, if nothing else, she liked to think she'd have cleared out Anton's office and found his secret a lot sooner. That was what he'd wanted. She was convinced of it now. The reason he'd been haunting her all this time was not because she'd told him to go to hell. It was because he wanted her to understand the things he couldn't bring himself to say. And maybe, just maybe, he wanted to say sorry.

So that was it. She was finished. It was the longest list she'd ever had to deal with, but it was complete. Nothing had been left out. She was all done with her regrets. There would be no more. She slipped the list into her pocket and went out the garden to fill the incinerator bin with the remains of Anton's passion project. Next came the tattered pieces of his books, his diary, his red scarf and the christening gown. A cool breeze ruffled her dress as she lit the fire. She felt it prick into goosebumps on her bare arms and legs. She knew it wasn't Anton but she blew him a kiss, just in case. 'Goodbye, Anton. Rest in peace.'

The sun was just sliding down behind the trees. It was going to be a lovely sunset. Maybe if she'd been at the allotment she'd have watched it from Samuel's plot, but she'd been going there a bit less lately. It was another habit, another crutch she was trying to break her dependency on.

When there was nothing left to burn, she took the list from her pocket and threw it in. She watched it being eaten up by the flames knowing she would never let herself be ruled by another list again. From now on she would live the way she wanted to. No more habits. No more routines. No more regrets.

The first few beats of the next song she'd selected started up on her phone. Its timing was perfect. Straight away, her feet began to move. And maybe it was because 'Supernature', the song she could never ever stop dancing to, was playing. Or maybe it was because these were her first steps towards freedom, but Ursula had the feeling this day was going to be special and everything she did for the rest of her life was going to be big.

59

SOME MONTHS LATER

The morning's frost was only just beginning to thaw but, for now, it sat on top of the rectangular stretch of grass like crisp filigree lace. Ursula was tempted to walk across it, to leave her footprints, albeit temporarily, on the unblemished white expanse. But that would have spoiled the loveliness of it, this place that was like a village green in the middle of the city. If you attuned your ears in the right way, it was possible to hear the distant hum of traffic coming from the main road. Directly opposite where she was standing, on the far side of the grass, she could see the back of two large houses, one of which she'd come to know quite well. It was where Rufus was living when she'd first met him. Houses faced the green on the three remaining sides. Clyde lived in one of them. It was him that told her about this place. He'd introduced her to Rufus too, in a roundabout way.

Anton's house and its contents had been sold. She'd left it all to the estate agent and solicitor to manage, preferring to spend autumn, Christmas, and the new year in Bala. Andi had been determined to get rid of all trace of Pablo and they'd repainted every room, starting with Ursula's bedroom. With everybody helping, they'd finished just in time for Christmas, and just in time for Ursula to make a new dress for the occasion, to replace the one Esme had ruined. In December, Zak's girlfriend gave birth to a beautiful baby boy; Andi was a grandmother now, and Don was helping her make plans that would keep Am-nawr afloat.

Ursula had been sad to leave Am-nawr but she had her own plans to look forward to. Her new life had started months ago, but today was definitely the newest of all new beginnings. She turned around to face a terrace house, cosy but with enough room for friends and family to stay, and for a sewing room of her own, if she wanted one. The estate agent's board was still in the small front garden, but the 'for sale' sign had been flipped over to 'sold'.

'What do you think, Rufus, will we be happy here?'

The bundle of grey-black fur at her side sniffed at the gate post. He was still a baby but he was going to be big when he was fully grown because he was Colonel's grandson. His mother, one of Colonel's daughters, lived over in that big house that backed onto the green, and his father was some kind of wolfhound lurcher. Rufus cocked a leg, sprayed the post and almost fell over as he did so. He was still learning his trade when it came to big-boy peeing. He recovered himself, nudged the gate open and gave her a look that seemed to be saying: 'Well, obviously.'

Ursula laughed. 'I think so too.'

A WORD FROM THE AUTHOR

Hello

I hope you enjoyed reading Ursula's story. If you did, would you mind leaving a review?

Your reviews are important. They help me to reach more readers and they help other readers to decide whether this book is for them.

You can leave a review at your local Amazon store.

To find out more about other stories written by me, read on...

Be the first to know about Hazel's latest news and the general goings on in her life. You can follow her in all the usual places or join her **Readers' Club** for monthly newsletters, and other giveaways.

https://hazelwardauthor.com

ALSO BY HAZEL WARD

BEING NETTA WILDE

A lonely woman. A single decision. A second chance at happiness.

★★★★★ 'A beautiful story about personal growth, love, loss, and friendships.'

★★★★★ 'An absolute blast of a read! A real feel good pick me up that kept me smiling until the end.'

★★★★★ 'Well written, poignant, funny, uplifting. Couldn't put it down!'

FINDING EDITH PINSENT

Two women. Two Timelines. One heart-wrenching story.

★★★★★ 'Outstanding!! Wow. Just wow.'

★★★★★ 'A rollercoaster ride and feelgood heart-warming experience.'

★★★★★ 'Edie is so realistic, you will fall in love with her.'

SAVING GERALDINE CORCORAN

One shameful secret. One hidden letter. Two unlikely guardian angels.

★★★★★ 'A truly powerful story told brilliantly.'

★★★★★ 'Sadness, love, humour, surprise. You name it I felt it.'

★★★★★ 'Superbly written and well worth reading, but be prepared to cry and laugh and cry again!'

EDUCATING KELLY PAYNE

How to learn about love ... the hard way.

★★★★★ 'The writing is phenomenal, the characters so real you can really see into their soul.'

★★★★★ 'I loved it! I'm wiping my eyes as I write.'

★★★★★ 'Kelly's journey is a cracker.'

CALLING FRANK O'HARE

One phone. One road trip. Too many memories.

★★★★★ 'Another wonderful book, never once skipped a few sentences, enjoyed every word.'

★★★★★ 'A thoroughly enjoyable read - sad, funny, insightful and moving.'

★★★★★ 'I loved the twists in this book, especially at the end.'

LOVING NETTA WILDE

One woman. Three men. Four troubled hearts.

★★★★★ 'The characters are so believable and it was inspirational to enlarge them by writing a new story about a different one of them in each successive book

★★★★★ 'I recommend highly, quite simply brilliant.'

★★★★★ 'Another gem from Hazel Ward. It's so well written and a very enjoyable read.'

MEETING ANNETTE GREY

Two strangers. One Park Bench. One life changing conversation.

★★★★★ 'Absolutely brilliant. Hazel brings her characters to life so you feel like they are all old friends.'

★★★★★ 'Hazel has an unerring talent to create characters, events and emotions so easily able to relate to.'

★★★★★ 'Lovely novella. A must read.'

Printed in Dunstable, United Kingdom

77490920R00231